the MOON & the SUN

VONDA N. MCINTYRE

Jo Fletcher
BOOKS

First published in the USA in 1997 by Pocket Books
This edition published in Great Britain in 2015 by

Jo Fletcher Books
an imprint of
Quercus Publishing Ltd
Carmelite House
50 Victoria Embankment
London EC4Y 0DZ

An Hachette UK company

A CIP catalogue record for this book is available
from the British Library

PB ISBN 978 0 85705 424 1
EBOOK ISBN 978 0 85705 423 4

10 9 8 7 6 5 4 3 2

Typeset by Ellipsis Digital Limited, Glasgow

Printed and bound in Great Britain by Clays Ltd, Elcograf S.p.A.

Map 'Plan général de Versailles, son parc, son Louvre, ses jardins, ses fontaines,
ses bosquets et sa ville par N de Fer 1700' originally by Nicolas de Fer, 1700

In Memoriam Avram Davidson 1923–1993

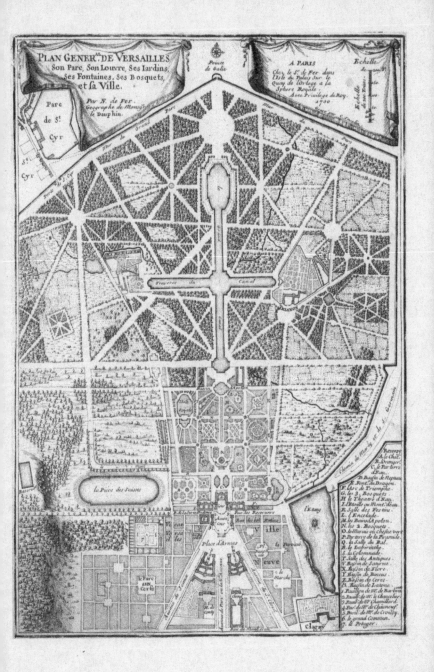

PLAN GENER.le DE VERSAILLES
Son Parc, Son Louvre, Ses Iardins,
Ses Fontaines, Ses Bosquets,
et sa Ville.

Par N. de Fer
Geographe de Monsig.r
le Dauphin.

A PARIS
Chez le Sr. de Fer dans
L'Isle du Palais sur le
Quay de l'Orloge a la
Sphere Royale.
Avec Privilege du Roy.
1700

Echelle

Parc
de St.
Cyr

St.
Cyr

la Piéce des Suisses

Place d'Armes

Ville
Neuve

le Parc
aux Cerfs

A. Reuvoy
B. à la Chal.
C. le Parterre d'eau.
D. Bassin de Neptune.
E. Font. du Dragon.
F. Lirc de Triomphe.
G. les 3. Bassins.
H. le Theatre d'Eau.
I. L'Etoille ou Mont. d'eau.
K. Salle des Festins.
L. L'Enceladc.
M. les Bains d'apolon.
N. les 2. Bosquets.
O. lahbirinte ou Chesne vert.
P. Parterre de la Piramide.
Q. la Sallc du Bal.
R. la Baltenville.
S. la Colonnade.
T. Salle des Antiques.
V. Bassin de Saporus.
X. Bassin de Flore.
Y. Bassin de Bacchus.
Z. Bassin de Ceres.
&. Bassin de Latone.
1. Pauillon de Me. le Dau
2. Pauillon de Me. le Chancelier
3. Pauil. de Mr. Chamillard
4. Pau. dest. de Chameuf
5. Pauil. de Me. de Crouisy
6. Grand Commun.
7. le Potager.

Clagny

Prologue

Midsummer Day's sun blazed white in the centre of the sky. The sky burned blue to the horizon.

The flagship of the King crossed abruptly from the limpid green of shallow water to the dark indigo of limitless depths.

The galleon's captain shouted orders; the sailors hurried to obey. Canvas flapped, then filled; the immense square sails snapped taut in the wind. The ship creaked and groaned and leaned into its turn. The flag of Louis XIV fluttered, writing *Nec Pluribus Impar*, the King's motto, across the sky. The emblem of Louis XIV, a golden sunburst, shone from the galleon's foretopsail.

Free of the treacherous shoals, the galleon plunged ahead. Water rushed against the ship's sides. The gilt figurehead stretched its arms into sunlight and spray. Rainbows shimmered from its claws and from the flukes of its double tail. The carven sea monster flung coloured light before it, for the glory of the King.

Yves de la Croix searched the sea from the ship's bow to the horizon, seeking his quarry along the Tropic of Cancer, directly beneath the sun. He squinted into Midsummer's Day and clenched his hands around the topdeck's rail. The galleon moved with the wind, leaving the air on deck still and hot. The sun soaked into Yves' black cassock and drenched his dark hair with heat. The tropical sea sparkled and shifted, dazzling and enrapturing the young Jesuit.

'*Démons!*' the lookout cried.

Yves searched for what the lookout had spied, but the sun was too bright and the distance too long. The ship cut through the waves, rushing, roaring.

'There!'

Dead ahead, the ocean roiled. Shapes leapt. Sleek figures cavorted like dolphins in the sea foam.

The flagship sailed toward the turbulent water. A siren song, no dolphin's call, floated through the air. The sailors fell into terrified silence.

Yves stood motionless, curbing his excitement. He had known he would find his quarry at this spot and on this day; he had never doubted his hypothesis. He should meet his success with composure.

'The net!' Captain Desheureux's shout overwhelmed the song. 'The net, you bastards!'

His command sent his crew scrambling. They feared him more than they feared sea monsters, more than they feared demons. The winch shrieked and groaned, wood against rope against metal. The net clattered over the side. A sailor muttered a profane prayer.

The creatures frolicked, oblivious to the approaching galleon. They breached like dolphins, splashing wildly, churning the sea. They caressed each other, twining their tails about one another, singing their animal sensuality. Their rutting whipped the ocean into froth.

Yves' excitement surged, possessing his mind and his body, overcoming his resolution. Shocked by the intensity of his reaction, he closed his eyes and bowed his head, praying for humble tranquility.

The rattle of the net, its heavy cables knocking against the ship's flank, brought him back to the world. Desheureux cursed. Yves ignored the words, as he had ignored casual profanity and blasphemy throughout the voyage.

Once more his own master, Yves waited, impassive. Calmly he noted the details of his prey: their size; their colour; their number, much reduced from the horde reported a century before.

The galleon swept through the fornicating sea monsters. As Yves had planned, as he had hoped, as he had expected from his research, the sea monsters trapped themselves in their rapture. They never noticed the attack until the moment of onslaught.

The siren song disintegrated into animal cries and screams of pain. Hunted animals always shrieked at the shock of their capture. Yves doubted that beasts could feel fear, but he suspected they might feel pain.

The galleon crushed through them, drowning them in their own screams. The net swept through the thrashing waves.

Desheureux shouted abuse and orders. The sailors winched the net's cables. Underwater, powerful creatures thrashed against the side of the galleon. Their voices beat the planks like a drum.

The net hauled the creatures from the sea. Sunlight gleamed from their dark, leathery flanks.

'Release the pigeons.' Yves kept his voice level.

'It's too far,' whispered the apprentice to the royal pigeon keeper. 'They'll die.' Birds cooed and fluttered in their wicker cages.

'Release them!' If none reached France from this flight of birds, the next flight would succeed, or the one after that.

'Yes, Father.'

A dozen carrier pigeons lofted into the sky. Their wings beat the air. The soft sound faded to silence. Yves glanced over his shoulder. One of the pigeons wheeled, climbing higher. Its message capsule flashed silver, reflecting the sun, signalling Yves' triumph.

Chapter 1

The procession wound its way along the cobbled street, stretching fifty carriages long. The people of Le Havre pressed close on either side, cheering their King and his court, marvelling at the opulence of the carriages and the harnesses, admiring the flamboyant dress, the jewels and lace, the velvet and cloth-of-gold, the wide plumed hats of the young noblemen who accompanied their sovereign on horseback.

Marie-Josèphe de la Croix had dreamed of riding in such a procession, but her dreams fell short of the reality. She travelled in the carriage of the duke and duchess d'Orléans, a carriage second in magnificence only to the King's. She sat across from the duke, the King's brother, known always as Monsieur, and his wife Madame. Their daughter Mademoiselle sat beside her.

On her other side, Monsieur's friend the Chevalier de Lorraine lounged lazily, handsome and languorous, bored by the long journey from Versailles to Le Havre. Lotte — *Mademoiselle, I must always remember to call her*, Marie-Josèphe said to herself, *now that I'm at court, now that I'm her lady-in-waiting* — leaned out the carriage window, nearly as excited as Marie-Josèphe.

The Chevalier stretched his long legs diagonally so they crossed in front of Marie-Josèphe's feet.

Despite the dust, and the smells of the waterfront, and the noise of horses and riders and carriages clattering along the cobblestones, Madame insisted on opening both windows and curtains. She had a great fondness for fresh air, which Marie-Josèphe shared. Despite her age — she was over forty! — Madame always rode on the hunt with the King. She hinted that Marie-Josèphe might be invited to ride along.

Monsieur preferred to be protected from the evil humours of the outside air. He carried a silk handkerchief and a pomander. With the silk he brushed the dust from the velvet sleeves and gold lace of his coat; he held the clove-studded orange to his nose, perfuming away the odours of the street. As the coach neared the waterfront, the smell of rotting fish and drying seaweed rose, till Marie-Josèphe wished she too had brought a pomander.

The carriage shuddered and slowed. The driver shouted to the horses. Their iron shoes rang on the cobblestones. Townspeople poured into the street, thumping against the sides of the carriage, shouting, begging.

'Look, Mademoiselle de la Croix!' Lotte drew Marie-Josèphe forward so they could both see out the carriage window. Marie-Josèphe wanted to see everything; she wanted to remember forever every detail of the procession. On either side of the street, ragged people waved and cheered, cried 'Long live the King!' and shouted 'Give us bread!'

One rider moved undaunted through the crowd. Marie-Josèphe took him for a boy, a page on a pony, then noticed that he wore the *justaucorps à brevet*, the gold-embroidered blue coat reserved for the King's most intimate associates. Realising her mistake, she blushed with embarrassment.

The desperate townspeople clutched at the courtier, plucked at his gold lace, pulled at his horse's saddle. Instead of whipping them away, he gave them the King's alms. He handed coins to the nearer people, and flung coins to the people at the edges of the throng, the old women, the crippled men, the ragged children. The crowd formed a whirlpool around him, as powerful as the ocean, as filthy as the water in the harbour of le Havre.

'Who is that?' Marie-Josèphe asked.

'Lucien de Barenton,' Lotte said. 'M. le comte de Chrétien. Don't you know him?'

'I didn't know—' She hesitated. It was not her place to comment on M. de Chrétien's stature at court.

'He represented His Majesty in organising my brother's expedition, but I had no occasion to meet him.'

'He's been away all summer,' Monsieur said. 'But I see he's kept his standing in my brother the King's estimation.'

The carriage halted, hemmed in, jostled. Monsieur waved his

handkerchief against the odours of sweating horses, sweating peop... and dead fish. The guards shouted, trying to drive the people back.

'I shall have to have the carriage repainted after this,' Monsieur grumbled wearily. 'And no doubt I'll miss some of the gilt as well.'

'Louis le Grand puts himself too close to his subjects,' Lorraine said. 'To comfort them with his glory.' He laughed. 'Never mind, Chrétien will trample them with his war horse.'

M. de Chrétien could no more dominate a war horse than could I, Marie-Josèphe thought. Lorraine's cheerful sarcasm amused and then embarrassed her.

She feared for the count de Chrétien, but no one else showed any worry. The other courtiers' mounts descended from the chargers of the Crusades, but Count Lucien, as befitted him, rode a small, light dapple-grey.

'His horse is no bigger than a palfrey!' Marie-Josèphe exclaimed. 'The people might pull him down!'

'Don't worry.' Lotte patted Marie-Josèphe's arm, leaned close and whispered, 'Wait. Watch. M. de Chrétien will never let himself be unhorsed.'

Count Lucien tipped his plumed hat to the crowd. The people returned his courtesy with cheers and bows. His horse never halted, never allowed itself to be hemmed in. It pranced, arching its neck, snorting, waving its tail like a flag, moving between the people like a fish through water. In a moment Count Lucien was free. Followed by cheers, he rode down the street after the King. A line of musketeers parted the crowd again; Monsieur's carriage and guards followed in Count Lucien's wake.

A bright flock of young noblemen galloped past. Outside the window, Lotte's brother Philippe, duke de Chartres, dragged his big bay horse to a stop and spurred it to rear, showing off its gilded harness. Chartres wore plumes and velvet and carried a jewelled sword. Just returned from the summer campaigns, he affected a thin moustache like the one His Majesty had worn as a youth.

Madame smiled at her son. Lotte waved to her brother. Chartres swept off his hat and bowed to them all from horseback, laughing. A scarf fluttered at his throat, tied loosely, the end tucked in a buttonhole.

od to have Philippe home!' Lotte said. 'Home and safe.'
  like a rake.' Madame spoke bluntly, and with a German
    spite having come to France from the Palatinate more than
    years before. She shook her head, sighing fondly. 'No doubt
w   manners the same. He must accommodate himself to being back
at court.'

'Allow him a few moments to enjoy his triumph on the field of
battle, Madame,' Monsieur said. 'I doubt my brother the King will
permit our son another command.'

'Then he'll be safe,' Madame said.

'At the cost of his glory.'

'There's not enough glory to go around, my friend.' Lorraine
leaned toward Monsieur and laid his hand across the duke's jewelled
fingers. 'Not enough for the King's nephew. Not enough for the
King's brother. Only enough for the King.'

'That will be sufficient, sir!' Madame said. 'You're speaking of
your sovereign!'

Lorraine leaned back. His arm, muscular beneath the sensual soft-
ness of his velvet coat, pressed against the point of Marie-Josèphe's
shoulder.

'You've said the same thing, Madame,' he said. 'I believed it the
only subject on which we concur.'

His Majesty's natural son, the duke du Maine, glittering in rubies
and gold lace, cavorted his black horse outside Monsieur's carriage
until Madame glared at him, snorted, and turned her back. The duke
laughed at her and galloped toward the front of the procession.

'Waste of a good war horse,' Madame muttered, ignoring Lorraine. 'What use has a mouse-dropping for a war horse?'

Monsieur and Lorraine caught each other's gaze. Both men laughed.

Chartres' horse leaped after Maine. The young princes were glorious. On horseback, they overcame their afflictions. Chartres' wild eye
gave him a rakish air; Maine's lameness disappeared. Maine was so
handsome that one hardly noticed his crooked spine. The King had
declared him legitimate; only Madame still made note of his bastardy.

His Majesty's legitimate grandsons raced past; the three little boys
pounded their heels against the sides of their spotted ponies and tried

8

to keep up with their illegitimate half-uncle Maine and their legitimate cousin Chartres.

'Stay in the shade, daughter,' Monsieur said to Lotte. 'The sun will spoil your complexion.'

'But, sir—'

'And your expensive new dress,' Madame said.

'Yes, Monsieur. Yes, Madame.'

Marie-Josèphe, too, drew back from the sunlight. It would be a shame to ruin her new gown, the finest, by far, that she had ever worn. What did it matter if it was a cast-off of Lotte's? She smoothed the yellow silk and arranged it to show more of the silver petticoat.

'And you, Mlle de la Croix,' Monsieur said. 'You are nearly as dark as the Hurons. People will start calling you the little Indian girl, and Madame de Maintenon will demand the return of her nickname.'

Lorraine chuckled. Madame frowned.

'The old hag never would claim it,' Madame said. 'She wants everyone to think she was born at Maintenon and has some right to the title of marquise!'

'Madame—' Marie-Josèphe thought to defend Mme de Maintenon. When Marie-Josèphe first came to France, straight from the convent school on Martinique, the marquise had been kind to her. Though Marie-Josèphe was too old, at twenty, to be a student at Mme de Maintenon's school at Saint-Cyr, the marquise had given her a place teaching arithmetic to the younger girls. Like Marie-Josèphe, Mme de Maintenon had come to France from Martinique with nothing.

Mme de Maintenon often spoke of Martinique to the students, her protégées. She recounted the hardships she had endured in the New World. She reassured the impoverished high-born girls that if they were devout, and obedient, as she was, His Majesty would provide their dowries and they too could escape their circumstances.

Monsieur interrupted Marie-Josèphe. 'Do you use the skin cream I gave you?' He peered at her over his pomander. His complexion was very fair. He whitened it further with powder, and accentuated his fairness with black beauty patches at his cheekbone and beside his mouth. 'It's the finest in the world – but it won't work if you insist on staying out in the sun!'

'Papa, don't be mean,' Lotte said. 'Marie-Josèphe's complexion is ever so much paler than when she arrived.'

'Thanks to my skin cream,' Monsieur said.

'Let her be,' Madame said. 'There's no shame in being a little leaf-rustler, as I was. As His Majesty says, no one at court enjoys the gardens anymore. Except me, and now Mlle de la Croix. What were you saying a moment ago?'

'It was nothing, Madame,' Marie-Josèphe said, grateful that Monsieur had interrupted her before she expressed her opinion of Mme de Maintenon. Expressing one's opinion at court was a gamble, and speaking kindly of Mme de Maintenon in Madame's presence was foolhardy.

'Whoa!' the coachman cried. The coach lurched to a halt. Marie-Josèphe slid forward, nearly falling from the seat. Her ankles touched the elegant long legs of the chevalier de Lorraine. Lorraine took her arm, most chivalrously, and continued to hold her when the coach steadied. His leg brushed against hers. He smiled down at her. Marie-Josèphe smiled back, then lowered her gaze, embarrassed by her thoughts. The chevalier was devastatingly handsome, despite being an old man. He was fifty-five, the same age as the King. He wore a long black wig, just like His Majesty's. His eyes were blazing blue. Marie-Josèphe drew back to give him more room. He shifted, seeking a comfortable position. His legs pressed her feet, trapping them against the base of the carriage seat.

'Sit up straight, sir!' Madame said. 'No one gave you leave to lie supine in my presence.'

Monsieur patted the chevalier de Lorraine's knee.

'I give Lorraine leave to stretch, my dear,' he said. 'My friend is too tall for my coach.'

'And I'm too fat for it,' Madame said. 'But I don't demand the entire seat.'

Lorraine drew himself up. The top of his wig brushed the roof.

'I do beg Madame's pardon.' He picked up his plumed hat and opened the door. As he stepped to the street, he drew the egret feathers across Marie-Josèphe's wrist.

Monsieur hurried after him.

Marie-Josèphe regained her breath and returned her attention to Madame and Lotte, where it belonged. 'I'll ride back to Versailles with Yves,' she said quickly. 'Everyone will have more room on the way home.'

'Dear child,' Madame said, 'that had nothing to do with the size of the coach.' She rose and climbed out. Monsieur handed her down, and Lorraine assisted Lotte. Marie-Josèphe followed quickly, anxious to see her brother again. Lorraine waited for her, treating her as if she were nearly on a level with the family of the brother of the King. He gave her his hand. His attentions both thrilled and embarrassed her. He left her off-balance. Nothing in Martinique had ever embarrassed her, when she had lived a quiet life keeping her brother's house and helping in his experiments and reading books on all manner of subjects.

She stepped into the street beside Madame, who was far too stately to acknowledge the dirt and the smells. The King wished to meet his expedition at the waterfront, and Madame was a part of his court, so Madame accompanied him and did not complain.

Marie-Josèphe smiled to herself. Madame did not complain in public. In private the Princess Palatine used plain speech and seldom held back her opinions about anything.

Monsieur touched Lorraine's elbow. Lorraine bowed over Marie-Josèphe's hand. He joined Monsieur, but Madame had claimed her place at her husband's side. Chartres leaped from his horse, threw the reins to a footman, and offered his arm to his sister.

Marie-Josèphe curtsied and stepped back. She must find her proper place at the end of the line of precedence.

'Come with us, Mlle de la Croix,' Madame said. 'The chevalier will escort you.'

'But, Madame—!'

'I know what it is, to miss your family. I haven't visited mine since I came to France twenty years ago. Come with us, and you won't miss your brother a moment longer than necessary.'

With gratitude and wonder, Marie-Josèphe stooped and kissed the hem of Madame's gown. Next to her, Lorraine bowed to Madame and Monsieur. Marie-Josèphe rose. To her surprise, the chevalier kissed Monsieur's hand, not Madame's. The chevalier de Lorraine offered Marie-Josèphe his arm, smiling his charming, enigmatic smile.

Entranced, Marie-Josèphe found herself near the front of the extravagant procession, where she had no right to be, in the company of one of the most handsome men at court.

The King's carriage stood at the head of a line of fifty coaches. The gold sunburst gleamed from its door. Eight horses stamped and snorted and jingled their harness. They were white, with coin-sized black spots. The Emperor of China had sent the spotted stallions to his brother monarch for his coach, and spotted ponies for his grandsons.

'Be careful, Mlle de la Croix,' Lorraine said softly as they passed the magnificent team. The pungent smell of horse sweat mixed with the odour of fish and seaweed. 'Those creatures are part leopard, and eat meat.'

'That's absurd, sir,' Marie-Josèphe said. 'No horse can breed with a leopard.'

'Don't you believe in gryphons—'

'The world holds unknown creatures, but they're natural beings—'

'—or chimeras—'

'—not mixtures of eagles and lions—'

'—or sea monsters?'

'—or demons and human beings!'

'I forget, you study alchemy, as your brother does.'

'Not alchemy, sir! He studies natural philosophy.'

'And leaves the alchemy to you – the alchemy of beauty.'

'Truly, sir, neither of us studies alchemy. He studies natural philosophy. I study a little mathematics.'

Lorraine smiled again. 'I see no difference.' She would have explained that unlike an alchemist, a natural philosopher cared nothing about immortality, or the transmutation of base metals to gold, but Lorraine dismissed the question with a shrug. 'The fault of my small understanding. Mathematics – do you mean arithmetic? How dangerous. If I studied arithmetic, I should have to add up all my debts.' He shuddered, leaned over, and whispered, 'You are so beautiful, I forget you engage in . . . unusual . . . activities.'

12

Marie-Josèphe blushed. 'I've had no occasion to assist my brother since he left Martinique.' *Nor to study mathematics*, she thought with regret.

Young noblemen leaped from their horses; their fathers and mothers and sisters stepped down from their carriages. The dukes and peers and the duchesses of France, the foreign princes, the courtiers of Versailles in their finery, arranged themselves in order of precedence to salute their King.

Beside the King's carriage, the count de Chrétien slid down from his grey Arabian. The other men of Count Lucien's rank all carried swords; a short dirk hung from his belt. He stood below the height of fashion in other ways. Despite his gold-embroidered blue coat, the sign of a favoured courtier, he wore neither lace nor ribbons at his throat. Instead, he wore an informal steinkirk scarf, its end tucked into a buttonhole. His small moustache resembled that of an army officer. Chartres still gloried in his success on the summer's campaign, but all the other courtiers stayed clean-shaven like the King. Count Lucien's perruke was auburn, knotted at the back of his neck in the military style. It should be black like the King's; it should fall in great curls over his shoulders. Marie-Josèphe supposed that someone who enjoyed the King's favour could dispense with fashion, but she thought it foolish, even ridiculous, for the Count de Chrétien to dress and groom himself like a captain of the army.

Leaning on his ebony walking stick, Count Lucien gestured to six footmen. They unrolled a gold and scarlet silk rug along the wharf, so His Majesty would be in no danger of coming in contact with slime or fish guts.

The courtiers formed a double line, flanking the Persian carpet, smiling and hiding their envy of Count Lucien, whom the King favoured, who served His Majesty so closely.

Marie-Josèphe found herself near the King's carriage, separated from it only by a few members of His Majesty's immediate family. The legitimate offspring of His Majesty stood nearest to the King, of course. Madame marched past Maine and his wife and his brother, insisting on her family's precedence before the children His Majesty had declared legitimate.

13

Count Lucien called for the sedan chairs. Four carriers in the King's livery brought his chair, and four more brought Mme de Maintenon's.

Count Lucien opened the door of His Majesty's carriage.

Marie-Josèphe's heart beat fast. She stood almost close enough to touch the King, except that the carriage door was in the way. Its golden sunburst gazed at her impassively. She caught a glimpse of the sleeve of the King's dark brown coat, of the white plumes on his hat, of the red high heels of his polished shoes. His Majesty acknowledged the cheering crowd.

One ragged fellow pushed forward. 'Give us bread!' he shouted. 'Your taxes starve our families!'

The musketeers spurred their horses toward him. His compatriots pulled him back into the crowd. He disappeared. His desperate shouts ended in a muffled curse. The King paid him no attention. Following His Majesty's example, everyone pretended the incident had never occurred.

His Majesty entered the sedan chair without stepping on the ground or on the Persian rug.

Mme de Maintenon, drab in her black gown and simply-dressed hair, entered the second sedan chair. Everyone said she had been a great beauty and a great wit, when the King married her in secret – or, as some claimed (and Madame believed), made her his mistress. Marie-Josèphe wondered if they complimented her in hopes of gaining her favour. As far as Marie-Josèphe could tell, Mme de Maintenon cared for the favour of no one except the King, and God, which amounted to the same thing; she favoured no courtier but the Duke du Maine, whom she treated as a son.

Count Lucien led the sedan chairs down the ramp to the wharf, limping a little. His cane struck a muffled tempo on the Persian carpet.

Mme de Maintenon's carriers took her sedan chair aside, waiting to enter the procession in her proper place. In public, the King's wife ranked only as a marquise.

The double line of courtiers turned itself inside out to follow the King: the widowed Grand Dauphin, Monseigneur, His Majesty's only immediate legitimate offspring, proceeded first. Monseigneur's little sons the dukes of Bourgogne, Anjou, and Berri, marched just behind him.

Monsieur and Madame, Chartres and Mademoiselle d'Orléans, and Lorraine and Marie-Josèphe entered the procession. The courtiers accompanied their King in strict order of rank. Only Marie-Josèphe was out of place. She felt both grateful to Madame and uneasy about the breach of etiquette, especially when she passed the Duchess du Maine, who favoured her with a poisonous glare.

The King's galleon rocked at the far end of the wharf, its sails furled, its heavy lines groaning around the stanchions. Apollo's dawn horses, gleaming gold, leaped from the stern, the motion of the ship giving them the illusion of life.

A breath of breeze crept in from the harbour, pungent with the smell of salt and seaweed. The King's sigil fluttered, then fell again, limp in the heat. Sailors unloaded Yves' belongings to the dock: crates of equipment, baggage, a bundle like a body in a shroud.

Yves swept down the gangplank. Marie-Josèphe recognised him instantly, though he had been a youth in homespun the last time she saw him. Now he was a grown man, handsome, elegant and severe in his long black robe. She wanted to run the length of the wharf to greet him. Saint-Cyr and Versailles had taught her to behave more sedately.

A half-dozen sailors trudged down the gangplank, bowed under the weight of shoulder-poles. A net hung between the poles, cradling a gilded basin. At the end of the narrow ramp, Yves placed his hand on the rim of the basin, steadying its sway. The captain of the galleon joined him, and together they strode up the dock. Yves kept his hand on the basin, protecting and possessing it.

A haunting air, sung in exquisite voice, flowed over the procession. The unexpected beauty of the melody so surprised Marie-Josèphe that she nearly stumbled. No one in the King's entourage would sing here, or now, without his order. Someone from the galleon must be singing, someone familiar with the music of foreign lands.

Yves approached. He reached into the gilded basin. The song exploded with a snort, a growl.

His Majesty's court gathered, flanking His Majesty's sedan chair.

Marie-Josèphe found herself next to Madame, who squeezed her hand.

'Your brother's safe, he's well,' Madame whispered. 'That is what's important.'

'He's safe, and well, Madame, and he was right,' Marie-Josèphe said, only loud enough for Madame to hear. 'That is what's important to my brother.'

Yves' small group met the King at the border of the Persian rug. The sailors did not step on the rug; the sedan chair carriers did not leave it.

'Father de la Croix,' Count Lucien said.

'M. de Chrétien,' Yves replied.

They bowed. Yves' pride and triumph shone behind his modest expression. His gaze passed across Louis' court. Every courtier stood on this filthy dock, as if it were the Marble Courtyard, because of him. Marie-Josèphe smiled, taking pleasure in his position as the King's natural philosopher and explorer. She expected him to smile back, to acknowledge, perhaps with surprise, her success in her brief time at Versailles.

But Yves scanned the court, and he did not even pause when he looked at her. Madame pressed forward, drawing Marie-Josèphe with her, trying to get a clear view inside the basin.

The song rose again, a whisper surging into a cry, into a shriek of anger and despair. Marie-Josèphe shivered.

The shape in the basin shuddered violently. Water splashed Yves and the sailors. The sailors flinched. The creature fought the canvas that swaddled it.

Count Lucien opened the sedan chair. His Majesty leaned out. His court saluted him with bow or curtsy. The men removed their hats. Marie-Josèphe curtsied. Her silken skirts rustled. Even the sailors tried to bow, laden as they were, and ignorant of etiquette. The creature shrieked again, and strands of its black-green hair whipped over the edge as the basin rocked and tilted.

'It lives,' Louis said.

'Yes, Your Majesty,' Yves said.

Yves pulled aside a flap of dripping canvas. The creature thrashed, splashing Louis' silk coat. Louis drew away, raising a pomander to his face. Yves covered the creature again.

His Majesty turned to the captain. 'I am pleased.'

The King withdrew into the sedan chair. Count Lucien closed the door, and the carriers quickstepped away. Marie-Josèphe curtsied again. Louis' court stood aside, bowing to their King as his palanquin passed.

Count Lucien handed a small, heavy leather sack to the galleon's captain. The count nodded to Yves, then followed the King's conveyance.

The captain opened the King's purse, poured gold pieces into his hand, and laughed with delight and satisfaction. Count Lucien had presented him with a double handful of louis d'or, the gold coins commemorating the King. For a man of the captain's station, it was a fortune.

'Thank you, Your Majesty!' the captain called after Louis' sedan chair. 'Thank you, royal jester!'

Members of the court gasped. The chevalier de Lorraine chuckled and bent to whisper to Monsieur. Monsieur hid behind his pomander and his lace to conceal his amusement.

Count Lucien made no response, though he must have heard the captain. His walking stick thudded solidly on the carpet as he climbed to the quay.

Yves grabbed the captain's arm to silence him. 'His excellency Lucien de Barenton, Count de Chrétien!'

'No!' The captain laughed and shook his head. 'Now *you're* playing the jester, Father de la Croix.' He bowed. 'A profitable voyage, sir. I'm at your service at any time – even when you hunt sea monsters.'

He strolled off toward the galleon.

Madame nudged Marie-Josèphe. 'Greet your brother.'

Marie-Josèphe curtsied gratefully, lifted her silk skirts above the shiny stinking fish scales, and ran toward Yves. Still he did not acknowledge her.

Marie-Josèphe's stride faltered. *Is he angry at me?* she wondered. *How could he be? I'm not angry with him, and I have some right to anger.*

'Yves . . . ?'

Yves glanced at her. He raised his dark arched eyebrows. 'Marie-Josèphe!'

His expression changed. One moment he was the serious, ascetic, grown-up Jesuit, the next her delighted older brother. He took three long strides toward her, he embraced her, he swung her around like a child. She hugged him and pressed her cheek against the black wool of his cassock.

'I hardly recognise you — I *didn't* recognise you! You're a grown woman!'

She had so many things to tell him that she said nothing, for fear her words would spill out all at once in a tangle. He set her down and looked at her. She smiled up at him. Sun-lines creased his face when he smiled. His skin had darkened to an even deeper tan, while her complexion was fading to a fashionable paleness. His black hair lay in disarrayed curls — unlike most of the men at court, he wore no perruke — while pins and the hot iron had crafted Marie-Josèphe's red-gold mane into ringlets beneath the lace-covered wire and the ruffles of her headdress, a fashionable fontanges.

His eyes were the same, a beautiful, intense dark blue.

'Dear brother, you look so well — the voyage must have agreed with you.'

'It was dreadful,' Yves said. 'But I was too busy to be troubled.'

He put his arm around her and returned to the gold basin. The creature thrashed and cried.

'To the quay,' Yves said. The sailors hurried up the dock. Their bare tattooed arms strained at the weight of basin and water and Yves' living prey. Marie-Josèphe tried to see inside the basin, but wet canvas covered everything. She leaned against Yves, her arm tight around his waist. She would have plenty of time to look at his creature.

They walked between the lines of courtiers. Everyone, even Madame and Monsieur and the princes and princesses of the Blood Royal, strained to see the monster Yves had captured for the King.

And then, as Yves passed, they saluted him.

Startled for a moment, Yves hesitated. Marie-Josèphe was about to dig her fingers into his ribs — Yves had always been ticklish — to give him a lively hint about his behaviour. As a boy he had always paid more attention to his bird collection than to his manners.

To Marie-Josèphe's surprise, and delight, Yves bowed to Monsieur, to Madame, with perfect courtliness and the restraint proper to his station.

Marie-Josèphe curtsied to Monsieur. She raised Madame's hem to her lips and kissed it. The portly duchess smiled fondly at her, and nodded her approval.

Yves bowed to the members of the royal family. He passed between the double line of courtiers. Graciously, he nodded to their acclaim.

Halfway up the dock, between the dukes and duchesses, and the counts and countesses, Marie-Josèphe and Yves passed the second sedan chair. Its windows were closed tight, and the curtains drawn behind the glass. Poor Mme de Maintenon, whose only task was to follow the King from Versailles to Le Havre and back, showed no interest in the creature and its triumphant captor.

'I wish I'd been with you,' Marie-Josèphe said. 'I wish I'd seen the wild sea monsters!'

'We were cold and wet and miserable, and hurricanes nearly sank us. You'd have been blamed – on a warship, a woman is as welcome as a sea monster.'

'What foolish superstition.' Marie-Josèphe's voyage from Martinique had been uncomfortable, yet exhilarating.

'You were much better off at the convent.'

Marie-Josèphe caught her breath. He knew nothing of the convent. How could he? If he had known, he would never have left her there in boredom and silence and lonely misery.

'I've missed you so,' she said. 'I worried!'

'Whenever I thought of you, I heard your little tunes. In my mind. Do you still write them?'

'Versailles hardly has room for amateur musicians,' she said. 'But you shall hear something of mine, soon.'

'I thought of you often, Marie-Josèphe . . . though not in such a dress.'

'Do you like it?'

19

'It's immodest.'

'It's quite proper,' she said, leaving out her own first reaction to the tight waist and low neckline. She had known nothing of court then.

'It's unsuited to your station. And to mine.'

'It's unsuited for a colonial girl. But you're now the King's natural philosopher and I'm Mademoiselle's lady-in-waiting. I must wear grand habit.'

'And here I thought,' Yves said, 'that you'd be safely teaching arithmetic.'

They climbed up the wharf to the quay.

'I couldn't remain at Saint-Cyr,' Marie-Josèphe said. 'All the instructresses must take the veil.'

Yves glanced at her, puzzled. 'That would suit you.'

The King's departure saved her from making a sharp retort; she, and Yves, and all the courtiers bowed as their sovereign climbed into his carriage. It drove away, surrounded by musketeers. The ragged townspeople streamed after the King, cheering, shouting, pleading.

Marie-Josèphe looked around hopefully for the chevalier de Lorraine, but he climbed into Monsieur's carriage. The other courtiers hurried to their coaches and horses and clattered after the King.

Only Count Lucien, several musketeers, the pigeon-keeper, the baggage wagons, and a plain coach remained on the quiet quay.

The pigeon-keeper hurried to meet his apprentice, who toiled up the dock with the baggage-carriers. The apprentice balanced an awkward load of wicker cages, most of them empty. His master took the cages that still sheltered pigeons.

'Put the basin there,' Yves said to the sailors. He gestured to the first wagon. 'Be gentle——'

'I want to see——' Marie-Josèphe said.

The last carriages rattled across the cobblestones.

Frightened by the clatter and the shouts and the snap of whips, the creature screamed and struggled. Its horrible singing cry cut off Marie-Josèphe's words and spooked the draft horses so they nearly bolted.

'Be gentle!' Yves said again.

Marie-Josèphe leaned toward the basin, trying to see inside. 'Now, behave!' she said. The creature shrieked.

The sailors dropped the basin. The carrying poles and the net fell across it. Water splashed the cobblestones. The sea monster groaned. The sailors ran toward the galleon, nearly knocking down the pigeon-keepers. The apprentice dropped the empty cages. The master, who held live birds in his huge tender hands and let the pigeons perch on his shoulders and head, slipped his pets beneath his shirt for safety.

'Come back—' Yves called to the sailors. They ignored him. Their compatriots, carrying Yves' other baggage, abandoned the crates and the luggage and the shrouded figure and fled to their ship.

Marie-Josèphe did her best not to laugh at Yves' discomfiture. The wagon drivers had their hands full reining in the horses: they could not help. The musketeers *would* not, for fetching and carrying was far below their station. And of course Count Lucien could not be expected to help with the baggage.

Angry and stubborn, Yves tried to lift the basin. He barely raised its corner. Some ragged boys, stragglers from the crowd, rode the quay's stone wall and jeered.

'You, boys!'

Count Lucien's command stopped their laughter. They jumped to their feet, about to run, but he spoke to them in a friendly tone and threw each a coin.

'Here's a sou. Come earn another. Help Father de la Croix load his wagons.'

The boys jumped from the wall and ran to Yves, ready to do his bidding. They were dirty and ragged and barefoot, fearless in the face of the creature's moans. The boys might have worked for a bread crust. They lifted the creature into the first wagon, the baggage into the second, and loaded the shrouded figure into the wagon full of ice.

A specimen for dissection, Marie-Josèphe thought. *My clever brother caught one sea monster for the King, and took another for himself.*

'Yves, come ride with me,' Marie-Josèphe said.

'It's impossible.' He climbed into the first wagon. 'I can't leave the creature.'

Disappointed, Marie-Josèphe crossed the quay to the plain coach.

21

The footman opened the door. Count Lucien courteously reached up to her, to help her in. The strength of his hand surprised her. Instead of being short, as she had expected, his fingers were disproportionately long. He wore soft deerskin gloves. She wondered if he would permit her to draw his hands.

She wondered why he had stayed behind. She felt nervous about talking to him, for he was important and she was not. And, truth to tell, she wondered whether to stoop to his height or stand straight and look down at him. She resolved the question by climbing into the coach.

'Thank you, M. de Chrétien,' she said.

'You're welcome, Mlle de la Croix.'

'Did you see the sea monster?'

'I am not much interested in grotesques, Mlle de la Croix. Pardon me, I cannot linger.'

The heat of embarrassment crept up Marie-Josèphe's face. She had insulted Count Lucien without meaning to, and she suspected he had insulted her in return.

The count spoke a word to his grey Arabian. The horse bowed on one knee. Count Lucien clambered into the saddle. The horse lurched to its feet, clumsy for an instant. Carrying its tail like a banner, the Arabian sprang into a gallop to take Count Lucien after his sovereign.

Chapter 2

Sunset spread its light across the park of the chateau of Versailles. The moon, waxing gibbous, approached its zenith. Heading for their stables, the coach horses gained their second wind and plunged through the forest along the hard-packed dirt road.

Marie-Josèphe leaned her head against the side of the coach. She wished she had gone with Madame, in Monsieur's crowded carriage. Madame would have all manner of amusing comments about today's journey. Monsieur and Lorraine would engage in their friendly barbed banter. Chartres might ride beside the carriage and tell Marie-Josèphe about his latest experiment in chemistry, for she was surely the only woman and perhaps the only other person at court who understood what he was talking about. Certainly his wife neither understood nor cared. The Duchess de Chartres did exactly as she pleased. It had not pleased her to come from the Palais Royale in Paris to join His Majesty's – her father's – procession.

If Chartres spoke to Marie-Josèphe then the duke du Maine might, too. And then the King's grandson Bourgogne and his little brothers would demand their share of paying attention to Marie-Josèphe.

Maine, like Chartres, was married; Bourgogne was barely a youth, and his brothers were children. Besides, they were all unimaginably above Marie-Josèphe's station. Their attention to her could come to nothing.

Nevertheless, Marie-Josèphe enjoyed it.

Bored and lonely and restless, Marie-Josèphe gazed out into the trees. This far from His Majesty's residence, the woods grew unconfined. Fallen branches thrust up through underbrush. The fragile swords of ferns drooped into the roadway. Sunset streaked the world with dusty red-gold rays. If she were riding alone she could stop and listen to the forest, to the twilight burst of bird song, to the soft dance of bat wings. Instead, her coach drove into the dusk, its driver and its attendants and even her brother all unaware of the music.

The underbrush disappeared; the trees grew farther apart; no branches littered the ground. Hunters could ride headlong through this tame groomed forest. Marie-Josèphe imagined riding along a brushstroke of trail, following the King in pursuit of a deer.

A scream of rage and challenge filled the twilit forest. Marie-Josèphe clutched the door and the edge of her seat. The horses shied and snorted and leaped forward. The carriage lurched. The exhausted animals tried to outrun the terrible noise. The driver shouted and dragged his team into his control.

The scream of the tiger in His Majesty's menagerie awoke and aroused all the other exotic animals. The elephant trumpeted. The lion coughed and roared. The aurochs bellowed.

The sea monster sang a challenge.

The wild eerie melody quickened Marie-Josèphe's heart. The shrieking warble was as raw, as erotic, as passionate, as the singing of eagles. The tame forests of Versailles hid the same shadows as the wildest places of Martinique.

The sea monster cried again. The Menagerie fell silent. The sea monster's song vanished in a whisper.

The carriage rumbled around the arm of the Grand Canal. The canal shimmered with ghostly fog; wavelets lapped against the sides of His Majesty's fleet of miniature ships. Wheels crunched on the gravel of the Queen's Road; the baggage wagons turned down the Queen's Road toward the Fountain of Apollo. Marie-Josèphe's coach continued toward the chateau of Versailles and its formal gardens.

'Driver!'

'Whoa!'

Marie-Josèphe leaned out the window. The heavy, hot breath of tired horses filled the night. The gardens lay quiet and strange, the fountains still.

'Follow my brother, if you please.'

'But, mamselle—'

'And then you are dismissed for the evening.'

'Yes, mamselle!' He wheeled the horses around.

Yves hurried from one wagon to the other, trying to direct two groups of workers at once.

'You men – take this basin – it's heavy. Stop – you – don't touch the ice!'

Marie-Josèphe opened the carriage door. By the time the footman had climbed wearily down to help her, she was running toward the baggage wagons.

An enormous tent covered the Fountain of Apollo. Candlelight flickered inside, illuminating the silk walls. The tent glowed, an immense lantern.

Rows of candles softly lit the way up the hill to the chateau, tracing the edges of *le tapis vert*, the Green Carpet. The expanse of perfect lawn split the gardens from Apollo's Fountain to Latona's, flanked by gravel paths and marble statues of gods and heroes.

Marie-Josèphe held her skirts above the gravel and hurried to the baggage wagons. The sea monster's basin and the shroud in the ice divided Yves' attention.

'Marie-Josèphe, don't let them move the specimen till I get back.' Yves tossed his command over his shoulder as if he had never left Martinique to become a Jesuit, as if she were still keeping his house and assisting in his experiments.

Yves hurried to the tent. Embroidered on the silken curtains, the gold sunburst of the King gazed out impassively. Two musketeers drew the curtains aside.

'Move the ice carefully,' Marie-Josèphe said to the workers. 'Uncover the bundle.'

'But the Father said—'

'And now *I* say.'

Still the workers hesitated.

'My brother might forget about this specimen till morning,' Marie-Josèphe said. 'You might wait for him all night.'

In nervous silence they obeyed her, uncovering the shroud with their hands. Shards of chopped ice scattered over the ground. Marie-Josèphe took care that the workers caused no damage. She had helped Yves with his work since she was a little girl and he a boy of twelve, both of them learning Greek and Latin, reading Herodotus – credulous old man! – and Galen, and studying Newton. Yves of course always got first choice of the books, but he never objected when she made off with the *Principia*, or slept with it beneath her pillow. She grieved for the loss of M. Newton's book, yearned for another copy, and wondered what he had discovered about light, the planets, and gravity during the past five years.

The workmen lifted the shrouded figure. Ice scattered onto the path. Marie-Josèphe followed the workmen into the tent. She was anxious to get a clear view of a sea monster, either one that was living or one that was dead.

The enormous tent covered the Fountain of Apollo and a surrounding circle of dry land. Beneath the tent, an iron cage enclosed the fountain. Inside the new cage, Apollo and his golden chariot and the four horses of the sun rose from the water, bringing dawn, heralded by dolphins, by tritons blowing trumpets.

Marie-Josèphe thought, *Apollo is galloping west to east, in opposition to the sun.*

Three shallow, wide wooden stairs led from the pool's low stone rim to a wooden platform at water's level. The tent, the cage, and the stairs and platform had been built for Yves' convenience, though they spoiled the view of the Dawn Chariot.

Outside the cage, laboratory equipment stood upon a sturdy floor of polished planks. Two armchairs, several armless chairs, and a row of ottomans faced the laboratory.

'You may put the specimen on the table,' Marie-Josèphe said to the workers. They did as she directed, grateful to be free of the burden and its sharp odours.

Tall and spare in his long black cassock, Yves stood in the entrance of the cage. His workers wrestled the basin onto the fountain's rim.

'Don't drop it – lay it down – careful!'

The sea monster cried and struggled. The basin ground against stone. One of the workers swore aloud; another elbowed him soundly and cast a warning glance toward Yves. Marie-Josèphe giggled behind her hand. Yves was the least likely of priests to notice rough language.

'Slide it down the stairs. Let water flow in—'

26

The basin bumped down the steps and onto the platform. Yves knelt beside it, unwrapping the net that surrounded it. Overcome by her curiosity, Marie-Josèphe hastened to join him. The silk of her underskirt rustled against the polished laboratory floor, with a sound as soft and smooth as if she were crossing the marble of the Hall of Mirrors.

Before she reached the cage, the tent's curtains moved aside again. A worker carried a basket of fresh fish and seaweed to the cage, dropped it, and fled. Other workers hauled in ice and a barrel of sawdust.

Her curiosity thwarted, Marie-Josèphe returned to Yves' specimen. She wanted to open its shroud, but thought better of revealing the creature to the tired, frightened workmen.

'You two, cover the bundle with ice, then cover the ice with sawdust. The rest of you, fetch Father de la Croix's equipment from the wagons.'

They obeyed, moving the specimen gingerly, for it reeked of preserving spirits and corruption.

Yves will have to carry out his dissection quickly, Marie-Josèphe said to herself. *Or he'll have nothing left to dissect but rotten meat on a skeleton.*

Marie-Josèphe had grown used to the smell during years of helping her brother with his explorations and experiments. It bothered her not at all. But the workers breathed in short unhappy gasps, occasionally glancing, frightened, toward Yves and the groaning sea monster.

The workers covered the laboratory table with insulating sawdust.

'Bring more ice every day,' Marie-Josèphe said. 'You understand — it's very important.'

One of the workers bowed. 'Yes, mamselle, M. de Chrétien has ordered it.'

'You may retire.'

They fled the tent, repelled by the dead smell and by the live sea monster's crying. The melancholy song drew Marie-Josèphe closer. Yves' workers tilted the basin off the platform. Water trickled into it.

Marie-Josèphe hurried to the Fountain.

'Yves, let me see—'

As Yves loosened the canvas restraints, the grinding and creaking

27

of the water pumps shook the night. The fountain nozzles gurgled, groaned, and gushed water. Apollo's fountain spouted water in the shape of a fleur-de-lys. At its zenith, the central stream splashed the tent peak. Droplets rained down on Apollo's chariot, dimpled the pool's surface, and spattered the sea monster. The creature screamed and thrashed and slapped Yves with its tails. Yves staggered backward.

'Turn off the fountain!' Yves shouted.

Snarling, the creature struggled free of the basin. Yves jumped away, evading the sea monster's teeth and claws and tails. The workers ran to do Yves' bidding.

The creature lurched away and tumbled into the water, escaping into its prison in the Fountain of Apollo.

Marie-Josèphe caught Yves' arm. A ripple broke against his foot and flowed around the soles of his boots, as if he walked on water. Water soaked the hem of his cassock.

My brother walks on water, Marie-Josèphe thought with a smile. *He ought to be able to keep his clothing dry!*

The fountains spurted high, then gushed half as high, then bubbled in their nozzles. The fleur-de-lys wilted. The creaking of the pumps abruptly ceased. No ripple, not even bubbles, marked the surface of the pool.

Yves wiped his sleeve across his face. Marie-Josèphe, standing two steps above him, almost reached his height. She laid her hand on her brother's shoulder.

'You've succeeded,' she said.

'I hope so.'

Marie-Josèphe leaned forward and peered into the water. A dark shape lay beneath the surface, obscured by the reflections of candlelight.

'It's alive now,' Yves said. 'How long it will survive . . .' His worried voice trailed off.

'It need not live long,' Marie-Josèphe said. 'I want to see it – call it to you!'

'It won't come to me. It's a beast, it doesn't understand me.'

'My *cat* understands,' Marie-Josèphe said. 'Didn't you train it, all those weeks at sea?'

'I had no time to train it.' Yves scowled. 'It wouldn't eat – I had to

28

force-feed it.' He folded his arms, glaring at the bright water. The sea monster drifted, silent and still. 'But I fulfilled His Majesty's wishes. I've done what no one has done in four hundred years. I've brought a living sea monster to land.'

Marie-Josèphe leaned closer to the water, straining to see. The creature was long, and sleek, longer and more slender than the dolphins that cavorted off the beach in Martinique. Its tangled hair swirled around its head.

'Whoever heard of a fish with hair?' she exclaimed.

'It's no fish,' Yves said. 'It breathes air. If it doesn't breathe soon—'

He crossed the rim of the fountain and stepped to the ground. Marie-Josèphe stayed where she was, gazing at the monster.

It gazed back at her, its eyes eerily reflecting the light. It extended its arms, its webbed hands.

Yves' shadow fell across the sea monster. The creature retreated, closing its golden eyes. Yves clenched his fingers around a goad.

'I won't let it drown.'

He poked the goad at the sea monster, trying to chivvy the creature into motion.

'Swim, damn you! Surface!'

Its hair drifted about its face. Its tail flukes quivered. The creature trembled.

'Stop, you're scaring it, you'll hurt it!' Marie-Josèphe knelt on the platform and plunged her hands into the water. 'Come to me, you're safe here.'

The creature's webbed fingers clutched her wrists and pressed heat against her skin. The sea monster's claws touched her like the tips of knives, but never cut.

The sea monster dragged her into the pool.

Yves shouted and jabbed with the goad. The monster floated, just out of reach. Marie-Josèphe struggled to her feet, coughing, soaked. The cold water lifted her full petticoats like the petals of a water lily. She pushed them down. Her underskirt collapsed against her legs, scratchy and ungainly.

'Hurry, take my hand—'

'No, wait,' she said. The creature slipped past her, fleeing, then turning back, its voice touching her through the water. 'Don't frighten it again.' She stretched one hand toward the sea monster. 'Come here, come here . . .'

'Be careful. It's strong, it's cruel—'

'It's terrified!'

The creature's voice brushed against her fingertips. Its song spun from the surface like mist. Barely moving, creeping, floating, the sea monster neared Marie-Josèphe.

'Good sea monster. Fine sea monster.'

'His Majesty approaches,' Count Lucien said.

Startled, Marie-Josèphe glanced over her shoulder. Count Lucien stood on the fountain's rim. He had come into the tent, crossed the laboratory floor and entered the sea monster's cage without her noticing him. Yves remained down on the platform at water level, and Count Lucien up on the fountain's rim; the two men stood face to face.

On the other side of the tent, the musketeers held the tent curtains aside. A procession of torches marched along the Green Carpet toward Apollo.

'I'm not ready,' Yves said.

Marie-Josèphe returned her attention to the sea monster. It hesitated, just out of her reach. If she snatched at it, it would leap away like a green colt.

'If the King is ready,' Count Lucien said, '*you* are ready.'

'Yes,' Yves said. 'Of course.'

The sea monster stretched its arms forward. Its claws brushed Marie-Josèphe's fingertips.

'Mlle de la Croix,' Count Lucien said, 'His Majesty must not see you in this state of disarray.'

Marie-Josèphe caught her breath, frightened to realise she might insult His Majesty. She waded toward the platform, clumsy in her soaked skirts, unsteady in her heeled shoes on the uneven bottom of the pond.

The sea monster swam around her, cut her off, and lunged upward before her. It gasped a great gulp of air. Marie-Josèphe stared at it, horrified and fascinated. It splashed down and lay still, gazing at her.

30

Though its arms and hands mimicked a human's, it was more grotesque than any monkey. Its two tails writhed and kicked. Webs connected its long fingers, which bore heavy, sharp claws. Its long lank hair tangled around its head and over its shoulders and across its chest – its breasts, for it did have flat, wide breasts and small dark nipples. Water beaded on its mahogany skin, gleaming in candlelight.

The monster gazed at Marie-Josèphe with intense gold eyes, the only thing of beauty about it. Grotesque and magnificent, like a gargoyle on a medieval church, its face bore ridged swirls on forehead and cheeks. Its nose was flat and low, its nostrils narrow. The creature's canine teeth projected over its lower lip.

'Splendid. Splendid and horrible.' His Majesty spoke, his voice powerful and beautiful. Count Lucien and Yves bowed to their sovereign. The King, in fresh clothes, fresh lace, and a new wig, studied his sea monster. His gaze avoided Marie-Josèphe. His court, from Monsieur and Madame to Mme de Maintenon to the grandchildren of France, stared into the fountain. Some gazed at the sea monster; Marie-Josèphe caused others even more amazement.

Frightened, the creature snarled and dove.

If Marie-Josèphe climbed out of the fountain, she would face the King squarely; he could not overlook her. Such a breach of etiquette might force Lotte to dismiss her. She might have to leave court. Trapped, about to burst into tears of embarrassment, seeking shadows, she backed away. Her petticoats nearly tripped her.

Count Lucien flung down his hat, took off his cloak, and held it open between Marie-Josèphe and the King.

Safely concealed, Marie-Josèphe stood still in the cold water. The sea monster, a dark shape, swam away. It grabbed the bars of its cage, rattled them, turned with an angry flick of its tail, and swam to the platform again. The sea monster peered from the water, revealing only its eyes and its tangled deep-green hair.

Most of the other members of court could see Marie-Josèphe perfectly well. But that did not matter. All that mattered was that His Majesty should not be offended.

Madame caught Marie-Josèphe's glance and shook her head with disapproval, but her lips twitched with heroically contained laughter.

Monsieur, in a gentlemanly fashion, avoided looking, but Lorraine gazed straight at her. He smiled. She wrapped her arms around herself, embarrassed to be seen in such a state by such an elegant courtier.

I suppose I'd laugh, too, Marie-Josèphe thought. *If I weren't so cold.*

'You gratify our faith in you, Father de la Croix.' His Majesty joined Yves on the platform within the fountain's rim. 'A live sea monster!'

'*Your* sea monster, Your Majesty,' Yves said.

'Monsieur Boursin, what is your judgment?' Louis said. 'Will it be suitable for our celebration?'

M. Boursin, drab in the plain clothes suited to his place in the King's household, hurried forward. He bowed, rubbing his hands together, tall and thin and cadaverous as the angel of death.

'Is it stout? Does it feed?'

Boursin peered into the pool. The sea monster swam around the sculpture of Apollo, singing a sorrowful song.

'It accepts only a little sustenance,' Yves said.

'Then you must fatten it.'

'You're a Jesuit,' Louis said heartily. 'You're clever enough to make it eat.'

The sea monster attacked the cage again, splashing, rattling the iron bars.

'Make it stop thrashing!' M. Boursin said. 'It mustn't bruise its flesh.'

Marie-Josèphe wished she could speak to the sea monster to calm it, but she dared not raise her voice.

'I cannot,' Yves said. 'It's a wild animal. No man can control it.'

'It will calm,' Louis said, 'when it has become accustomed to its cage.'

His Majesty stepped to the ground, the high heels of his shoes loud on the wooden stairs. Yves and M. Boursin followed.

'M. de Chrétien,' His Majesty said courteously to Count Lucien.

'Your Majesty.'

'Mlle de la Croix,' Louis said, when he had left the cage, when his back was still turned.

Marie-Josèphe caught her breath. 'Y-yes, Your Majesty?'

'Are you hoping for a visit from Apollo?'

The courtiers laughed, and Marie-Josèphe blushed at the reference. The laughter died away.

'N-no, Your Majesty.'

'Come out at once, before you catch your death.'

'Yes, Your Majesty.'

She struggled onto the platform. Count Lucien continued to conceal her with his cape, using his walking stick to raise it as she climbed the steps. The water was cold, the air on her wet skin colder. Shivering, dripping pond water, she stepped over the fountain's rim, slipped past the courtiers, and hid in the shadows among the laboratory equipment.

Keeping his back turned, the King joined Mme de Maintenon.

'How do you like my sea monster, my dear?'

The chevalier de Lorraine strode past Count Lucien to Marie-Josèphe, sweeping his long dark cloak from his shoulders. Beneath it he wore a blue coat, the same shade as Count Lucien's, though with less gold lace. The blue coat marked him as a member of Louis' inner circle. Monsieur followed Lorraine with quick glances, trying but failing to keep his attention on the King.

'The creature's horribly ugly, Sire,' Mme de Maintenon said.

'No uglier than a wild boar, madame.'

Lorraine swung his cloak around Marie-Josèphe's shoulders. The fur-lined velvet, the warmth of his body, and the scent of his perfume enclosed her.

'Thank you, sir.' Her teeth chattered.

Lorraine bowed to her and rejoined Monsieur. Monsieur touched his arm. Diamond rings flashed in the candlelight.

'I think it's a demon, Sire,' Mme de Maintenon said.

'Your grace, it's a natural creature,' Yves said. 'Holy Mother Church has examined its kind, and judged it merely an animal. Like His Majesty's elephant, or His Majesty's crocodile.'

'Nevertheless, Father de la Croix,' His Majesty said, 'you might have captured a beautiful one.'

Yves strode to the dissection table, forcing Marie-Josèphe to retreat farther into the shadows. Count Lucien continued to hide her

33

from His Majesty. Lorraine's cloak concealed her soaked dress, but her hair hung in snarls around her face. Her headdress tilted at a ridiculous angle, stabbed her with its wires, and pulled her hair as it fell to the ground.

Yves unfolded the canvas shroud from his dead specimen. Ice scattered across the planks.

'The sea monsters are all ugly, Your Majesty,' Yves said. 'Females and males alike.'

The courtiers clustered around him, anxious to see the dead creature. On the wall of the tent, shadows jostled for position near the shadow of Marie-Josèphe's brother. Yves was the moon to His Majesty's sun, and the other courtiers hoped to capture some of the reflected light.

'It reeks of foul humours.'

Marie-Josèphe peeked over the edge of Count Lucien's cloak. Monsieur covered his nose with his handkerchief. Marie-Josèphe could hardly blame anyone not used to dissections, for wishing he had brought along his pomander.

'Stay out of sight, Mlle de la Croix,' Count Lucien said, with strained patience. He would prefer, of course, to be in his proper place beside the King. Louis, ever the gentleman, overlooked his absence.

Marie-Josèphe shrank back behind the concealing cloak, where she could see only the shadows of her brother, the King, and the courtiers.

'The preserving spirits do have a strong odour, Monsieur,' Yves said.

'I confess — if my confessor will excuse a moment's infidelity to him—'

The shadow of Louis nodded toward Father de la Chaise, his confessor, and his voice bore only the faintest hint of mockery. Father de la Chaise bowed low.

'I confess that I doubted your claims, Father de la Croix,' the King said. 'And yet you found the creatures, in the wild sea of the new world. Your predictions were correct.'

'All the evidence pointed to a single place and a single time of their gathering,' Yves said modestly. 'I was merely the first to collect the reports. The monsters converge in the shelter of Exuma Island, where the midsummer sun crosses over a great ocean trench. There they mate, in animal depravity.'

An expectant silence fell.

'We need hear no more of that,' the Marquise de Maintenon said severely.

'Every subject's fit for a natural philosopher to study!' The duke de Chartres broke in with the obsessive enthusiasm that earned him annoyance from the court and suspicion from the lower classes. 'How else will we ever understand the truth of the world?'

'What is fit for a natural philosopher may trouble the minds of others,' His Majesty said. 'Or lead us astray.'

'But the truth—'

'Be *quiet*, boy!' Madame's tone was soft but urgent.

Marie-Josèphe felt sorry for Chartres. His position warred with his desire for knowledge. He would be happier if he was, like Marie-Josèphe, no one.

Happier, Marie-Josèphe thought – *but he would not have all the best scientific instruments*.

'Since the time of St. Louis,' His Majesty said, 'no one has brought a live sea monster to France. I commend you, Father de la Croix.'

His Majesty's deft change of subject eased the tension.

'Your Majesty's encouragement guaranteed my success,' Yves said.

'I shall commend you to my holy cousin Pope Innocent.'

'Thank you, Your Majesty.'

'And I shall observe your study of the dead monster.'

'I-I—'

Marie-Josèphe silently begged Yves to reply with adequate grace and appreciation.

'Your Majesty's interest honours my work beyond imagination,' Yves said.

His Majesty turned to Count Lucien. They conferred for a moment; the King nodded.

'Tomorrow. You may begin your study after Mass.'

'Tomorrow, Your Majesty? But it's essential – the carcass already decomposes.'

'Tomorrow,' His Majesty said calmly, as if Yves had not spoken. 'After Mass.'

Marie-Josèphe wanted to appear from behind Count Lucien's cloak and add her pleas to her brother's, so His Majesty would understand that Yves must waste no time. But she could not add to her breach of etiquette. She could not show herself to the King; she should not even speak to him unless he spoke first.

Yves' shadow bowed low against the silken tent wall.

'I beg Your Majesty's pardon for my excess of enthusiasm. Thank you, Sire. Tomorrow.'

The shadows moved and melded and separated into pairs.

'I remember,' Louis said, 'when I was young like Father de la Croix, I too could see in the dark.'

His Majesty's courtiers laughed at his joke.

As the King and Mme de Maintenon led the courtiers from the tent, Count Lucien lowered his cloak and swung it around his shoulders. He clenched and unclenched his hands.

Lorraine paused before Marie-Josèphe.

'You may keep my cloak, Mlle de la Croix—'

Her teeth chattered as she spoke. 'Thank you, sir.'

'—and perhaps you'll reward me when I retrieve it.'

The heat of embarrassment did nothing to drive away Marie-Josèphe's shivering.

Monsieur slipped his hand around Lorraine's elbow and drew him away. They followed the King. Monsieur whispered; Lorraine replied, and laughed. Monsieur looked away. Lorraine spoke; Monsieur glanced at him with a shy smile.

The fountain mechanisms creaked and grumbled. The Fountain of Apollo remained still, but the Fountain of Latona at the upper end of the Green Carpet would shower water into the air, for the pleasure of the King.

'Count Lucien,' Marie-Josèphe said. 'I'm grateful—'

'His Majesty must not be exposed to unseemly sights.'

The count bowed coolly. He tramped toward Yves, passing the equipment and the dissection table, disguising his slight lameness

36

with the support of his walking stick. Marie-Josèphe rubbed warmth into her chilled body.

Count Lucien offered Yves a leather sack twice the size of the purse he had given the galleon captain.

'With His Majesty's regard.'

'I am grateful, Count Lucien, but I cannot accept it. When I took religious orders, I took a vow of poverty as well.'

Count Lucien gave him a quizzical glance. 'As did all your holy brothers, who enrich themselves—'

'His Majesty saved my sister from the war in Martinique. He gave me the means to advance my work. I ask nothing else.'

Marie-Josèphe stepped between them and held out her hand. Count Lucien placed the purse, with its heavy weight of gold, in her palm. Her fingertips brushed his glove.

He withdrew his hand, longer and finer than hers, without acknowledging the touch. Marie-Josèphe was embarrassed by her rough skin.

He has never scrubbed the floor of a convent, Marie-Josèphe thought. She could not imagine him in any but elegant surroundings.

'Thank you, Count Lucien,' Marie-Josèphe said. 'This *will* advance my brother's work. Now we may buy a new microscope.' Perhaps, she hoped, even one of Mynheer van Leeuwenhoek's, with enough left over for books.

'Learn your sister's lesson, Father de la Croix,' Count Lucien said. 'All wealth and all privilege flow from the King. His appreciation – in *any* form – is too valuable to spurn.'

'I know it, sir. But I desire neither wealth nor privilege. Only the freedom to continue my work.'

'Your desires are of no consequence,' Count Lucien said. 'His Majesty's wishes are. He has given permission for you to attend his awakening ceremony. Tomorrow, you may join the fifth rank of entry.'

'Thank you, M. de Chrétien.' Yves bowed. Conscious of the honour Yves had been given, Marie-Josèphe curtsied low.

The count bowed to the brother, to the sister, and left the tent.

'Do you know what this means?' Marie-Josèphe exclaimed.

'It means the King's approval,' Yves said, his smile wry. 'And time stolen by ceremony that I'd rather use in study. But I must please the King.' He put his arm around her shoulders. 'You're shivering.'

She leaned against him. 'France is too cold!'

'And Martinique is too remote.'

'Are you glad His Majesty called you to Versailles?'

'Are you sorry to leave Fort-de-France?'

'No! I—'

The sea monster whispered a song.

'It sings,' Marie-Josèphe said. 'The sea monster sings, just like a bird.'

'Yes.'

'Give it a fish – perhaps it's as hungry as I am.'

He shrugged. 'It won't eat.' He scooped seaweed from the basket and flung it through the bars of the cage. He flung a fish after it. He rattled the gate to test that it was fastened.

The sea monster's eerie melody wrapped Marie-Josèphe in the balmy breeze of the Caribbean. It stopped abruptly when the fish splashed into the water.

Marie-Josèphe shivered violently.

'Come!' Yves said suddenly. 'You'll catch the ague.'

Chapter 3

The sea monster floated beneath the surface, humming, its voice a low moan. The edges of the small water reflected the sound.

A rotting fish fell into the pool. The sea monster dove away, then circled back, sniffed at it, scooped it up, and flung it away. It sailed between the cold black bars and hit the ground with a dead *splat*.

The sea monster sang.

Marie-Josèphe took Yves up the narrow dirty stairs, through the dark hallway and along the threadbare carpet, to the attic of the chateau of Versailles. Her cold clammy dress had soaked the fur lining of Lorraine's cloak. She could not stop shivering.

'Is this where we're to live?' Yves asked, dismayed.

'We have three rooms!' Marie-Josèphe exclaimed. 'Courtiers scheme and bribe and connive for what we've been given freely.'

'It's a filthy attic.'

'In His Majesty's chateau!'

'My cabin on the galleon was cleaner.'

Marie-Josèphe opened the door to her dark, cold, shabby little room. Light spilled out. She stared, astonished.

'And my room at university was larger,' Yves said. 'Hello, Odelette.'

A young woman of extraordinary beauty rose from the chair where she sat sewing by candlelight.

'Good evening, M. Yves,' said Marie-Josèphe's Turkish slave, with whom Marie-Josèphe shared a birthday, and to whom she had not been allowed to speak for five years. She smiled at her mistress in a matter-of-fact way. 'Hello, Mlle Marie.'

'Odelette!' Marie-Josèphe ran to Odelette and flung herself into her arms. 'How—where—Oh, I'm so glad to see you!'

'Mlle Marie, you're soaked!' Odelette pointed to the dressing-room

39

door. 'Go away, M. Yves, so I may get Mlle Marie out of these wet clothes.' Odelette had never, from the time they were all children, shown Yves a moment's deference.

Yves offered her a mock bow and left to explore his rooms.

'Where did you come from? How did you get here?'

'Was it not your will, Mlle Marie?' Odelette unfastened the many buttons of Marie-Josèphe's grand habit.

'It was, but I never dared hope they'd send you. Before my ship sailed, I wrote to the Mother Superior, I wrote to the priest, I wrote to the governor—' The clammy wet silk fell away, leaving her bare arms exposed to the cold night air. 'And when I reached Saint-Cyr, I asked Mme de Maintenon for help – I even wrote to the King!' She hugged herself, trying to ward off the chill. 'Though I don't suppose he ever saw my letter!'

'Perhaps it was the governor. I attended his daughter during her passage to France, though the Mother Superior wanted to keep me.'

Odelette picked loose the wet knots of Marie-Josèphe's stays. Marie-Josèphe stood naked and shivering on the worn rug. Her ruined gown and silver petticoat lay in a heap. Odelette hung the Chevalier's cloak on the dress-rack.

'I'll brush it, and it might dry unstained. But your beautiful petticoat—!' Odelette fell into their old habits of domesticity as if no time had passed at all. She rubbed Marie-Josèphe with a scrap of old blanket and chafed her fingers and arms to bring back some warmth. Hercules the cat watched from the window seat.

Marie-Josèphe burst into tears of anger and relief. 'She forbade me to see you—'

'Shh, Mlle Marie. Our fortunes have changed.' Odelette held a threadbare nightshirt, plain thin muslin, not at all warm. 'Into bed before you catch your death, and I have to send for a surgeon.'

Marie-Josèphe slipped into the nightshirt. 'I don't need a surgeon. I don't *want* a surgeon. I'm just cold. It's a long walk from the Fountain of Apollo when your dress is soaking wet.'

Odelette unpinned Marie-Josèphe's red-gold hair, letting it fall in tangled curls around her shoulders. Marie-Josèphe swayed, too tired to keep her feet.

'Come, Mlle Marie,' Odelette said. 'You're shivering. Get in bed, and I'll comb your hair while you go to sleep.'

Marie-Josèphe crawled between the featherbeds, still shivering.

'Come, Hercules.'

The tabby cat blinked from the window seat. He yawned, rose, stretched hugely, and dug his claws into the velvet cushion. One leap to the floor and one to the bed brought him to her side. He sniffed her fingers, walked on top of her, and kneaded her belly. The feathers softened his claws to a soft pressure and a faint sharp scratching sound. He curled up, warm and heavy, and went back to sleep.

'Put your arms beneath the covers,' Odelette said, trying to pull the covers higher.

'No, it isn't proper—'

'Nonsense, you'll die of a cold in your chest.' Odelette tucked the covers around her chin. Odelette spread Marie-Josèphe's hair across the pillows and combed out the tangles. 'You mustn't go out anymore with your hair poorly dressed.'

'I wore a fontanges.' Marie-Josèphe yawned. 'But the sea monster knocked it loose.' She lost track of what she was saying. 'You should see the sea monster. You will see it!'

I'm still too excited to go to sleep, Marie-Josèphe thought. Then, a moment later, Odelette laid her heavy braid across her shoulder. Marie-Josèphe had already dozed, and had not felt Odelette finish her hair. Odelette blew out the candle. The smoke tinged the air with burned tallow. A shadow in the darkness, Odelette moved toward the window.

'Leave it open,' Marie-Josèphe said, half asleep.

'It's so cold, Mlle Marie.'

'We must get used to it.'

Odelette slipped into bed, a sweet warmth beside Marie-Josèphe. Marie-Josèphe hugged her.

'I'm so glad to have you back with me.'

'You might have sold me,' Odelette whispered.

'Never!' Marie-Josèphe did not admit, to Odelette, how close she had come in the convent to repent of owning a slave. She *did* repent. The arguments had convinced her and guilt now troubled her. She

41

had understood in time that the arguments were meant to persuade her to sell Odelette, not to free her. The sisters thought Odelette's abilities too refined for the work in a convent, and would have preferred the money her sale would have brought.

I must free her, Marie-Josèphe thought. *But if I free her now, I can only send her out into the world, a young woman alone and without resources. Like me, but without the protection of good family or a brother, without the friendship of the King. Her only resource is her beauty.*

'I'll never sell you,' she said again. 'You'll be mine, or you'll be free, but you'll never belong to another.'

A phrase of music, exquisitely complex, soared in and filled the air with sorrow.

'Don't cry, Mlle Marie,' Odelette whispered. She brushed the tears from Marie-Josèphe's cheeks. 'Our fortunes have changed.'

'Can you hear the singing?' Marie-Josèphe asked.

Did I ask the question? Marie-Josèphe wondered. *Or did I only dream it? Do I hear the sea monster's song, or do I dream it, too?*

A dreadful racket of tramping boots, rattling swords, and loud voices woke Marie-Josèphe. She tried to make it a dream – but she had been having a different dream. Hercules stared toward the door, his eyes reflecting the faint light, his tail twitching angrily.

'Mlle Marie?' Odelette sat up, wide awake.

'Go back to sleep, I'm sure it's nothing.'

Odelette burrowed under the covers, peeking out curiously.

'Father de la Croix!'

Someone pounded on the door of Yves' room. Marie-Josèphe flung off the bedclothes and snatched Lorraine's cloak from the dress stand. She opened the door to the corridor.

'Be quiet! You'll wake my brother!'

Two of the King's Musketeers filled the low, narrow hallway, the plumes of their hats brushing the ceiling, their swords banging the woodwork when they turned. Mud from their boots clumped on the carpet. The smoke of their torch smudged the ceiling. Burning pitch overcame the odours of urine, sweat, and mildew.

'We *must* wake him, mademoiselle.' The shorter of the two was still a head taller than Marie-Josèphe. 'The sea monster – the tent is full of demons!' Indoors, and in a lady's presence, the musketeer corporal snatched off his hat.

Yves' door opened. He peered out sleepily, his dark hair tousled and his cassock buttoned partway and crooked.

'Demons? Nonsense.'

'We heard it – leathery wings flapping—'

'We smelled brimstone!' said the taller musketeer.

'Who's guarding the sea monster?'

They looked at each other.

Yves made a sound of disgust, slammed his door behind him, and strode down the hallway with the musketeers in his wake.

'Mlle Marie—' Marie-Josèphe waved Odelette to silence. She hung back so Yves would not order her to stay behind. When the men disappeared, she followed.

She hurried down the back stairs and through the mysterious and deserted and dark chateau. Gentlemen of His Majesty's household had already claimed the partially burned candles, a perquisite of their office. Her hands outstretched, she made her way through Louis XIII's small hunting lodge, the heart of Louis XIV's magnificent, sprawling chateau.

Hugging Lorraine's cloak around her, she hurried onto the terrace. The moon had set but the stars shed a little light. The luminarias marking the King's pathway had burned to nothing. The fountains lay quiet. Marie-Josèphe ran across the cold dew-damp flagstones, past the Ornamental Pools, and down the stairs above the Fountain of Latona. Beyond, on the Green Carpet, the musketeers' torch spread a pool of smoky light.

Motion and a strange shape in the corner of her eye startled her. She stopped short, catching her breath.

The white blossoms of an orange tree trembled and glowed in the darkness. Gardeners, dragging the orange-tree cart, slipped from the traces to bow to Marie-Josèphe.

She acknowledged the gardeners, thinking, *of course they must work at night; His Majesty should see his gardens only in a state of perfection.*

They took up the cart again; its wheels crunched on the gravel.

When His Majesty took his afternoon walk, fresh trees, their blossoms forced in the greenhouse, would greet him. His Majesty's gaze would touch only beauty.

Marie-Josèphe hurried to the sea monster's tent. The lantern inside had gone out; the torch outside illuminated only the entry curtain and its gold sunburst.

'Say a prayer before you go in!' said the musketeer corporal.

'An incantation!'

'He means an exorcism.'

'There isn't any demon,' Yves said.

'We heard it.'

'Flapping its wings.'

'Wings like leather.'

Yves grabbed the torch, flung aside the curtain, and strode into the tent. Out of breath from running, Marie-Josèphe slipped past the musketeers and followed her brother.

The tent looked as they had left it, the equipment all in place, melted ice dripping softly to the plank floor, the cage surrounding the fountain. The odour of dead fish and preserving spirits hung in the air. Marie-Josèphe supposed the guards might have mistaken the unpleasant smells for brimstone.

She believed in demons – she believed in God, and in angels, so how could she not believe in Satan and demons? – but she thought, in these modern days, demons did not often choose to visit the earthly world. Even if they did, why should a demon visit a sea monster, any more than it would visit His Majesty's elephant or His Majesty's baboons?

Marie-Josèphe giggled, thinking of a demon on a picnic in His Majesty's Menagerie.

Her laughter brought her to Yves' attention.

'What are you laughing at?' he said. 'You should be in bed.'

'I wish I were,' Marie-Josèphe said.

'Superstitious fools,' Yves muttered. 'Demons, indeed.'

The torchlight reflected from a splash of water on the polished planks.

'Yves—'

A watery trail led from the fountain to the cluster of lab equipment. The gate of the cage hung open.

44

Yves cursed and hurried to the dissection table. Marie-Josèphe ran into the cage.

The sea monster floated a few strokes from the platform, its hair spreading around its shoulders. Its eyes reflected the torchlight, uncanny as a cat's. It hummed softly, eerily.

'Yves, it's here, it's safe, it's all right.'

'Stay there – there's broken glass. Are you barefoot?'

'Are you?'

Shards of glass flung sharp sounds as Yves swept them into a pile.

'My feet are like leather – we never wore shoes on the galleon.'

He joined her in the cage, holding the torch out over the water. A spark fell and sizzled. The sea monster spat at it, whistled angrily, and dove.

'It slithered around out here. It climbed the stairs! I didn't think it could make progress on land. It knocked a flask over, it fled back to the fountain . . . I must have left the gate ajar.'

'You tested it,' Marie-Josèphe said. 'You latched it and rattled it.'

He shrugged. 'I couldn't have. Tomorrow I'll get a chain.'

Yves sat abruptly. He slumped forward, his head down, hair hanging in rumpled black curls. Marie-Josèphe snatched the torch before it fell. Concerned, she sat beside her brother and put her arm around his shoulder.

He patted her hand. 'I'm only tired,' he said.

'You work so hard,' Marie-Josèphe said. 'Let me help you.'

'That wouldn't be proper.'

'I was a good assistant when we were children – I'm no less able now.'

She feared he would refuse, and that would be the end of it. *I no longer know my brother*, she thought, distressed. *I no longer know what he'll say, what he'll do, before he knows it himself.*

He raised his head, frowned, hesitated. 'What about your duties to Mademoiselle?'

Marie-Josèphe giggled. 'Sometimes I hold her handkerchief, if Mlle d'Armagnac doesn't snatch it first. She'd hardly notice I was gone. I need only tell her you need me – so your work might please the King . . .'

His brow cleared. 'I'd be grateful for your help. You haven't become squeamish, have you?'

'Squeamish!' She laughed.

'Will you document the dissection?'

'I'd like nothing better.'

'The dissection will occupy my time. Will you take the charge of the live sea monster? Feed it—'

'Yes. And I'll tame it, too.'

'You'll need all your ingenuity to persuade it to eat.' His beautiful smile erased the exhaustion from his face. 'I'm certain you'll succeed. You were better with the live things than I ever was.'

Delighted to be part of his life, part of his work, once again, Marie-Josèphe kissed his cheek.

Yawning, he pushed himself to his feet. 'There's time still for a bit of sleep.' His smile turned wry. 'Not even the Jesuits reconciled me to waking early.'

'I'll take that duty, too,' Marie-Josèphe said. 'I'll wake you in time to attend the King.'

'That would be a considerable kindness,' Yves said.

He ushered Marie-Josèphe out of the cage, closed the gate, and latched it and rattled it just as he had done earlier in the evening. The sea monster's lament followed them.

'Oh!' Marie-Josèphe jumped back from something cold and slimy beneath her foot.

'What is it – did you step on glass?'

She picked up a dead fish.

'Your sea monster doesn't like its fish.'

Chapter 4

Marie-Josèphe walked through the silent dawn gardens of Versailles. At first light, the gardeners had vanished, but the courtiers still slept and the visitors had not yet arrived. She was alone in the beauty, surrounded by flowers, perfumed by a cloud of orange perfume.

She strode down the Green Carpet toward Apollo, planning her day. She would feed the sea monster, then return to the chateau in plenty of time to wake Yves and break their fast with bread and chocolate. He would attend His Majesty's awakening. She could not accompany him, because women did not participate in the grand lever. Instead, she would wait for him in the guard room with the other ladies and the less-favoured men, and join the procession to Mass.

The morning delighted her. The world delighted her. When she kicked a small stone down the path, she thought, *with a few strokes of my pen, with a calculation, I can describe the motion of its rise and fall. I can predict its effect on the next stone, and the next. M. Newton's discoveries allow me to describe anything I wish, even the future paths of the stars and the planets. And now that I am free of the convent, no one will forbid me to do so.*

A breeze rustled the leaves of the potted orange trees. Marie-Josèphe considered how to predict the fluttering motion, and though the solution eluded her for the moment, she felt certain she could discover it with some time and consideration.

M. Newton must have solved such a simple problem, she thought. *Dare I write to him again? Would he bother to reply at all, when he condescended to communicate with me once, and I failed to answer? I wish I had seen the contents of his letter.*

The chateau of Versailles stood on a low hill; the Green Carpet led downward to the sea monster's tent.

A much easier walk than last night! she thought. She wore her riding habit, more practical and easier to walk in than court dress.

As she neared the laboratory tent, a half-dozen heavy wagons rumbled along the Queen's Road toward the fountain. Barrels weighed each one down.

Count Lucien cantered his grey Arabian past the wagons. The fiery horse scattered gravel from its hooves, flicked its jaunty black tail, and drew up beside the tent. Count Lucien saluted Marie-Josèphe with his walking stick. Under his supervision, the workmen raised the tent's sides and the drivers lined up the wagons.

Marie-Josèphe entered the tent, unlatched the cage door, and hurried in. From the Fountain's rim, she sought the sea monster.

The creature's long dark hair and iridescent leathery tails shimmered beneath the hooves of Apollo's dawn horses.

'Sea monster!'

The creature flicked its tails, pushing itself deeper beneath the sculpture. Marie-Josèphe reached for a fish, then thought better of it. The ice had melted around the basket, and the dead things reeked.

'Lackey!'

Unlike the sea monster, the lackey came running, pulling his forelock and keeping his gaze on the ground.

'Yes, mamselle?'

'Get rid of those smelly things. Where are the fresh fish? And the new ice?'

'Coming along from the kitchen, mamselle, here, just now.' He pointed. Several men approached, one with a wicker basket, two others pushing barrows full of ice.

'Good. Thank you.'

He bobbed a bow and ran to hurry the others along. They set a wicker basket of fish inside the cage, then went to work shovelling fresh ice onto Yves' specimen.

Marie-Josèphe ran over the rim of the Fountain and down to the platform. The sea monster had not tried to escape a second time, for the planks were dry.

It must be terrified, Marie-Josèphe thought, sighing. *Frightened animals are so hard to train.*

She splashed the water with one hand, patting the surface as she would pat her bedcovers to call Hercules.

'Come, sea monster. Come here.'

The sea monster watched her from beneath the dawn chariot.

Marie-Josèphe swished a fish through the water. The sea monster raised her head, opened her mouth, and let the water flow over her tongue.

'Yes, good sea monster. Come, I'll give you a fish.'

The sea monster spat the water noisily into the pool.

'Can you make it eat?'

Startled, Marie-Josèphe turned. 'Count Lucien! I did not . . . I mean, I thought . . .'

He stood on the fountain's rim, looking at the sea monster. She had not heard him approach. He turned his cool gaze to her.

'Did you not recognise me,' Count Lucien asked, 'without my moustache?'

His tone was so dry that she was afraid to laugh, afraid she might be misinterpreting his joke.

He had shaved his fair moustache. Perhaps someone had told him courtiers these days wore moustaches only during military campaigns, and shaved them off – to be cleanshaven like His Majesty – when they returned to Versailles. He had changed his informal steinkirk tie for proper lace and ribbons, and his tied-back military wig for a fashionably styled perruke. Its curls cascaded down the shoulders of his gold-embroidered blue coat. Most of the other courtiers wore black perrukes, like the King's, but Count Lucien's was auburn. The colour flattered his fair complexion, and his pale grey eyes.

'I recognise you,' Marie-Josèphe said stiffly. 'But you attend to the King's business, so I did not expect to speak with you.'

'The sea monster is the King's business, Mlle de la Croix,' he said. 'Your brother has the charge of it—'

'I have the charge of it, sir, while he studies the dead specimen.'

'In that case, you must expect to speak to me quite often. Can you persuade the beast to feed?'

'I hope so.'

'Your brother force-fed it.'

'I'm sure I can tame it to eat from my hand.'

'The sea monster need not be tame. His Majesty requires only that it be sleek.'

49

He bowed and left her, climbing down from the Fountain's low rim awkwardly, like a child, and leaning on his walking stick.

On the other side of the Fountain, a driver backed his wagon to the cage. Workmen rolled the barrels down the wagon-bed. The rolling barrels thundered. A gardener appeared from nowhere and raked the wagon tracks out of the gravel.

A workman crashed his sledgehammer against the barrel top, staving it in. Sea water gushed into the pool.

As other workmen in other wagons broke more barrels, the cool scent of the ocean drifted through the air. Ripples and bubbles roiled the surface of the fountain.

With a thrust of its powerful tails, the sea monster propelled its body upward. Water spilled from its open mouth, dripped from its dark hair, and trickled down its body. A tangled lock of its hair had turned light green.

Should I worry about the faded colour? Marie-Josèphe wondered. *Could it be a sign of illness?*

The sea monster trilled a musical cry and ducked its head beneath the surface.

It dove into the pool, leaving hardly a ripple. When it surfaced, a live fish, a silver sea fish, struggled between its teeth. The sea monster flicked the wriggling fish into the air and caught it in its mouth. The tail twitched between the sea monster's lips. The sea monster swallowed. The fish disappeared.

'Live fish!' Marie-Josèphe said. 'It wants live fish!'

The sea monster dove again and raced toward the wagons, toward the fresh sea water. When the cage stopped it, it grabbed the bars and shook them. The iron rattled and rang, like spears clashing. The sea monster screamed and thrust its arm between the bars, snatching at the driver's ankle.

'Get away, you devil!' The driver stumbled back, surprised and frightened. He fell against a barrel. It rolled, spun, and crashed to bits against the cage. Staves and iron straps rained into the pool. The sea monster screamed again and shook the bars till they shuddered and clanged.

Terrified, the driver grabbed up his whip. Its lash cracked in the air near the sea monster's hands.

50

'You damned demon!' The whiplash exploded again.

The sea monster screamed in terror and splashed away beneath the water.

'Stop!'

Marie-Josèphe ran out of the cage and around the edge of the fountain toward the driver. The huge draft horses stamped and snorted.

'Stop!' Marie-Josèphe cried again. The sea monster shrieked and whistled.

Panicked and furious, the driver raised his hand as if to crack the lash again, as if to whip Marie-Josèphe. Marie-Josèphe froze, too astonished for fear.

Count Lucien's ebony walking-stick caught the driver's wrist at its height, stopping the downstroke. The big man pushed against the cane, too frantic to understand that a touch of restraint, rather than violence, had stopped him.

'Driver!' Count Lucien said.

The driver realised what he had almost done, what he had done.

Count Lucien lowered his cane and sat back in the saddle. The grey Arabian stood stock-still, only its ears moving, swivelling toward its rider, flicking toward the driver, toward the moans and trills of the sea monster.

'Mlle de la Croix has the charge of His Majesty's sea monster,' Count Lucien said.

'Sir, I—mamselle, your pardon—' In horror and remorse, the driver flung the whip to the ground.

'You are dismissed.' Count Lucien's tone made his meaning clear: the driver was not to return.

The driver was half again Count Lucien's height, three times his weight; the knife on his belt exceeded the length of the count's dirk.

His size made no difference. His punishment could have been far worse, and might be if the musketeers arrived before he fled. The driver grabbed his reins and shouted a curse at his horses. They plunged forward. The wagon rumbled. The gardener hurried out again to sweep the tracks clear.

'Count Lucien—' Breathless, her knees wobbly, Marie-Josèphe could think of nothing to say.

'You will not be further troubled.'

He nodded to her. As he rode away, he leaned down, hooked the whip with his walking-stick, wrapped it into a loose coil, and laid it across the pommel of his saddle.

The musketeers reached her, breathless.

'What happened, mademoiselle?' asked the lieutenant.

'As you see,' Marie-Josèphe said, gesturing to the broken barrel, the spilled sea water. 'An accident.'

At the chateau, Lucien saw Zelis, his grey Arabian, safely off to the stables with his groom, then climbed the stairs from ground floor to first floor, the royal floor. Orange blossoms perfumed the air.

For all its magnificence, the chateau of Versailles was an awkward and unpleasant dwelling, built over a marsh, hot and close in summer, smoky and cold in winter. The King of France paid for his glory with the sacrifice of his comfort.

The musketeers bowed to him and stood aside; Lucien passed unchallenged into the hallway behind His Majesty's bedroom. His Majesty permitted only his sons and a few highly-favoured noblemen to use the private entrance.

A footman opened the private door. Lucien entered and took his place at the King's bedside, behind the gold balustrade that separated the curtained bed from the ordinary onlookers of his awakening.

Silence suffused the cold, dim official bedroom. Tapestries of white silk and gold thread gleamed like autumn dawn. White plumes crowned the bed.

Lucien bowed to Monsieur, to Monseigneur, to the grandsons. He returned Lorraine's salute. With cool politeness, he acknowledged the bows of M. Fagon the first physician and M. Félix the first surgeon.

Eight o'clock chimed. Servants opened the window-curtains, flooding the room with eastern sunlight and cold air from the open windows. Sunshine doubly gilded the tapestries and the brocade bed-curtains, shimmered from the golden-tan parquet floor, illuminated the fine paintings and the mirrors, accentuated the high relief of the image of France watching over the King's sleep.

Lucien and Lorraine drew aside the tapestries of the King's

four-poster bed. The first valet bent over the King to whisper, 'Sire, it is time.'

Of course the King was already awake. He always appeared majestic; it would not do, to rise bald, snuffling and scratching and rubbing the sleep from his eyes like an ordinary mortal. He seldom slept in his own bed, and Mme de Maintenon never slept in the King's official bedroom. His Majesty's custom was to sleep in her apartment and return to his own bed for his morning rituals.

His Majesty sat up, with the unnecessary help of Monsieur.

'Good morning, my dear brother,' Louis said. 'I am awake.'

'Good morning, sir,' Monsieur replied. 'I am glad to see you so well this morning.'

Monsieur handed his brother a cup of chocolate. The King possessed a hearty appetite, but he never ate in the morning. The liquid in his cup lay cold and congealed, brought all the way from the distant kitchens; at the chateau of Versailles, food never reached the table hot.

His Majesty deliberately traded comfort for splendour; he sacrificed his privacy for the ability to keep the aristocracy in his sight and under his control. Each member of the nobility was a potential enemy, as he had learned all too well during the civil war of his uncle's instigation. Lucien owed part of his own position at court to his father's unshakable political loyalty to His Majesty.

When I am middle-aged, Lucien thought, *crippled like my father and retired to Barenton, I hope and expect to be able to claim a similar honour*.

Lucien drew aside the bedclothes. Monsieur offered his hand to His Majesty to help him out of bed. His Majesty accepted Monsieur's help. Wearing nightgown and short wig, in the presence of the courtiers favoured with First Entry, he stepped down from the enclosure of his tall bed.

Lorraine held the dressing gown for His Majesty.

At the door to the first chamber, the usher knocked his staff on the floor.

'His Majesty has awakened.'

His Majesty's confessor joined the King in kneeling at his bedside. The courtiers watched the King pray, gossiping all the while.

Lucien, Monsieur, Lorraine, the doctor, and the surgeon accompanied

53

His Majesty to his privy chair. Lucien watched His Majesty carefully for any hint that his affliction had returned. Since the operation, His Majesty's morning ablutions had ceased, mercifully, to cause him such pain. Lucien had feared for his sovereign's life. Louis was a stoic, seldom admitting any discomfort. But during that year of illness, his body had tortured him cruelly.

The surgeon had been as unmerciful.

Fagon and Félix did cure His Majesty of the anal fistula, Lucien had to admit. The surgeon tried out the cure on any number of peasants and prisoners. He killed not a few of them, and buried them at dawn. He forbade the bells to ring, so no one would know of the failures.

He saved a few, Lucien thought, *I'll give him that. He did return the King to us. What will happen when His Majesty dies, and Monseigneur reigns . . .*

How His Majesty could spawn such an insignificant heir as Monseigneur was a mystery that did not bear examination.

Lucien took comfort in the robustness of his King. His Majesty was an old man, but an old man restored to health.

Monsieur offered His Majesty a bowl of spirits of wine. His Majesty dipped his fingers. Lucien brought him his towel. He wiped his hands.

Fagon examined the King, as he did every day.

'Your Majesty is in excellent health.' Fagon spoke loudly enough for the courtiers to hear. They murmured their approval. 'If Your Majesty wishes, I will shave Your Majesty today.'

'I'm flattered, M. Fagon,' Louis said. 'When did you last shave anyone's chin?'

'When I was an apprentice, Sire, but I have kept my razor sharp.'

The royal barber stepped aside, hiding his disappointment at being displaced on this day of all days. Dr. Fagon shaved His Majesty's face. He removed His Majesty's small morning wig and shaved the gray stubble of what remained of his natural hair, without a misplaced motion.

'Excellent work, sir. Perhaps you are wasted as a doctor.'

If Fagon were insulted, he concealed his reaction.

'All my talents are perpetually at Your Majesty's service.'

As the rising ceremony progressed, the usher allowed successive groups of courtiers into His Majesty's bedroom. When Fifth Entry arrived, Lucien noted with disgust that Father de la Croix had disregarded His Majesty's invitation.

For anyone to rebuff such an honour is appalling, Lucien thought. *For a Jesuit to do so is remarkable.*

Monsieur divested His Majesty of his nightgown and handed him his shirt. Lace cascaded from the throat and the cuffs. His stockings were of the finest white French silk, his pantaloons of black satin. Pearls encrusted the scabbard of his sword, and his swordbelt, in an intricate design. Embroidered golden fleurs de lys covered his long coat. All the fabric of his clothes came straight from the finest French manufactories, made especially for today: for today was a day to impress the Italians, who liked to pretend their cloth and lace, their leather and designs, were the height of fashion.

Monsieur knelt before his brother and helped him slip into his high-heeled shoes. Though His Majesty no longer dressed in the colours of flame and sunlight, as he had early in his reign, he continued his custom of wearing red shoes for state occasions. Diamonds encrusted the heavy gold buckles. The tall heels lifted His Majesty to a height of more than five and a half feet.

A footman brought a short ladder; Lucien climbed it. The royal wig-maker handed him the King's new periwig, an elegant, leonine construct of glossy black human hair. Lucien placed it on the King's head and arranged the long perfect curls across his shoulders. The wig added another three inches to his stature. Somewhere near Paris, a peasant girl had earned her father a year's wages by sacrificing her hair.

Monseigneur the Grand Dauphin handed His Majesty his hat. The white ostrich plumes glowed in the morning light.

A murmur of appreciation rippled across the courtiers beyond the balustrade; as one, they bowed to their King.

The King led his family and the most favoured members of his court out to face the day.

The workers grumbled, but Marie-Josèphe persuaded them to strain the sea water from the last few barrels. Along with bits of seaweed and a few periwinkles, the screen produced a half-dozen live fish.

'Just pour the water in the fountain, mademoiselle,' said the musketeer lieutenant. 'The demon will catch the fish, like it caught the other.'

'It must come to me to take its food,' she said.

The musketeer grimaced. 'Watch your fingers,' he said.

'It could have bitten me last night,' she said. 'It could have drowned me. I'm safe enough.'

'You can never tell, with demons,' he said, as if he had considerable experience with demons.

'Can you bring me more live fish?' she asked one of the workers.

'Live fish, those aren't easy to get, mamselle.' He ran his hand through his thin brown hair.

'Count Lucien will pay you well if you bring live fish.'

'And whip you if you don't.' A tanned young worker with a sweaty scarf tied across his forehead laughed at his comrade. 'With Georges' whip.'

'He never would!' Marie-Josèphe exclaimed. But then she thought, *He very well might, if he thought someone had slighted His Majesty.*

'How many live fish do you want, mamselle – and how much are you paying?'

'Bring me as many as you'd eat for dinner – if you could eat only fish and if you could eat only dinner.'

The workers dragged the last staves of the broken barrel out of the water and threw them into a wagon-bed. The clatter frightened the sea monster farther under one of Apollo's dolphins. The workers touched their hats, clambered into the wagons, and drove away.

Several gardeners hurried to rake the wagon tracks and the hoofprints from the path, to clean away every clod of horse manure, and to vanish again, leaving potted flowers and trees in precise lines, carrying with them any wilted blooms.

The musketeers busied themselves lowering the sides of the tent, closing Marie-Josèphe off alone with the sea monster. She sat still in the silence, in the silken sunlight that poured through the top and sides of the tent. The sea monster, underwater, drifted closer.

Marie-Josèphe regarded the live fishes doubtfully. They twitched and quivered. If she did not feed them to the sea monster herself, soon, she might as well tip them into the fountain. Otherwise they would die. She rolled her embroidered velvet sleeve up above her elbow, reached into the jar, and grabbed one of the fish.

Gripping the wriggly thing tight, Marie-Josèphe knelt and swished the fish through the water.

'Come, sea monster.'

The sea monster lunged forward, but quickly turned aside. Ripples lapped around Marie-Josèphe's wrist.

'Come here, sea monster. Come get a nice fish.'

The sea monster swam back and forth, a few armslengths from the stairs.

'Please, sea monster,' she said. 'You must eat.'

The live fish writhed feebly. Marie-Josèphe opened her hand. The sea monster darted so close that her claws brushed Marie-Josèphe's fingers. Marie-Josèphe gasped with delight. The creature snatched the fish and shoved it into her mouth.

'Good sea monster!' Enthralled, Marie-Josèphe captured another fish. 'Fine sea monster!'

Frightened by her own boldness, the sea monster fled to Apollo to nestle beneath the hooves of the dawn horses.

Perhaps Apollo is driving the wrong way in order to retard time, Marie-Josèphe thought. *Perhaps if he drives against the sun, time will go backwards, and we shall all live forever.*

She glanced over her shoulder, toward the glow of the sun shining through the translucent tent wall.

She caught her breath. The sun was high, much higher than she expected. She flung the fish into the pond, ran up the stairs and out of the cage, slammed the door, and hurried outside.

When did Count Lucien ride away? she wondered. *It was only a few minutes ago, was it not?*

She tried to convince herself that she was not very late as she ran up the Green Carpet to the chateau.

She burst into Yves' room, hoping his bed would be empty, hoping he had gone, hoping Odelette had awakened him. But he lay snoring softly in his dark room.

'Yves, dear brother, wake up, please, I'm so sorry—'

'What?' he mumbled. 'What is it, what's wrong?' He sat up, his curly dark hair sticking out at all angles. 'Is it seven already?'

'It's at least half past eight, I'm so sorry, I went to feed the sea monster, I forgot the time.'

Anger would have been easier to bear than his stricken expression, his silence.

'I'm so sorry,' she said again.

'It was important,' Yves said.

Marie-Josèphe hung her head. Her error made her feel like an errant child, not a grown woman, and she had no excuse, no defense.

'I know,' she whispered.

The silence weighed upon her.

'Where is Odelette?'

'I sent her to attend Mademoiselle in my place,' Marie-Josèphe said. 'She had no way to know you should be awakened! This is all my fault, my responsibility.'

Yves put his arm around her shoulder.

'Never mind,' he said, his voice falsely cheerful. 'I'd much rather sleep, than rise at dawn to watch an old man get out of bed and use his open chair.'

Marie-Josèphe tried to laugh, but bit her lip instead to hold back her tears.

'No one will even notice that I wasn't there,' Yves said heartily. 'Did the sea monster feed?'

'It ate a few fish,' Marie-Josèphe said miserably.

'That's wonderful!' Yves exclaimed. 'And much more important to the King's approval. I knew you'd succeed.'

'You are so good to me,' Marie-Josèphe said. 'To suffer my error without anger – to make it sound like an achievement!'

'Never think another thing about it,' he said. 'Now, leave me to dress, in proper modesty.'

She kissed his cheek. As she passed through the dressing chamber that joined their bedrooms, he called out, 'Sister, can you find bread and chocolate? I'm famished.'

Chapter 5

Marie-Josèphe trudged back down the hill to the Fountain of Apollo and the sea monster. Beyond everything else, her error had caused her to miss going to Mass with His Majesty and his court in the chateau's small chapel. She whispered a prayer, and promised God that she would go to evening Mass, even though no one else would attend.

She returned to the Fountain of Apollo and entered the tent. The sea monster's song drew her, but she hesitated. Determined to put aside her worry and embarrassment, so as not to communicate her distress to the creature, she spent some minutes arranging Yves' instruments for the dissection. The specimen lay beneath a layer of melting ice; water dripped down the legs of the dissection table to form a puddle speckled with bits of sawdust.

Marie-Josèphe settled a sheet of paper on her drawing box so she would be ready when Yves began his work. Thinking again about the fluttering leaves, she scribbled an equation of the calculus in Herr Leibniz's notation. A moment told her that the solution was insufficient, and that the problem was worth pursuing.

The sea monster whispered, and softly cried. Marie-Josèphe rubbed out the equation so no one could read it. Once more in possession of her equanimity, she entered the sea monster's cage. The creature peered at her from beneath the sculpture. Its long dark hair, with its odd light green tangle, swirled around its shoulders.

'Come to me, sea monster.' She scooped a fish from the jar – the poor things gasped at the surface; they would all soon expire – took it from the net, and dipped the slippery twitching animal into the pool.

The sea monster dove toward her, its sad song rising eerily. Marie-Josèphe agitated the water with the fish.

The sea monster lunged forward, snatched the fish – claws scraped lightly against Marie-Josèphe's hand – and stuffed it into her mouth as she dove back and away. Droplets splashed Marie-Josèphe's face and beaded on her riding habit. She flicked them off before they could stain the velvet. Encouraged, if not satisfied, she caught another fish.

The sea monster grew bolder. Soon it dared to take its food delicately from Marie-Josèphe's hand. The touch of its swimming webs was like silk. Instead of fleeing, it floated within her reach as it ate. Marie-Josèphe moved her hand closer, closer, hoping to accustom the creature to her touch.

Noise and motion startled them both. The tent sides fluttered as a rider galloped by and pulled up in a scatter of gravel. The sea monster snarled and spat, reared in a backward dive, and sped to its sanctuary beneath Apollo. Marie-Josèphe sighed with frustration.

Chartres flung aside the tent curtains, clanged open the cage door, and tramped over the rim of the fountain. The high heels of his shiny gold-buckled shoes struck the platform sharply. Marie-Josèphe curtsied to the duke. Chartres grinned and bowed over her hand.

'Good morning, Mlle de la Croix.'

Flustered and flattered, embarrassed by her water-wrinkled fingers, by the fish scales – and the fishy odour – on her hand, she extricated herself from his grasp, and curtsied.

'Good morning, sir.'

His light brown curls – his own hair, not a wig – gleamed against the collar of his dove-grey coat. He continued to wear his informal steinkirk tie; he kept his moustache. Lotte had confided, giggling, that he sometimes darkened its colour with her kohl.

He peered out into the fountain, squinting. She felt sorry for him for being partly blind.

'Where is it? Oh—there—no—'

'Under the dawn horse's hooves,' Marie-Josèphe said. 'See? If you're quiet and still, it might come out.'

She captured a fish, thrust it into the cold pond, and swished it back and forth. It gave a weak twitch.

'Let me feed the beast!' Chartres said.

I can risk my own hand to the monster's teeth, she thought. *I can't risk the duke's. If it bites him, Madame would never forgive me.*

She offered him the fish, but let it slip from her hand as if by accident.

'Sir, I'm sorry—'

'I'll get it!' To her astonishment, he fell to his knees and plunged his hand into the pool, soaking the lace at his wrist. The fish sank out of his reach. It recovered and swam forward. The sea monster appeared, swimming face-up. It snatched the fish from below and darted away. Chartres nearly fell from the platform in excitement. Marie-Josèphe grabbed his wet sleeve and pulled him back.

'It's magnificent!' he exclaimed. 'I do want to help Father de la Croix.' He knelt beside her, oblivious to the effect of splinters on his silken hose. 'If you talk to your brother he might let me hand him his instruments. Or hold the viewing mirror. Or—'

Marie-Josèphe laughed. 'Sir, you may claim a seat in the first rank. You'll see everything. You can concentrate on the dissection completely.'

'I suppose so,' he said, reluctantly. 'But your brother mustn't hesitate to consult me – and of course he may use my observatory – You'll tell him about my equipment?'

'Of course, sir. Thank you.' Chartres had the newest compound microscope, a telescope, and a slide rule that Marie-Josèphe coveted to the point of sin.

People whispered and gossiped about what Chartres did in his observatory, about poisons and magic and conjurings. They were so unfair, for he knew a great deal of chemistry and had not the least interest in poisons or in demons.

'Sir,' she said, offhand, hiding her anxiety, 'have you seen my brother?' What if His Majesty had noticed Yves' absence and grown angry? What if he had called him to task, what if the King had deprived her brother of his position, of his work?

'No – but look, perhaps that's him now.'

The guard drew aside the white silk at the entryway.

Monseigneur the Grand Dauphin, heir to the throne, Chartres' cousin, entered the tent. The Dauphine had died some years before; Monseigneur was said to keep a mistress, Mlle Choin, in private apartments; she never came to court.

His Majesty's young grandsons, Monseigneur's sons, the dukes of Bourgogne, Anjou, and Berri, marched along behind their father the

61

Grand Dauphin, playing at dignity while elbowing each other and craning their necks for a glimpse of the sea monster.

Madame and Lotte entered; Maine strolled in. Madame froze him with politeness. His Majesty might legitimise Louis Auguste and his brother Louis Alexandre and his half-sisters all he liked; Madame would never consider any of them, even her daughter-in-law, anything but bastards.

If Madame's opinion distressed them, which Marie-Josèphe doubted, they hid their concern. Maine was particularly handsome today, in a fine new red coat with gold embroidery and silver lace. His hat spilled out a snowdrift of egret plumes. The coat disguised his uneven shoulders. He walked carefully, so his limp hardly showed.

More courtiers poured into the tent, and visitors, too, His Majesty's subjects from Paris and the countryside, far more people than Marie-Josèphe expected to come to the dissection. The courtiers milled about, seeking vantage points behind the royal family's seats. The visitors stood behind the aristocrats, along the wall of the tent.

Several people strolled over to the cage and peered through the bars. One even lifted the latch, but a musketeer stopped him.

'You may not enter, sir,' the musketeer said. 'Much too dangerous.'

'Too dangerous for me, not too dangerous for her?' The visitor pointed toward Marie-Josèphe, then laughed. 'Or perhaps she's the sacrifice to Poseidon's sea monster?'

'Keep a respectful tongue in your head, if you please,' the musketeer said.

'His Majesty's invitation—'

'—is for the public dissection.'

The townsman opened his mouth to reply, then shut it again. He bowed and took a step back.

'You are correct, officer,' he said. 'His Majesty's invitation is for the dissection. His Majesty will show us his living sea monster when he chooses.'

'Perhaps when it's tamed,' the musketeer said.

Marie-Josèphe threw a fish into the pool. The sea monster plunged toward it, splashing and snarling. Its teeth snapped together. Marie-Josèphe felt a little sorry for the fish. Watching in vain for Yves, she climbed the stairs with Chartres and left the sea monster's cage, locking it behind her.

She curtsied to the royal family, then kissed Madame's hem and embraced Lotte, who stooped to kiss her lips and her cheek. Lotte moved carefully so as not to dislodge her fontanges. Its ruffles rose over her beautifully-dressed hair; its ribbons and lace spilled down her back.

'Good morning, my dear,' Madame said. 'We missed you at Mass.'

'Perhaps she was with M. de Chrétien instead,' Lotte said with a delighted laugh.

'Hush, daughter,' Madame said.

'Please forgive me, Madame,' Marie-Josèphe said, wondering what Lotte found so amusing.

'Forgive you for missing that wretched priest's most boring sermon in weeks? Child! I envy you.'

Madame's complaints about the churchmen of Versailles always distressed Marie-Josèphe. She knew God would understand that Madame meant nothing blasphemous or heretical. Marie-Josèphe was not so sure the other members of court understood, especially Mme de Maintenon, especially since Madame used to be a Protestant. But, then, Mme de Maintenon used to be a Protestant, too.

'Do you like my hair? Your Odelette is a wonder!' Lotte said. 'An octavon, is she? Why have we not seen her before?'

'I beg your pardon, Mademoiselle, she's a Turk — she recently followed me to France, from Martinique.'

'She dressed my hair so beautifully — and with a touch of her hand she renewed this old fontanges.'

'I cannot afford to buy you a new one every time the fashion changes,' Madame said dryly. 'Nor even every day.'

Monsieur and Lorraine joined them. Marie-Josèphe curtsied, her heart beating faster when Lorraine took her hand between his, raised it to his lips, kissed it, and restrained her hand for a moment before letting her go. When she drew away, startled and shocked and excited by his provocative touch, he smiled, his eyes half-closed. He had the most beautiful long dark eyelashes.

Monsieur bowed coolly to Marie-Josèphe. He led his family and

63

Lorraine away to their places. Monsieur took his seat, carefully arranging his coat-skirts. Chartres threw himself onto a chair beside his sister.

'Mlle de la Croix,' he asked, 'is it true that the sea monsters eat people?'

'Oh, yes,' Marie-Josèphe said in as serious a tone as she could find. 'I'm sure it is true.'

'And people,' Lorraine said, 'return the favour.'

The fountain machinery creaked to life, clanking and groaning. In the distance, water gushed and flowed.

'Ah,' Madame said. 'His Majesty is coming.'

In a panic, Marie-Josèphe thought, *Where is Yves? If His Majesty is here, the dissection must proceed . . . unless His Majesty is furious, and has come to banish me—*

Stop it, she said to herself. *Who are you to think the King himself would punish you? At most he would send Count Lucien. More likely he would send a footman.*

'Pardon me, please, Madame, Mademoiselle.' She curtsied quickly. Holding up the velvet skirts of her riding habit, she ran across the tent to the entrance.

A horrible possibility occurred to her. What if Yves expected her to remind him of the time of the dissection? What if she had failed him again, twice in a single day? She should have gone back to the chateau an hour ago. If she left now, His Majesty would be kept waiting, which was inconceivable. She could not begin the dissection herself – she was capable of performing it, but she would be horribly outside her place to do so.

She thought, *I'll ask one of the musketeers—*

She nearly ran into Count Lucien. She stopped long enough to curtsy to him.

'Take your place, please, Mlle de la Croix,' he said. He glanced around the tent, his casual gaze taking in everything, approving everything, seeking any sights improper for His Majesty to see.

'But I—my brother—'

Musicians followed Count Lucien into the tent; he gestured to a spot that would make His Majesty the focus of their music. The musicians took their places. Their notes sought the proper tone, found it, combined into melody.

'Father de la Croix will arrive in good time,' Count Lucien said.

The musketeers again drew aside the curtains. The trumpeter played a fanfare that swept across the tent.

His Majesty entered, riding in a three-wheeled chair pushed by two deaf-mutes. A cushion supported His Majesty's gouty foot. Yves strolled at the King's right hand. Mme de Maintenon's sedan chair followed close behind.

The fanfare ended; the musicians struck up a cheerful tune. Yves gestured and spoke and laughed, as if he were speaking to a fellow Jesuit of his own age and rank.

Count Lucien stood aside, bowing. Marie-Josèphe slipped out of His Majesty's path and curtsied deeply. All the members of the royal family rose. Silk and satin rustled, sword-belts clanked, egret plumes whispered. Nobility and commoners alike bowed low to their King.

His Majesty accepted the accolades as his due. Footmen ran ahead to remove his armchair, making way for his wheeled cart. The carriers lowered Mme de Maintenon's sedan chair beside him. Though the side curtains remained drawn, the chair's window opened a handsbreadth.

'The ship came about so quickly,' Yves said, 'that the sailor tumbled over the railing to the main deck – and when he landed, flat on his—' Yves hesitated, then said in the direction of Mme de Maintenon's open window, 'I beg your pardon, Your Grace, I've been too long among rough sailors, I mean to say he landed in a seated position – he never spilled a drop of his wine ration.'

The King chuckled. No response emanated from Mme de Maintenon's chair.

The King graciously indicated to the women of the royal family that they might be seated; he smiled at his brother and granted Monsieur a chair.

'I missed you, Father de la Croix, this morning.' His Majesty returned his attention to Yves. 'I'm disappointed, if I don't see my friends when I arise.'

A flush of embarrassment crept up Marie-Josèphe's neck and across her cheeks. She took a step forward, involuntarily, determined to draw the blame to herself. Count Lucien reached up and laid his hand on her arm.

'I must tell His Majesty—' she whispered.

'Now is not a proper time to speak to His Majesty.'

'I beg your pardon, Your Majesty,' Yves said. 'I wished to prepare for the dissection, so it will go perfectly. I deprived myself of your awakening ceremony. It was inexcusable of me to overlook Your Majesty's feelings in the matter.'

'Inexcusable, indeed,' His Majesty said, kindly, to Yves. 'But I will excuse you, this one time. As long as I see you tomorrow when I wake.'

Yves bowed. The King smiled at him. Marie-Josèphe trembled with guilty relief.

Mme de Maintenon rapped sharply on the window of her sedan chair. The King leaned toward her, listened, and spoke to Yves again.

'And I expect to see you at Mass as well.'

'Your Majesty hardly need mention it.'

Yves bowed in deep gratitude to His Majesty.

Count Lucien spoke softly to Marie-Josèphe. 'You must impress upon your brother the importance—'

Marie-Josèphe interrupted him. 'He knows, sir. The fault is entirely mine.'

'The responsibility is his.'

'You missed Mass, too, Count Lucien,' Marie-Josèphe said, stung into a retort by the criticism of her brother. 'Perhaps His Majesty will scold you as well.'

'He will not.' Count Lucien limped across the tent floor, to stand in his place beside the King.

All the while, the musicians played in the background. The sea monster trilled along with them, its song winding strangely within their melody.

'Marie-Josèphe!' Yves said. 'I need you.'

She hurried between the rows of courtiers and joined him beside the dissection table.

'There you are,' he said. 'Are you ready?'

'I am ready.' She kept her voice neutral, hurt by his peremptory tone, but accepting its justice. She hurried to stand at her drawing box. It held sheets of paper and her charcoals and pastels. The dry charcoal whispered against her fingers. At the convent, in Martinique, she had been forbidden to draw; at Saint-Cyr she had not had time for practice. She hoped she could do justice to Yves' work.

'Remove the ice,' Yves said.

Two lackeys scooped away the ice and the insulating layer of sawdust from the dissection table, revealing the shroud. Others stood nearby with large mirrors, holding them so His Majesty could see the proceedings without craning his neck. The operating theatre at the college of surgeons in Paris would have been more convenient for everyone else, perhaps, and would have allowed more spectators to see clearly. But at Versailles the convenience of His Majesty overruled other considerations.

At one end of the front row of spectators, Chartres watched eagerly, leaning forward, poised to leap and snatch and capture every shred of knowledge Yves offered. He caught Marie-Josèphe's gaze, wistfully, as if to say, *I could have moved that ice. I could hold that mirror.*

Marie-Josèphe tried not to giggle, thinking of the consternation if Chartres performed such menial tasks.

'His Majesty gave me the resources to discover the yearly gathering-place of the last of the sea monsters,' Yves said, 'and to capture two of them alive. The male creature resisted to its death. The female sea monster survives, for it possesses no such will to freedom.'

The quartet split its melody and soared in harmony, a daring departure from the usual measured music. Marie-Josèphe shivered at the beauty and the daring. Madame – who was herself an excellent musician – whispered a startled exclamation to Lotte; even His Majesty glanced toward the quartet. The violinist faltered. The musicians had not changed the familiar piece.

The female sea monster was singing.

It is like a bird, Marie-Josèphe thought, delighted. *A mockingbird, that can imitate what it hears!*

The violinist found his place. The sea monster's voice soared above the melody, then dropped far below. The soft rumble touched Marie-Josèphe's bones with a chill.

The tang of preserving fluid, and the dangerous sweet scent of flesh near rotting, rose from the canvas and filled the air. Monsieur raised his pomander, sniffed it, then leaned toward his brother and offered him the clove-studded orange. His Majesty accepted the protection from the evil humours, nodded thanks, and sniffed the pomander.

'I will first do a gross dissection, proceeding through the sea monster's skin, fascia, and muscles.' As oblivious to the music as to the odours, Yves pulled the canvas aside.

The live sea monster's song stopped.

The male sea monster was even uglier than the female, its face coarser, its hair pale green, tangled, and uneven. Its ugliness did not startle Marie-Josèphe; she had helped Yves dissect frogs, snakes, and wharf-rats, slimy worms, sharks with evil toothy grins.

But she was surprised by the creature's halo: broken glass and shards of gilt metal radiated like a sunburst around its head. She sketched, as if her hand were connected directly to her eyes: the shape of the head, the tangled hair, the rays of broken glass alternating with kinked, gilded strips.

Yves swept away the glass and the metal, as if it were random debris. He picked up a lock of the creature's hair. A twist of gilded metal fell from the tangle. Yves pushed it aside with the other rubbish.

Peering over the edge of the fountain and through the bars of its cage, the live sea monster whistled and sighed.

Marie-Josèphe slipped the sketch of the halo to the bottom of her stack of paper, and began another drawing.

'God has given the creatures hair,' Yves said, 'so they may disguise themselves in beds of seaweed. They are shy and retiring. They eat small fish, but the bulk of their diet no doubt is kelp.'

Marie-Josèphe sketched quickly: the wild hair, uneven in places as if it had been cut; the strong jaw; the sharp canine teeth projecting over the lower lip.

'When you're done with cutting the beast,' said Monseigneur, 'we can roast bits of it.'

'My apologies, Monseigneur.' Yves bowed toward the Grand Dauphin. 'That's impossible. The carcass is preserved for dissection, not for eating.'

'No doubt pickling the thing does away with all the merits of sea monster flesh,' Lorraine said.

68

'Save your appetite for my banquet, Monseigneur.' His Majesty spoke without amusement at the banter. Everyone fell silent and watched intently, even as he did, straining to see the creature or its mirror image.

Yves picked up a dissection knife and slit the dead sea monster's skin from sternum to pubis.

The live sea monster screamed.

The musicians played louder, trying to drown out the shrieks. They failed.

'The sea monster's skin is thick and leathery,' Yves said, raising his voice above the cries and the music. 'It provides some protection against predators, such as sharks and whales and kraken. Your Majesty will have noticed that the skin of its tails is thickest – most heavily armoured – proving that the beast's defence is escape.'

The line of Marie-Josèphe's charcoal wavered as the live sea monster's shrieks rose. Her vision blurred.

It can't still be hungry, Marie-Josèphe thought. *What's wrong, sea monster? You sound so sad. I cannot come to you. I must stay in my place and document my brother's work.*

She finished the sketch of the face. The servant at her side took it away to pin it to the frame behind her, so all the court could see. She lifted her hand to stop him, but it was too late.

She had sketched the creature with open eyes: large dark eyes, almost no whites, large pupils. She had sketched it alive, with an expression of grief and fear.

Marie-Josèphe shivered, then threw off her disquiet.

What nonsense! she thought. *Animals' faces have no expressions. As for the eyes – I drew the living sea monster's eyes.*

Yves peeled back the skin.

The female sea monster moaned and cried. Creatures from His Majesty's menagerie answered, roaring and trumpeting, gibbering and snorting in the distance. His Majesty turned his head toward the Fountain of Apollo; the simple movement informed his court that the clamour distressed and annoyed him. The musicians played more loudly. No one knew what to do, Marie-Josèphe least of all.

'We see a layer of subcutaneous fat – blubber, as it is known in whales and sea cows.' Yves projected his voice above the cacophony.

69

'The sea monsters carry a relatively small amount of blubber, indicating that they do not dive to great depths or accomplish great sea journeys. We may be sure that they reach their midsummer gathering by riding the great warm current. My conjecture is that they conceal themselves in shallow water, and seldom venture far from their birth islands.'

Marie-Josèphe sketched the male sea monster's torso. The layer of fat softened the lines of its body, but could not conceal its well-developed muscles and powerful bones.

'Mlle de la Croix.'

Marie-Josèphe jumped, startled. Count Lucien stood at her shoulder, speaking softly. With all the racket, he could have spoken in a normal voice without distracting Yves any more than he was distracted already. As for His Majesty and the courtiers, they assiduously ignored Marie-Josèphe and Count Lucien's conversation.

'The creature must be silenced,' Count Lucien said. 'For His Majesty's sake—'

'I fed it,' Marie-Josèphe whispered. 'That isn't the cry it made when it was hungry. I don't know – maybe it doesn't like the music.'

'Don't be impudent.'

She blushed. 'I wasn't—'

But he was right to chastise her. If the din drove His Majesty away, his regard for Yves would fall. Yves' position, and his work, would suffer.

'It sings like a bird,' she said. 'If the cage were covered, the sea monster might fall silent like a bird.'

Count Lucien's disgusted glance at the cage said more than if he had cursed her for a fool. The cage enclosed the Fountain and rose nearly to the tent peak. To cover it completely would require a second tent.

Count Lucien limped toward the sea monster's cage, gesturing to several footmen to attend him.

'Bring that net.'

The stout ropes of the net clattered against planking.

The sea monster's wailing never faltered. Marie-Josèphe wanted to wail, herself, for if they wrapped the sea monster in the net, if they silenced it, gagged it, all Marie-Josèphe's taming would go to waste.

Marie-Josèphe sketched frantically to keep up with Yves' lecture.

Derma, sub-derma, subcutaneous fat, fascia. She would draw the skin in detail – perhaps Chartres would allow her to use his microscope until she could buy a new one – in large scale, before it lost its integrity.

Beyond the Fountain, footmen took down the silken tent sides and carried them to the cage. Count Lucien pointed; they fastened the white silk to the bars, hanging it first between the sea monster and His Majesty. The thin curtain hardly baffled the sound, nor would it cut off enough light to make the creature sleep. Marie-Josèphe supposed it was worth a try. Heavy canvas could not be brought from the town of Versailles in under an hour, from Paris in less than a day.

The sea monster's cries faded. Everyone – except the King – glanced toward the cage with surprise.

Random whistles dissolved to quiet; a murmur of relief passed across the crowd. Count Lucien gestured; the servants returned to their places. The count bowed in Marie-Josèphe's direction. She smiled uncertainly. It must be chance, not her suggestion, that the sea monster had chosen this moment to sink into silence. The answering roars of the menagerie animals tapered off, ending with the hoarse coughing roar of a tiger.

The quartet played more softly. Count Lucien returned to his place; Yves returned to his lecture; Marie-Josèphe returned to her drawing. The King watched the dissection of chest and shoulder muscles with great interest.

The line of sketches stretched across the frame. Half a dozen, a dozen: the sea monster's body, its leg, its webbed, clawed foot. Marie-Josèphe's hand cramped.

'I will next expose the internal organs—'

His Majesty spoke a word to Count Lucien, who motioned for the King's deaf-mutes to take their places. The seated courtiers leaped to their feet. The rush and rustle of silk and satin filled the tent.

'—which should resemble—' Caught in his work, Yves picked up a new, sharp dissection knife.

'Father de la Croix,' Count Lucien said.

Yves straightened, looked blankly at Count Lucien, and recalled where he was, and in whose presence.

'Most intriguing,' His Majesty said. 'Immeasurably interesting.'

'Thank you, Your Majesty,' Yves said.

'M. de Chrétien,' the King said.

Count Lucien came forward. 'Yes, Your Majesty.'

'Order the Academy of Sciences to publish Father de la Croix's notes and sketches. Commission a medal.'

'Certainly, Your Majesty.'

'Father de la Croix, M. de Chrétien will inform you when I shall be free to observe again. Perhaps your Holy Father will wish to attend as well.'

Marie-Josèphe's heart sank: another delay. If the King did not free Yves to do his work, the sea monster might never be properly described.

Yves bowed. Marie-Josèphe curtsied. Charcoal dust from her hand smeared the skirt of her riding habit.

'At Your Majesty's convenience,' Yves said.

When His Majesty had left the tent, when the musicians had followed him, still playing, and his court had accompanied him, when his servants and guards and the visitors had departed, Marie-Josèphe was left all alone with Yves and Count Lucien.

Marie-Josèphe sank onto a chair. Not His Majesty's, of course; for her to sit in it would be ill-mannered. She sat in the seat that was still warm from the presence of the Chevalier de Lorraine.

The new shoes Marie-Josèphe had been so pleased with pinched her feet intolerably.

'When may I expect to continue, Count Lucien?'

Without replying, Count Lucien looked thoughtfully at the display of Marie-Josèphe's drawings.

'Mlle de la Croix, can you draw life as well as death?'

'Oh, yes, M. de Chrétien, life is much easier.'

'You may submit a drawing of the sea monster – a live sea monster, if you please – for His Majesty's medal. I don't promise your drawing will be chosen.'

'But when may my brother continue his work?'

'Sister,' Yves said, 'Count Lucien has offered us a singular honour. Be so kind as to offer him some gratitude.'

72

'I do!' she said. 'Of course I do, I'm flattered, sir, and I thank you. But drawings and medals don't decay. The sea monster, the dissection—'

'His Majesty dictates the progress of the dissection,' Yves said. He plucked a long shard of glass from the lab table and flung it into the garbage bucket. It shattered with a sound like bells. Yves folded the canvas over the dead sea monster's flayed body.

'You said yourself, only a few of the creatures remain. What if this is the only one you ever have to study?'

'It would be a shame. Still, the world holds many unknown creatures.' Yves directed the lackeys in packing ice around the specimen.

'In two or three days, the dissection might proceed,' Count Lucien said offhand.

'Not today?' Marie-Josèphe asked.

'I cannot see how that is possible. Today, His Majesty welcomes your Holy Father.'

Yves nodded, agreeing with Count Lucien. 'I must attend His Holiness. The sea monster will have to wait.'

The lackeys covered the ice with a thick layer of sawdust.

'Tomorrow, then?' Marie-Josèphe asked.

Count Lucien laughed. 'I assure you, His Majesty will be occupied from morning till after midnight. Ceremonies, entertainments, the luncheon in his Menagerie. Planning Pope Innocent's crusade against heretical shopkeepers. His Majesty expects to conduct his regular council meeting, and he must practice for Carrousel.'

'Must His Majesty observe?' Marie-Josèphe asked.

'His Majesty wishes to observe,' Count Lucien said, settling her question.

'But if he's so busy, would he even notice if Yves—'

'Your brother will gain precious little knowledge,' Count Lucien said dryly, 'locked in the Bastille.'

'Marie-Josèphe,' Yves said, 'I have no intention of opposing His Majesty's wishes.'

'Count Lucien,' Marie-Josèphe said, 'do you explain to His Majesty. My brother's work preserves the glory of capturing the sea monsters. His Majesty's glory!'

'You expect too much of me, Mlle de la Croix. It might be best,'

73

Count Lucien said, with some impatience, 'to continue after Carrousel, when the live sea monster will no longer scream.'

'By then, nothing will be left but the sea monster's bones, and the vermin its flesh generates!'

'Regrettable,' Count Lucien said.

'Forgive my sister, please, M. de Chrétien,' Yves said. 'She understands little of ceremony.'

Embarrassed, Marie-Josèphe fell silent. The lackeys swept up the wet, slushy pulp around the dissection table. Their brooms scratched softly against the planks.

'Is your understanding any better, sir?' Count Lucien asked. 'You disappointed His Majesty when you missed his awakening. I advise you not to disappoint him again. He expects you at Appartement, for his entertainments, this evening. Don't throw away these honours.'

Marie-Josèphe jumped to her feet. 'I can't allow His Majesty to think that was my brother's fault!' she cried.

The sea monster echoed her exclamation.

'Hush, Marie-Josèphe,' Yves said. 'No need to involve M. de Chrétien. His Majesty forgave me—'

'For my error!' The sea monster whistled, as if to emphasise Marie-Josèphe's mistake.

'What does it matter? All's well.'

Count Lucien considered, his brow furrowed for a moment. 'M. de la Croix has the right of it,' he said to Marie-Josèphe. 'His Majesty need not be troubled twice to forgive a single transgression. I must caution you against another lapse.'

Count Lucien bowed to Yves, to Marie-Josèphe, and took his leave. He leaned on his walking stick heavily, after the long hours of inactivity. Though the sides of the tent remained open, he departed through the entrance, and the musketeers held the curtains aside. Outside, his Arabian bowed. He clambered into the saddle and galloped away.

When he was out of earshot, Marie-Josèphe said, 'I'm so sorry, I've made such a dreadful tangle of today – of your triumph.'

'Truly,' Yves said, 'it's forgotten.'

She gave him a quick, grateful hug.

'Go feed the creature – hurry. And bid it be silent!'

Marie-Josèphe entered the sea monster's cage and captured a fish. It twisted in the net, weak and nearly dead.

'Sea monster! Dinner! Fish!' She swept the net through the water. Her fingers dipped beneath the surface, into the low vibration of the sea monster's voice.

Beneath the hooves of the dawn horses, the sea monster lifted her head. Her hair, her forehead, her eyes rose above the water. She peered at Marie-Josèphe.

'Will it scream again if I take down the curtains?' Yves asked.

'I don't know, Yves – I don't know why it started screaming. Or why it stopped, or why it sings.'

He shrugged. 'It doesn't matter – the noise won't trouble the King.'

The lackeys pulled down the makeshift curtains and remade the sides of the tent.

'It was in such distress,' Marie-Josèphe said. 'Come here, sea monster. Are you all right? Are you hurt?'

Silent, the sea monster swam toward her. Marie-Josèphe let the live fish free. The sea monster darted forward, netted it between its webbed hands, and ate it in one bite.

'It's so quick!'

'It wasn't quick enough to escape the net.'

Marie-Josèphe threw it another fish. The sea monster kicked its tails, jumped halfway out of the water, and caught the fish in the air. It disappeared into the pool, crunching the fish's bones and fins between its teeth.

'But you said—it was mating, it was entranced—'

'I don't care to discuss that.' Yves' face flushed beneath his fading tan.

'But—'

'I will not discuss fornication, even animal fornication, with my sister who is straight from the convent!'

Yves' tone startled her. When they were children, they had discussed everything. Of course, when they were children, neither had known a thing about fornication, animal or otherwise. Perhaps he still knew nothing, and his ignorance embarrassed him, or the truth of it frightened him, as what Marie-Josèphe had learned in the convent frightened her.

She netted the last fish and offered it to the sea monster from her bare hand. The sea monster swam within an armslength. The fish thrashed in Marie-Josèphe's fingers.

'Come, sea monster. Fish, good fish.'

'Fishhhhh,' said the sea monster.

Marie-Josèphe caught her breath, delighted. 'She talks, just like a parrot.'

She let the fish swim into the sea monster's hands. The sea monster crunched it between her teeth, and submerged.

'I can train her—'

'To be silent?' Yves said.

'I don't know,' Marie-Josèphe said thoughtfully. 'If I were sure what distressed her. She sounded so sad – she almost made me cry.'

'No one minds if you cry. But the sea monster's wailing distressed His Majesty. Come along, we must hurry.'

Marie-Josèphe packed her drawing box while he chained the gate and fastened it with a padlock. She drew out her sketch of the male sea monster's face, with its halo of glass and gold.

'What are these decorations? Where did the glass come from? The gilt?'

'A broken flask. Debris from the Fountain.'

'The live sea monster put them here? Is that what she was doing last night? Why?'

He shrugged. 'The sea monsters are like ravens. They collect shiny things.'

'It looks like—'

'—nothing.'

Yves took the sketch from her hand, crumpled it, and thrust it against the slow-match. The paper ignited. The halo around the dead sea monster's head blackened and crumpled. Yves threw Marie-Josèphe's sketch into a crucible and let it burn.

'Yves—!'

His smile dazzled her. 'Come along.' He folded her hand in the crook of his elbow and led her from the tent.

Behind them, the sea monster whispered, 'Fishhhh . . .'

Chapter 6

Marie-Josèphe stretched her arms up into the new court dress as Odelette lifted it over her head.

The beautiful blue satin and silver lace banished all Marie-Josèphe's regrets for the ruined yellow silk. One of Lotte's servants had brought the dress; Odelette had worked magic on it, taking it in and rearranging the trim.

The boned bodice and skirt slipped down over camisole, stays, and stockings, petticoat and underskirt. Odelette did up the fastenings, tucked back the skirt to reveal the petticoat, and deftly adjusted the ruffles.

Marie-Josèphe was so grateful to Lotte. Mademoiselle's gift allowed her to attend the Pope's arrival in a proper dress.

Marie-Josèphe wondered if she would be allowed to meet the Holy Father, to kiss his ring. Surely she would not; that privilege must be reserved for important members of court. She would see him, which she had never hoped to do, for his visit to France was extraordinary.

He is such a good man, she thought. A good man, a holy man. When His Holiness and His Majesty are reconciled, they'll stop the evils of the world.

Odelette brought out an elaborate new fontanges decorated with leftover lace from the dress and Marie-Josèphe's last few ribbons.

'There's no time for you to arrange it,' Marie-Josèphe said. 'I'll be late to attend Mademoiselle.'

'I worked so hard to make it beautiful,' Odelette said.

'And it is – Bring it with us, you may present it to Mademoiselle.'

Odelette reluctantly put the headdress aside and arranged Marie-Josèphe's hair simply, with a single false diamond as ornament.

Odelette sighed. 'Wish for the King to give you a real diamond, Mlle Marie,' she said. 'Everyone knows all you have is paste.'

'Everyone knows I have no money,' Marie-Josèphe said. 'If I had a diamond, they would wonder where I got it.'

'They all borrow money. From the King, from each other, from the merchants. No one thinks a thing about it.'

Odelette plunged a lamb's-wool puff into a jar of powder. About to powder her mistress' bare throat and the curve of her breasts, she stayed her hand.

'No,' she said thoughtfully, 'no, powder will hide the blue veins beneath your skin, that prove you are fair.'

The floury powder rose up in a cloud. Marie-Josèphe sneezed.

'Good,' she said. 'I'm pale enough.'

Odelette patted her own forehead and cheeks and throat with the wool puff, mottling the smooth tan of her perfect skin with smears of white.

'You're the most beautiful woman at court,' Odelette said. 'All the princes will look at you and say, Who is that lovely princess? I must marry her, and the Ambassador from Turkey must marry her attendant!'

Marie-Josèphe laughed. 'I love you, Odelette.'

'It might happen,' Odelette said. 'It happens in all the fairy tales.'

'Princes marry princesses, and Turkey isn't likely to send an ambassador to France.' Though France and Turkey both made war against the same enemy, the King hardly considered the Turks his allies. In the past his armies captured and sold Turkish prisoners, like Odelette's mother, into slavery. 'The gentlemen will say, Who is that colonial girl? I could not marry anyone so plain and unfashionable – unless she had an enormous dowry!'

Odelette brought Marie-Josèphe her high-heeled, pointed shoes; Marie-Josèphe stepped into them.

'There. You're perfect, Mlle Marie. Except your hair.'

Marie-Josèphe glanced at the pale creature in her mirror. She hardly recognised herself.

Marie-Josèphe and Odelette hurried through the cramped and smelly attic corridors. Odelette carried the fontanges like a fantastic cake.

They descended, down and down the narrow stairs, to the royal level, above the ground floor. Threadbare carpets and dark hallways gave way to polished parquet, rich tapestries, carved stone, gilded wood. Art and fine crafts filled the chateau, so His Majesty would always be surrounded by beauty. Artists and artisans of France produced almost everything His Majesty used, and His Majesty's notice made French crafts fashionable in all the capitals of the world. Even France's enemies designed their palaces to resemble the chateau of Versailles.

In the chateau, Marie-Josèphe often found herself staring helplessly at paintings whose beauty and technique she could never hope to match. Paintings by Titian, by Veronese, filled her with wonder. Today she forced herself to pass them with only a glance.

At Lotte's apartments, a footman announced her. 'Mlle Marie-Josèphe de la Croix.' He held open one side of the double door. 'You may enter.'

Lotte ran out of a cloud of multicoloured silk and satin and velvet, out of the midst of her ladies-in-waiting in their finest gowns and their best jewels.

'Mlle de la Croix!' She embraced Marie-Josèphe, stood back, and looked her up and down.

'You will do,' she said severely, mimicking Madame.

'Thanks to you, Mademoiselle.' Marie-Josèphe curtsied to Lotte and to the other ladies, who all outranked her by every measure.

'What an exciting day!' Lotte plucked at Marie-Josèphe's skirt to accentuate the flounces. 'But, poor Marie-Josèphe, were you covered with fish guts?'

'No, Mademoiselle, only a little charcoal on my fingers.'

'Is this the famous Odelette?' asked Mlle d'Armagnac, the season's most celebrated beauty. Her skin was as fair as porcelain and her hair as pale as summer wine. 'What is that confection?'

The ladies crowded around Odelette, captivated by her handiwork. Lotte laid claim to the new headdress. The ruffled tower reached an armslength above her head, and the ribbons spilled down her back. Mlle d'Armagnac brought silver ribbons, to match Lotte's petticoat; Odelette wove them into the arrangement.

'It's wonderful!' Lotte cried. 'You're so clever.' She hugged Marie-Josèphe, gave Odelette a gold louis, and sailed out of her rooms. Marie-Josèphe followed, nearly lost in the crowd.

At Madame's apartments, both halves of the tall carved entry doors swung open. Lotte's rank demanded that courtesy. In the anteroom, Madame's ladies-in-waiting curtsied. Lotte nodded and smiled at them. Halfway to her mother's private chamber, she turned back.

'Where is Mlle de la Croix? I want Mlle de la Croix.' Marie-Josèphe curtsied. Lotte kissed her lightly, took her arm, and whispered, 'Are you ready to face my mama?'

'I treasure your mama,' Marie-Josèphe said sincerely.

'And she likes you. But she can be so stuffy!'

In Madame's private chambers, a single candle burned on the desk. Madame sat writing, wrapped in a voluminous dressing-gown. The fire in the grate had gone out. The room was dim and cold. Marie-Josèphe curtsied low.

Madame looked up from her writing desk and laid aside her pen.

'My dearest Liselotte,' Madame said, 'come and let me look at you.' Madame and Mademoiselle shared the same pet name, within their family.

As Marie-Josèphe curtsied, two little dogs rushed from beneath the skirts of Madame's dressing gown. They yapped hysterically, their claws tapping and scratching on the parquet. The reek of their droppings clung in all the corners. The dogs, like walking rag-piles, jumped and pawed Marie-Josèphe's petticoat.

She drew back, rising even before Madame acknowledged her, to avoid a paw in the face. She surreptitiously toed Elderflower away. The ancient pug yapped more loudly, snapped at her skirt, lost interest and wandered off, snuffled at the floor, snorted for air. Younger-flower, the other pug, followed him slavishly. Even compared to Elderflower, Youngerflower was not very bright.

Madame rose, embraced Lotte, fondly patted her cheek, and stepped back to gaze at her.

'Your gown was so costly – His Majesty's Carrousel will be the ruin of us all – but you are beautiful, and the habit suits you.'

The low neckline showed off Lotte's magnificent bosom; dove-grey satin, silver lace, and diamonds flattered her blue eyes. Healthy, sturdy, cheerful, and kind, Lotte favoured her mother's side of her family, the German side, while her intensely handsome brother, in both his strengths and afflictions, could be taken only for a Bourbon.

Madame looked Marie-Josèphe up and down. 'Mlle de la Croix, I believe I have seen that gown before.'

'It looks so well on Marie-Josèphe, Mama,' Lotte said. 'And her wonderful Odelette worked magic to change it.'

'She changed it so much, you could wear it again.'

'No, Mama, not a second time, not with the Foreign Princes here!'

'Where is the palatine I gave you?'

Marie-Josèphe feigned surprise and distress. 'Oh, Madame, I beg your pardon, the new gown drove every other thought out of my head!' Fond as she was of Madame, she had no intention of copying her old-lady styles, hiding her decolletage beneath a scarf or a tippet.

'Every other thought but the current fashion.' Madame shook her head, resigned. 'Very well. You will do.' Madame sounded exactly like Lotte's imitation.

Lotte choked down a laugh. Marie-Josèphe hid her own amusement by dropping into another curtsy.

'Dear daughter,' the portly duchess said, 'I began to wonder where you were.'

Lotte laughed. 'Why, Mama, I had to rescue Mlle de la Croix from the monster fish!'

Marie-Josèphe approached Madame, knelt, and kissed the hem of her gown. 'Please forgive me, Madame. I didn't mean to make Mademoiselle late.'

'Forgive you twice in one day?' Madame smiled. 'I'm not your confessor, child! But I wonder if you have too many duties to bother with an old woman's family.' She took Marie-Josèphe's hand and raised her to her feet.

'Don't make me give up Marie-Josèphe, Mama,' Lotte said. 'I would offend M. de Chrétien. Besides, I have great plans for her!'

'And His Majesty has great plans for her brother, who needs her. Father de la Croix is more important to His Majesty than we are.' Madame opened her hand in a gesture that took in the whole room, with its faded hangings, the stubby candles. 'I don't begrudge him his place.'

'Madame, you should see our rooms!' Marie-Josèphe said, though she could hardly imagine Madame climbing to the attic, and devoutly hoped Madame would not try. 'I could fit my whole chamber within your bed-curtains, and my brother's is no larger.'

'Ah, that won't last long, my dear. I honour your brother for his success.' She sighed. 'I only wish I could provide for my children properly and pay my bills.'

'Mama, you're exaggerating as usual,' Lotte said. 'Why, we're rich, since dear Grande Mademoiselle died.'

' "Dear" Grande Mademoiselle – Never mind, I mustn't speak ill of the dead. La Grande Mademoiselle left your brother rich. Monsieur is rich. But I have hardly enough to keep my household, and I can hardly maintain Monsieur's position with one new dress every other season.'

'Mama, you have a brand new grand habit! We must hurry, why haven't your ladies got you dressed?'

'They fussed so, I sent them away and wrote my letters until you should come.'

Lotte took charge, sending Odelette to fetch Madame's stays and stockings, putting Marie-Josèphe in charge of Madame's petticoat. Together they dressed the Princess Palatine. Their conversation turned to the sea monsters.

'I wrote to the Raugrafin Sophie,' Madame said. 'I told her of your brother's triumph, Mlle de la Croix, and of watching him butcher the monster fish.'

'The creatures aren't really fish, Madame. They're like whales, or sea-cows. He's dissecting it – to look inside, to reveal the wonder of how its body works—'

'Dissection, butchery.' Madame shrugged.

'Chartres has all the family talent for alchemy.' Lotte shuddered theatrically. 'I couldn't understand it – if I did I'm sure I'd never again eat or drink or breathe.'

'You'd have no more choice in it,' Madame said, 'than you have in emptying your bowels or breaking wind.'

'Mama!' Lotte laughed, her beautiful laugh like spun silver. 'Now you stop breathing for a moment, so we may lace your stays.'

Elderflower, in his wandering, bumped into Madame's feet and plopped down. Marie-Josèphe and Odelette helped Madame into her petticoat. Its edge fell over Elderflower, concealing him. Youngerflower, losing sight of the older dog, ran around the room yapping in a panic.

Ignoring Youngerflower, Madame bent down and pushed aside lace and ruffles to pat Elderflower's long soft ears.

'He's getting feeble. I'll be so sad when he dies – and what will Youngerflower do when he's gone?'

'Mama, don't be silly, Elderflower's no more feeble than you are!'

'We should both retire to a convent, where we'd be in no one's way, and no one would have to think of us. A convent would accept a little dog, don't you think? They wouldn't deprive me of my few pleasures.'

They would deprive you of everything they could, dear Madame, Marie-Josèphe thought, but she could not say such an irreverent thing out loud.

'Madame, I think you would not enjoy a convent.' She and Odelette lifted the great construction of Madame's court dress and settled it upon her.

'Mama, they wouldn't let you hunt, if you retired to a convent. They might not let you write your letters. What would Raugrafin Sophie do without them?'

'I'd have nothing to write about, from the convent. I'd have to take the veil, and a vow of silence.'

'You'd never see the King—'

'I see him—' Madame's voice caught. 'I see him seldom enough anyway.'

'And besides, you must find me a prince, you promised!'

Lotte's enthusiasm brought a smile, tinged only a little with sadness, to Madame's lips. She held out her arms; she and Lotte embraced again.

'I must, it is true,' Madame said. 'For I failed your brother in the matter of his marriage – his father failed him, his uncle the King failed him, and our family is full of mouse droppings!' Madame sighed deeply. 'If Chartres had fewer foolish notions, fewer dangerous occupations—'

83

'Mama, you forget—'

'That Father de la Croix has the same sort of notions? I forget nothing, Liselotte. He can afford his new-fangled ideas.'

Madame sat down. Elderflower clawed his way into her lap; snuffling and sputtering, the evil pug sat its bottom on her velvet skirt and pawed the gauze covering her bosom. Madame petted the creature fondly.

'Everything's different for a Grandson of France. What His Majesty approves in a Jesuit, he cannot approve for his nephew.'

'Madame, your son loves science,' Marie-Josèphe said. 'Forbidding him his studies would cause him infinite distress.'

'And allowing him to continue might cost him his life. The suspicions could drag your brother down as well. And you, you must take care.'

'Suspicions!' Marie-Josèphe shook her head in confusion. 'Who could suspect Yves of any base act? Who could suspect Chartres? Madame, he is sweet and good and intelligent—'

'My husband is sweet and good and intelligent as well,' Madame said. 'For all his faults and even for his sins. That kept no one from gossiping that he poisoned Henriette d'Angleterre – or that he should be burned.'

'Nonsense, mama. Everyone who knew the first Madame says she died because she never ate anything. She pined away for love of—'

'Hush, you know nothing of her, you were no more than a glimmer of duty in your father's eye.'

'And you were still in the Palatinate with Aunt Sophie!'

Madame bent to lean her forehead against Elderflower's soft golden fur. Youngerflower snuffled around her feet, his nose to the floor, seeking his elder companion without success.

Madame sighed. 'And how I wish I had stayed there!'

She gazed at Lotte for a long minute. Her rough breath slowed and deepened and she did not cry. Marie-Josèphe's heart broke for Madame, so far from home.

'I will find you a prince, Liselotte,' Madame said. 'My duty is to find him, and your duty will be to marry him. I hope you will not hate me on that day . . . I hope you will be happier than I.'

'Mama, never worry about my wedding day. You'll be proud of me, I promise. Oh, what shall we do about your hair?'

'Give me a ribbon to tie it with,' Madame said, glancing critically at Lotte's headdress. 'You have plenty to spare. No one will notice me.'

'Marie-Josèphe, mama needs your help.'

'I can only defer to Odelette, Mademoiselle.'

She drew Odelette forward and held the pins and ribbons while she worked. Lotte joined her, playing the part of hairdresser's assistant with enthusiasm.

'Mama, please smile,' Lotte said. 'You look magnificent. Will you send for some chocolate and cakes to sustain us for the afternoon?'

'I should not smile because my teeth are too ugly and I should not have cakes because I am too fat,' Madame said. 'But I will do both, my dear, to please you.'

As Odelette finished dressing Madame's hair, Monsieur and Chartres and Lorraine arrived, trooping into Madame's private chamber like a trio of jewelled and bewigged peacocks. As if from nowhere, servants appeared with more pastries, with plates of fruit, with wine.

Moving with her usual stolid energy, Madame rose from her chair to curtsy to her husband. Monsieur formally returned her salute.

'I've brought my hairdresser for you, Madame.' Monsieur stroked a curl of his massive black wig and sipped wine from a silver goblet. 'Do let him—'

'I've been fussed over quite enough.' Madame waved Monsieur's hairdresser away.

Lorraine and Chartres looked on, drinking wine, critical and amused. Bowing, disappointed, the hairdresser withdrew.

'Have you a new hairdresser?' Monsieur asked. 'The arrangement is adequate – more than adequate. With the addition of a ruffle or two—'

'I am far too old for a fontanges. No, thank you, Monsieur. I prefer my hair plain – and so does your brother the King.'

Monsieur and Lorraine exchanged a glance; even Marie-Josèphe knew that the King, in his wilder youth, paid his serious attentions to beauties.

'Who did your hair?' Monsieur asked his daughter. 'It's quite delightful.'

'Mlle de la Croix, Papa,' Lotte said. 'I'm so lucky to have her – she might have been trapped at Saint-Cyr forever!'

'Odelette is entirely responsible,' Marie-Josèphe said.

Odelette curtsied shyly. Monsieur felt around in his pockets, came up with nothing but crumbs, unpinned a diamond from his waistcoat, and gave it to Odelette.

'Where is Father de la Croix?' Madame asked. 'He promised us a few moments – a story or two of his voyage.'

'He will be here soon, Madame.'

'If he's late, Mlle de la Croix,' Chartres said, 'I'll be pleased to escort you.'

'You'll escort your sister,' Madame said severely. 'As your wife doesn't see fit to grace my rooms.'

'Why, Madame,' Lorraine said, 'Mlle de Blois fears she'll be swept up – with the other mouse droppings.'

'Madame Lucifer has better things to do than spend her time with me,' Chartres said. 'To my everlasting gratitude.'

'I so want to hear your brother's adventures,' Madame said. 'If I miss them, I'll wait another decade for any excitement.'

'If you miss a single story, Madame,' Marie-Josèphe said, 'he'll tell them all over again for you. I promise.'

'You are a good child.'

'Mlle de la Croix, I have a present for you.' Chartres limped toward her, his blind eye wandering. Marie-Josèphe always feared he would fall at her feet.

He pulled the stopper from a beautiful little silver bottle and thrust it at her.

'What is it, sir?'

'Perfume – of my own making.' He dropped to one knee before her. Embarrassed, Marie-Josèphe stepped back.

'Do get up, sir, please.'

He grasped her hand, to dab perfume on her wrist, but Lotte stopped him.

'Let her smell it first, Philippe,' she said. 'It might not suit her.'

'How could it not?' Chartres said.

Marie-Josèphe wondered if it was quite proper for a married man to give a gift of perfume to his sister's lady-in-waiting. For her to criticise his manners would be even more improper. She wondered why his wife avoided him, for despite his strange blind eye he was handsome, and he always had something new and interesting to talk about.

'Pure essence of flowers.' Chartres waved the stopper beneath her nose, releasing a delicate tendril of scent.

'Roses! Sir, it's lovely.'

Chartres splashed the perfume on Marie-Josèphe's wrist. As he reached for her bosom, Madame snatched the bottle. Chartres pouted.

'A prince should not do a maid's job.' Madame gave the flask to Marie-Josèphe. 'Let your girl scent you up, Mlle de la Croix, if you wish.'

'I only want to show Mlle de la Croix I'm a chemist,' Chartres said. 'I could help her brother. I could study with him.'

Odelette dabbed essence of roses behind Marie-Josèphe's ears and on her throat and between her breasts. The tincture evaporated, chilling her skin, enveloping her in fragrance.

'You may think yourself a chemist, Philippe,' Monsieur said. 'But you're only a novice perfume maker.'

Chartres' uneven gaze followed Odelette's hands. Lorraine smiled at Marie-Josèphe, mocking and sympathetic. The skin around his eyes crinkled with the most attractive laugh-lines.

'Sometime you must try one of my perfumes,' Monsieur said. He waved his lace handkerchief before her face. A pungent and musky odour obliterated the fragrance of roses. 'Now, who is superior, father or son?'

'I beg your pardon, Monsieur – but my nose is filled with the scent of roses, and I cannot compare another fragrance.' She dared not tell Monsieur his favourite perfume overwhelmed her and made her think of Lorraine.

'You look far too plain for the importance of the day.' Monsieur peered into a mirror, plucked off one of his own beauty patches and pressed it just above the corner of Marie-Josèphe's mouth.

'Thank you, Monsieur.' She curtsied, hardly knowing what else to do.

'Now that I've proven myself a chemist,' Chartres said, 'will you recommend me as your brother's assistant?'

'She will not, sir,' Monsieur said.

'You come to supper smelling of sulphur,' Madame said. 'Now you propose to add fish guts? It isn't proper for you to dirty your hands.'

'Or his reputation,' Lorraine said, a dark hint of warning in his voice.

'Be quiet, my dear.' Monsieur spoke with worried intensity and returned his attention to his son. 'Dabbling in alchemy is beneath you.'

'Yes, it is, sir!' Chartres exclaimed. 'What I study is chemistry. It's important work. We may discover how the world functions—'

'And what use is that, sir?' his father asked. 'Will it advance the fortunes of our family?'

'I married Madame Lucifer to advance the fortunes of our family,' Chartres said.

'For all the good that did us,' Madame said.

His complexion dangerously choleric, Monsieur raised his voice. 'You have duties enough already.'

'And what are those, sir?' Though Chartres' voice held only innocence, his blind eye wandered wildly.

'To please the King,' Monsieur said.

Marie-Josèphe caught her breath with relief when Yves arrived, only a moment before Monsieur and Madame and their ladies and gentlemen departed to make their way through the chateau to the Marble Courtyard. He bowed gallantly; the ladies clustered around him, hiding behind their fans with feigned shyness. He stood out among the courtiers, whether he was with ladies or gentlemen, because of the plainness of his robe, because of his beauty. But he had left no time to amuse Madame with sea monster stories.

He folded Marie-Josèphe's hand into the crook of his elbow; they joined the procession. She was proud to be with her brother, yet she admitted to herself a shred of envy at Mlle d'Armagnac's place, fluttering her fan at Chartres, taking the Chevalier de Lorraine's arm.

'What have you put on your face?' Yves whispered.

'Monsieur placed it there.'

'It isn't the sort of thing my sister should wear.' With gentle caution, he plucked the beauty patch from her upper lip.

'I'm sorry.' Marie-Josèphe kept her voice low. 'I didn't know how to say he might not give it to me.'

'As for your dress . . .' With a concerned frown, he tugged at the lace peeking above her low neckline, pulling the decorated edge until the camisole's plain muslin showed. She pushed his hand away, hoping no one had seen, but Mlle d'Armagnac watched, and whispered to Lorraine.

'Madame approved it – she's the soul of propriety.' She did not mention Madame's palatine. She tucked the muslin out of sight, leaving only the silk lace trim revealed. Marie-Josèphe had been astonished to discover that Lotte's camisoles were of muslin, except the trim. Madame was not only the soul of propriety, but the soul of making the most of a sou.

'You always were a quick study,' Yves said. 'A few months in France, two weeks at Versailles, and already an expert in court etiquette.'

'Two weeks at Versailles, all summer at Saint-Cyr – where they speak only of the King, religion, and fashion.'

Yves gazed at her quizzically. 'I'm only teasing. You've done well – but I'm here now. You needn't worry anymore.'

What Yves said was true. His success overshadowed Marie-Josèphe's small progress. She could fade behind his light. She could keep his house; if she were lucky he would let her continue to assist in his work. She was selfish, and foolish, to wish and hope for more. Humbled, she squeezed his arm and leaned her head against the rough wool of his cassock. Yves patted her hand fondly.

At Yves' side, Marie-Josèphe waited in the Marble Courtyard, standing in her place behind Mademoiselle. Courtiers and clerics packed the square, covering its bold concentric black-and-white pattern of newly-polished marble tiles.

The chateau glowed, its columns and vases polished, the gilt on the doors and windows and balconies renewed, the marble busts cleaned and repaired. Huge pots of flowers lined the courtyards that opened out, each one successively larger, to the Gate of Honour and the Place d'Armes. Thousands of spectators filled the courtyards.

A double line of flowering orange trees in silver pots flanked His Holiness' route, along the Avenue de Paris, across the Place d'Armes, up to the gilded gate. Larger orange trees marked a path across the cobblestones of the Ministers' Place, through the Forecourt, and between the wings of the chateau to the edge of the Marble Courtyard. The visitors stood respectfully behind the orange trees, leaving the pathway clear.

Marie-Josèphe had never seen so many people. They all wore finery, even if the finery were cobbled together. The men wore swords, as decent dress required: massive medieval family heirlooms, battered souvenirs of past wars, gilt or potmetal blades rented from the stands along the road from the town of Versailles.

Marie-Josèphe's feet hurt. The sun dipped behind the roof of the chateau, plunging the courtyard into cool shadow. Marie-Josèphe shivered despite the press of bodies and the clear late-summer day. With her handkerchief, she patted the perspiration from Mademoiselle's brow.

A cheer gathered in the distance. Marie-Josèphe forgot her pinched feet and her shivers.

Noise struck her as the voices of thousands of people rose, rejoicing in the reconciliation between Louis and the Church of Rome. The courtyard, set between the wings of the chateau, concentrated and focused the cheers, as if the busts of philosophers and heroes were shouting their acclaim, as if Mars and Hercules on their pediment cried out to celebrate Christianity's ascendance.

Magnificent in their bright uniforms, a troop of Swiss Guards dismounted at the Gate of Honour and marched between the trees. His Holiness' coach followed. Though His Majesty had given His Holiness dispensation to drive a carriage to the entrance of the chateau, the guards must walk.

Louis could have commanded Innocent to approach him on foot; he had, after all, forced one of Innocent's holy predecessors to abase himself and apologise for the loutish actions of his guards. This King of France had forced Rome's representatives to yield precedence to his own. But he was a great diplomat; he would not require an old and pious and humble man to walk. He would not risk his treaty.

The coach proceeded between the orange trees, keeping a stately pace. As Innocent passed, nodding to the crowd, a tide of cheers followed him. The crowd closed in after the carriage, filling the space between the orange trees. Green leaves and white blossoms quivered violently.

The great doors of the chateau swung open, and the King appeared.

Louis crossed the Marble Courtyard at a leisurely pace, magnificent in brown velvet studded with tigers-eyes and trimmed with gold lace, a green satin waistcoat heavily embroidered with gold, and diamond garters and shoe buckles. For this very particular occasion, he wore the Order of the Holy Ghost outside his coat. Dazzling diamonds covered the long blue sash. Rubies and sapphires decorated the gold scabbard of His Majesty's ceremonial sword. Spanish point lace edged his hat, and the most wonderful white plumes swept over his shoulder.

Marie-Josèphe curtsied deeply. All around her, silk rustled and velvet whispered as the other courtiers bowed. Marie-Josèphe risked a peek.

Below, in the forecourt, the Swiss Guards formed a double line to flank His Holiness' carriage. The horses, stepping high, trotted to the low course of stairs at the edge of the Marble Courtyard.

His Majesty reached the top of the steps.

His Majesty allowed the cheering to crescendo. He stood in grandeur, flanked by two generations of his heirs, by the deposed King James and Queen Mary of England, by his ministers and his advisers. Mme de Maintenon, drab and serene, stood at the very back of the King's party.

Marie-Josèphe caught her breath. His Holiness' white robes shone from the dimness of the coach.

His Holiness descended. His Majesty stood straight, gazing at the old man who held a key to winning the war against the League of Augsburg. The crowd fell silent.

The two most powerful men in the western world faced each other.

Cardinals and bishops followed Innocent out of the carriage. They bowed to His Majesty. When they rose, so did Marie-Josèphe and the other courtiers.

'Welcome, Cousin. Our estrangement has caused great sorrow.' His Majesty honoured the Pope with his courtesy.

'Cousin, I rejoice at the reconciliation of France with Rome. I rejoice at our alliance.'

'Together, we will crush the Protestants. We will eradicate their heresy from France. From Europe. From the world. For the glory of God.'

The enormous crowd erupted in a spontaneous cheer of devotion to God and King.

Transfixed, Mme de Maintenon clasped her hands before her lips. Her dark eyes shone with tears. Marie-Josèphe felt a little sorry for her, despite her position: married – everyone said – to the King, but secretly, never acknowledged, and therefore open to the charge of adultery and fornication. Her persuasion was the cause of this unprecedented meeting. And yet she must stand behind the bastard princes, silent, nearly overcome with emotion.

As the cheering continued, one of the bishops brought forward a container of gold encrusted with pearls and diamonds. He handed the reliquary to His Holiness, who accepted it reverently. Pope Innocent raised the tall domed receptacle to his lips, then handed it to His Majesty.

Louis accepted the magnificent offering. His Holiness had brought a bone, or a bit of flesh, from the preserved body of a saint, to reside forever in France. Perhaps His Majesty would keep it in the chapel at Versailles, where the courtiers could see it, touch the reliquary, acquire goodness and piety by its influence.

His Majesty handed the reliquary to Count Lucien, who accepted it and gave it to Father de la Chaise. His Holiness frowned at Count Lucien, then made his expression benign again. And indeed Marie-Josèphe thought Count Lucien had handled the saint's relic rather offhandedly. Innocent's gift merited a golden altar, or at least a velvet pillow.

Count Lucien signalled. A half-dozen footmen staggered forward, bent beneath the weight of a magnificent ebony prayer bench of the most fashionable style. Inlays of exotic woods and mother-of-pearl, outlined with gold, illustrated scenes from the Parables.

His Majesty's artisans have outdone themselves, Marie-Josèphe thought.

The King and the Pope saluted each other, Innocent bowing with genuine humility, His Majesty deigning to incline his head to his fellow prince. The courtiers with His Majesty, the churchmen with Innocent, bowed deeply each to the other side. When they rose, Mme de Maintenon's expression shone like the sun, with unutterable joy. In public she kept her own council; she raised her black lace fan before her face, but it betrayed her by trembling.

His Majesty could give his hand only to the Emperor, the only man in Europe whose rank equaled his own. He did not breach etiquette for the sake of Pope Innocent, as he had for his deposed ally James of England.

Though Innocent forbore to offer his ring to Louis to be kissed, he searched His Majesty's escort, and stretched his hand toward Mme de Maintenon.

Mme de Maintenon hurried forward, her black silk skirt and petticoats rustling against the black and white marble. A powerful unacknowledged queen on a distorted chessboard, she knelt – gracefully, despite her age – before Innocent and pressed his hand, his ring, to her lips.

'Perhaps he'll stone her,' Madame muttered, only loud enough for Lotte – and Marie-Josèphe, just behind her – to hear. Marie-Josèphe felt rather shocked, but Lotte pressed her lips together, and her shoulders shook.

'Rise, sister.' Innocent treated Mme de Maintenon with exquisite and kindly politeness, supporting the faction that believed she and the King had married.

His Majesty and Pope Innocent and Mme de Maintenon walked together across the Marble Courtyard to the chateau entrance, the Royal Family and the bishops and cardinals falling in behind, the courtiers bowing as they passed. Another cheer from the crowd rose around them and echoed from the walls, making the busts of heroes and saints shout and cry as they never had in life.

Chapter 7

Marie-Josèphe accompanied Mademoiselle and Madame back to Madame's apartments. Put out of sorts by Mme de Maintenon's triumph, Madame grumbled all the way.

'Innocent will take all His Majesty's time,' she said, 'Planning wars, estranging me further from my relatives . . . I fear His Majesty will never invite us on another hunt, or even a walk.'

'We could walk by ourselves, Mama,' Lotte said.

'It isn't the same.'

'Oh, Madame,' Marie-Josèphe said, 'how can His Majesty do anything ordinary today?'

'His entertainments this evening will be ordinary enough, I have no doubt. No pope will stop the gambling or the drinking, and he certainly cannot stop the boredom!' Madame sighed, then brightened as she led the way into her dim, cold apartments. 'I must finish my letter to Electress Sophie.'

'You'll have to admit to Aunt Sophie that the Marquise de Maintenon came away unstoned.'

Madame made a sound of disgust. 'The old whore! By your leave, Mlle de La Croix.'

'I beg your pardon, Madame?'

'And I beg yours! I cannot help my improper language, for I ran wild when I was young.'

'I heard no improper language,' Marie-Josèphe said.

Madame laughed, and Lotte joined in.

'So the old hag hasn't taken you in, with her piety and her mouse turds! I knew you were a sensible young woman.'

'You give me too much credit, Madame.' Marie-Josèphe's cheeks warmed intensely with her embarrassment. 'If you spoke improperly I couldn't tell – I don't know what that word means.'

'Which word?' Lotte asked dryly. 'Turd, hag, or whore?'

'The last,' Marie-Josèphe whispered.

'It is charming that you do not know it,' Madame said. 'I must get to my letters.'

Marie-Josèphe and Lotte curtsied as Madame disappeared into her private chamber.

Lotte took Marie-Josèphe's arm. Together they left Madame's rooms. Odelette followed. Dusk was falling; as they passed, servants lowered the crystal chandeliers and lit masses of new candles.

In Lotte's apartments, the ladies-in-waiting claimed Odelette to dress their hair. Lotte drew Marie-Josèphe to a corner by the window so they could whisper together.

'You have led such a sheltered existence!' Lotte said.

'You know that I have.'

'A whore is a woman who sells herself for money.'

'In Martinique we would call her a slave. Or a bondservant, if she sold herself.'

'Not a slave, not a bondservant! A woman who sells her body.'

Marie-Josèphe shook her head, confused.

'Who sells her body to men. To any man.' Exasperated, Lotte said, 'For sex!'

'Sex?' Marie-Josèphe tried to make sense of it. 'Do you mean, fornication? Sex without marriage?'

'Marriage! Silly goose.'

'I—' Marie-Josèphe fell silent. It would be improper for her to defend herself against her royal mistress' ridicule, though she felt hurt that Lotte would take such pleasure in making fun of her.

You raised yourself too high, Marie-Josèphe told herself. *If Lotte slaps you down, then you deserve it.*

'I don't mean it!' Lotte said. 'Marie-Josèphe, I'm sorry. You must let me teach you everything about the world – how could the nuns keep you in such ignorance?'

'They hoped only to preserve my innocence,' Marie-Josèphe said. 'The holy sisters are innocent themselves. They know nothing of—' Her voice fell to a whisper.

'Whoring,' Lotte said out loud. 'I'll tell you of Ninon de L'Enclos – I met her, if His Majesty found out! – Or mama – but of course she isn't a whore, she's a courtesan.'

'What is that?'

Lotte explained. To Marie-Josèphe, the difference could dance on the head of a pin with a thousand angels.

In the convent, the nuns had repeated dire and ambiguous warnings that Marie-Josèphe never understood. Only once had she asked what 'fornication' meant, exactly; a week alone in her room with nothing to eat but bread and water could not cure her unwomanly curiosity, but the punishment made her devious about how she found out answers. The punishment left her with the holy knowledge that intimate relations between a man and a woman were evil, obligatory in marriage, and unpleasant.

When she was Lotte's age, Marie-Josèphe had wept for her dead mama and papa, who had loved each other while they lived, who loved her and Yves, who had been required to submit to distress and pain to create their children and their family. She wept because she and her future husband would have to do the same thing, if she wished to recreate the enchantment of her childhood. She hoped she was strong enough, and she wondered why God had made the world this way. She wondered if God had made a joke. But when she asked the priest at confession, he laughed. Then he told her people should not love each other, for such love was profane. People should love God, whose love was sacred. Then the priest assigned her such a heavy penance that she suspected she had nearly earned a beating.

Once Mother Superior lectured her students about fornication. She left them in such a state of confusion and excitement that at bedtime they whispered instead of sleeping. When the holy sisters checked their charges at midnight, they heard the whispers. That night, and for a month afterwards, the sisters laid themselves down next to the students, rigid and wakeful, to prevent forbidden words and to enforce the proper sleeping position among their charges: on their backs, their hands on top of the covers.

'Now you know of Mlle de L'Enclos,' Lotte said, 'who is a wit, who was the toast of Paris, a courtesan.'

'She committed mortal sin,' Marie-Josèphe said, appalled.

'Then everyone at court will go to hell!'

'Not everyone! Not Madame—'

'No, not poor mama,' Lotte said.

'And not His Majesty!'

'Not now, it's true, but when he was young, why, Marie-Josèphe, he was the worst!'

'Oh, hush, how can you speak of His Majesty that way?'

'Where do you think the mouse turds came from?'

Marie-Josèphe tried to reconcile her belief that children resulted only from marriage, with the indisputable fact that the duke du Maine – and his brother and sisters and his half sister – existed.

'His Majesty can do as he wishes,' Marie-Josèphe said.

And perhaps, Marie-Josèphe thought, God makes the business of creating children less horrible, for his representative on Earth. That would explain why His Majesty had created so many.

'Not according to the Church – not according to Mme de Maintenon! The courtiers say she has him locked up in a chastity belt.'

Embarrassed, Marie-Josèphe held her silence. She, the elder, should be the more knowledgeable. Lotte had ventured into territory about which Marie-Josèphe was ignorant.

'And I'm not going to hell – not for that reason, in any event,' Marie-Josèphe said, trying to regain a foothold. 'Nor are you—'

'Are you sure?' Lotte said slyly.

Marie-Josèphe forged ahead, unwilling to understand Lotte's innuendo. '—or my brother—'

'Your beautiful brother!' Lotte exclaimed. 'Yves is wasted on the priesthood, what a shame! Every woman at court is entranced by his eyes.'

'Or—or—' Marie-Josèphe stumbled, knocked off-balance. 'Or Count Lucien!'

Lotte stared at Marie-Josèphe, argued into concurrence. Then, to Marie-Josèphe's astonishment, Lotte burst into a great rollicking unladylike laugh.

'Dear Marie-Josèphe!' she said. Her laugh turned to a snort and she caught her breath. Marie-Josèphe had no idea why she was laughing.

'You're jesting with me, and here I thought you were serious, I thought, My friend is so learned in some ways, and so ignorant in others. But you knew everything all along.' She sighed. 'So I suppose I mustn't try to enhance my reputation with you, for you'll know I'm exaggerating and I'll lose your respect.'

'You couldn't,' Marie-Josèphe said, grateful for a handhold in shifting sands. 'That could never happen.'

'I wonder,' Lotte said softly.

Marie-Josèphe and Yves reached the foot of the magnificent Ambassadors' Staircase and joined the line of courtiers, progressing toward the heart of the chateau, where the King entertained his guests. So many people stood crushed together on the double staircase that Marie-Josèphe could barely see the elaborate decorations, the sculpture, the multicoloured marble.

She wore the same blue gown – she had no other fine enough for this evening – but after Odelette created another lacy tier for Lotte's fanciful headdress, Mademoiselle had insisted on lending Marie-Josèphe her third-best fontanges. Marie-Josèphe held her head high, thinking, Tonight I'm not quite so far out of the stream of fashion.

They reached the Salon of Venus. The Master of Ceremonies thumped his staff on the floor.

'Father de la Croix and Mlle de la Croix.'

Marie-Josèphe walked into the brilliance of His Majesty's state apartments.

Banks of candles gleamed and flickered, rising from gold and silver candlesticks on every surface, casting the spectrum of the rainbow through the faceted crystals of the chandeliers. The candlelight reflected from the windows, from the gold sunburst reliefs, from the gold leaf of the wall carvings and the inlays on the furniture. Light leaped and sparkled over jewels, along the gold embroidery on the men's coats, across the gold and silver lace adorning the gowns and petticoats of the noblewomen. It illuminated the triumphant paintings on the walls and ceilings. It gleamed across the marble floors.

Music whispered through the room, mingling with gossip and

chatter. Even a measured piece of court music threatened to set Marie-Josèphe wildly cavorting, dazzled, across the polished floor.

On the ceiling, Venus, Crowned by the Graces, cast garlands of flowers to enthrall the gods at her feet; she was so lovely, the petals so real, that Marie-Josèphe could imagine reaching into the air and capturing a wreath touched by dew. Her perfume might emanate from those blossoms. Motifs of love decorated the Salon of Venus. Under the gaze of the goddess, anything was possible, even for a colonial spinster without connections or resources. After all, Mme de Maintenon had come from Martinique with even less.

A crush of people, a brilliant gathering of royalty and nobility, filled the Salon of Venus. Everyone in the world dreamed of attending the celebration of the fiftieth year of Louis XIV's reign. The foreign princes of Condé and Conti and Lorraine had arrived even before Pope Innocent, to pay their respects. The nobility of distant lands, from across the Mediterranean, from across the Atlantic, from the other end of the Silk Road, soon would attend His Majesty.

At the announcement of Yves' name, a murmur of recognition buzzed through the room like a swarm of bees. Everyone turned to look, to bow or smile or nod to him. Yves acknowledged the greetings in a most courtly manner, gracious yet dignified.

Courtiers surged toward Yves in a wave. Before they reached him, their tide broke and parted like the Red Sea.

Louis strolled through the ruptured wave. It rippled as he passed, as his subjects and his guests bowed low. The plumes of the men's hats brushed the floor and the lace of the women's petticoats whispered into drifts, colourful spume strewn at the monarch's feet. The sea of courtiers closed behind him, but the royal family insisted on its precedence. If Madame could not exactly part the waters of the courtiers, she could sail through them like a great ship.

Monsieur trailed in Madame's wake, bringing the chevalier de Lorraine with him; Lotte followed, on the arm of Charles, duke de Lorraine. The foreign prince was a wealthier and more highly-placed distant relative of the chevalier, but he was not nearly as handsome. Nevertheless, Lotte glowed in Charles of Lorraine's attention. Her exuberance overcame the essential plainness of her mother's side of the family.

Louis stopped some paces from Yves.

Yves saluted the King, graciously, yet with reserve. Marie-Josèphe dropped into a deep curtsy.

'Father de la Croix,' His Majesty said. 'I'm delighted to see you at my evening entertainments.'

'Thank you, Your Majesty.'

Yves strode to His Majesty, and bowed again.

'You must tell us your adventures, Father,' Louis said. 'Tell us all how you captured the sea monsters.'

'Yes, Your Majesty.'

Louis turned his entire attention to Yves. Louis was the sun. His natural philosopher reflected the light of his King. Invisible in the shadow of her brother's accomplishments, Marie-Josèphe was free to observe. Royalty surrounded Yves like a whirlpool, leaving Marie-Josèphe in a safer eddy.

'Tell us everything, Father de la Croix.' Madame took Yves' arm, as if the King, or Monsieur and the Chevalier, might snatch him away and keep his stories all to themselves. 'Don't leave out a single monster, a single leviathan – a single sea breeze!'

'It will be my pleasure, Madame, though in truth the voyage held more discomfort and boredom than adventure.'

Courtiers jostled past Marie-Josèphe, crowding between her and the inner circle. Lords and ladies alike exclaimed over Yves' voyage, his bravery, his triumph over the dangerous monsters.

'How handsome he is,' whispered the young duchess de Chartres, 'Mme Lucifer' as her husband, her cousin Philippe d'Orléans, called her. Mlle d'Armagnac, attending Mme de Chartres, murmured her agreement.

Mme de Chartres and her husband exchanged neither word nor glance; Madame nodded to her with scrupulously correct coolness. While Mme Lucifer gazed at Yves and fluttered her fan, Mlle d'Armagnac gazed at Mme Lucifer's husband Chartres and fluttered her eyelashes.

The Chevalier de Lorraine towered above His Majesty's legitimised daughter. 'He will break your hearts, my ladies.' His voice was low, amused, overpowering.

Marie-Josèphe made way for people of higher rank. In the shadows by the doorway, out of the crush, she reminded herself that she had Yves all to herself most of the time. She could hear of his adventures when they were alone. Tonight belonged to him, and he belonged to the court. He had earned every moment of his time in the illumination of the King's regard.

The air was thick with smoke, sweat, and perfume. The aroma of savoury pastries drifted from the Salon of Abundance. Marie-Josèphe's stomach growled. She ignored her hunger; she had no choice. She had eaten nothing all day but chocolate and pastry; her head ached from too many sweets and her stomach growled for soup, meat, salad. But the court would not be invited to the collation for hours yet.

Marie-Josèphe slipped across the threshold into the empty Salon of Diana, glad of a moment beyond the crowd. The billiard tables waited for His Majesty's pleasure. A second chamber group played to the empty room.

A flurry of inchoate music strayed in from the Salon of Mars. Marie-Josèphe peeked through the doorway. The musicians of still another orchestra tuned their instruments. M. Coupillet, one of His Majesty's music masters, hovered nervously before them.

Signor Alessandro Scarlatti of Naples loomed over his young son Domenico, who sat at a magnificent harpsichord. The scenes on its sides, inlaid in polished wood and mother of pearl, glowed in the candlelight. Greed was a sin, covetousness was a sin, but Marie-Josèphe coveted playing the harpsichord.

Scenes of war and triumph surrounded her. On the ceiling, ravening wolves pulled the chariot of the god Mars into battle. Symbols of war and victory covered every surface. Marie-Josèphe wished His Majesty had chosen the Salon of Diana as his music room, for she much preferred the mythical huntress, and M. Bernini's white marble bust of the King, gazing upward across the chamber with youthful arrogance. She wished she had known His Majesty when he was young. He was handsome now, still – of course – but he had been so beautiful thirty years ago.

Signor Scarlatti barked an order at young Domenico. Marie-Josèphe made out a bit of the Italian, mostly 'No, no, no!' Domenico stopped and put his hands in his lap. Signor Scarlatti proclaimed the tune in wordless speech, including the grace notes. Signor Scarlatti rapped the glowing finish of the harpsichord with his baton. 'Doodle-doodle-doodle—! Capisci?'

'Yes, father.' Domenico began again; Signor Scarlatti folded his arms and glared down while he played. Marie-Josèphe thought Domenico a wonderful prodigy, and a sweet mischief.

Signor Scarlatti spied Marie-Josèphe. 'Is it . . . the little arithmetic teacher?' He strode to Marie-Josèphe and kissed her hand.

'Good evening, Signore,' Marie-Josèphe said.

'You have come up in the world,' he said.

'I've changed my clothes,' Marie-Josèphe said.

'And you have progressed from Saint-Cyr to Versailles.' He gazed at her soulfully. 'Now that you are so far above me, can I even hope for a kiss?'

Marie-Josèphe blushed. 'My brother would not like me to kiss gentlemen. Especially married gentlemen.'

'But if I please you . . . if I please him . . . if I please His Majesty—'

'Sir, I didn't know my little song – my gift to you! – would make a debtor of me.' She extricated her hand.

He chuckled. 'Then you've not been at court for long.'

'You know I have not. Please forget I ever asked a favour of you – please forget I ever spoke to you!'

'You are unkind – you break my heart,' he said. The lilt of his French tempered his complaint.

'Signorina Maria!' Domenico ran to her and wrapped his arms fiercely around her waist, almost disappearing in the ruffles of her petticoat.

'Master Démonico! You play so beautifully!'

He laughed, as he always did, at the nickname she had made for him when he and his papa visited Saint-Cyr to play for the students. She knelt to embrace him.

'He would play more beautifully if he practiced.' Signor Scarlatti sighed. 'Here we have practiced—' He glanced back at his son.

'Though not enough! He ran off – to play games! The day he's to play for the King! You would think he was three years old, not six.'

'I'm not six! I'm eight!'

'Hush! At Versailles, you are six. Practice!'

The boy drew Marie-Josèphe along with him to the harpsichord. She sat beside him.

'I saw your sea monster, Signorina Maria!' he said.

'Did she frighten you?'

'Oh, no, she's beautiful, she sings such stories!'

'You have a story to sing, yourself, young man,' Signor Scarlatti said. 'And if you don't play properly, what will our patron say? The viceroy will send us away from Naples.' He bent close to Marie-Josèphe. 'But then I might stay in France, to worship you until you reward me.'

'Your playing will please the King,' Marie-Josèphe said to Domenico, and then, to Signor Scarlatti, 'and his reward will be more than I could ever hope to give you.'

'I'd exchange all his riches for a single kiss,' Signor Scarlatti said.

His importuning went beyond friendly jesting; Marie-Josèphe reminded herself that while he was rich and famous, she was a lady.

'Signore,' Marie-Josèphe said sternly, 'when you have all his riches – and his titles – we might speak again.'

Signor Scarlatti struck his breast. 'Touché,' he said. 'You have bested me. You may hang my heart on your wall as a trophy.'

'I much prefer your heart where it is, Signore, so you may give it to your music.'

'I am ready,' he said. 'Domenico—Domenico is not so ready. He disappoints me, he disappoints M. Coupillet, but no one else will notice. M. Galland admires our preparations. My greatest ambition is to please you.'

'To please His Majesty,' Marie-Josèphe said.

'And His Majesty,' said Signor Scarlatti.

Marie-Josèphe kissed Domenico's cheek. 'You could never fail to please everyone, with your playing,' she said to the child, and hurried back into the crowded Salon of Venus, into the merciful warmth and the smoky light.

103

In an alcove, partly hidden by curtains and orange trees, Mme Lucifer huddled with Mlle d'Armagnac.

You must think of Mme Lucifer as the Duchess de Chartres, Marie-Josèphe reminded herself. Marie-Josèphe de la Croix must not use a nickname for a member of the royal family, especially a nickname so pointed. Madame would be amused, but she would have to be horrified in public.

A cloud of tobacco smoke billowed from behind the curtains. Mme de Chartres puffed luxuriously on a small black cigar, then handed it to Mlle d'Armagnac, who drew in a mouthful of smoke and puffed it out contentedly. Marie-Josèphe wished she could dare to approach, to join them.

'It's the little nun,' Mme Lucifer said.

'So it is, Mme de Chartres.'

Marie-Josèphe smiled shyly, hoping they would condescend to offer her a taste of the tobacco.

'Do you suppose she's on her way to confession?' Mlle d'Armagnac said. Smoke dribbled from between her lips and mixed with the sweet scent of orange blossoms.

'Our confession, perhaps.' Mme Lucifer advanced upon Marie-Josèphe. The jewels on her bodice glittered as wildly as her eyes. 'Will you report our transgression to your brother, my dear – or to my father the King?'

'It isn't my place to speak to His Majesty at all,' Marie-Josèphe said. 'My brother's work absorbs him. He doesn't preach, or hear confession.'

'What other unpriestly disciplines does he engage in?' Mlle d'Armagnac spoke in a more friendly fashion.

'Nothing my brother does is unpriestly!'

'What a pity,' said Mlle d'Armagnac. 'Why, Mme de Chartres, think how many sins one could commit with such a handsome priest.'

'I'm counting them, my dear – and I could commit one more than you.'

'Why, two more, I believe – as you are married.'

Both ladies laughed. Mlle d'Armagnac handed the cigar to Mme Lucifer, who slipped behind the orange trees.

The herald strode to the door of the Salon of Mars and thumped his staff three times on the parquet.

'The entertainments begin!'

Mme Lucifer snatched Mlle d'Armagnac's sleeve to pull her out of sight.

His Majesty approached, leading the way to the Salon of Mars and to this evening's performance. His Holiness walked at his right hand. Yves walked at his left – with the King, with the Pope, in front of the king and queen of England. Marie-Josèphe was so astonished that she stood before the doorway like a gaping fool. At the last moment she scurried out of the way and dropped into a deep curtsy.

His Majesty paused. She found herself looking at his white silk stockings, his high-heeled red shoes, his feet, renowned for their beautiful shape and small size, now cruelly swollen by the gout.

'Mlle de la Croix,' he said sternly, 'do you smell of tobacco?'

She rose. Mme Lucifer's jibe at Yves tempted Marie-Josèphe to invite His Majesty to turn around and look behind the orange trees. But if Mme Lucifer had been so kind as to offer her the cigar, she would have smelled of tobacco, so she could not proclaim a perfect innocence.

'It is – it is a custom of Martinique,' she said, which was quite true.

'A pagan custom,' His Holiness said. 'Adopted from wild Americans.' Marie-Josèphe was close enough to kiss his ring, but he did not offer her that honour.

'A nasty one, at best. I disapprove of smoking, especially by ladies,' Louis said. He sighed unhappily. 'Even more than I disapprove of the fontanges, but what influence have I, at my own court? I see that you have brought one horrid custom from your homeland, and attached yourself to another horrid custom here in France.'

'I beg Your Majesty's pardon,' she whispered, wilting beneath the disapproving gaze of the King.

His Majesty proceeded. But as he moved forward, he reached toward the trees with his walking stick and pushed the branches aside, revealing Mme Lucifer and Mlle d'Armagnac. Tendrils of cigar smoke wafted out to encircle His Majesty and His Holiness.

Mme Lucifer glared defiantly before dropping into a curtsy. His

Majesty shook his head sadly, with fond disapproval, and continued into the music salon. His court streamed after him. Chartres, the embarrassed young husband, ignored his disgraced wife.

Marie-Josèphe wondered what His Majesty thought of her behaviour, if he thought of her at all, if it pleased him that she had shielded his daughter, or angered him that she had tried to deceive him.

Madame Lucifer snarled a horrendous curse, flung the cigar stub to the shining parquet, and sucked her burned finger. Beneath the lit cigar, the floor sizzled. In a moment the wax would burn away; the cigar would singe the wood.

Count Lucien flicked the cigar into the air with his walking stick and thrust it into the silver tub of an orange tree. His expression contained more amusement than annoyance. It escaped no one that Mme Lucifer might have spared herself the King's silent scolding if she had thought as quickly as the Count de Chrétien. Despite their mother's celebrated wit, the children of Athénaïs de Montespan and Louis XIV were seldom accused of excessive quickness of thinking.

As Lotte swept past, she drew Marie-Josèphe into the line of courtiers. She gave up concealing her laughter, chuckling with delight. Madame, with years more experience controlling her public reactions, gave one quick snort of amusement, then pressed her lips tight together.

'How quick you are!' Lotte exclaimed. 'How brave!'

'I only told the truth,' Marie-Josèphe said.

Madame Lucifer, still sucking her burned finger, glared at her as she passed. If Marie-Josèphe hoped for gratitude, what she received was a frown of suspicion.

'But if I must be scolded for smoking,' Marie-Josèphe said softly to Lotte, 'I would rather have smoked!'

'Madame would slap me pink if I dared smoke,' Lotte said. 'And you too.'

'Even Madame may not slap me,' Marie-Josèphe said. 'The nuns slapped me quite enough, Mademoiselle.'

Chapter 8

The music began.

Under the direction of M. Coupillet, the chamber orchestra played a quiet prelude. The wonderful harpsichord and a lectern stood nearby.

His Majesty listened, never moving, even to ease his gouty foot on its feather cushion. He sat straight and proud in his armchair. Beside him, His Holiness maintained a serene presence that made him nearly a match for the King. Though he did not adorn himself with jewels or gold, his pure white robe glowed against a background of brilliant Cardinal red.

The King, Pope Innocent, and the king and queen of England sat in armchairs in the front row. Behind and beside him, His Majesty's family sat in armless chairs. Duchesses and a few favoured courtiers perched on ottomans. Count Lucien stood near the King, behind an empty ottoman. Marie-Josèphe had noticed that he never sat when he could stand, but that he did not walk if he could ride.

Yves stood with the younger courtiers, behind the grand dauphin, the legitimate grandsons, the princes of the blood, and the illegitimate duke. Chartres, defying custom, remained at Yves' side.

Nervously waiting for the prelude to end, Marie-Josèphe stood behind Mademoiselle. The salon grew warm; Marie-Josèphe welcomed the heat. Lotte fanned herself with a delicate sandalwood fan. A drop of sweat ran from her temple down her flushed cheek. Marie-Josèphe drew out her handkerchief and delicately dabbed away the perspiration.

M. Coupillet ended the prelude with a grand flourish.

'Signor Scarlatti the younger,' said the master of ceremonies, 'playing the harpsichord.'

Little Domenico Scarlatti, dressed in satin and ribbons and a perruke, walked stiffly to the harpsichord. He bowed elegantly to His

Majesty. The audience rustled and murmured, remarking on the child's youth and reputation.

'M. Antoine Galland,' said the master of ceremonies, 'reading his translations of Arabian stories, made at the command of His Majesty.'

M. Galland was a skittish young man. He nearly forgot to bow; he nearly dropped his slender leatherbound book as he opened it onto the lectern. He caught it; candlelight sparkled from its jewelled decorations. M. Galland bowed again to His Majesty. At the King's gracious nod, M. Coupillet brought the orchestra to attention. The musicians and the little boy played.

M. Galland read aloud, his voice whispery.

Marie-Josèphe hardly perceived the words of the story, though M. Galland's translation was the centrepiece of His Majesty's entertainment. Marie-Josèphe wished only to listen to her own imagination made real by Domenico, by M. Coupillet and the orchestra.

Her little song spun and danced with the candlelight. The notes painted a background of distant deserts and gardens, dangerous adventures, exotic scents and songs.

After years of music that played only within her mind, she immersed herself in the melody that flooded the court of the Sun King. Music could never sound as she imagined it, unless angels – or demons – performed it.

Perhaps I was right, she thought, *and Démonico is angel, or demon*.

Marie-Josèphe let her eyes close. She pretended she was alone. The rustle of silk and satin and velvet, the murmur of restless courtiers with aching feet, the whispers about her handsome brother, all vanished behind a melodic picture of a daring and erotic story from mysterious Arabia.

'"Scheherazade, my wife",' M. Galland said, his voice now confident and loud, '"thou shalt live one more night, the Sultan proclaimed, Thou shalt tell me one more story. Then thou shalt die, for I know the treachery of women".'

The story and Marie-Josèphe's song ended with Domenico's flourish at the harpsichord.

Breathless, Marie-Josèphe opened her eyes. Her heart pounded.

Elevated by the orchestra, by little Domenico's performance, the piece was unimaginably wonderful.

M. Galland, Domenico, and Signor Scarlatti bowed to His Majesty. As they leaned into the silence, Marie-Josèphe fastened her attention on the King. She hoped for some sign from him, some indication of pleasure.

His Majesty applauded his musicians, his translator. His approval freed everyone to express their appreciation, or to feign it. Acclaim filled the Salon.

M. Coupillet presented Domenico, Signor Scarlatti, the other musicians. M. Galland bowed again.

Pope Innocent barely reacted. Marie-Josèphe wondered if such a holy man was permitted to take pleasure in any worldly entertainment.

How sad if he cannot, Marie-Josèphe thought.

Lotte fanned her face and neck urgently. She paused, fanned, snapped the fan shut with an impatient snick, snapped the fan open, and fanned again. Marie-Josèphe brought herself back to her duties, snatched Lotte's handkerchief from her sleeve, and dabbed perspiration from Lotte's cheek. Mademoiselle's rouge was not too badly smeared.

'An excellent story, M. Galland,' His Majesty said. 'A rousing tale.'

'Thank you, Your Majesty.' M. Galland bowed again, blushing. He handed his book to a page, who gave it to the master of ceremonies, who presented it to Count Lucien. Count Lucien in turn offered it to His Majesty.

'In honour of Your Majesty's patronage,' M. Galland said, 'I caused to have made a copy of the first story in my translation of the *Tales of Scheherazade: The Thousand and One Arabian Nights.*'

His Majesty took the book from Count Lucien, admired the lavish binding, and returned it to the count. 'I accept it with pleasure.'

'I am grateful for your approval, Sire.'

'Signor Scarlatti.'

Scarlatti stepped quickly forward and bowed again.

'Signor Scarlatti, my compliments to your patron monsieur the Marquis del Carpio, and my thanks to him for sending you and your son.' His Majesty smiled at little Domenico. 'Charmingly played, my boy.' Domenico bowed stiffly from the waist, like a little string toy. His Majesty gave the boy a gold coin from his own hand.

'M. Coupillet.'

The music master hurried forward, bowing repeatedly.

'A charming piece, M. Coupillet, unfamiliar to me. Composed for this occasion?'

'Yes, Your Majesty,' Coupillet said.

'Excellent, excellent – though rather daring.'

Marie-Josèphe waited, first baffled, then with growing outrage. His Majesty believed M. Coupillet composed the piece, and M. Coupillet said nothing!

'Signorina Maria composed it,' little Domenico said.

A ripple of shock passed through the audience, that the son of a commoner would speak unbidden to the King. Domenico, clutching his gold piece between the thumb and forefinger of each hand, holding it before his chest like a talisman, stared wide-eyed with fright and shrank down as if he wished he were six, after all.

'Is this true, M. Coupillet?'

'To a small extent, Your Majesty,' M. Coupillet said. 'I revised—I embellished it particularly, of course, Your Majesty, so it would not debase court standards.'

His Majesty turned his deep blue gaze upon Marie-Josèphe. She wished she had never played the piece for Domenico at St Cyr. His Majesty's attention was terrifying, be it reproach or approval.

'Mlle de la Croix!'

She thought, wildly, as she curtsied, *I should go to him – make my way around the courtiers – through them – leap over Lotte and her tabouret!*

When she rose, Count Lucien stood before her, offering her his arm, and a path led through the crowd. She laid her hand on his wrist and gratefully let him guide her, let him draw her solidly to the ground. Without him, she might float to the ceiling, join the painted clouds, and ride away in the chariot with Mars and his wolves.

His Majesty smiled. 'Mlle de la Croix, you are a lady of many talents – tamer of sea monsters, companion to Apollo – and a new Mlle de la Guerre.'

'Oh, no, Your Majesty!' Marie-Josèphe said. 'Mlle de la Guerre is a genius, I'm only an amateur.'

'But you are here, and she is in Paris, creative twice over: a child for her husband, and an opera – I never see her, but perhaps she will dedicate the opera, at least, to me.'

His Majesty rose, pushing himself upright and lifting his foot gingerly from its cushion. Everyone who was seated, rose. The royal family, the foreign princes, and the rest of the courtiers gathered around to listen, to be close to the King and to his protégée of the moment.

Marie-Josèphe had no idea what to do, so she curtsied again. *Surely one cannot salute the King too often*, she thought. She curtsied to the King; she curtsied to the Pope.

Pope Innocent stretched out his hand. She fell to her knees and kissed his ring. The warmth of the heavy gold brushed her lips like a living breath, the power of God conducted through the body of His Holiness. The world blurred beyond the tears that filled her eyes.

Count Lucien offered her his assistance. She rose, shaky with hunger and awe, clutching the count's arm.

'You composed this music?' Innocent asked.

'Yes, Your Holiness.'

'You are a true child of your parents, whom I loved,' His Majesty said. 'As beautiful, as intelligent as your mother, as charming and talented as my friend, your father. Do you play, do you sing, as beautifully as he did?'

'I wish I did, Your Majesty.'

'And you, Father de la Croix, do you too possess the musical talents of your father?'

'My sister is by far the more talented musician,' Yves said.

'How is that possible?' the King asked, astonished. 'Never mind, your father no doubt passed on other of his many rare qualities.'

'Constraint was not among them,' Pope Innocent said, 'or he would have given Signorina de la Croix the sense to repress this piece. It is indecent.'

'I—I beg your pardon, Your Holiness?' Marie-Josèphe said.

'Well you should,' His Holiness said. 'Music should glorify God. Are you not familiar with the Church's edict? Women should remain silent.'

'In church, Your Holiness!' Marie-Josèphe was all too aware of the rule, which had imprisoned the convent in miserable silence.

'At all times — music is completely injurious to your modesty. Cousin, you must censor this pagan excess!'

The warmth of Marie-Josèphe's joy drained away to pale incomprehension. Then she flushed scarlet. *Why didn't I let Monsieur powder me,* she thought wildly, *to conceal my humiliation?*

Innocent is a holy man, Marie-Josèphe thought, *free of the corruption that dishonoured his predecessors. If he thinks my composition improper — is it possible that he's right?*

She trembled, confused and distressed; she might as well be a girl, back in the convent, her hands stinging from the switch and her eyes stinging with tears, unable to understand why she had received punishment instead of a reply when she asked a question.

I thought the sisters were misguided, Marie-Josèphe thought, *for I could not believe God wished us to exist in silence and heartache. I thought they lived too far from the guidance of Mother Church and the Holy Father. But I was wrong, and they were close to truth.*

His Majesty took his time answering Innocent. First he nodded to Count Lucien, who presented M. Galland, Signor Scarlatti, and M. Coupillet with fat leather pouches clinking heavily with coins. Musicians and translator backed away, bowing, easing out of sight.

'I consider the piece charming, cousin,' His Majesty said again. His voice remained courteous, yet the chill of his disapproval spread through the salon until he smiled at Marie-Josèphe, a true smile, though he never parted his lips to reveal his toothless gums. 'It brings back happier times. Younger days. It reminds me of a bit of music I composed — do you recall it, M. de Chrétien?'

'Presented upon the return of Your Majesty's embassy to Morocco,' Count Lucien said. 'The ambassador considered it a most signal honour. As did we all, Sire.'

'I've not composed in many years,' His Majesty said. 'Ah — how staid age has made me! But that will soon change!' The King laughed.

Pope Innocent's pale and ascetic face coloured, as if Louis had laughed at him.

'The story reeked of heathen indecency,' Innocent said. 'The music spelled out intrigue and debauchery!'

'Your Holiness,' Yves said, 'Your Holiness, I beg your pardon, but my sister is an innocent.'

She blessed her brother for his defence, but Pope Innocent looked Marie-Josèphe up and down: her headdress, her dress, her decolletage. He shocked Marie-Josèphe when he noticed what any ordinary man would see.

'Is she, Father de la Croix? You should take more care with her moral instruction.'

Marie-Josèphe thought, in despair, *I only meant to please my brother, and instead I've exposed him to censure.*

'The piece is unfit for ladies,' Innocent said. 'Or for righteous men.'

'Cousin,' Louis said, 'the ladies of France are wise in the ways of the world.'

'They are too wise,' Innocent replied. 'And too worldly. They have been too long estranged from our influence.'

'As you are estranged from theirs,' Count Lucien said. 'Your Holiness.'

Innocent glared down at Count Lucien, but he spoke to Louis.

'I had no idea jesters still attended the Kings of France. You are magnanimous, cousin, to continue to employ your late queen's pets.'

If the courtiers were entertained by the struggle of two powerful wills over the newest and most powerless members of court, the direct insult to one of their own froze them into silence and left even His Majesty astounded.

Innocent stretched his hand toward Count Lucien, offering him his ring to kiss.

Count Lucien regarded the ring with distaste.

'Will you dance us a jig, Signor Jester?'

'Will you play accompaniment, Signor Pope, on your celestial harp?' His tone perfectly pleasant, Count Lucien stood at his ease with his ebony walking stick in the crook of his arm.

113

'Monsieur de Chrétien governs Brittany – a difficult province – in my name,' His Majesty said. 'He is my valued adviser, and my trusted friend – and he does not dance.'

'Brittany. Difficult indeed.' Innocent's expression clouded. 'A province rife with pagan heresies.' When he glanced again at Count Lucien, his disapproval solidified, like rain turning to hail.

Count Lucien never flinched.

'Mlle de la Croix!' His Majesty said, indifferent to the uneasy silence. 'In honour of – in memory of – your father, you shall compose a cantata for my anniversary.'

'Oh – Your Majesty!' Marie-Josèphe was overwhelmed with apprehension, then with determination. His Majesty's approval outweighed His Holiness' irritation.

'Your subject,' Louis said, 'shall be the capture of the sea monster. Who better to write it than the sister of the hunter?'

'Thank you, Your Majesty.' She dropped into a deep curtsy. Her legs trembled. She knelt on the satiny parquet with her skirt spread around her and her head bowed.

'Hunting is not a suitable occupation for a Jesuit priest,' Innocent said. 'And composing is not a suitable occupation for his sister.'

'Indulge me, cousin. I am an old man, and I desire a sea monster, a banquet, and a cantata for my celebration. Come. Supper will calm us, and settle our discord.'

I must rise, Marie-Josèphe thought, staring at the polished floor, unable even to lift her head.

'Mlle de la Croix,' Count Lucien said coolly. 'You must rise.' She wondered if he could read her thoughts the way he read His Majesty's. He took her hand in his long, slender fingers.

'Allow me to help you,' Lorraine said from her other side. He took her other hand and raised her easily.

His Majesty led the way toward the Salon of Abundance and the midnight collation. His Holiness accompanied him, after a single glance that singled Yves out and excluded Marie-Josèphe as well as Count Lucien. Marie-Josèphe looked down at Count Lucien and up at Lorraine.

'Thank you, sirs,' she whispered.

Count Lucien bowed over her hand. Limping a little, his walking stick only tapping the floor, he left her leaning on Lorraine's arm.

'Chrétien is a worse stickler for etiquette even than the King,' Lorraine said.

Monsieur appeared at his side and took his arm.

'Come, Philippe. We must join my brother.'

Lorraine bowed, gave Marie-Josèphe to Yves, and strolled away with Monsieur. Ravenous, Marie-Josèphe tried to follow, but Yves held her back. All the courtiers streamed after His Majesty. Beyond them, M. Coupillet stared at Marie-Josèphe with an expression of poisonous jealousy. He turned his back and set the chamber orchestra to playing one of his own cantatas, a pretty piece without a single daring note.

'What were you thinking of?' Yves demanded.

Shocked by M. Coupillet's behaviour, distressed by His Holiness' disapproval, Marie-Josèphe replied defensively to Yves. 'Of pleasing you. Of pleasing His Majesty.'

'You should have known—'

'What should I know? How could I know? It was just a little song, little Domenico heard me play it and played it for his papa, M. Coupillet heard it, he admired it—' *He surely does not admire it anymore*, she said to herself.

'Before, you wanted to help me,' Yves said. 'You said you wanted to help me with my work – nothing else was more important to you! – now you've succumbed to frivolity—'

'I haven't! I do want to help you. How could I refuse the King?'

'He should not have asked you. When His Holiness objected, he should have submitted himself—'

'He's the King! He has a right to anything he wants. He's offered our family another honour – it doesn't compare to yours, but allow me something of my own. In honour of Papa!'

'Father de la Croix. Mlle de la Croix.'

Count Lucien stood in the doorway.

'I am concerned,' he said, 'that His Majesty may be disturbed by your argument. Father de la Croix, one of his . . . observers . . . may report your comments to him.'

'A— a family disagreement, no more,' Marie-Josèphe said.

He must have heard what Yves said, Marie-Josèphe thought. *Is it treason, to say the King must submit himself to the Pope? Or would it only anger His Majesty, which amounts to the same thing?*

'Resolve your disagreement elsewhere, if you please.'

'Thank you for your advice, Count Lucien.' With relief, Marie-Josèphe thought, *he's not warning us that he will report our indiscreet words to the King. He's warning us of the others who report to the King in secret.*

He bowed sharply and disappeared. Marie-Josèphe, faint with hunger, wanted only to abandon the argument with Yves and join the other courtiers at midnight supper. But her brother led her deeper into the State Apartments. The Salon of Mercury was only dimly-lit, and deserted. Marie-Josèphe wondered if they should be here, all alone except for Mercury. The messenger of the gods raced across the ceiling; wavering candlelight ruffled the feathers of the roosters drawing his chariot.

'The Academy must have the sea monster drawings,' Yves said. 'As soon as I finish the dissection. How will you do both?'

'It's only a little song. A few minutes of music.'

'The drawings are more important.'

'They'll be ready,' Marie-Josèphe said. 'I won't fail you. You trusted me when we were children. Can't you forgive me a single error? Don't you trust me anymore?'

'You've changed,' he said.

'So have you.'

'His Holiness disapproves.'

'But His Majesty commands.'

Together, in silence. Marie-Josèphe and Yves crossed the Salon of Mercury. Marie-Josèphe thought, *My drawings will be perfect, and erase the constraints between us.*

In the Salon of Mars, M. Coupillet conducted a saraband. A single couple, all alone, danced to the measured music. Surely that was Lorraine, there was no mistaking his tall and elegant figure. He and his partner came together, pivoted, and parted to the form of the dance.

116

Indifferent to the notice of the orchestra and careless of the attention of Marie-Josèphe and Yves, Lorraine and Monsieur danced. Monsieur gazed up at his friend; Lorraine bent to kiss him. The heavy dark wings of his wig shadowed Monsieur's face. When Lorraine glided into the next step of the saraband, his gaze caught Marie-Josèphe's.

He smiled at her, and continued to dance.

Yves lengthened his stride and hurried Marie-Josèphe from the music room. He pressed his lips together in an angry line. He walked her all the way past the billiards tables in the Salon of Diana, and only stopped as they were about to enter the crowded Salon of Venus, where the King's guests ate hungrily. The exquisite smells from the Salon of Abundance beyond made Marie-Josèphe's mouth water.

Yves faced her, his eyes blue-black in anger.

'You shouldn't have been exposed to such a sight,' he said. 'His Majesty's brother takes advantage—!'

'Of what? Monsieur is the kindest man imaginable. What's made you so angry?'

'The kiss—' Yves stopped. 'You don't know why I'm angry? Good.'

'Why shouldn't Monsieur kiss his friend? Lotte kisses me.' Lotte's kisses had at first startled her, for affection had been forbidden in the convent. The sisters admonished the students to reserve their love for God.

She treasured Lotte's affection. If Yves tried to forbid it, he would have to do worse than thrash her.

'Because—Men shouldn't kiss each other. This is an unfit subject. We won't speak of it again.'

Marie-Josèphe wished he would not say such things. When they were children, exploring the beaches and marshes and fields of Martinique, nothing was beyond their curiosity. Marie-Josèphe regretted some of the changes in her brother. But she had changed, too, from the adoring little girl willing to follow him into any mischief, to the grown woman who still adored him, but was not so willing to follow him into courtly caution.

He led her through the warmth and light and noise of Venus, and on to Abundance. She was so hungry her hands trembled.

117

I shouldn't let him think I agree with everything he said, Marie-Josèphe thought, *but if I argue we'll have no chance of any supper.*

His Majesty was no less generous than Plenty, whose image lounged on the ceiling fresco, cushioned by a bank of clouds, thinly veiled in a drift of silken scarves. Angels and cherubim surrounded her, helping distribute wine and a cornucopia of fruit. His Majesty's table groaned with the weight of roast beef and fowl, fruits and pastries.

A footman appeared before Marie-Josèphe and offered her a plate of the most delicate dishes: roast squab, peaches, pears. Marie-Josèphe picked up one of the squabs and ate it in two bites. The crisp skin crackled between her teeth; the succulent flesh dissolved in her mouth. Tiny bones gave texture to the meat. The footman handed her a linen napkin. She wiped the grease from her lips.

When she had eaten three squabs and a peach, she felt steadier. She nibbled at the pear, which she had never tasted before she came to court. Pears and peaches and apples did not grow well in Martinique; and most of the fields were given over to sugar cane.

Monsieur and Lorraine strolled into the Salon, arm in arm. Lorraine guided his friend toward Marie-Josèphe and Yves. He smiled at Marie-Josèphe as if they shared a romantic secret. She curtsied to Monsieur, to Lorraine. Yves offered the smallest, stiffest of bows. Lorraine returned their salute; Monsieur smiled and nodded.

Footmen hurried to serve Monsieur and his companion, bringing Monsieur a gold plate and Lorraine a plate of silver. Knowing the tastes of their masters, the footmen brought the duke d'Orléans pastries and sweets, Lorraine a joint of rare beef. Lorraine bit into the meat. His strong white teeth tore a morsel from the bone. Red juice dripped down his fingers and onto the silver lace at his cuff.

He is very handsome, even though he is so old, Marie-Josèphe thought. *The King has lost his teeth, but the chevalier has all his. I wonder if he has his hair, as well?*

He wore a beautiful black periwig of the most current fashion. The curls tumbled down upon his shoulders. No one gossiped that he wore a wig because his hair had fallen out early. He wore it because it was the style, a style the King himself had begun when an illness thinned his hair. Lorraine's clothes were of the finest brocade and lace, and his high-heeled shoes showed off his fine legs in their white silk stockings. He was so tall that Marie-Josèphe found him awkward to talk to when they both were standing.

His eyes were a beautiful blue.

'Have a taste of this pastry, dear Philippe.'

Lorraine turned his attention to Monsieur. When his gaze left Marie-Josèphe, the light itself dimmed as if an imperceptible wind had blown out half the candles. But the crystal chandeliers still burned brightly, perfuming the room with the scent of hot beeswax.

Monsieur offered his friend a tidbit of pastry, dripping with cream. A fleck of sugar clung to Monsieur's upper lip, like a beauty patch.

'It's quite extraordinary,' Monsieur said.

'Not just now, Philippe,' Lorraine said. 'It does not go with the seasoning.' He gestured with the joint of beef. He put down the bone and brushed the sugar from Monsieur's face.

How daring, Marie-Josèphe thought, *to call Monsieur by his given name. Perhaps it is an amusement between them, because they enjoy the connection of the same Christian name. But he never addresses Monsieur so familiarly in Madame's presence, and surely he wouldn't breach etiquette when His Majesty was in earshot.*

Lorraine, and even Monsieur, must dread seeing the King's face go cold with disapproval. A single word of censure from His Majesty could ruin one's place at court.

And I cannot even imagine what Count Lucien would say! Marie-Josèphe thought. *Such a strange man, his thoughts so dedicated to His Majesty. Perhaps he would reach up and rap Lorraine's knuckles with his walking stick, like Sister Penitence at the convent.*

Lorraine wore a sword, while Count Lucien carried only a short dirk. Marie-Josèphe imagined having a sword, back at the convent, when the sisters rapped her knuckles if she daydreamed, and slapped her face if she hummed, and thrashed the girls if they slept two in a bed for fear of the dark.

If I'd had a sword, she thought, *no one would have rapped my knuckles, much less thrashed me.*

Chapter 9

'Mlle de la Croix, you are transforming yourself,' Monsieur said. 'In candlelight, your complexion is quite pale. Even your hands. Don't you agree, Philippe?'

'She is entrancing in any light,' Lorraine said.

'I owe any improvement entirely to you and your family, Monsieur,' Marie-Josèphe said. 'And I am very grateful.' Monsieur meant his comments kindly, and Marie-Josèphe was grateful, but she wished he would not mention her colonial background every time he saw her.

Chartres strolled up, Madame on his arm. He tossed off a glass of wine in a single gulp, and traded the empty goblet for a full one. Chartres' eyes glittered fiercely and his face was flushed.

He drank the second glass of wine just as quickly, and snatched a third glass from a footman.

'That's more than sufficient, dear son,' Madame said.

'It's less than enough, dear Mama,' Chartres said, and drank the third glass of wine.

'Father de la Croix, save us all from boredom!' Madame said. 'Tell us more of your adventures.'

Chartres cut in before Yves could reply. 'I want to assist you—'

'My son fancies himself a natural philosopher.' Monsieur's lightly edged tone warned Chartres against this forbidden course.

Chartres flushed scarlet, reacting with an intensity foreign to his usual distracted air. '—in dissecting the sea monster!'

'One person is adequate to perform a dissection, sir.' Yves spoke offhand, for he did not know Chartres' interests. A natural philosopher of his erudition had no use for an inexperienced assistant.

'It's beneath your station,' Madame said to Chartres. 'Digging around in the guts of a fish.'

'Madame is perfectly correct,' Yves said, bowing courteously to the duchess. 'For an ordinary dissection, even I would direct an underling in the cutting. But for the King's sea monster—' He spread his hands modestly. 'For the King, I'll do the work myself.'

'Don't you wish me to serve the King, Mama?' Chartres said, poisonously, to his mother.

'Yes – in a manner suited to your position.'

'I fear I wouldn't know what to do with extra hands, M. de Chartres,' Yves said quickly. 'You can learn all there is by watching and by studying the notes and the drawings.' He brightened suddenly. 'Perhaps – can you draw?'

Marie-Josèphe caught her breath.

He plans to punish me, she thought, *by taking away my tasks – by giving them to Chartres.*

'Yes!' Chartres said. 'I mean . . . a little.' Under his mother's disapproving scowl, he dropped his gaze. 'I mean . . . not well.'

'He means "No," ' Madame said, 'and that's enough about that.'

Greatly relieved, yet at the same time sorry for Chartres, Marie-Josèphe cast a sympathetic glance at the young duke, a grateful glance at Madame. But Chartres scowled, only his blind eye wandering toward her, and Madame had not spoken for Marie-Josèphe's benefit.

Lorraine, glancing over Marie-Josèphe's shoulder, suddenly bowed.

The duchess de Chartres and Mlle d'Armagnac swept into the group, as brilliant as chandeliers in their diamond-studded bodices. Mme de Chartres acknowledged Lorraine's salute with a dismissive gesture.

'Good evening, Papa,' Mme Lucifer said to Monsieur. 'Good evening, Mama.'

'Good evening, Mme de Chartres,' her father-in-law said. 'Mlle d'Armagnac.' Madame, her mother-in-law, nodded with exquisitely polite coolness. Mme de Chartres ignored her husband; he ignored her. He drank a fourth glass of wine. Mlle d'Armagnac glanced at Chartres over the edge of her fan, lowering her gaze flirtatiously when he responded, right in front of her friend Mme de Chartres.

Marie-Josèphe wondered what it must have been like to grow up as Mlle de Blois, with no one to call Mama or Papa. For surely Mme

Lucifer could never have called the King Papa. Mme de Maintenon had raised Mme de Montespan's children. Ever since Montespan had been banished, they were doubly estranged from their natural mother.

It was said that Mme de Maintenon loved His Majesty's natural children as her own, and guarded their interests jealously. She had made brilliant marriages for them, much better than they could expect. She had offended many members of court in doing so, not the least of them Madame.

'We've come to spirit Father de la Croix away,' said Mme Lucifer. 'All the ladies want to meet him.' She and Mlle d'Armagnac herded Yves off into the crowd.

'The manners of trollops,' Madame muttered. 'You must warn your brother, Mlle de la Croix, if you hope he will keep his vows.'

'He would never break them, Madame!' Marie-Josèphe said. 'He would never do such a thing.'

'Not for – any temptation?' Monsieur asked.

'No, Monsieur, not for anything.'

'What about the dissection?' Chartres asked. 'When will it continue?'

'I don't know, sir,' Marie-Josèphe said. 'When the King wishes.'

'My uncle the King may delay it until the creature rots,' Chartres said with disgust.

Though she had said – feared – the same thing, Marie-Josèphe thought it politic to change the subject.

'Sir, I've written to Mynheer van Leeuwenhoek, begging to purchase one of his microscopes. His lenses are said to be marvelous.'

'Van Leeuwenhoek!' Chartres said. 'You should buy a proper French microscope, with a compound lens. Mlle de la Croix, your eyes are too pretty to be ruined by van Leeuwenhoek's difficult machine.'

'Which he will have to smuggle to you,' Lorraine said, 'if he does not keep your money and send you nothing.'

'Smuggle it, sir?'

'Perhaps he'll pack it in obscene Dutch broadsheets,' Monsieur said, 'and smuggle two loads of contraband for the price of one.'

Lorraine laughed.

'We are at war with the Dutchmen, after all, Mlle de la Croix,' Madame said.

'One campaign next summer will put an end to that,' Chartres said.

'Do not expect another command,' Monsieur said.

'But I led my cavalry to a victory!'

'That was your mistake,' Monsieur said.

'Natural philosophy transcends war.' Into the silence, Marie-Josèphe said, timidly, 'Does it not?'

'It should!' Chartres said.

'M. de Chrétien's go-betweens may transcend war,' Lorraine said. 'As they transcend borders.'

'So, no doubt,' Monsieur said, 'you'll get your micro-whatever-it-does.'

'It reveals things that can't be seen, father,' Chartres said.

'As the Bible does?' asked Madame.

'Very small things, Madame,' said Marie-Josèphe. 'If we looked at – at Elderflower's fleas, we might see fleas on the fleas.'

'We must do that straightaway,' Lorraine said.

'I would not wish to do it at all,' said Madame.

Another footman appeared at Lorraine's elbow. Chartres reached for the wine the servant carried, but the chevalier whisked it away so gracefully that Chartres could not object.

'You've drunk nothing all evening, Mlle de la Croix,' Lorraine said. 'This will ease your mind from your worries of war and natural philosophy.'

Marie-Josèphe had no need to ease her mind, but she was thirsty, so she accepted the goblet. The red wine reflected light in patterns along the silver rim.

She sipped it, expecting the bitter, watery taste of the convent's communion wine. Maroon velvet slipped over her tongue. The scent of fruit and flowers filled her nostrils. She sipped again, savouring the taste with her eyes closed. She thought, *I could drink this merely by breathing*.

When she opened her eyes, Lorraine gazed down at her, charming her with his amused smile.

'You like it,' he said.

'Of course she likes it,' Monsieur said. 'It's a delightful vintage.'

'You've given me my first glass of wine,' she said.

'Your first!' Monsieur was horrified.

'How else might I be your first?' Lorraine said softly.

Marie-Josèphe blushed. 'You misunderstand me, sir.'

'What did you drink, on your colonial island?' Monsieur asked, peering at her as curiously as if she were one of Yves' specimens.

'In the convent, sir, we drank small beer, or water.'

'Water!' Monsieur exclaimed. 'You are fortunate to have your life.'

'Such delightful innocence,' Lorraine said.

Marie-Josèphe sipped the wine, and glanced up at Lorraine from beneath her eyelashes.

'You flatter me, sir—'

'I? I'm known to speak only the strongest of truths.'

'—and the nuns always warned me against flattery.'

'Ignore my devotion and my admiration, I beg you, Mlle de la Croix. A broken heart will distract me.'

Chartres snorted and downed another glass of wine.

'Ignore his meagre wit,' Madame said. 'He seeks only to divert himself from the tedium. The nuns would forgive even Lorraine, if they had endured one of His Majesty's parties.'

'They endured—' Marie-Josèphe hesitated, to steady her voice '—we all endured the silence of the cloister.'

Lorraine bowed to her, and kissed her hand.

'You illuminate court, my dear Mlle de la Croix. As your mother did.'

She drew her hand from his, made self-conscious by Monsieur's opinion of her skin.

'Come along, my dear Chevalier,' Monsieur said, loudly, heartily. 'You must give my brother the King a challenge at billiards.' He took Lorraine's elbow and guided him around. Chartres followed, stumbling slightly, not only from his lameness. Marie-Josèphe curtsied, but the three men had already turned away.

Lorraine looked over his shoulder and stretched out his hand to her with a pathetic sigh.

Madame seized Marie-Josèphe by the arm.

'If your brother will not save me from boredom, you must!' she said. 'Come along, we'll find a quiet corner.'

'Madame, how can you be bored?'

'How can you not, Mlle de la Croix? Never mind, you'll understand after you've attended a year of these interminable evenings. I'd rather be writing letters, or working on my collections. I do so look forward to Father de la Croix's medal. I hope it will be very dramatic.'

She found a bench in an alcove by the window and settled into it. She could not offer Marie-Josèphe a seat in her presence in public, even had she wished to, even had the idea occurred to her.

'I can tell you nothing of my brother's voyage,' Marie-Josèphe said. 'I've had hardly a minute of his time since he returned.'

'Then you must tell me something else extraordinary – something to write to Raugrafin Sophie, back home.'

'The sea monster sings – just like a bird. And it speaks like a parrot.'

'Does it now! Perhaps you can train it to entertain His Majesty.'

'I could, if I had time, though it's very fierce. It frightened one of the workmen, and he nearly struck us both.'

'He struck you!'

'No, no, he failed, because Count Lucien – now do not laugh! – stopped the brute.'

'Why would I laugh? M. de Chrétien punished the villain, I hope!'

'Yes. He goes unarmed – but he shielded me with his cane.'

'That is no less than I would expect from someone of Count Lucien's breeding.'

'Madame . . . may I ask you something?'

'My dear, you honour me! Even my children never ask my advice – as you might notice, from Chartres' horrible marriage.'

'I fear it might be indiscreet.'

'Ah, indiscreet? Even better.'

'Is Count Lucien very brave, or is he foolhardy?'

'How, foolhardy?'

'He placed himself, unarmed, between me and the brute. He ignores fashion. And he spoke to His Holiness in such a way—!'

'What use would a sword have been? He could hardly challenge someone of the lower classes, even if His Majesty allowed duels, which he does not. No doubt the assailant realised himself lucky, for Count Lucien could have ordered his servants to thrash the man.'

Madame nodded toward the other corner of the room, where Count Lucien spoke with Mme la marquise de la Fère. The auburn perruke and gold lace of the King's pet courtier shone in the candlelight.

'As for fashion — how do you find him objectionable?' Madame smiled mischievously. 'Mme de la Fère finds him satisfactory, and her taste is impeccable. Perhaps you compare our fashions to those in Martinique?'

'Oh, no, Madame! Martinique has no fashion. We begged news of every ship that entered the harbour of Fort de France. The officers were of little help. The passengers — they sometimes told us what was fashionable in Paris, the previous season.'

'I care nothing for fashion,' Madame said quite truthfully. She did not dress as drably as Mme de Maintenon, being not nearly so ostentatiously devout, but she seldom wore many jewels on her court habit, seldom chose bright colours and always covered her ample bosom with a palatine. 'I would delight in living in Fort de France.'

'I lived the last five years in a convent. There was no question of fashion in the convent.'

'How did you come, then, to judge M. de Chrétien's attire?'

'The young ladies at Saint-Cyr, Madame. When they did not speak of religion — though that was seldom — they spoke of court, and of His Majesty, and of every new style.'

Madame chuckled. 'The old trollop hasn't pressed them under her heel as well as she believes. I'm glad to hear it.'

'They say, at court only a young officer — on leave from his regiment — should cultivate a moustache and tie his hair, and untie his cravat. I suppose M. de Chrétien cannot quite carry a sword, but—'

'Tonight he is clean-shaven, and his perruke is in the proper style.'

'Perhaps someone whispered to him,' Marie-Josèphe said hesitantly, 'not to appear as an officer?'

'Whyever not?' Madame, too, lowered her voice. 'I do not say His

Majesty would overlook any officer, who attended him in boots still dusty from the battlefield, and with his perruke knotted. But I do say he would not rebuke M. de Chrétien.'

'Count Lucien visited the battlefield?'

'He commanded a regiment, like any young nobleman with the King's regard. At Steenkirk last summer, at Neerwinden these weeks past. He rode all night to reach Versailles in time to accompany the King to Le Havre.'

Marie-Josèphe looked across the room, now seeing Count Lucien as an officer, raising a sword instead of his walking-stick. Mme de la Fère spoke. Delighted, he laughed. The lady smiled. Her fan slipped aside, revealing the scars of smallpox on her cheeks.

Count Lucien sipped his wine. Marie-Josèphe feared he would look around and see her, pale with mortification, and know her thoughts instantly. He did not. Unlike Lorraine, or Monsieur, or Chartres, he directed his attention to his partner in conversation, and did not seek beyond Mme de la Fère for better entertainment, or a higher rank, or a lady with a perfect complexion.

'Did you think,' Madame asked, 'that he took no part in the campaign?'

'I confess, Madame, that I did,' Marie-Josèphe said. 'Or, rather, I confess that I did not think at all, but made an assumption and did not confirm it.' She tried to smile. 'My brother would criticise my methods. They would not do at all during an experiment.'

'Is M. de Chrétien brave, is he foolhardy? I beg my son not to be foolhardy, yet I would not like it said he was not brave. He is brave. Chartres bore his wound most gallantly. It was not very severe – but even a small wound can carry off a loved one, once the doctors have their way.'

'M. de Chartres is gallant, Madame,' Marie-Josèphe said. 'I'm sure his leg will be as good as new by winter.'

'His leg?'

'Did you not say his leg was wounded?'

'No, indeed, his arm. One musket ball ripped his coat to shreds and the next—' Madame touched her biceps, holding her arm, wounded by the thought of her son's pain. 'He pulled the ball out himself and allowed M. de Chrétien to dress the wound. It healed so cleanly that I'm inclined to forgive the count many of his faults.'

'What faults are those, Madame?'

With her chin, Madame gestured across the room. The exquisite Mlle de Valentinois and Mlle d'Armagnac, who contended for the position of court's most beautiful young woman, had joined Mme de la Fère in conversation with Count Lucien. They flirted outrageously.

'Mlle Past, Mme Present, and Mlle Future, to begin with,' Madame said, 'though Mlle Future hasn't a brain in her head, so she'll not last long. More important – his religion.'

'His religion! Madame, do you mean he's—' She lowered her voice. 'Is he a heretic?'

'The King's adviser – a Protestant? Certainly not. He's an atheist.'

Marie-Josèphe could not believe it. She smiled uncertainly, expecting Madame to laugh and assure her she had made a joke. But Madame continued her story.

'Then they returned to the cavalry,' Madame said. 'Chartres wasn't wounded in the leg – that was M. de Chrétien.'

Marie-Josèphe thought, *Madame does not realise, thank heavens, I believed Chartres' lameness the result of injury and Count Lucien's a fault of his birth.*

'Chartres could have returned to court when he was injured, but of course he wouldn't. No more would Chrétien. Men are a mystery, my dear.'

'Yes, Madame.'

'And so I cannot answer your question,' Madame said. 'No woman, since St. Jeanne, knows the difference between foolhardiness and bravery on the field of battle. And you see what happened to her!'

Marie-Josèphe slipped through the knots of people, giddy with exhaustion, dazzled by candlelight and the glitter of gold and jewels. She looked for Lotte, at Madame's bidding.

Tobacco smoke and desperate laughter filled the gaming room. Gold coins and counters spilled across the tables. The players held their cards tight, as if they could squeeze from them another king or queen; or lounged nonchalantly back with their cards nearly slipping from their languid fingers.

'Damn and blast!' Mme Lucifer slammed her cards on the table. 'Christ's blood and God's breath!'

M. de Saint-Simon, an unprepossessing young man one would hardly notice if he had not been a duke and peer, drew his winnings toward him.

'Madame, I beg you – respect the good father's sensibilities.'

Yves stood at Mme de Chartres' shoulder. She swore again and glanced up at him.

'Poor Father Yves!' she said. 'Are we damned?'

'The sailors inured me to profanity, madame.'

'I would make a good sailor,' Madame Lucifer said.

Everyone at the table laughed, except Saint-Simon.

Marie-Josèphe slipped into the Salon of Mars. The chamber orchestra played softly, the measured music marking out His Majesty's court, describing the luxury France could sustain, even in the face of war and a poor harvest.

The dove-grey of Lotte's new gown shimmered in a window alcove, only partly concealed by the curtains. Marie-Josèphe hurried toward her, but stopped at the last moment. Lotte was not alone. Duke Charles bent toward her, whispering, and she laughed. The glow of her delight fairly lit up the alcove.

Madame would not approve, I'm sure, Marie-Josèphe thought, *and yet what harm could there be in conversation? Still, I mustn't embarrass my friend.*

She walked past the half-drawn curtains.

'Mademoiselle? Mademoiselle, where are you? Madame wants you.'

Her strategy worked.

'Marie-Josèphe!'

Marie-Josèphe turned back. Lotte and Charles of Lorraine strolled toward her. Marie-Josèphe curtsied.

'Your mama asks for your attendance,' she said.

'Poor Mama, all she really wants is to go to bed. No, no,' Lotte said. 'Charles and I will attend her. I know where she sits. If you come with us you'll be trapped too. Do you mind, Charles?'

The duke bowed graciously. The clothes of the foreign prince lacked the sumptuousness of the court of Versailles, but he had a kind face.

'I will be delighted to attend Madame,' he said, 'and I hope she will look upon me with favour.'

They departed. Marie-Josèphe belonged only to herself. She moved along the edges of the rooms. In the paintings of great masters, gifts from foreign governments, heroes mythical and real gazed into the distance or fought their battles, reclined on velvet and satin or galloped through clouds. His Majesty graced many of the scenes, majestic as Apollo, as Zeus, as a Roman emperor, as himself, Louis le Grand, on his war horse, on his throne.

Queen Marie Thérèse and the young dauphin, Monseigneur as he was as a little boy, strolled together through their portrait in matching dresses of red and gold and black, embroidered all over with pearls. Marie Thérèse carried a mask, to conceal her identity at a ball.

What a shame, to conceal such a beautiful complexion for any reason, Marie-Josèphe thought. The Queen was so fair, her hair, even her eyebrows, the pale blonde of white gold, her eyes grey. Fancifully, Marie-Josèphe curtsied to the portrait of the late queen.

Marie-Josèphe entered the Salon of Diana, hardly noticing where she walked as she admired the paintings. She stopped. His Majesty was playing billiards with James of England, Monsieur, and the chevalier de Lorraine. The other courtiers watched with rapt attention.

Should I curtsy? she wondered. *Have I missed a ceremony out of ignorance?*

But no one noticed her; it would be best to draw no attention to herself. She could not stroll through this room, admiring the paintings, but she could watch His Majesty, a much greater privilege. The salon was blissfully hot, and pungently smoky, but her new shoes hurt.

I haven't been awake this late, Marie-Josèphe thought, *since—since before Yves left Martinique, when we slipped out at night to run to the beach, to collect living shells that crept out in the light of the phosphorescence.*

In the convent, she had been obliged to go to bed not long after dark, and to get up long before dawn, and there was no question of running onto the beach.

His Majesty played a masterful shot. His ball clattered into the pocket. Monsieur and Lorraine clapped, and all the spectators followed suit.

James thumped his billiard cue on the floor and cursed.

'God's blood, Cousin Lewis, you've beat me again! You have damnable luck, sir.' He spoke with an accent, and he lisped, and he offended everyone except His Majesty with his lack of propriety toward the King.

'A hard-fought match, sir,' Monsieur said, speaking over James' comment.

'Thank you, my dear brother,' Louis said, as other courtiers surrounded him with their congratulations.

Marie-Josèphe stayed where she was, for she should not put herself forward in this company of princes and dukes.

Nearby, Count Lucien leaned on his ebony stick and sipped a glass of wine. He bowed. She returned his salute. She wanted to talk to him, not to apologise for her mistaken assumptions about him, for she had not – she hoped! – given him any reason to know of them, but to make up for her uncharitable thoughts with courtesy.

'Does your leg pain you much, Count Lucien?' she said. 'I hope it will soon heal completely.'

'Sieur de Baatz's salve will put it right in a week or two,' he said. 'The old gentleman's mother's recipe kept the surgeons from me.'

'Madame is so grateful to you for Chartres' survival. And I'm grateful, too.'

'For Chartres' survival?'

'For your bravery this morning.'

Count Lucien bowed slightly. Nearby, at the billiard table, courtiers verbally replayed the King's game. Marie-Josèphe wondered why Count Lucien was not at His Majesty's side.

'Don't you play billiards, Count Lucien?' Marie-Josèphe asked.

'I have done,' he said. 'Tonight, I forgot my billiard cue.' In a voice as dry as the Arabian desert, he added, 'The one with the curve.'

131

He sketched the long curve in the air, the shape of a stick that would allow him to reach the table.

Marie-Josèphe's face flushed. 'I beg your pardon,' she said. 'I am so sorry—I didn't mean—'

'Mlle de la Croix.'

She fell silent.

'Mlle de la Croix, it was years ago that I noticed I'm a dwarf. It's common knowledge. You needn't be embarrassed to notice it yourself.'

She had feared she had offended him once more; now she feared he would laugh at her. He took another sip of wine, savouring it, gazing up at her over the rim of his silver cup, never gulping it as Chartres did. He stood quite steady. Only the deliberation of his movements revealed the effect of the wine. His heavy sapphire ring glowed against the silver of his goblet.

'May I draw you?' Marie-Josèphe asked.

'For a gallery of oddities? Shall my likeness hang among ape-men and sea monsters?'

'No! Oh, no! Your face is beautiful. Your hands are beautiful. I would like to draw you.'

Count Lucien drank the last drops of wine; a footman appeared from nowhere to take away his goblet. The count waved away another glass.

He will refuse me, Marie-Josèphe thought, *and once again I've said the wrong thing*.

'Your time is otherwise engaged,' Count Lucien said. 'And His Majesty's bedtime ceremony occupies mine.'

Lucien bowed to Mlle de la Croix and limped away.

Sieur de Baatz's salve will soothe the wound, Lucien thought. *Exercise will loosen my joints and ease the ache of my back*.

The Marquise de la Fère caught his gaze as he passed; he paused to kiss her hand. Speaking to him alone, she was not so self-conscious of her marred complexion.

'My carriage waits on your pleasure, my dear Juliette,' he said.

'And yours.'

'I must ride Zelis home,' he said. 'I'll follow when we've put His Majesty to bed.'

132

'Your groom can ride—But I forget, no one rides your favourite desert horses but you.'

'My groom could lead Zelis home, but I've stood in Diana's Salon all evening. My groom cannot shake the kinks out of me.'

She smiled at him, her vast brown eyes limpid in candlelight.

'Of course not, my dear,' she said. 'That's my task.' She fluttered her fan and her eyelashes elaborately, mocking coquettes. He laughed, kissed her hand again, and joined the group of nobles who would see His Majesty comfortably put to bed.

Yves wrenched his attention back to Mme de Chartres, wondering how anyone so young and of such questionable birth could be so arrogant. She demanded more royal prerogatives than the legitimate members of the royal family. His Majesty was good manners incarnate, the grand dauphin became invisible in his self-deprecation, and His Majesty's grandsons behaved like any little boys, only better dressed.

'You brought me bad luck tonight, Father de la Croix, and I demand that you make amends for it.'

'I don't believe in bad luck, Mme de Chartres,' he said. 'Or in any kind of luck at all.'

'You stood with me at the card table, and I lost – so I place my losses at your feet.'

'Would you place your winnings at my feet, if you had won?' he asked.

She closed her Chinese sandalwood fan; she stared at him with a straightforward gaze. Golden Chinese ornaments glittered and dangled in her hair, their pendants touching delicately, ringing faintly.

'Why, Father de la Croix, I would place anything you asked at your feet – if you only would ask.'

She behaved as if he were flirting, though he had meant the question in the most straightforward way. He had been among men, sailors or other Jesuits or university students, for so long that he had forgotten what little he had ever known about polite conversation in the society of women. Mme de Chartres gave a second meaning to his every courtly compliment.

Despite the honours His Majesty had shown him this evening, despite the admiration of the courtiers and the attention of the beautiful women – he could appreciate their beauty, could he not, for God had created it, after all – Yves wished he were back in his room. He had notes to write up from the sea monster dissection. He must be sure Marie-Josèphe did not neglect the sketches. And he must get some sleep, during the dark hours, so he could use the hours of daylight to complete his study of the carcass.

The Master of Ceremonies strode into the room, clearing the way for His Majesty. Mme de Chartres drew aside, falling into a deep curtsy. Yves bowed, surreptitiously watching His Majesty pass.

Am I meant to watch His Majesty's bedtime as well as his rising? Yves thought. He shrugged off the sudden apprehension, for M. de Chrétien would have told him of the added duty. His Majesty passed, with King James at his left and His Holiness on his right hand, Count Lucien in the King's wake with the other noblemen. His Holiness glanced at Yves, his brow furrowed; Count Lucien passed him without word or gesture.

The King's presence had filled the state apartments. Now the rooms felt empty, and in a moment they would be dark, for the courtiers left behind now hurried away, yawning and complaining of the lateness, the tedium. The servants of His Majesty's gentlemen swarmed into the apartments, snuffing out the candles before they could burn one hairsbreadth shorter.

'Come with me,' Mme de Chartres said.

'I'm honoured to escort you to your husband,' Yves said.

'My husband! What would I want with my husband?' She laughed at him and swept away, calling back over her shoulder without caring if anyone heard, 'You disappoint me, Father de la Croix.'

Yves knew what she desired. He was not a virgin, not quite, a circumstance he regretted, but since taking orders he had never broken his vow of celibacy. Mme de Chartres' eagerness to break her marriage vows disturbed him past any threat of temptation.

He was alone for the first time during the entire interminable evening. He had told the story of the sea monster's capture two dozen times, the story of the sailor's unspilled wine almost as often. Few of

His Majesty's nobles had ever been to sea. They expected a wealth of adventures, exciting stories, not the truth of discomfort, boredom to equal anything they complained about at Versailles, and hours or days or weeks of terror and misery when the seas turned ugly.

Yves walked through the dark apartments, abandoned by anyone of any importance. As the gentlemen's servants collected the burned candles for their masters, His Majesty's servants replaced them with fresh tapers. No candle could be lit a second time for the King. Attending His Majesty for one single quarter of a year, the usual term, could light one's house until the seasons turned. This was one of the considerable perquisites for the courtiers who attended the Sun King.

Yves descended the magnificent Staircase of the Ambassadors, for he could not reach his tiny rooms in the chateau's attic except by returning to the ground floor and climbing a narrow staircase. A figure in blazing red appeared from the darkness.

'Father de la Croix.'

'Your eminence.' Yves bowed to Cardinal Ottoboni.

'The Holy Father requires your presence,' the cardinal said, in Latin.

Yves replied in the same language. 'I am at His Holiness' service.'

Cardinal Ottoboni swept out onto the terrace. He pointed into the garden. His Holiness stood between the parterres d'eau, gazing along the length of the garden toward the peak of the sea monster's tent.

'Attend me, Father de la Croix,' His Holiness said.

Yves hurried to Innocent's side. Ottoboni remained on the terrace. Innocent led Yves out of earshot, toward the Orangerie, into a cloud of fragrance. They gazed in silence at the rows of small trees.

'I am distressed,' Innocent said.

'I am sorry, Your Holiness.'

'I'm distressed by your worldly concerns.'

'I only seek God's truth, and His will, in nature.'

'It isn't your place,' His Holiness said, 'to determine God's truth, or His will.'

Innocent's voice remained kind, but Yves did not mistake the sternness of his words.

'I'm distressed by your sister's pagan composition.'

'Your Holiness, I beg you, she meant nothing by it – it was perfectly innocent.'

'My son, indulge me – and my fear for both your souls.'

'I'm grateful for your attention, Your Holiness.'

'Our cousin's court surrounds you with danger. With debauchery, adultery, and bastardy. Heresy abounds. Atheists, monsters, advise the King.'

'My vows and my faith are my protection, Your Holiness.'

'When is the last time you said Mass, or heard confession?'

'Not for many months, Your Holiness.'

'Your vows and your faith require attention,' His Holiness said.

Innocent paced between the beds of flower embroidery. Yves followed, careful not to outwalk the Holy Father, who was decades his elder and in frail health.

'Perhaps Father de la Chaise would permit me to assist him at Mass – to hear confession—'

'Perhaps Father de la Chaise would condescend to hear your confession,' Innocent said. 'I will not ask how long it has been since you made it.'

Innocent reached the stairs leading to the terrace. He took Yves' elbow for support as they returned to the chateau.

'A year of meditation, perhaps, would benefit you,' Innocent said. 'A retreat to a monastery, a year of silence—'

Yves struggled to keep his silence now. He had no doubt he would be sent away, if he protested. And if he were sent away, he would lose the King's patronage and all it meant for his work.

'I shall observe,' Innocent said, 'and consider what will do you the most good.'

Innocent offered Yves his hand. Yves fell to his knees and kissed the Pope's ring.

Marie-Josèphe ran up the narrow stairs to the attic of the chateau. The hour was late. She and Lotte had attended Madame's simple preparations, and Marie-Josèphe had attended Lotte during her bedtime routine.

136

How can I sleep tonight? Marie-Josèphe thought. *After an evening of such magnificence, such excitement—*

She remembered, again, the Chevalier's lips against her fingers, her surprising shiver of pleasure at his touch. She wondered what it would be like to kiss him. The nuns had warned her against kisses, against the sin and danger and pain that kisses led to. But a kiss to the hand, at least, proved not to be horrible at all.

Laughter followed her; footsteps sounded on the threadbare carpet. A lady masked in the iridescent colours of a hummingbird and a gentleman masked as a goat — or a satyr — climbed the stairs. They pressed together side-by-side in the narrow passageway. Marie-Josèphe recognised Chartres instantly; she thought the lady was Mlle d'Armagnac. She was certainly not Mme Lucifer. Chartres nuzzled her throat with the nose and horns of his mask until she threw back her head and laughed again, throaty and breathless.

The lady's fashionable headdress stood crooked and her hair tumbled around her face. Ribbons tangled with the fantastic feathers of her mask. She pulled her fontanges free, hurled it down the stairs, ribbons and lace trailing through the dust, and flung herself against Chartres. They stumbled sideways up the stairs, kissing, gasping, hands fumbling desperately each on the other's body. Chartres tore at the lacings of Mlle d'Armagnac's bodice. He yelped. 'Do not unman me, mademoiselle!'

Marie-Josèphe was about to flee when Chartres, capricorn-masked, caught her in his gaze. She dropped into a curtsy.

'Sir,' she said, 'I beg your pardon.'

Mlle d'Armagnac snatched her hands from beneath the gold-laced skirts of Chartres' coat and embroidered waistcoat. One of his stockings drooped down his leg, rumpling around the knee-roll. Mlle d'Armagnac glared at Marie-Josèphe and straightened her mask to conceal her identity. Her disarranged habit exposed her breasts. A jewelled beauty patch sparkled just below her left aureole. She tugged at her bodice to cover herself.

'I do not know you,' Chartres said coldly to Marie-Josèphe, glaring dark and wild from beneath the horned half-mask. His skewed gaze was as perverse as any goat's.

137

'But, M. de Ch—'

'You have mistaken me for someone else.' He grinned and raised his mask. 'Unless, Mlle de la Croix, you'd care to accompany us?'

'No!' she exclaimed, horrified.

'What a shame. Good evening.' He lowered the mask over his blind erratic eye, reclaiming the visage of a satyr. He bent to kiss and nip Mlle d'Armagnac's breast, baring it again. She stroked his long curled hair and pulled him closer, tighter, gazing at Marie-Josèphe all the while. When he rose, the beauty patch stuck to his chin.

They both laughed and ran up the stairs, squeezing past Marie-Josèphe on the landing, ignoring her curtsy and her embarrassment. Mlle d'Armagnac's door opened. Silk rustled, then tore, a high harsh rip; the door slammed.

The staircase, the hallway, the whole of the chateau lay silent and dark.

Marie-Josèphe fled. She plunged into her room and pressed the door shut. Odelette sat up in bed, blinking sleepily in the light of a single candle.

'Mlle Marie, what's happened?' Odelette slid from beneath the featherbed and hurried to her.

'Nothing. I saw—'

'Didn't you know?' Odelette said, when Marie-Josèphe described what she had seen. 'Didn't you notice? They pair off in the eaves – like sparrows fucking.'

'Don't speak so coarsely, dear Odelette.'

'Should I say, making love? Do they love each other? I see that they fuck. I don't see that they love.'

'Say—say, fornicating.'

Odelette laughed. 'Mlle Marie, the common word is less ugly. Come along, let me put you to bed.'

Marie-Josèphe allowed Odelette to help her out of her court habit and undress her hair.

'Did you find a prince tonight, Mlle Marie?'

'Yes.'

'Did he find you?'

'Perhaps he did,' Marie-Josèphe said. 'But . . . he has no ambassador, so I wonder if you can approve him?'

'The ambassador always finds the stolen princess,' Odelette whispered. Marie-Josèphe hugged her, wishing Odelette's fairy tale could possibly come true.

In her shift, Marie-Josèphe gazed across the garden, toward the sea monster's tent, listening for the sea monster's song. But the gardens lay quiet in the night.

'Come to bed, Mlle Marie, before it gets cold again.'

'I couldn't possibly sleep,' Marie-Josèphe said. 'And I must feed the sea monster. Help me into my riding habit, and keep the bed warm till I return.'

'Tell me of your prince.' Odelette shook out the riding habit.

'Is my brother in his room?'

'In his room, asleep, and both doors are closed. He'll never hear what you tell me.'

'You saw my prince,' Marie-Josèphe said. 'The handsome man in Madame's apartment.'

'There were no handsome men in Madame's apartment.' Odelette buttoned the tiny jet buttons.

'Chartres is handsome—'

'He's as misshapen as a snake.'

'He isn't! And Monsieur is—'

'Pretty.'

'I suppose you're right. Pretty.'

'As I said. No handsome men.'

'I couldn't aspire so high – a member of the royal family? I meant the Chevalier de Lorraine.'

'Monsieur's friend.'

'Yes.' She prepared to defend Lorraine against the charge of being too old. Uncharacteristically, Odelette kept her silence.

'He is handsome, is he not?'

'He is handsome, Mlle Marie.'

'But you don't like him?'

'He is handsome.'

'What does it matter?' Marie-Josèphe exclaimed. 'I have no dowry, he'd never think of me.' She hesitated. 'But . . . he kissed me – on the hand, I mean, quite properly. Almost properly. He made no improper advances – nothing very improper, not like . . . like Chartres.' She plunged on. 'Chartres bared Mlle d'Armagnac's breasts – on the stairway! And she . . . she placed her hands very near M. de Chartres' . . .' She sought the proper term. 'His organ of generation.'

'She seized his cock.'

Marie-Josèphe tried to be offended. Instead, she giggled. 'On the stairway. How do you know these words, Odelette? You never knew them in Martinique.'

'From the convent, of course.' Odelette jumped into bed and pulled the covers up to her chin. 'From Mother Superior.'

Chapter 10

The sea monster's eerie plaintive song filled the moonlit gardens. Marie-Josèphe hurried along the Green Carpet. She hugged Lorraine's cloak close against the chill and damp. The wolf fur warmed her, and it smelled of Lorraine's musky scent, the scent Monsieur had also offered her.

She wished she were a great lady who could order a coach to take her here and there, or a rich one who could afford to keep a horse. She liked to walk in the gardens, but the hour was late and the night was chilly, and she still had so much to do.

She laughed aloud in wonder that she was living at the centre of the world.

And I've begun to train the sea monster, she thought. *If I have a few days, I might be able to train it to keep silent when His Majesty next sees it. But if His Majesty delays the dissection for those few days, the male sea monster will decompose, and all the training will be for nothing.*

Marie-Josèphe's lantern swung. A wild shadow dance sprang from her feet. She skipped. The shadow leaped, its cape flying in the beautiful night.

I shall have to work on the sketches later, Marie-Josèphe thought. *A few hours—*

But the moon, almost three-quarters full, had fallen halfway to the horizon. The night was half over.

Before her the tent glowed faintly; across the garden, near the Fountain of Neptune, torches flickered as gardeners set out potted flowers in great drifts, keeping the gardens beautiful for His Majesty.

A dark-lantern flashed open, blinding her with its light. Marie-Josèphe jumped, startled and frightened.

'Who goes there?'

'Mlle de la Croix,' she said, amused by her fear of the sea monster's guards. 'Come to feed the sea monster.' She held up her lantern, beaming its light, in turn, into the musketeer's eyes.

The dark-lantern rotated, spilling its light between them. Marie-Josèphe lowered her lantern. The light cast a long shadow behind the musketeer and illuminated his face, demonically, from below.

'Do you have authorisation to enter?'

'Of course I do – my brother's.'

'In writing?'

She laughed. Yet he barred her way, standing before the entry.

Inside the tent, the sea monster whistled and growled.

'Father de la Croix said, "Let no one enter".'

'He didn't mean me,' Marie-Josèphe said.

'He said no one.'

'But I *am* no one. He's the head of our family – why would he think to separate himself from me?'

'What you say is true.' The musketeer stood aside. 'Be cautious, mamselle. If it isn't a demon – and I don't say it isn't – it is angry.'

She entered the tent, grateful not to have to climb the hill and call Yves from his bed to vouch for her. Shutting her lantern so she would not frighten the sea monster, Marie-Josèphe paused to let her eyes adjust. A pale blur loomed nearby: New screens of heavy white silk woven with gold sunbursts and fleurs de lys shielded the dissection table from the live sea monster's sight. The white and the gold glimmered.

Marie-Josèphe unlocked the sea monster's cage. Small fish swam and splashed in a jug of sea water. A strange, faint glow suffused the Fountain. Could Yves have left a lit candle on the stairs, reflecting from the water?

'Sea monster?' Marie-Josèphe whispered. 'It's only me, come to give you some supper.'

Ripples spread across the pool. Marie-Josèphe caught her breath.

The ripples glowed with eerie phosphorescence. The glow spread. The luminescence reflected from the gilt of Apollo's dolphins and tritons.

In Fort de France, on Martinique, the ocean glowed like this. The barrels must have captured glowing sea water, and brought it to Versailles.

'Sea monster?' Marie-Josèphe hummed a melody the sea monster had sung. She wondered if the songs of sea monsters had any meaning, like the cries and yowls of her cat Hercules.

Perhaps I'm saying, I'm glad to be out of the awful gold basin, the awful canvas, Marie-Josèphe thought. That would be very confusing for the poor sea monster.

She sat on the edge of the fountain and hummed a different melody.

A wake like a shining arrow flowed toward Marie-Josèphe. The sea monster swam to the platform, her tails undulating gently, only her eyes and hair revealed above the surface. Marie-Josèphe sat on the lowest step, her feet on the wet platform, and held out a fish to the captive creature.

Shall I hold tight to the fish? she wondered. *No, if I force the sea monster to stay near, I'm likely to frighten it.*

Instead of snatching the fish and thrashing away into the darkness, the sea monster swam very close, turned, and swept past beneath Marie-Josèphe's hand. The pressure of the water stroked her skin.

'Sea monster, aren't you hungry?'

The sea monster surfaced an armslength away.

'Fishhhh,' she said.

'Yes, exactly, fish!'

The sea monster dove again. Marie-Josèphe sat very still, her fingers growing numb in the cold water.

Beneath the glowing surface of the pool, the sea monster's dark shape rose beneath her hand. The sea monster, floating face-up, gazed at her through luminescent ripples and placed her webbed claws directly beneath Marie-Josèphe's fingers.

Marie-Josèphe released the fish into the sea monster's grasp.

The sea monster rolled, stroking her arm along Marie-Josèphe's palm. Her warmth radiated against Marie-Josèphe's skin. Marie-Josèphe laid her hand on the creature's back, as if she were gentling a colt.

The sea monster trembled.

'There's nothing to be afraid of.' Marie-Josèphe did not like to lie, even to a creature.

143

Floating face-down, the sea monster quieted beneath her touch.

Marie-Josèphe smoothed one lock, then another, of the creature's dark green hair. The glossy strands lay across the sea monster's skin, iridescent black in the faint light. The sea monster hummed, like a cat who purred in song. Marie-Josèphe picked up a third strand of hair. The tangle would not straighten, for the hair was knotted.

The sea monster rolled over again, drawing the tangled strand from Marie-Josèphe's grasp. Floating on her back, she neatly bit off the fish's head, munched it, ate the other half. Her double tail fanned the water beside Marie-Josèphe's foot. Marie-Josèphe bent to look more closely. The tails were nothing like fish tails, and not much like seal fins. Darker, thicker skin covered the sea monster from pelvis downward. A mat of dark-green hair covered her female parts. The upper bones of her tails were rather short, the lower bones longer, with powerful muscles front and back. The joint between them bent both ways. The joint connecting long lower bones to large feet resembled Marie-Josèphe's wrist. The feet ended in long, webbed toes and wickedly powerful claws.

The sea monster used one toe to flick a drop of water toward Marie-Josèphe's face. It spattered her cheek and dribbled down her face.

'Don't splash me, sea monster,' she said. 'I already ruined one gown in your pool, and I cannot afford another. Come, leave off playing. Eat another fish. I have so much to do, I must hurry.' Her stomach growled. The squabs were very long ago and very small. She smiled at the sea monster. 'You're lucky, you know – I wish someone would bring me a fish to eat!'

The sea monster took the fish, bit off its head, and offered the body and tail to Marie-Josèphe.

Shocked, Marie-Josèphe scooted backwards. Safe beyond the fountain's rim, she gazed down at the sea monster.

Be calm, she said to herself. *It cannot have understood that you are hungry. It brought you a fish, as Hercules might bring you a mouse.*

The sea monster sang a few notes.

'Thank you,' Marie-Josèphe said, speaking to the sea monster as she would speak to her cat. 'You may eat it now.'

'Fishhhh.' The sea monster popped the piece of fish into its mouth. A bit of the tail stuck out between her lips. She crunched it and swallowed, and the translucent fin disappeared.

Marie-Josèphe petted her goodbye. The sea monster grasped her wrist. Gently, firmly, the sea monster sang and drew Marie-Josèphe closer to the water.

'Let go,' Marie-Josèphe said. 'Sea monster—' She twisted her hand, but the sea monster's claws pinioned her. The creature sang again, loud and insistent. She pulled Marie-Josèphe's hand beneath the water. 'Let – me – go!' Scared, she tugged her hand from the sea monster's grip, careless of the sharp claws.

The sea monster freed her. She fell back, clambered to her feet, and scrambled away. The sea monster gazed after her with only her eyes above water. The creature continued to sing, but the song vibrated strangely through the water and the stone, and trembled against the wooden platform like a primitive drumbeat. Marie-Josèphe felt more than heard it. She shivered, clanged the cage door shut and locked, snatched up the lantern, and hurried from the tent.

'Good night, Mlle de la Croix. Your monster is well-fed, I hope.'

'I hope so,' she said shortly, barely acknowledging his bow. She trudged up the Green Carpet, past the masses of dewy potted flowers, toward silent fountains. She was not used to being frightened by animals; her fear distressed her. Her wrist ached from the sea monster's grip. Yet the creature had freed her when it could have clawed her arm to shreds and scars.

The sea monster's song followed her, discordant and eerie. She shivered. The statues loomed, white ghosts, and their shadows spread black pools through the darkness. Marie-Josèphe's happiness and pride dissolved into the sea monster's fierce music.

'Yves—?' Her brother stood pale as the marble, pale as death, bleeding from his hands and forehead. He stood in a pool of blood. She saw him as clearly as if the music were light. And then she did not see him at all.

The music stopped.

'Yves? Where are you?'

Marie-Josèphe's tears blurred the bright chateau windows, the

145

torches' flames. She dashed the back of her hand against her eyes and raised her skirts above her ankles and fled.

She rushed through the chateau, tears streaming down her face, her shoes wet with dew. She had enough presence of mind to use the back stairs, hoping no one would see her.

I must stop, she thought frantically, *I must stop crying, I must walk instead of run, I must sweep along with the hem of my skirt brushing the floor, so no one will see me and say, She's just a peasant, hiking her skirts up around her knees.*

She ran up the stairs to the attic, choking back her sobs, her breath ragged. She threw open the door to Yves' dressing room. A single candle lit it. Yves buttoned his cassock, while a servant in the King's livery stood impatiently nearby.

Marie-Josèphe flung herself into her brother's arms.

'Sister, what's wrong?' He held her, comforting her with his strength.

'I thought you were dead, I thought—I saw—'

'Dead?' he said. 'Of course I'm not dead.' He smiled. 'I'm not even asleep, much as I'd like to be. What's frightened you so?'

'Your worship,' the servant said.

'Hush, I'll be along.'

Yves hugged her again, solid and dependable. He found a handkerchief and wiped the tear stains from her cheeks, as if she were a child who had stubbed her toe.

'I thought . . .' The visions that had spun around her in the darkness of the garden vanished in the candlelight of his room. 'I was feeding the sea monster—'

'In the dark? No wonder you were frightened. You shouldn't go into the gardens alone at night. Take Odelette with you.'

'Yes, you're right, it must have been the dark,' Marie-Josèphe said, all the time thinking, *How strange, I never feared the dark before.*

'Please, your worship—'

'Don't call me that!' Yves said to the servant. 'I'm coming.'

'Where are you going?' Marie-Josèphe asked.

'To His Majesty. To the sea monster.'

★

146

The Fountain luminesced, filling the tent with an eerie glow like fox-fire. Triton's trumpet shone, and the hooves of the dawn horses, and their muzzles, as if they galloped on cold fire and breathed it from their nostrils.

Marie-Josèphe lit the lanterns; the glow vanished. The sea monster whistled and hummed and splashed, luring Marie-Josèphe to her.

'I can't play with you now, sea monster,' Marie-Josèphe whispered. 'His Majesty is coming!' She checked the screens of heavy silk to be sure the sea monster could not see past them, then pulled aside the dead monster's canvas shroud, exposing the carcass, spilling sawdust and melting ice to the floor. Preserving fluids and caked blood stained the canvas. The monster's ribs lay exposed, stripped of skin and muscle. One arm was flayed to the bone, and the leg on the same side.

Outside the tent, His Majesty's wheeled cart creaked; hooves crunched in gravel; footsteps tramped. Yves greeted the King and Count Lucien. The King's deaf-mutes pushed his chair into the tent. Count Lucien walked beside His Majesty. Four carriers followed with a sedan chair hung with white velvet and gold tassels. Marie-Josèphe hugged Lorraine's dark cloak around her and stood by her drawing box, hoping to attract as little attention as possible.

'I think it best to examine the sea monster's internal organs in private,' the King said.

'Your Majesty,' Yves said, 'the sea monsters are ordinary animals.'

The deaf-mutes lifted the cart onto the plank floor and pushed it to the lab table. The sedan chair followed; the carriers lowered it and fled the tent, bowing.

His Majesty did not bother to dismiss his deaf-mutes; he treated them, as always, as if they hardly existed. Count Lucien remained by his side, leaning easily on his staff. Marie-Josèphe returned his polite nod with a quick curtsy. Yves helped His Holiness from the palanquin and conducted him to an armchair.

Exhaustion paled the old man's face, and he leaned heavily on Yves' arm. His Majesty swung himself out of the cart and hobbled to the dissection table, leaning only a little on Count Lucien's shoulder. He gazed with fascination at the creature. His Majesty showed no signs of having been up all night; even the swelling of his gout had eased.

'Every feature I've studied so far,' Yves said, 'every muscle, every bone, has its match within every other furred creature known to natural philosophy.'

'Father de la Croix,' His Majesty said, 'I did not charge you to find what is common about the sea monsters. I charged you to find what is unique.'

'I will look, Your Majesty.' Yves took up his heaviest lancet. 'Are you ready, sister?'

Marie-Josèphe settled a fresh sheet of paper.

Yves sliced open the creature's belly, exposing its viscera. The intestines and stomach lay flat and shrivelled, empty of food. Perhaps the male sea monster had successfully resisted being force fed. Marie-Josèphe regretted the creature's death, but she was glad the organs would not explode upon His Majesty and His Holiness when Yves pierced them.

'The intestines are rather short for a creature that must sustain itself mostly on seaweed, with an occasional garnish of fish,' Yves said, 'by which I surmise that seaweed is easily digested.'

He cut the intestines out delicately, measuring and inspecting, taking small samples, placing the organs in jars of spirits. Marie-Josèphe drew as best she could in lantern light. The sea monster's intestine sported an appendix, unusual in most animals. Yves dissected out the kidneys, the pancreas, the bladder; he even sought stomach-stones and kidney-stones. He found nothing unusual or notable in the lower abdomen. He might have been dissecting any carcass, or even the corpse of a man.

His Majesty watched with increasing impatience; His Holiness with increasing discomfort. Count Lucien watched unmoved.

With a heavy pair of shears, Yves cut open the ribs at the breastbone. He separated the rib cage, exposing the lungs and the heart.

'It is as I thought,' Yves said. He probed delicately into the chest, moving aside lobes of the lungs to expose the heart and the various glands. 'The creature presents no attributes of the fish, neither gills nor swim-bladder. It is very like the dugong. And as you have seen,

148

Your Majesty, the sea monster possesses internal organs normal to all mammals.'

'Father de la Croix, whether the monster is a fish or a beast is of no interest to me. What is of interest is its organ of immortality.'

'I've found no evidence of such an organ, Sire. Immortality, like the transmutation of gold, is the province of alchemy, abhorred by the Church and by natural philosophy.'

'You dismiss ancient tales cavalierly, Father de la Croix,' His Majesty said. 'How did you come to accept this undertaking, if you believe my quest futile?'

'I wished to please Your Majesty,' Yves said, taken aback by the King's sharp tone. 'The quest for the sea monsters was anything but futile. As for the organ of immortality, it exists, or it does not exist. My beliefs are immaterial.'

Pope Innocent stared at him, exhaustion transformed by outrage.

'That is to say, I might form a hypothesis, but it must be tested . . .' Yves' voice trailed off. His quest for knowledge had for an instant overcome his restraint; he was doing himself no credit with Pope Innocent.

'If you believe the organ does not exist,' His Majesty said, ignoring Yves' embarrassment, 'you surely will not find it.'

'If the monsters impart everlasting life to those who consume them, Sire,' Yves said, 'why, how many sailors would be a thousand years old?'

Louis waved away the objections. 'Sailors live a hard life. Protection against old age and disease would never save a man from accident or drowning.'

'Cousin,' Innocent said, 'perhaps your natural philosopher has the right of it. God drove us from Eden, after all, where we were immortal. Now we are mortal, but we live in the hopes of joining Him in everlasting life.'

'If God created an immortality organ, and commanded us to use beasts as we will – then it is His will that we become immortal.'

Innocent frowned thoughtfully, troubled. 'Earthly immortality would be a burden, not a satisfaction.' He hesitated. 'Yet, if one were called to continue God's work—'

'As I am,' His Majesty said.

'—one would submit . . . however burdened by Earthly flesh.'

Yves continued his exploration of the heart and the lungs. At the top of the chest, beneath the upper ribs, the highest lobe of the lung resisted his probe. He exclaimed wordlessly and pulled the lobe farther into view.

'This is unique.'

Marie-Josèphe glanced from the gutted sea monster to her brother, to Innocent, to His Majesty. All of them stared at the unusual lobe of the lung. The colour differed, and the texture. A tangle of blood vessels covered its surface.

Only Count Lucien paid no attention to the carcass. He paid his attention to the King, gazing at his sovereign with hope, and relief, and love.

Yves lifted the unusual structure and cut it free of the normal lung.

'You have found it,' Louis said. 'What else could it be?'

Marie-Josèphe hurried up the Green Carpet after Yves, holding her drawing box tight against her chest, protecting the record of her brother's discoveries. Yves strode along before her. Far ahead, His Majesty's deaf-mutes pushed his rolling cart at a run, and Pope Innocent's chair carriers struggled to keep up. Count Lucien's elegant grey Arabian trotted beside them. Early mist swirled at their heels. Yves might keep up with them, but Marie-Josèphe never could. She broke into a run, glad she was not wearing court dress. Ten paces ahead, Yves paused and waited impatiently. Torches gilded the chateau, cast shadows across the gardens, and haloed Yves' hair.

'Hurry, or we'll get no sleep at all – you do want me to attend His Majesty's awakening?' He smiled, teasing her.

She looked at the ground, embarrassed all over again for failing him yesterday.

They climbed the back stairs to the attic and their tiny apartment. As they ascended, a young courtier muffled in cloak and half-mask passed, creeping quietly down. He ignored their salute, as if the mask made him invisible.

Yawning and stretching, Yves disappeared into his bedroom to nap for a few hours.

Odelette and Hercules slept soundly in Marie-Josèphe's bed, cuddled together, warm and safe. Marie-Josèphe put aside the temptation to join them in their comfortable nest.

If I fall asleep now, she thought, *I shall never wake in time to rouse Yves. Besides, I've not done a moment's work on the dissection sketches*.

In Yves' dressing room, she lit tallow candles and settled herself at the table to begin the painstaking task of redrawing the sketches with pen and ink. As she arranged the papers, she found the equation she had scribbled and scratched out. Her thoughts wandered to the problems that fascinated her, the description of God's creations – God's will, perhaps – in precise terms. She wrote a second equation for predicting the motion of rustling leaves; she saw that it would not work, either, even when she added the effect of gravity.

This is as difficult a problem as predicting the actions of my dear leaf-rustler, Madame! Marie-Josèphe thought, amused.

She rubbed out the equation, and turned her attention to Yves' drawings.

At six o'clock, Marie-Josèphe put several finished drawings away and slipped into her room to change clothes; she and Odelette must attend Lotte; they must all help Madame dress; they must gather in the antechamber outside His Majesty's bedroom and join the procession to Mass.

I mustn't fail my duties to Mademoiselle, Marie-Josèphe thought. Not two days in a row. I must attend Mass—

She had promised to attend last night; she had forgotten.

Odelette's soft breathing was the only sound. Hercules slipped in through the open window, leaving the curtain a handsbreadth open; he stretched and yowled, demanding breakfast. Gray morning light from the west-facing window woke Odelette. She blinked, her long lashes brushing her cheeks, beautiful even a moment out of sleep.

'Have you sat up all night, Mlle Marie?' Odelette whispered. 'Come to bed, you can rest a little while.'

'It's time to get up,' Marie-Josèphe said. 'Help me change my

151

dress – and you must do my hair. Mademoiselle wants you this morning.'

Sitting up, Odelette cried out. She drew her hand from beneath the covers. Blood smeared her fingertips.

'Quick, Mlle Marie, before I stain the bedclothes—'

Marie-Josèphe flung open her storage chest, snatched up a handful of soft clean rags, and took them to Odelette.

Odelette thrust the pad between her legs to soak up her monthly flow, then curled miserably beneath the blankets. She always suffered terribly from her monthlies.

'I'm so sorry, Mlle Marie—'

'You must stay in bed,' Marie-Josèphe said. She put Hercules beside Odelette and stroked his soft fur, the tabby stripes of two textures, till he gave up asking for his breakfast and snuggled warm against Odelette's sore back. 'In bed, with our bed-warmer.' Odelette smiled, though her lips trembled. 'And I'll send you some broth. You must drink it, but share a little with Hercules.'

'Mlle Marie, you must wear a towel today.'

She and Odelette had always begun their monthlies on the same day. They had been apart so long, surely that rule had been lost with distance? But when Marie-Josèphe counted, Odelette was right. Marie-Josèphe tied a rolled towel between her legs and struggled into her grand habit. She must not spoil another dress.

Poor Odelette, her women's troubles pained her so. Marie-Josèphe kissed her cheek.

Marie-Josèphe unbraided her hair and dressed it simply, without lace or ribbons. She looked like a naive colonial girl, but she could do no more without Odelette's help.

In Yves' room, she sat on the edge of his bed and shook him gently.

'Yves – brother, it's time to get up.'

'I'm awake,' he mumbled.

Marie-Josèphe smiled fondly and shook him again. He sat up, rubbing his eyes and stretching.

'I am awake,' he said.

'I know.' She kissed his cheek. 'I must fly, to Mademoiselle.'

152

She hurried down the attic stairs. She felt lucky not to suffer from her monthlies as Odelette did. If she had to keep to her bed, she would miss greeting His Majesty after his morning ceremony, she would miss following the King to Mass.

She would miss caring for the sea monster, and Yves might give her place to Chartres.

Lucien's carriage flew along the Avenue de Paris and past the lines of visitors waiting to enter His Majesty's gardens. The carriage followed the same route as Pope Innocent's, all the way to the steps of the Marble Courtyard.

Despite the inconvenience – His Majesty seldom concerned himself with the convenience of his courtiers – the King permitted few carriages to enter the forecourt of the chateau. Lucien accepted the perquisite as the King intended, as a sign of esteem. He rode in his carriage more often than he might otherwise have done, to publicly take advantage of His Majesty's favour.

His footman placed the steps and held the door. Lucien climbed down, leaning easily on his walking staff. He had not slept, but he had refreshed himself. Thanks to Sieur de Baatz's salve, his leg had nearly healed; thanks to Juliette, thanks to the distractions of calvados and stimulation, the pain in his back was quite tolerable.

His eight matched coach horses stood rock-still, bay coats and harness gleaming.

'Return to my chateau and put yourself at the disposal of Mme la Marquise,' Lucien said to his coachman. 'She will wish to attend today's picnic at His Majesty's Menagerie.'

'Yes, sir.'

Lucien crossed the black and white marble of the courtyard, entered the chateau through its central doors, beneath the balcony of the King's apartment, and took his usual route to His Majesty's bedroom.

Waiting by his brother's bed, Monsieur stifled a yawn. The duke d'Orléans often rode to Paris after the King's evening entertainments, for he found Versailles constraining. On occasion, Lucien joined him. Though he did not share all Monsieur's tastes, he appreciated the duke's ability to enjoy himself. But for Lucien, the events of the previous night had been more rewarding than any diversion Monsieur might imagine.

This morning, everything was as it should be. No one could suspect last night of being extraordinary; no one could suspect the King had stayed awake all night seeking immortality. His Majesty performed the rituals of his awakening with his accustomed grace and dignity.

Lucien noted, with approval, that Yves de la Croix had ceased to spurn the privilege of fifth entry. The Jesuit bowed to His Majesty with adequate elegance. Lucien feared de la Croix had been brought too high too quickly, that his abrupt elevation would result in disaster for him and for his sister. Other men waited years for Fifth Entry.

Unlike His Majesty, de la Croix did look as if he had been up all night. Dark circles shadowed his eyes.

Perhaps the King had dozed since returning from the secret dissection, or perhaps he had lain awake considering the implications of Yves de la Croix's discoveries.

His Majesty might never die, Lucien thought. *If he never dies, the realm will never be subjected to Monseigneur's reign. If he never dies, he will escape the influence of Mme de Maintenon. He will reinstate the Edict of Nantes. He will cease making war on his own people.*

Lucien joined His Majesty's procession from the official bedchamber. The King's gout troubled him today, but he concealed his discomfort.

In the first chamber, dozens of less favoured courtiers crowded together. Inured to their magnificent surroundings, bored by the paintings and frescoes, the carved marble and the gilded representations of Apollo and the sun, they stood, yawning sleepily, gossiping, trading insults veiled as compliments. When His Majesty appeared, they fell silent and saluted their sovereign.

When they rose, Mlle de la Croix gazed at His Majesty, in awe, like the colonial girl she remained. Her cheeks flushed with excitement. Lucien sympathised with her amazement. He loved Louis, as he had loved Queen Marie Thérèse. He missed the queen; he still grieved for her, though she was ten years gone. Having spent most of his life at court, he knew better than to display everything he felt. He hoped Mlle de la Croix would learn, soon, not to reveal herself quite so plainly.

As he always did, Lucien left the procession when His Majesty approached the chapel.

As His Majesty disappeared into the chapel to perform his religious devotions, Lucien wondered, *Does immortality extend life into endless sickness and aging? Or . . . might it convey perfect health, and everlasting youth?*

Marie-Josèphe curtsied low with the other courtiers as His Majesty strode from his room. His brother and his son and his grandsons and the Foreign Princes Condé and Conti and Lorraine and the legitimised duke du Maine and the Chevalier de Lorraine and Count Lucien followed. In their brilliant company, Yves was as drab as a crow. She wished, sometimes, that he was a young courtier rather than a Jesuit, that he practiced war instead of learning, that he dressed in diamonds and silk.

But, then, she thought, *I would be even less a part of his life, and I would be nothing to his work, because he would have none. He would marry, his wife would manage his household, he would have no room for a spinster sister.*

She sighed, then thought, *I might not be a spinster, if he were not a priest. He would promote my marriage; our family might have the resources to allow it.*

She shrugged off her fantasies. As the King passed, people stepped forward to press letters into his hands, to beg him for favours, for pensions, for a position in his household. Even ordinary folk could petition him, as he paraded with his family on his way to Mass.

Mme de Maintenon and the other women of the royal family joined His Majesty. Marie-Josèphe surveyed Mademoiselle as she passed, criticising herself. She had not dressed Lotte's hair as beautifully as Odelette would have done.

A roar of greeting and affection rose from the crowd of visitors as soon as the King appeared. Lesser nobles, tradesmen and their wives, all those who presented themselves at the gate decently dressed, had the right to enter the chateau grounds and see their sovereign. The

155

crowd parted for him, but pressed close as soon as he had passed. Marie-Josèphe pushed through the crush of bodies, trying to keep her place, trying not to feel afraid.

'Your Majesty, a boon to ask—'

'Please, Your Majesty, heal my son—'

The procession paused as the King accepted the petitions of his subjects and passed the letters to Count Lucien. He laid his hand on the swollen throat of a child, when the mother begged for a cure for the King's Disease.

The crowded, echoing chapel was a relief after the crush of the courtyard. Marie-Josèphe took her place in the pew behind Madame's. Hugging her shawl close, Madame kissed Marie-Josèphe's cheek.

'Perhaps the new chapel will be warmer,' Madame said, but her tone was not very hopeful.

Marie-Josèphe had to smother a giggle. References to Hell freezing over often accompanied speculations about the new chapel's eventual completion. She wondered if hell, frozen, would be warmer than the old chapel. She wished she could tell Madame the joke. In her own way, Madame was very pious, but she loved God rather than the rituals and ceremonies of the church. She had been a heretic, a Protestant, in her youth; court gossips claimed her conversion was a fraud, entered into only to allow her to marry Monsieur.

Marie-Josèphe thought she might tell Count Lucien the joke, but Count Lucien was nowhere to be seen.

Yves joined Marie-Josèphe. She squeezed his arm fondly.

'Aren't you glad you attended His Majesty this morning? Was it wonderful, in his room? I wish I—'

'Shh,' he said gently.

The choir's voices, as one, rose to the frescoed ceiling. Marie-Josèphe shivered at the pure beauty of the singing.

Splendid new cloths draped the altar, and a thousand new wax candles burned in silver candelabra. Marie-Josèphe admired the altar, then turned with the rest of His Majesty's court to face the back of the chapel.

156

'What are you doing?' Yves whispered, horrified. He faced the altar, with a foolish expression of confusion.

Marie-Josèphe tugged at his sleeve. 'I should have explained,' she whispered. At Mass, His Majesty's court always faced him, while he faced the altar and the priest.

Yves resisted her, but yielded to the combined stares of Madame and the princes of the blood royal. He turned around.

Above, His Majesty arrived in his balcony at the rear of the chapel.

The King gazed down at his court, who worshipped him to worship God. With a gesture of elegant magnanimity, he directed them toward the altar. Obediently, respectfully, they all turned again, as His Holiness Pope Innocent XII came to the altar to conduct Mass.

Chapter 11

The coolness of the chateau gave way to the warmth of the terrace above the gardens. The sun had already sped halfway to noon. *It's warm today!* Marie-Josèphe thought gratefully.

Potted flowers traced the verges of the pathways; the blossoms of a thousand orange trees perfumed the air. Bees bumbled softly through the flower-embroidery.

The fountain mechanisms creaked and groaned, shivering the quiet into pieces. The fountains all burst into sprays and streams: Latona and Poseidon, Neptune, the dragons. Usually the fountains played only for His Majesty, but they would play continuously until after Carrousel.

People filled the gardens, flowing down the Green Carpet and pooling around the Fountain of Apollo and the sea monster's tent. They carried Marie-Josèphe like a stream, as if she were lighter than air.

The poor sea monster will be so hungry, Marie-Josèphe thought, *I did hope to feed her as soon as the servant brought the fish. But perhaps it's just as well. I induced her to eat from my hand . . .* Marie-Josèphe rubbed her sore wrist and thought, apprehensively, *If she's very hungry, perhaps I can induce her to obey me.*

Marie-Josèphe slipped past and between groups of visitors — mothers and fathers and children, elderly grandparents, two and three and even four generations marvelling at the magnificence of their King's home and the perfection of his gardens. Strolling through the soft, warm afternoon in their best clothes, husbands wearing rented swords, wives defying the sumptuary laws with daring silver lace at sleeve or petticoat, the children in leading-strings and ribbons, the townspeople of Versailles and Paris and every town in France hoped for a glimpse of Louis le Grand.

The rolled-up towel chafed Marie-Josèphe's legs.

Do I dare take the nuisance off until tomorrow? Marie-Josèphe wondered. *Uncomfortable business! Another of God's jokes, at which you can laugh only if you aren't the subject.*

At the convent, her confessor had been shocked when she asked about God's jokes. God performed miracles, and He meted out punishment — such as women's monthlies — but He did not play jokes.

How sad, Marie-Josèphe thought, *to be omnipotent, to be immortal, to possess no sense of humour.*

At the bottom of the slope, people shouted and clustered closer around the sea monster's tent. Marie-Josèphe snatched her skirt above her ankles and broke into a run, afraid something had happened to the creature.

'Wait your turn!' snarled a man in broadcloth and homespun as Marie-Josèphe tried to slip past him.

'Papa, Papa, I want the sea monster!' His young son pulled at his coattail. 'Papa, Papa!' The three other boys, all so young they were still in dresses, joined the cry. Their mother hushed her brood, without effect.

The tradesman turned; Marie-Josèphe could not be sure if he intended to slap her or the child who had started the appeal.

'Sir!'

Her velvet and lace protected her; she stood out in the crowd of visitors as a member of His Majesty's court.

'I beg your pardon, mademoiselle.' He stepped away, pulling his wife and the four young children with him. They vanished into the crowd, the eldest child still begging for the sea monster.

'Guard!' Marie-Josèphe called.

After a moment, one of the musketeers opened a way for her and led her through the crowd and into the open tent.

'What are you doing?' she asked. 'Why have you let everyone in?'

'His Majesty ordered it,' the musketeer said. 'His Majesty's subjects are to be allowed to see the monster.' The musketeers let the visitors file in through one open side of the tent. They looked at yesterday's sketches — not those from the secret dissection, which she had left safe in the chateau — and peered through the bars of the cage and exited through a second raised section of the tent wall.

159

The water lay as still as glass.

The musketeer ushered Marie-Josèphe through the gate of the cage to the edge of the fountain.

'There's nothing in the fountain but Apollo,' one of the visitors said.

'We cannot make the creature show itself,' the musketeer replied.

'Shoot at it, that will bring it out.'

'She's frightened,' Marie-Josèphe said. 'Wouldn't you be, if a thousand people clustered around your bed?'

'It doesn't bother His Majesty,' said the musketeer.

'The sea monster is a wild creature.'

'So it was said of His Majesty,' said the musketeer. 'In his youth.'

More live fish flapped and splashed. The servant had brought dozens of fish, far more than any person would eat for dinner, even if dinner were the only meal. Marie-Josèphe netted one. She smiled at the servant's wishful thinking, but grew solemn at the thought of his hunger.

'Sea monster! Fish, nice fish!' She swished the net around in the water.

Beneath the hooves of the dawn horses, the sea monster flicked her tails. A few visitors saw the movement and gasped. They shouted to each other, pointed, called out to Marie-Josèphe to show them more.

'Be quiet, I beg you,' she said. 'If you're quiet, she might come out of hiding.'

A ripple moved through the fountain. The sea monster's long dark hair streamed behind her, protecting her back from the sun, disguising her glowing copper skin. Marie-Josèphe took the fish from the net and held it in her hand.

The sea monster hesitated.

'Good sea monster. Come a little closer, come have your fish.'

'Fishhh!' the sea monster said.

The sea monster surfaced. Marie-Josèphe offered her the fish. She snatched it and gobbled it messily in several bites. Fish guts and bits of fin dribbled into the water.

The audience gasped and murmured in awe and surprise and disgust. Startled, the sea monster slipped back beneath the water. Marie-Josèphe hoped that in the time she had she could train the sea monster not to fear the noise. His Majesty would want to view the creature again; he would want to show off his quarry to the visiting heads of state. He would want the sea monster to be well behaved.

'It's all right, sea monster,' Marie-Josèphe said. 'The noise means nothing, no more than waves on a beach. It won't hurt you. Come, let me feed you another fish.'

If I wish her to trust me, I must trust her, Marie-Josèphe said to herself.

Marie-Josèphe dipped her hand into the water. The sea monster swam closer, radiating intense warmth.

The sea monster rose suddenly from the pool. Water splashed against the stairs. Her long tangled hair whipped around her bare shoulders, tumbling over her flat breasts. The paler green strand of hair stuck out at an awkward angle.

Visitors gasped and cried out and applauded. The musketeer clattered away to face the visitors, ready to bully or cajole them: The peace of the King's gardens must not erupt into riot. But instead of fleeing, the visitors pressed closer, fascinated, entertained. The lucky ones peered through the bars of the cage; the rest tried to see over the heads of the front rank.

The sea monster sank back into the water. Marie-Josèphe stroked the creature's hair. The sea monster suffered her touch. Marie-Josèphe reached back with her free hand; the musketeer handed her a netted fish. She offered the wriggling creature to the sea monster. The sea monster fumbled at the net, failing to extricate the fish.

Marie-Josèphe untwisted the fabric, pulled the fish from the opening, and handed it to the sea monster.

The sea monster ate the fish in two quick bites and looked around for more. Marie-Josèphe continued to feed her, luring her closer, till the sea monster slithered half out of the water and rested her elbows on the platform. The visitors whispered and murmured in awe.

Marie-Josèphe let the sea monster swim away, then called her back and gave her another fish. After three repetitions of the simple command, the sea monster floated just out of Marie-Josèphe's reach, singing, but coming no closer. Marie-Josèphe imagined that she should be able to understand the song, then chided herself.

I might as well try to understand a mockingbird, she thought.

'Come, sea monster!' she commanded.

The sea monster stopped singing. She snorted and spat and splashed water with her tail from ten feet away. She snarled. She swam no closer.

'You should beat it!' said the musketeer. 'Then it would obey.'

'I'd only frighten her,' Marie-Josèphe said. 'She'll not be beaten while she's in my charge.' She dangled the fish above the water. 'Come, sea monster—'

The sea monster kicked a wave toward the platform; it splashed Marie-Josèphe's shoes and the hem of her riding habit.

The sea monster sang a peremptory phrase, dove, and disappeared.

Why, Marie-Josèphe thought, *she's bored! She's learned the lesson already, why should she practice it?*

Instead of insisting that the sea monster return, Marie-Josèphe let the fish swim free, living prey. But after she had let it loose, she thought, *If the sea monster only obeys when she chooses, can I make any claim to have trained it?*

The sea monster surfaced, whistling, swimming at a distance. The audience exclaimed. She splashed her tails on the surface. She surged closer to Marie-Josèphe.

Marie-Josèphe rose. 'You may have more fish later, if you come when I call.' On a foolish whim she added, 'And an extra portion if you show yourself again to the visitors!' She smiled to herself, and thought, *If only creatures really were so easy to train.*

Lucien climbed the great stone staircase to Mme de Maintenon's apartment. Forced blooms glowed with fresh spring colours in gilded pots.

The guard opened one side of the double doors and bowed Lucien through Mme de Maintenon's doorway.

Mme de Maintenon furnished her apartment as austerely as a cell in a convent. No matter what gifts His Majesty lavished on her, she lived among drab colours. She refused flowers and jewels alike. Even His Majesty's council table was plain black lacquer with the most moderate gilt and inlay.

Lucien shrugged off the uneasiness that enclosed him in these

162

rooms. He could do nothing about the darkness, the drabness, or Mme de Maintenon's dislike of him, except to refuse to allow any of it to afflict him.

A single spot of colour brightened the room: a gleaming tapestry covered Mme de Maintenon's lap. Embroidered silk fell in thick soft folds like the fabric in a great master's canvas. Gold couching and intricate embroidery in red and orange and yellow, the colours of fire, covered all the silk but the central section.

Despite the room's close atmosphere, Mme de Maintenon nestled in her cushioned wicker chair, shielded from drafts by its woven sides. She placed careful stitches, covering the last bit of white with the colours of blood and sunlight.

Mme de Maintenon retained the exquisite complexion and the dark lustrous eyes that had made her a great beauty in her youth, but she had accepted age and increasing infirmity as Louis had not.

Lucien bowed. 'Mme de Maintenon.' He made it a matter of pride, even of arrogance, to speak to her always in a friendly and respectful manner. No matter what the provocation, no matter what opportunities she offered him – few enough, at that; she was no fool – he resisted exercising his wit against her. 'I trust you're well.'

'Well enough to do good works, sir,' she said. 'The ache of one's bones makes no difference there.'

She did not ask after his health or his family. She never did; and she had never, in his memory, spoken his title. No one else of his acquaintance found any irony in applying the title Count de Chrétien to an atheist.

'Winter approaches,' she said softly, 'and people will starve – but His Majesty spends the summer making war and the autumn creating entertainments. Oh – forgive me for mentioning my distress, you would not understand it.' She bent again to her embroidery.

Lucien regarded her with irritation and sympathy. She knew nothing of what he understood or believed; she never deigned to find out, for she knew what any atheist must think. The whole glorious autumn stretched ahead, yet she anticipated winter.

He wanted to say to her, Madame Scarron, was your life with your crippled late husband so dreadful? Did M. Scarron never spend a

163

moment attending to your pleasure, or amusing you with his cele-brated wit? If his infirmities prevented him from pleasuring you, could you find no moment of satisfaction in distracting him from his pain? Are you punishing my cherished sovereign in return?

But he did not say it; he would never say it. Not to the wife of his King.

'You are engaged in an intricate task,' he said, with a pang of unaccustomed wistfulness. The Queen used to embroider constantly – he treasured a handkerchief she had given him, though it was so covered with silk flowers that it was useless – for, in truth, the sweet sad fool-ish lady had no occupation, no place at her husband's court.

'It is a gift,' Mme de Maintenon said softly. She smoothed the white silk. She held it up for him to see.

People in torment writhed across satin. A man screamed from the rack; blood flowed from a woman's entrails as an Inquisitor drew her bowels from her body. The central figure, a wild-eyed man in medi-eval garb, twisted against the stake, flesh burning in the splash of scarlet silken flames.

Lucien inspected it without reacting. 'Free-thinkers, libertines, and dangerous heretics all.'

'My girls at Saint-Cyr embroidered it.'

'Strong images, madame, to inflict upon schoolgirls.'

'Exactly – strong, and instructive. While they worked, they con-sidered heresy, and disobedience and its consequences. I must finish it quickly.' She bent to the embroidery again, placing another scarlet stitch of fire. 'I usually do the eyes last. For this image I did them first.' She plunged the needle into the cloth. 'This is Éon de l'Étoile. Arch-heretic, the Leader of Satan's Army.'

'He was never burned,' Lucien said.

'Indeed, surely, he must have been. He made war upon the Church, he plundered monasteries, he called himself God's son—'

'He fed the peasants with the riches of the Church.'

'Riches he obtained by thievery and murder.'

'The Church imprisoned him, and he died,' Lucien said. L'Étoile had, of course, been a madman. 'His followers never denounced him. They were burned – but he was not.'

164

'I resign the field in favour of your intimate knowledge of a pagan land.' Mme de Maintenon fixed another flame at l'Étoile's feet. 'No matter. He should have been burned.'

'His Majesty the King!'

The guard threw open both doors for Louis. His Majesty hobbled in, favouring his gouty foot.

Lucien bowed to His Majesty; he acknowledged the greeting of Father de la Chaise and the profound salute of the marquis de Barbezieux. Louvois' vindictive and brutal son succeeded his father as the King's military adviser. Only once had he taken liberties when speaking to Lucien. In the face of the King's sudden indifference to his interests, he proved he was not entirely stupid: he begged the Count de Chrétien for forgiveness – and intercession.

Father de la Chaise always behaved with perfect courtesy to Lucien, hoping, futilely, to convert him and save his soul.

M. de Barbezieux carried his tooled leather campaign desk, while Father de la Chaise carried the Pope's gift, the reliquary, with great reverence.

Mme de Maintenon gasped. 'Sire, the saint's relic, it should be in the chapel, under guard—'

'Don't you want to look at it, Bignette?' His Majesty asked. 'Once Father de la Chaise takes it away, we will never see it except on the saint's day.'

She made as if to rise from her chair, then sank back within its protection. Father de la Chaise brought the reliquary to her. She whispered a prayer.

'It is beautiful.' She bit off the last strand of flame-coloured silk, and held out the tapestry to Father de la Chaise. 'Father de la Chaise, my girls made this – you must take it, so it may lie beneath His Holiness' precious gift.'

'That will be glorious, madame.'

Louis invited his advisers to sit at the council table. Father de la Chaise placed the domed cylinder before His Majesty. Louis idly caressed its chased gold sides and the pearls on its top.

'A rare gift from His Holiness,' Barbezieux said.

Lucien snorted with disgust. 'The saint had no use for the

relic . . . and His Majesty has no need of it. Or its cage.' He wondered what lunatic had first dismembered a body and enclosed it, bit by bit, in magic amulets.

Louis chuckled, then chided Lucien gently. 'None of your atheistic wit, Chrétien. Innocent has made peace with me. I shall assume he means no insult with his cage.'

His Majesty called for Quentin, his personal valet, who tasted the wine, poured for Barbezieux and de la Chaise, then for Lucien, and finally, when His Majesty's guests had also tasted the wine without being poisoned, for the King.

Barbezieux toyed with his goblet.

'Your health, Your Majesty.' Lucien drank, appalled by the young minister's rudeness, amused by his discomfiture. *He believes the slander*, Lucien thought, *that Mme de Maintenon poisoned his father. He fears the same.*

His Majesty accepted the wishes for his health, then drank from his own goblet and settled into work.

'Chrétien,' the King said, 'Brittany lacks a bishop. Were I to nominate one, His Holiness will invest him with the others, as soon as he signs the treaty. To whom do you wish the appointment offered?'

'To Nemo, Sire.'

His Majesty raised a questioning eyebrow. 'To no one?'

'If M. de Chrétien has no nominee, Your Majesty, the position and the revenue might best be given to—'

Lucien interrupted Father de la Chaise. 'It suits my family for the appointment to remain empty.' He finished his wine; Quentin poured again.

'Sir, you're trading the spiritual health of Brittany for a few bits of gold,' de la Chaise said. 'Your people need direction. Your family is sufficiently wealthy, and Brittany already bears the reputation—'

'Enough, sir. I asked for M. de Chrétien's suggestion, and he has given it. About my decision, I will see.'

A new bishop would send much of the revenue from his lands to Rome. Without a bishop's household and responsibilities to support, the parishioners would pay their taxes to His Majesty, and be left with something to eat after what threatened to be a poor harvest.

You're too proud for your own good, Lucien said to himself. *You neglect to explain yourself to His Majesty because you think Mme de Maintenon will give herself credit for your decision, because she might believe she shamed you into unaccustomed acts of charity.*

Explaining himself to His Majesty was unnecessary. Lucien's sovereign possessed great political astuteness; His Majesty often understood the motives of his subjects and his advisers before they understood themselves.

'What have you for me today, M. de Barbezieux?'

'Orders, Your Majesty, for quartering troops among the Protestants.' Barbezieux drew papers from his campaign desk.

'Very good.' Louis signed the documents. Barbezieux and de la Chaise looked on with approval. Already busy with another bit of needlework, Mme de Maintenon smiled.

Lucien said nothing, for nothing he could say would make Louis change his mind. He had already tried, harder than was prudent. The proposal was meant to hasten the conversion of the heretics, but as far as Lucien had seen, it had caused only disaster and treason and the enrichment of men who did not deserve any rewards. Yet instead of withdrawing the failed orders, the King extended them. His Majesty's intolerance – Mme de Maintenon's, as Lucien preferred to believe – prevented him from seeing how severely the draconian measures against Protestants damaged France and His Majesty himself.

It's easier to be an atheist, Lucien thought. *And less dangerous. The King's troops do not have permission to quarter themselves in my house, to loot it, to abuse without limit the members of my household.*

'Is that all? Good day, then, gentlemen,' the King said to Barbezieux and de la Chaise. 'M. de Chrétien, you will stay for a glass of wine.'

Barbezieux and de la Chaise bowed and withdrew.

Quentin refilled His Majesty's goblet, and Lucien's. Mme de Maintenon refused refreshment. Lucien sipped the wine; it was too fine a vintage to gulp even for medicinal purposes.

His Majesty closed his eyes, revealing for a moment his exhaustion, his age.

'Give me some simple task, M. de Chrétien,' His Majesty said. 'Nothing to do with statecraft or religion. Something I may grant with a purse, with a wave of my hand.'

'There's the matter of Father de la Croix, Your Majesty. The dissection.'

'Did he not complete it?'

'He completed the important part, Your Majesty. Apparently some few small muscles and sinews remain for him to observe.'

'His first attention must be to the matter we investigated last night.'

'Of course, Your Majesty.'

His Majesty waved his hand. 'Otherwise, as his time permits, he may do as he likes with the carcass.'

'I will tell him, Your Majesty. He'll be grateful.'

They sipped their wine in companionable silence, as if they were campaigning or at Marly, where etiquette weighed less heavily.

'You trouble me, M. de Chrétien,' His Majesty said.

'Trouble you, Sire?'

'You ask me for nothing.'

'No wonder I trouble you, Sire,' Lucien said. 'Nothing is difficult to give, being so insubstantial.'

His Majesty chuckled, but would not be diverted. 'All around me people beg for rank, for position, for pensions. For themselves, for worthless family members.'

Lucien wondered if he were being used to convey a message to Mme de Maintenon, who had obtained endless perquisites for her feckless brother. It was equally likely – more likely – that His Majesty spoke without considering her feelings.

'I'm afraid, M. de Chrétien, that if you are dissatisfied, you'll flee my court again to the adventures of Arabia.'

'I have no reason to return to Arabia, Your Majesty,' Lucien said. 'I went there only because you commanded me to leave your sight.'

'I often wished for your good counsel, while you were gone. Will you not take some reward, if only a token?'

You have given me a place in your confidence, Lucien thought, *which honours me beyond wealth or rank.*

'Your Majesty, I ask for nothing more than I already have.'

'Someday, Chrétien, you'll ask me for a great favour. My honour will require me to grant it, whatever the cost.'

Marie-Josèphe closed up the cage and crossed the plank floor to Yves' laboratory. The guards had moved the screens, surrounding it, hiding the shroud and protecting the equipment and the samples. She slipped past the curtains. Inside, everything was just as Yves had left it. Marie-Josèphe breathed a sigh of relief. His Majesty had not bothered to tell her brother that the sea monster would be put on display – for, after all, why should he? It was his sea monster. And he had, no doubt, been certain that his guards would protect the laboratory from casual curiosity or inadvertent damage.

The shroud was piled with fresh ice and a layer of sawdust. A hint of decay tinged the air. If His Majesty would only give Yves a single session, he could complete the gross dissection and preserve samples for study.

She sat at the laboratory table. The sea monster's internal organs, including the anomalous lobe of the creature's lung, lay preserved in spirits in heavy glass jars. The tissue looked quite ordinary, no different from that of the porpoise she had helped Yves dissect when they found it stranded and dead on the beach back home.

Shouldn't an organ of immortality shine with light and glow with gold? Marie-Josèphe wondered. *If the precepts of alchemy are true, after all, if base metals may transmute to the perfect metal gold, if living beings may achieve immortality . . .*

She had never believed in transmutation or immortality. The discipline of observation and description and deduction and interaction spoke to her more clearly.

She prepared samples of kidney and liver, pancreas and lung, mounted them, and made a careful drawing of each, studying them with Yves' old microscope. The sea voyage had done the mechanism no good. She hoped Mynheer van Leeuwenhoek would condescend to sell her one of his instruments. His lenses were said to be the best in the world, though devilishly difficult to focus.

She opened the final jar and carefully prepared a sample of the anomalous lung. Its texture was firmer than ordinary lung, its tissue denser.

At the microscopic level, the anomalous tissue differed greatly from ordinary lung. Instead of air sacs, the tissue lay in delicate overlapping leaves. She picked up her pen and began to draw.

'Mlle de la Croix.'

She lifted her gaze from the microscope. Count Lucien stood within the makeshift room of white silk, aloof and elegant as always. They exchanged salutes; he not only bowed, but tipped his hat.

'I see you are a scholar,' he said.

'I cannot claim such a distinction. I'm only preparing samples for Yves to study.'

'Where is your brother? I have a message for him.'

'I'm sure he's writing up his notes—'

She cut off her careless words even before he raised his hand to silence her about last night's secret meeting.

'—about the other matter,' she said. 'Has His Majesty set the time of the next dissection? Please, tell me.'

'His Majesty desires your brother to concentrate his efforts upon . . . the other matter. But inasmuch as his time allows, M. de la Croix may conduct the dissection when His Majesty is not present.'

'Thank you, Count Lucien.'

'I'll convey your gratitude to His Majesty.'

'You see? – I didn't ask too much of you, after all.'

'I'd gladly take credit if I deserved it. The decision rested completely with His Majesty. But, Mlle de la Croix, have I asked too much of you?'

'In what way?'

'The submission for His Majesty's medal.'

'It's nearly finished.' *I'm not lying*, she thought, hiding her dismay. *Not exactly lying. The dissection sketches have prepared me to draw a proper likeness of the living sea monster.*

'When may I have it?'

'Tomorrow. I promise.'

'Very well.'

'Sir, may I beg a favour of you? A word of advice? It will take a moment of your time, no more.'

'Certainly.'

'Before I entered the convent—' She stopped, and waved her words away; Count Lucien had no time to spare for her history. 'I would like to resume a correspondence . . .' She hesitated, afraid he might laugh at her presumption.

'With an admirer?' He smiled, in a kindly fashion. 'Secret letters?'

'Certainly not, sir! It would be improper – my brother wouldn't approve. I corresponded about optics, and the laws of motion, and asked a few ignorant questions about the nature of gravity. I only want to know who to give the letter to, so M. Newton will receive it.'

'M. Newton,' he said.

'Yes, sir.'

'The Englishman.'

'The mathematician and philosopher.'

Count Lucien chuckled. Marie-Josèphe blushed.

'I'm sorry you think it absurd, that a mere woman dare approach a man of—'

'I don't think it absurd at all.' He shook his head. 'If your brother's reaction to an admirer concerns you, you'd not wish to witness His Majesty's reaction to an English correspondent. No matter how learned.'

'It's only a letter about a curious mathematical problem.'

'Mlle de la Croix. By writing to M. Newton, you'd put yourself in danger. I have no doubt you'd put M. Newton in danger as well. We are at war with England. Do you trust a censor to understand your curious mathematical problem? More likely, he'd judge your letter to be in cipher, and your M. Newton to be a spy.'

'As the nuns judged me to be writing spells,' she said.

'I beg your pardon?'

'Nothing. I'd never wish to put M. Newton in danger. I'm so sorry, I didn't realise—'

'You should never have to,' he said, with sympathy. 'It would be better if we weren't at war, if you could carry on your correspondence without concern. I regret to tell you, it isn't possible.'

171

'Thank you for your good advice,' she said, downcast.

'Pardon me, I must take my leave.'

'Count Lucien . . .'

He glanced back.

'Will my letter to Mynheer van Leeuwenhoek cause any difficulty for him?'

Count Lucien gave her a long look of disbelief, listened to her explanation of dashing off her request and entrusting it to an officer of the ship from Martinique, told her that he hoped the letter might have been lost, and said he would see if anything could be done.

In response to her thanks, Count Lucien bowed and left the makeshift room.

Marie-Josèphe stared at the laboratory table, distressed, grateful to Count Lucien for saving her from another misstep, angry that an innocent exchange of knowledge might be considered treason.

A cheer rose outside. Marie-Josèphe peeked out, expecting to see the visitors salute Count Lucien, who so often dispensed the King's alms. But the count had already ridden away. Instead, the visitors crowded around the sea monster's cage, cheering again in response to a splash and a trill of song.

The sea monster's song, such a constant sound that she hardly noticed it while she was working, had been going on for some time. So had the applause.

The sea monster is showing herself to the visitors! Marie-Josèphe thought, delight overshadowing her distress. *I've succeeded in gentling her, she's no longer frightened of people.*

She wanted to show off the sea monster's trick of coming when she was called, but she could not delay telling her brother Count Lucien's good news. She stepped out of the laboratory tent.

The sun had reached its zenith. If she did not hurry, she would be late to help Mademoiselle dress for His Majesty's picnic at the Menagerie. She ran out of the tent and hurried up the Green Carpet, passing groups of people strolling down the slope toward the Fountain of Apollo and the sea monster.

Chapter 12

By the time Marie-Josèphe reached Mademoiselle's apartments, she was out of breath and damp with sweat. She hesitated in the cold shadows of the corridor until her breathing eased, then indicated her presence by tapping her fingernails on the door.

'Marie-Josèphe!'

Lotte ducked from beneath Mlle d'Armagnac's attempt to rearrange her hair and emerged from the bright crowd of ladies-in-waiting and friends. She raised Marie-Josèphe from her curtsy.

'You must help – my hair has driven Mlle d'Armagnac to tears. Where's your girl? She's such a wonder! Where have you been?'

'Tending to the sea monster, Mademoiselle.'

'Make a lackey throw it a fish. Send for little Odelette, will you? And – your dress! You can't attend His Majesty's luncheon in your riding habit!'

Lotte's ladies-in-waiting, all beautifully gowned for His Majesty's luncheon, arranged Mademoiselle's grand habit and petticoats and polished her jewels with silk handkerchiefs.

'I'm responsible for the sea monster, Mademoiselle. My brother charged me with keeping it and studying it.'

'What good will studying it do? My dear silly thing, next you'll be speaking Latin and reciting lectures on the planets like those boring old sticks from the Academy.'

I'd love to hear such a lecture, Marie-Josèphe thought – *and to know I still remember my Latin!*

'Odelette is ill, Mademoiselle. Your hair looks beautiful. I cannot do better than Mlle d'Armagnac.'

'Shall I call the barber to see your girl? Perhaps she should be bled.'

'Perhaps she should be whipped,' said Mlle d'Armagnac, annoyed to have her talents at enhancing beauty compared unfavourably to those of a servant. 'Isn't that what you do to lazy slaves, in the wild colonies?'

173

'No!'

Marie-Josèphe told the lie without a second thought because Mlle d'Armagnac made her angry, because her own family's slaves had never been whipped, and because Odelette would never be whipped if Marie-Josèphe had anything to say about it. Nor would she be bled.

'Please, no, Mademoiselle, this is—' Marie-Josèphe could not bring herself to tell the King's niece that Odelette always bled too heavily for her health. 'It's an old complaint.'

'Ah,' said Lotte, 'it's like that, is it?'

'She'll be better this evening or tomorrow. I'll tend to her as soon as you're dressed.'

'You'll do no such thing,' Lotte said, 'you'll attend me, and go to the picnic.'

'But—'

'Shh!' Lotte called for a servant to take broth and warm flannel to Odelette.

'And to remind my brother of the luncheon, if you please, Mademoiselle. His work engrosses him so.'

'If we cannot whip the slave for dereliction, perhaps we can whip the brother,' Mlle d'Armagnac said, and all the ladies giggled at her daring wit.

'Of course, fetch Father de la Croix.' To Marie-Josèphe she said, 'You both must see the Menagerie.'

'Mademoiselle, I haven't anything to wear.'

Lotte laughed, threw open her cupboard, pulled out dresses, and chose a beautiful brocade. Marie-Josèphe might have been in a whirlwind for all the power she had: Lotte's other ladies stripped her to her shift and stays and dressed her in the new gown, leaving her only a moment to blush furiously, fearing they might notice the rolled-up towel. She wished she had risked taking it off, for as yet it had been of no use.

'This is my best court gown from last summer,' Lotte said. 'I was a little thinner, and you're not so scrawny as some fashionable ladies – lace it up, it will look fine! Now, you mustn't bother that it's a year old, with this season's petticoat no one will notice.'

Marie-Josèphe doubted that. She was grateful for Lotte's generosity, but she wondered, shamed by her envy, if she would ever have a new dress of her own.

Mademoiselle's carriage rumbled down the road toward His Majesty's Menagerie. Marie-Josèphe sat beside Lotte, squeezed in among the other ladies in their full court dresses. Weariness overtook her. She tried to recall when she had last eaten, when she had last slept.

The gilded gates of the Menagerie swung open. The sound and smell of exotic animals filled the courtyard. Chartres, on horseback, accompanied by Duke Charles, met Lotte and escorted her through the gates toward the central octagonal dome. Marie-Josèphe followed with the other ladies, noticing their significant glances, hearing their whispers about the attraction between Mademoiselle and the Foreign Prince.

They climbed to the balconies overlooking the animal pens. Cages of birds from the New World decorated the passageway: Bright screeching parrots and macaws, and hummingbirds that shrieked even more loudly.

At the central dome, servants held aside sheer white curtains. His Majesty's guests stepped into a jungle.

Drifts of orchids covered the walls and ceiling, hot with colour and lush as flesh. Scarlet tanagers and cardinals screamed and fluttered on the branches, not caged, but entrapped with silken threads around their legs. A few had broken free and flew madly back and forth. Gamekeepers rushed back and forth as madly as the birds, trying to capture them before they soiled the food, trapping them in bags, tying them more tightly to the branches of the orchids.

The central dome was filled with tables laden with baked peacocks, their iridescent tails spread wide, with bowls of oranges and figs, roast hare, ham, and every sort of sweet and pastry. Marie-Josèphe could hardly bring herself to pass; the scents made her mouth water. Dizzy, she followed Mademoiselle past the curtain onto one of the balconies overlooking the animal enclosures.

A more pungent odour overwhelmed the smell of the food. In the tiny stone enclosure beneath them, a tiger paced two steps, flung itself around, paced two steps back. It stopped, looked upward, snarled, and

175

launched itself toward Marie-Josèphe. Its claws scraped the wall beneath the balcony railing. Lotte and the other ladies shrieked. Marie-Josèphe caught her breath in terror, frozen by the tiger's glare.

On the ground again, the tiger growled and paced and jerked its tail and sprayed a cloud of acrid musk, the hot juniper reek of cat spray. The other ladies giggled, pretending to be frightened, pretending to be shocked. They had all been here a hundred times before.

'Did it frighten you?' Lotte asked. 'It frightened me the first time I saw it.'

'It doesn't frighten me,' Chartres said. He pitched a purloined orange at the furious tiger. The tiger swatted at its flank as if at a mosquito, catching the orange with its claw, ripping it in half, crushing it against the ground.

'I thought nothing could frighten you!' Lotte said to Marie-Josèphe. 'I thought you'd pull off one of its whiskers to study.'

'I'd never pull the whisker off such a creature.'

'Are its claws so much sharper than the sea monster's?'

'Sharper – and it has bigger teeth. It wouldn't sing to me when I spoke to it!'

The ladies laughed. As if she had commanded it, music sparkled upward from the grotto beneath the octagonal tower.

'The musicians are in the grotto.' Lotte whispered, 'It's full of water pipes – if you know where the faucets are, you can soak anyone who walks through! My uncle the King used to douse anyone who dared enter. Such fun!'

The tiger diverted her from the fun. It hurled itself at the dividing wall between its compound and the next. The camels lurched away, grunting and spitting with fear. The stench of their shit mixed with the tiger's scent-mark. Their fear aroused the lions in the next compound. The lions roared and the tiger challenged them; the camels huddled in the centre of their enclosure. On the other side of the dome the elephant trumpeted in fury. An ancient aurochs, its red hide turned roan with age, tossed its wide horns and bellowed continuously. Leashed birds – bluebirds and bluejays – on the balcony shrieked and beat their wings. Torn feathers fluttered to the ground.

In the distance, the sea monster cried out in answer.

On the circle of balconies overlooking the enclosures, courtiers shouted and applauded. Chartres was not the only one to torment the creatures with oranges, or stones.

Everyone, even the animals, suddenly fell silent.

His Majesty had arrived.

All the court gathered in the central dome: the men, bareheaded, nearest His Majesty; the women at the back of the group, conscious of the honour, for women did not usually attend His Majesty's public dinner. Marie-Josèphe looked for her brother, but Yves was nowhere to be seen. The bound birds cried and beat their wings. A cardinal broke free, hit the curtain like a powder-puff, fell stunned, recovered in mid-air, flew into the curtain again, and tumbled to the floor, its neck broken. A servant scooped it up and out of His Majesty's sight.

His Majesty sat alone at a small, elegant table beneath an arch of scarlet and gold orchids; Monsieur stood nearby with his napkin. The most favoured courtiers served his food: Count Lucien poured his wine. His Majesty ate as he performed every task: calmly, majestically, deliberately. He gazed straight forward, chewing steadily through course after course of his first meal of the day: a platter of thick soup, fish, partridge, ham and beef, a plate of salad.

After the partridge, His Majesty turned to Monsieur.

'Will you be seated, brother?'

Monsieur bowed low; a servant hurried to bring a chair of ebony and mother-of-pearl. Monsieur sat beside his brother, facing him, holding his napkin ready.

When His Majesty had finished his ham, he glanced toward M. du Maine, standing in the front row with Monseigneur the Grand Dauphin and the legitimate grandsons.

'M. du Maine, the weather is fine for Carrousel, is it not?'

M. du Maine replied with a bow even deeper than Monsieur's. The legitimate son watched the bastard favourite with a foolish expression of transparent envy.

His Majesty ate alone. Out of respect for the King, Marie-Josèphe resisted the temptation to pilfer a bit of meat from the tables behind her. No one paid her any mind; if she dared, she could take the edge off her hunger. She might also find herself curtsying and trying to fashion a proper greeting through a mouthful of food. She imagined Count Lucien's disapproval. She would die of embarrassment.

But I'm hungry enough to eat one of the sea monster's fish, she thought. *Alive. Wriggling*.

His Majesty finished, put down his knife, wiped his mouth, and dipped his fingers into a bowl of spirits of wine to clean them. When he rose, all his court bowed.

An instant later – as if by coincidence, but surely by careful plan – Pope Innocent, with his retinue of Bishops, Cardinals, and Yves, paraded into the dome. The courtiers bowed again.

'Cousin, welcome,' His Majesty said.

His Majesty, accompanied by his brother and his sons and grandsons, and His Holiness, accompanied by his bishops and cardinals and his French Jesuit, strolled together out of the hexagonal room onto the balcony overlooking the lion's enclosure. The musicians on the balcony – several strings and a harpsichord – struck up a bright tune.

His Majesty's ravenous courtiers set to.

'Mlle de la Croix, may I offer you your second glass of wine?' Lorraine, looking particularly elegant, loomed above her. Marie-Josèphe admired his smile, his eyes, his new brocade waistcoat.

'You're too late for that,' she said. His eyes widened and he made one quick bark of laughter. She became frightfully aware of the daring cut of her bodice. 'I would like a glass of wine, sir, thank you.'

He brought wine, plump strawberries from the greenhouse, sliced cold peacock, the grease congealed beneath its skin.

He caressed her shoulder, her collarbone, with a peacock feather. The feather moved down her breast. She stepped away. Lorraine put the feather in her hair, so it draped along the side of her face and down her back.

'Exquisite,' he said.

Marie-Josèphe sipped her wine. It tasted of summer, of sunlight, of flowers. The wine went directly to her head. Lotte had strolled onto the balcony of the giraffes with Duke Charles, leaving Marie-Josèphe with the chevalier, the duke's older, poorer, lower-ranking, but much more handsome relative. Lorraine stroked her cheek; he slid his hand beneath her simply-dressed hair and caressed the back of

178

her neck. She shivered. Intrigued, surprised, she let herself relax against his touch. He leaned toward her. Frightened, she slipped from beneath his hand.

The chevalier de Lorraine laughed softly.

Nearby, Count Lucien drank wine with the flawlessly beautiful Mlle de Valentinois, Mme de la Fère, and Mlle d'Armagnac. Mlle d'Armagnac flirted so outrageously that Marie-Josèphe felt outraged on Count Lucien's behalf.

'Chrétien has parted from Mlle Past,' Lorraine said, 'and Mme Present departs soon; he stands poised on the brink of Mlle Future.'

'I don't understand you, sir.'

'Do you not?' He smiled. 'Pay them no mind – Chrétien has too much to teach you, and Mlle Future has too little.'

The chevalier moved in front of her and drew her toward him. Marie-Josèphe found herself gazing into his eyes.

'Have you had smallpox?' the Chevalier asked.

'Why – yes, sir,' Marie-Josèphe said, astonished by the question. 'When I was very little.'

'Then you are beautiful,' he said. 'As beautiful as you appear.'

'Mlle de la Croix.'

Marie-Josèphe started, nearly spilling her wine on the Master of Ceremonies. Lorraine chuckled and took his hand from her neck.

'His Majesty asks you to play a tune.'

'If I—? Sir, play for His Majesty? I cannot!'

Lorraine pressed her gently forward. 'Of course you can. You must.'

Flustered, overwhelmed, Marie-Josèphe followed the Master of Ceremonies to the lion balcony. She curtsied low. His Majesty smiled and raised her to her feet.

'Mlle de la Croix!' he exclaimed. 'More beautiful than ever – and with a sensible hair ornament. It would please me to hear you play.'

She curtsied again. Yves looked troubled. His Holiness regarded her without expression. Behind them, M. Coupillet stood with his back turned, facing his musicians. He did not acknowledge her. Courtiers emerged from the jungle, gathering on the balcony behind her. One dishevelled agitated yellow finch arrowed through the doorway, gold silk threads streaming from its claws. It disappeared.

179

Little Master Domenico jumped up from the harpsichord and bowed chivalrously to Marie-Josèphe.

'Thank you, Master Domenico.' She could not help but smile, though she dreaded playing after his prowess at the keyboard. She had practiced a little at Saint-Cyr, but for five years before that she had been forbidden to touch any instrument.

Marie-Josèphe seated herself. She touched the ebony keys; they flowed like silk against her fingertips.

She played. She made a mistake; her fingers tangled. She stopped, her cheeks blazing hot.

She began again.

The music rippled around her like waves, like wind, like clouds. The sea monster's songs touched her heart, touched her fingertips, touched the keys of the magnificent instrument she controlled.

The music ended. She sat before the harpsichord like a supplicant, praying. She trembled. She hardly had the strength to lift her hands.

'Charming,' His Majesty said. 'Perfectly charming.'

More drunk with attention than with wine, Marie-Josèphe ran up the narrow stairs to her attic room. The peacock feather tickled her neck. The towel rubbed her inner thighs raw.

Her room was stuffy, but a candle glowed beside the bed. Odelette bent over a meringue of lace and ribbons, a new headdress.

'It's so dark in here!'

'I was cold, so I closed the curtains.'

'The afternoon sun will shine in now, and warm you.' Marie-Josèphe opened the curtains, flooding the room with light. Hercules leaped onto the window seat.

A servant scratched at the door – two servants, one returning her riding habit from Mademoiselle's apartment, the other bringing bread and soup and wine. Marie-Josèphe gave each serving man a sou and sent them away with the empty broth bowl, and pretended not to notice their amazed disgust at her pitiable gratuity.

'I'm so glad you're feeling better,' Marie-Josèphe said to Odelette. She stuck the peacock feather into a curlicue of the mirror frame.

'I feel worse,' Odelette said. Her voice quivered. Tears streaked her cheeks. Marie-Josèphe sat on the edge of the bed, as if her slave were a great lady receiving callers.

'What's wrong?'

'Mignon said you'd beat me. She said you said I'm lazy.'

'I never would! I didn't! You aren't!'

'She said—' Odelette repeated a garbled version of Marie-Josèphe's exchange with Mlle d'Armagnac.

'Oh, my dear . . .' She took the unfinished fontanges from Odelette's hands. 'Do you need a clean towel?' Odelette nodded. Marie-Josèphe fetched fresh cotton and put the blood-stained cloths in cold water to soak.

'Mlle d'Armagnac made a stupid remark.' Marie-Josèphe tore the bread into bits and soaked it in the soup. 'So I said I'd tear her hair out if she ever tried to beat you.'

Odelette ate a bite of bread. 'You didn't!'

'No,' Marie-Josèphe admitted. 'But I did say you'd not be beaten – and I would tear her hair out.'

Odelette managed to smile. Marie-Josèphe dampened a cloth with rose-water, wiped away Odelette's tears, and helped her drink a cup of wine.

'Can you help me with these buttons, just for a moment?' Marie-Josèphe asked. 'Are you able?' She slipped out of Lotte's beautiful gown and back into her riding habit, putting aside the uncomfortable towel until tomorrow.

I've changed clothes as often as the King! she thought, though she reminded herself that he always changed into new clothes, while she only changed back and forth.

Odelette did up the buttons on Marie-Josèphe's riding habit, while eyeing the gown.

'It's out of fashion,' Odelette said, 'but I could make something of it.'

'You are so dear. You aren't to touch it until you feel better. Now, lie down. Hercules, come! Odelette needs a tummy-warmer.' Hercules, lying upside-down in the sun with his legs splayed in an undignified manner, blinked, rolled over, stretched, and leaped to the bed.

Marie-Josèphe tucked the covers around Odelette and fed her soup and bread.

'How could you think I'd beat you?'

'We've been apart for so long. I thought, perhaps Mlle Marie has changed.'

'I'm sure I have, but not like that. We've all changed, all three of us.'

'Will it be as it was?'

'It will be better.'

Marie-Josèphe trudged down the Green Carpet. The lovely path became longer each time she trod it, like a magical road with no end. She listened for the sea monster, but a concert near the fountain of Neptune overwhelmed other sounds. She passed few visitors; they had gathered on the other side of the garden, near Neptune, to enjoy the concert and the ballet His Majesty had been pleased to order for his subjects.

In the tent, ice melted into puddles around the dissection table and dripped loudly into the silence.

Yves stood at the laboratory table, sharpening his scalpels. Servants dug chipped ice away from the dead sea monster.

'Sister, I won't want your help today.'

'What?' she cried. 'Why?'

'Because I must dissect the parts that are improper for public view. I shall ask the ladies not to attend.'

Marie-Josèphe laughed. 'Every other statue at Versailles is nude! If human nakedness is no mystery, why should anyone bother about a creature's?'

'I won't dissect it before ladies. Nor will you draw it.'

'Then who will?'

'Chartres.'

Marie-Josèphe was offended. 'He draws the way you compose! I've drawn the sex of animals for you, a hundred times—'

'When we were children. When I didn't know any better than to allow it.'

'Next you'll say, I should put breeches on my horse.' His indignant

182

expression amused her so, she could not help but tease him. 'And then you'll say, no lady should ride a horse, that isn't wearing breeches!'

'Ladies wearing breeches?' Count Lucien said.

Count Lucien approached from the entrance of the tent. A servant followed, carrying an ornately framed portrait of the King. The servant placed the portrait on the King's armchair, bowed deeply to it, and backed away as if it were His Majesty himself.

'Horses wearing breeches,' Marie-Josèphe said.

'Odd fashions you have on Martinique.' Count Lucien swept off his hat and bowed to the portrait.

'Horses don't wear breeches on Martinique!' Yves said.

'Forgive us, Count Lucien. I've teased my brother cruelly and he is out of temper. How are you?'

'I'm in a remarkably good mood for a man who spent an hour arguing with the censors of the Black Cabinet.'

He handed her a letter.

'What is it?'

'Your correspondence from Mynheer van Leeuwenhoek.'

'Count Lucien, you are a treasure.'

His shrug encompassed the diplomacy he had employed to liberate the letter from His Majesty's spies.

She read the Latin: Mynheer van Leeuwenhoek, intrigued by the interest of a young French gentleman in his work, regretted the impossibility of selling any of his instruments—

For a moment she thought he referred to Yves; but she had written on her own behalf.

Perhaps M. van Leeuwenhoek, who is no doubt a heretic, she thought, *mistook my confirmation name for my Christian name.*

Disappointed, she continued.

—but, once the regrettable hostilities between their respective governments had ended, Mynheer van Leeuwenhoek would be pleased to invite M. de la Croix to visit his workshop.

Marie-Josèphe sighed, and smiled sadly at Count Lucien. 'I'll not be expecting contraband, after all,' she said. *Nor*, she thought, *any obscene Dutch broadsheets. It's wicked of me*, she thought, *but I would like to see them.*

183

'I know it,' he replied, then added, in response to her surprise, 'I beg your pardon, Mlle de la Croix, but I was obliged to read the letter, in order to explain to the censors why you should be allowed to have it.'

'Thank you, sir. Do you see? I ask only what you can give.'

Count Lucien bowed.

Count Lucien spoke to the servants; they rearranged the silken screens to reveal the dissection table to the audience, but conceal it from the living sea monster.

Marie-Josèphe thought, *Count Lucien would concern himself with the sea monster's distress only if its crying will disturb the King!*

'Is His Majesty coming after all?' She clapped her hands to her hair, which had begun to escape its pins.

'He is here,' Count Lucien said, nodding toward the portrait. 'This once, he will not notice your coiffure.'

M. Coupillet, the music-master, shouldered past visitors coming in to watch the dissection.

'A moment of your sister's time, Father.'

'She is already occupied, sir,' Yves said.

'I am anxious, Father de la Croix,' M. Coupillet said. 'I am anxious, M. de Chrétien. Mlle de la Croix, I say that I am anxious. We must discuss the cantata.'

'I've begun it – I can work on it at night.'

'You'll be busy, Mlle de la Croix,' Count Lucien said. 'Composition at night, decomposition during the day.'

Marie-Josèphe laughed.

'Will you need an instrument?' Count Lucien asked.

'Of course she needs an instrument,' M. Coupillet exclaimed. 'No wonder she's done no work! Do you think she's able to compose entirely in her mind?'

'May I beg the use of a harpsichord?' Marie-Josèphe kept her attention on Count Lucien, afraid she would be rude to M. Coupillet.

'Whatever you require – it's His Majesty's wish.'

'A very small harpsichord, sir, if you please – it's a very small sitting room.'

'Sister, bring your drawing box,' Yves said to Marie-Josèphe. 'We will begin.'

She curtsied quickly to Count Lucien and to the portrait of the King. She hurried to her place, relieved that Yves had given up the idea of sending her away. She wished he would send M. Coupillet away.

M. Coupillet followed her. 'If I may suggest – allow me to oversee the cantata's progress.' He averted his gaze from the dead sea monster. 'You are, after all, an amateur and a woman. Without my help, you risk offending His Majesty with incompetent work.'

'You needn't defile your talent by lending it to my poor efforts,' Marie-Josèphe said. She was nervous enough about failing the King's commission without being insulted.

'There, there, Mlle de la Croix, how can you berate me for seeking your gratitude? You tax your intelligence with natural philosophy, with music – why, next you'll wish to study the classics! No wonder you're confused and exhausted.'

'Even in France,' Count Lucien said, 'many would say women cannot excel as artists, as scholars—'

Marie-Josèphe looked away, hoping to hide her shock.

'Do you see, Mlle de la Croix, M. de Chrétien agrees—'

'So would they say,' Count Lucien said, to Marie-Josèphe, 'no dwarf can ride to war.'

M. Coupillet drew himself to his full, outraged height. Count Lucien merely smiled at him with sympathetic condescension. The music master wilted, stepped back, and made a stiff bow.

'Good day, mademoiselle,' Count Lucien said.

'Good day, Count Lucien,' Marie-Josèphe said, amazed with gratitude that he had compared her intellectual endeavors to his own exploits at Steenkirk and Neerwinden. 'Thank you for everything.'

Count Lucien departed, pausing to bow, and to sweep the plumes of his hat across the floor, before His Majesty's portrait.

'Your attention,' Yves said, 'if you please.'

'Yes, I'm ready. Good day, M. Coupillet, I cannot spare you any more time.'

'Ladies of delicate temperament may wish to avoid this demonstration.' Yves exposed the genital area of the sea monster.

A few gentlewomen left, along with M. Coupillet. The rest stayed, leaning their heads together to whisper and laugh at Yves' scruples.

At sunset, a footman respectfully carried away the portrait of the King; the open tent emptied of spectators. Marie-Josèphe finished a last sketch of the sea monster's generative organs, now dissected out of the smooth furry pouch that had held them protected within the creature's body. Exposed, they resembled the male organs of the marble statues lounging in the gardens of Versailles.

Yves went away to write up his notes, leaving Marie-Josèphe to arrange the shroud, and direct the replacement of ice and sawdust, and feed the living sea monster.

When everyone else had left, Marie-Josèphe unlocked the cage and netted a fish. Red-gold sunlight doubly gilded Apollo and his horses.

'Sea monster!'

The sun fell below the horizon, leaving soft dusk behind. In silence, a footman arrived, lit the candles, and departed. A damp breeze fluttered the flames. The tent flapped. Marie-Josèphe shivered. The guards hurried around the tent, closing its open sides. The breeze stopped.

The sea monster whistled.

Marie-Josèphe swished the net through the water.

'Sea monster! Fishhh!'

An arrow of ripples streaked across the fountain.

The sudden warmth of menstrual blood pressed out and dribbled between Marie-Josèphe's legs, stinging her raw skin.

A blasphemy passed her lips that, a month ago, never would have crossed her mind. Once again, as usual, even about inconvenient matters, Odelette was right. Marie-Josèphe's impatience with the bother had made her foolish.

I'll feed the sea monster quickly and then run back up the hill, Marie-Josèphe thought. *And beg Odelette's pardon if I've stained my petticoat. I mustn't stain my skirt! Poor Odelette despairs of saving the silver petticoat, and I cannot afford to spoil more clothes.*

The sea monster surfaced. Marie-Josèphe stroked her hair. The sea monster screamed and splashed backwards.

Marie-Josèphe waved the desperately wriggling fish back and forth, trying to distract the sea monster from her strange disquiet.

'Sea monster, be easy.'

The sea monster floated, only her eyes and forehead above the surface. Underwater, her nostrils flared and contracted. Her hair swirled around her shoulders. Marie-Josèphe leaned forward, trying to see why the sea monster was in distress.

The sea monster snorted violently. The surface bubbled above her mouth and nose. She swam backwards, then moaned and sighed and swam to the stairs, approaching uncertainly, her song a question, a comfort.

She opened the net and let the fish swim away uneaten. She took Marie-Josèphe's hand between her webbed fingers.

Marie-Josèphe stayed very still. The sea monster lowered her face to Marie-Josèphe's hand. Marie-Josèphe trembled, afraid the creature was about to bite her, praying she was not. The sea monster's warm lips touched her skin. The beast flicked out her tongue and licked Marie-Josèphe's knuckles.

Marie-Josèphe laughed with relief.

'You're like my old pony,' she said to the sea monster. 'You just want to lick the salt off my skin!'

As Marie-Josèphe fed the sea monster, she petted her, continuing to tame her to her hands and voice.

'Say "sea monster",' Marie-Josèphe said to the creature, holding out a fish.

'Fishhhh.' The sea monster's parroting speech dissolved in a long complex song of melody and whistles. She snapped up the fish in two quick bites.

'Say, "Marie-Josèphe".'

'Fishhhh!'

'Say, "Your Majesty honours me",' Marie-Josèphe said, recklessly, flinging a fish into the pool in frustration. Again in frustration, she sang back at the sea monster.

The sea monster fell silent and stared at her.

Marie-Josèphe continued, singing the wordless song she had played for His Majesty.

The sea monster drifted closer and hummed an exotic, compelling, haunting second melody that broke every rule of music.

Tears spilled down Marie-Josèphe's cheeks.

I have nothing to be sad about, she thought. *Why am I crying? Because it's my time of month . . . ?*

She scrubbed the tears away with the back of her hand.

But my time of month never made me sad before, she thought. *Only impatient with the inconvenience, with being told I must not do this, I must not do that.*

The sea monster took her hand. Hearing footsteps, Marie-Josèphe waved the net behind her, hoping the guard would understand that she wanted a fish.

She continued to sing. The sea monster embroidered variations on the melody.

The net left her hand and returned. The sea monster must have seen the morsel, for she ended her song, accepted her reward, and submerged with the fish held delicately between her claws.

'Thank you, sir.' Turning, Marie-Josèphe nearly ran into Count Lucien, standing behind her on the fountain's rim.

'Your song was extraordinarily beautiful.'

'I thought you were the musketeer!' Marie-Josèphe said, too flustered to reply to his compliment.

He took the net from her hand and scooped up another fish. The sea monster swam to the stairs and snarled. Marie-Josèphe quickly threw her the treat.

The sea monster tossed the fish in the air, caught it, and let it swim free. Marie-Josèphe laughed, delighted by the sea monster's play.

Beside the stairs, the sea monster rolled over and over in the water and splashed spray with her tail.

I wonder, she thought, *how His Majesty would like a sketch of the sea monster juggling fish? I wonder how Count Lucien would like it?*

'Stop it, sea monster!' Marie-Josèphe brushed droplets from the sleeve of her habit. 'What do you want? You aren't even hungry.'

'It wants to play,' Count Lucien said. 'With the fish. Like a cat with a mouse.'

Marie-Josèphe scooped up the last live fish and threw them into the pond. They darted away. The sea monster whistled and dove, chasing them, letting them escape, flicking spray into the air.

'Good-night, sea monster!' Marie-Josèphe whispered.

The sea monster surfaced by the platform. Marie-Josèphe gave her a final caress. The sea monster took her hand and held it to her lips, wailing and touching Marie-Josèphe's fingers delicately with her tongue.

Marie-Josèphe thought, *Why would the sea monster lick salt from my hand, when she's swimming in salt water?*

The sea monster crawled up the steps to the edge of the small water, crying with despair and warning. The fearless, foolish woman of land walked bleeding toward great predators whose roars and snarls filled the darkness and the dawn. If the predators of land could smell as keenly as the sharks of the ocean, the woman was doomed.

The sea monster echoed the land-woman's simple song of childish babble. Only silence replied.

The sea monster's song of warning burst through the gardens, filled them, and faded away.

Calm once more, the sea monster washed thick salt tears from her eyes.

Singing a different song, soft and lyrical, she swam to shelter beneath the hooves of Apollo's horses.

Chapter 13

Marie-Josèphe was all too aware of the slickness of blood between her legs as Count Lucien escorted her from the tent. It was very awkward; the count courteously tried to allow her to precede him, while she tried not to turn her back on him. She hoped her burgundy habit would not show bloodstains.

Count Lucien might not realise I'm bleeding, even if he saw a stain, Marie-Josèphe thought. *Do men take any notice? As for Count Lucien, he might not know what it means.*

Then she wondered, *Why is he here?* and answered her own question: *to observe His Majesty's sea monster.*

Outside the tent, the setting sun turned the Grand Canal molten gold. The moon, nearing full, loomed beyond the chateau. A groom on a dun cob held the reins of Count Lucien's grey Arabian and a splendid bay of the same breed.

Marie-Josèphe curtsied to Count Lucien. 'Good night, Count Lucien.' She rose, expecting his horse to bow so he could mount; expecting him to ride away.

'Can you ride, Mlle de la Croix?'

'I haven't ridden for a long—' Then she thought – she hoped! – he might invite her, in the name of His Majesty, to ride with the hunt. 'Yes, sir, I can.'

'Come speak to this horse.' He nodded toward the bay.

His requests, the requests of an agent of His Majesty, were more important than Marie-Josèphe's embarrassment. She approached the horse, apprehensive. Stallions were said to go mad in the presence of a bleeding woman.

But the bay, like the grey, was a mare.

She let the bay mare lip her palm and caress her with the soft warmth of its muzzle. At the scent of fish, the Arabian blew out its breath, snorting softly. Marie-Josèphe blew gently into the mare's nostrils. The bay pricked its ears forward and breathed against Marie-Josèphe's face.

'How did you learn that?' Count Lucien asked.

Marie-Josèphe had to think back to her childhood, to the happiest times of her life.

'My pony taught me.' She smiled and blinked and glanced away, surprised by her tears. 'When I was little.'

'The Bedouins speak to their horses in that manner,' Count Lucien said. 'At times I thought they were kinder to their horses than to each other.'

'She's beautiful,' Marie-Josèphe said. 'Do you always ride mares?' She scratched the bay mare delicately beneath the jaw. The horse stretched its head forward, leaning into Marie-Josèphe's fingertips.

'It's the custom, with this breed,' Count Lucien said. 'The mares are fast and strong and fierce. They'll turn their fierceness to your will, if you request it. If they trust you.'

'So will His Majesty's stallions,' Marie-Josèphe said.

'You must compel the fierceness of a stallion. You must waste its strength – and your own.' Count Lucien's clear grey gaze lost itself in the distance. He brought himself back; his voice recovered its usual straightforward tone. 'Your time is valuable to His Majesty. You mustn't waste it trudging up and down the Green Carpet. Jacques will keep Zachi at His Majesty's stables, and bring her to you at your request.'

Marie-Josèphe stroked the sleek neck of the bay Arabian mare, made shy by the attention, by the responsibility, by the doubt that she could ride this magic creature. The creature renounced its claim to magic by lifting its tail and depositing a load of droppings on the path. A gardener ran up and cleaned away the mess with a shovel, as if he had been waiting. Perhaps he had.

'I haven't ridden since I was a little girl,' Marie-Josèphe admitted. 'I wasn't allowed, in the convent, because—'

She thought, she hoped, the reason was foolish. She did not want to sound foolish to Count Lucien, or embarrass him. She did not want to find that the reason was true, for if riding truly destroyed a maiden's virginity, then no husband would ever believe her pure.

191

'We weren't allowed.'

'We'll see if you remember.' Count Lucien nodded to Jacques, who jumped down from the cob and placed the mounting-stairs beside Zachi's stirrup. 'If you don't, a sedan chair would answer better.'

Marie-Josèphe could not bear the thought of riding in a sedan chair if she had the choice of Zachi. She hesitated. She feared her blood would stain the saddle.

I should have made an excuse, some excuse, any excuse, she thought. *There's nothing to do now but brazen it out.*

She had never ridden en Amazone, only astride like a boy. She was surprised at how sure she felt in the side-saddle, with her left foot in the stirrup and her right knee hooked around the pommel. She settled herself on the bay.

The grey Arabian bowed, going down on one knee to lower the stirrup. Count Lucien mounted.

'Wait at the stables,' Count Lucien said to the groom. Jacques bowed and swung up on his cob without bothering about stairs or stirrup. He slung the mounting stairs across the pommel of his saddle and urged the cob into a trot toward the chateau and the stables beyond.

The grey and the bay set off at a leisurely walk up the hill toward the chateau. Even at a walk the mare moved with intense energy. A hard hand on the bit made her jig and fret. Marie-Josèphe eased her nervous grip on the reins. Zachi calmed. Her ears swiveled back toward Marie-Josèphe; the mare only waited for a single word, a single touch, and she would spring free into a gallop and fly out of the garden and into the woods.

Marie-Josèphe maintained a sedate pace. It could not be proper to gallop through the King's gardens.

'Will you lend a horse to my brother?' Marie-Josèphe asked.

'No,' Count Lucien said.

The edge in the count's voice piqued Marie-Josèphe's curiosity.

'Why not?' *Will he say*, she wondered, *that Yves' legs are so long he needs no horse?*

'Because I never knew a priest,' he said, 'who could use a horse without ruining it.'

I should defend Yves, Marie-Josèphe thought. *But, it's true . . . he isn't a fine rider.*

Dusk softened the edges of the fountains and turned the statuary to white ghosts. The sea monster sang; in the Menagerie, a lion roared.

Marie-Josèphe shivered. When they passed the spot where she had seen the apparition of Yves, she glanced nervously sideways.

A rippling shadow stalked the edge of the path.

'Count Lucien, run!'

The King's tiger, sleekly striped, obscure in twilight, glared silver-eyed. Blood dripped from its teeth and claws. Zachi shied and spun and snorted.

Panicked, Marie-Josèphe dug her heel into Zachi's ribs. The mare leaped into a gallop. Gravel spattered from her hooves. Marie-Josèphe urged the mare faster. The Arabian bolted back down the path, past the sea monster's tent and through its discordant melody, along the Allé de la Reine toward the Menagerie.

Marie-Josèphe feared to look back, feared to see the bloody teeth of the tiger, feared she had abandoned Count Lucien to his death. Terror spun around her.

Zachi slowed to a canter, to a prancing trot. Sweat dappled the mare's shoulders, but she moved as if she could run for an hour, and another. She arched her neck and snorted, swiveled her small fine ears, and switched her black tail. Marie-Josèphe huddled in the saddle, shivering. Tears streaked her face, cold in the night air.

'You outran it,' Marie-Josèphe said to Zachi. 'You saved us—'

Zachi pranced, no longer frightened, but nervous among the musky smells of the Menagerie.

Zelis cantered down the path. Count Lucien drew his mare to a stop beside Marie-Josèphe.

'I see that you can ride,' Count Lucien said calmly.

'Thank God you're all right!' Marie-Josèphe said. 'I shouldn't have fled – I'm so sorry – I must find the keeper of His Majesty's tiger—'

'Mlle de la Croix,' Count Lucien said, 'what are you talking about?'

'Didn't you see it? The tiger?'

193

'There was no tiger.'

'I saw it. Zachi saw it – she was as frightened as I!'

The bay mare showed no sign of terror.

'Zachi will take any excuse to run,' he said. 'I saw nothing. Zelis saw nothing. There is no tiger.'

'It must have escaped from its cage.'

'There is no tiger.'

'But I saw it – today, at luncheon!'

'After luncheon, His Majesty's butchers took the tiger. There is no other.'

Marie-Josèphe sat back, startled. 'They killed it – already?'

'The furriers must prepare its pelt. Dr. Fagon must prepare its medicinal organs. M. Boursin must prepare its meat for the Carrousel banquet.'

'Then – what did I see?' Marie-Josèphe whispered.

Count Lucien turned his horse toward the chateau; Zachi followed.

'A shadow in the darkness—'

'It wasn't a shadow.'

Count Lucien rode in silence.

'It wasn't!' Marie-Josèphe said.

'Very well.'

'I don't see ghosts, I'm not—I—'

'I have said that I believe you.'

What did I see? she asked herself. *What did I see tonight, what did I see when I thought Yves was dying?*

Count Lucien brought a silver flask from his pocket. He opened it and offered it to her.

'And I'm not drunk!' she said.

'If you were, I wouldn't offer you more spirits. If you were, you wouldn't be shivering.'

She drank. The scent of apples softened the harsh spirits. She took another sip.

'Save some for me, if you please,' Count Lucien said.

She handed him the flask. He took a substantial swallow.

'What is it?' Marie-Josèphe asked.

'Calvados,' he said. 'From the orchards of Brittany.' He smiled.

'Were it known that I drink calvados instead of brandy, I'd be marked as hopelessly unfashionable.'

'You stand at the height of fashion. Everyone says so.'

Only when he chuckled did she recognise her joke, however small, however inadvertent; she had amused, not offended, Count Lucien.

The horses walked companionably along the path. The sea monster had fallen silent; the tent stood dark and quiet. Marie-Josèphe's vision took on brightness and clarity. The stars sparkled.

'You aren't used to spirits,' Count Lucien said.

'I've drunk it,' Marie-Josèphe said. 'But only once, when my brother and I were children. Our father distilled it from molasses. I distilled it again. For Yves' work. It tasted awful, it made us dizzy, and then it made us sick. After that, we only used it to preserve specimens.'

Count Lucien laughed. 'You are a scholar — you've discovered a use for rum!' He offered her the flask.

'Thank you,' she said. 'I will have some more.'

Zachi pranced when they passed the spot where the tiger had appeared, but nothing, not even shadows, marked the verge of the path.

Zachi did see something, Marie-Josèphe thought. *I wonder what I saw, that wasn't a tiger?*

'Zachi thinks you might let her race again.'

'Not now,' Marie-Josèphe said. 'You must think—I know better than to run a horse in the dark—'

'The desert breed sees in the dark like cats,' Count Lucien said. 'You asked no more than Zachi was willing to give you.'

'Did you live with the Bedouins? In the desert?'

'I spent several years in the Levant. In Arabia, in Egypt, in Morocco.'

'On the King's secret business?'

'Should I tell you, if it were secret business?' He chuckled. 'I was only a youth, and at the time His Majesty wasn't inclined to give me any commissions, secret or otherwise.'

'Morocco and Egypt and Arabia,' Marie-Josèphe said, tasting the words. 'What an adventure — I envy you!'

The chateau loomed ahead, rising on the crest of its low hill like a

195

crown. The attic and ground floor windows glowed with candlelight; the windows of the first floor, the royal floor, glittered with the reflected light of mirrors and crystal chandeliers. Marie-Josèphe and Count Lucien rode into the passageway between the chateau proper and its northern wing.

Marie-Josèphe wrestled with her velvet skirt and the unfamiliar saddle. A word from Count Lucien brought a footman. She dismounted, made awkward by apprehension. She was afraid to look at the seat of the saddle.

In the years since her parents had died, she had felt despair and grief and hopelessness, fury and outrage, even moments of peace and happiness, but never helpless fear.

'Thank you for your courtesy, sir,' she said to Count Lucien. 'I'm more grateful than you can know.'

'Fulfill your duties to His Majesty,' Count Lucien said, 'so he knows your gratitude.'

She handed him Zachi's reins. The bay Arabian lipped gently at her sleeve. Marie-Josèphe stroked the mare's soft muzzle.

'Does Zachi bow?' Marie-Josèphe asked.

'Yes, Mlle de la Croix,' Count Lucien said. 'All my horses bow.'

Marie-Josèphe crept into her room, moving quietly so as not to wake Odelette. Hercules blinked at her, his eyes reflecting green in the candlelight.

She struggled out of her hunting habit. Her chemise was a little stained, but the blood had not soaked into her underskirt or spoiled her petticoat. Marie-Josèphe sighed with relief and surprise, for her flow usually began heavily. She tied a rolled towel between her legs. She rinsed out her chemise and the rags she had put to soak, and hung them to dry.

The bed offered a warm place beside Odelette. She put aside the temptation, wrapped Lorraine's cloak around her shoulders, and carried candle and drawing box to Yves' dressing-room.

The light of her candle flickered across a boxy shape covered in drapery. Marie-Josèphe pulled the brocade aside, uncovering an extraordinary harpsichord. The polished wood shone; the delicate frieze of inlay danced along its side. She opened the keyboard. Each ebony key reflected an orange flame. The harpsichord smelled of exotic wood, beeswax, rare oil.

She sat on the matching bench and brushed her fingertips across the keys. They caressed her like silk, like Lorraine's manicured hands.

Marie-Josèphe played a chord.

She winced at the discord. She looked for the tuning key, but it was nowhere to be found.

Tears of disappointment and frustration sprang to her eyes. She tried to reassure herself. The instrument was not so very out of tune. She could compose on it, she could correct the tones in her mind. But she would compose without the pleasure of a true instrument.

Jumping up, she ran back down the stairs to the main floor, the royal floor of the chateau.

'Where's Count Lucien?' she asked the first servant she saw. 'Have you seen Count Lucien?'

'He went to his carriage, mamselle. Through the Marble Courtyard.'

She ran down to the Marble Courtyard, crossing it on tiptoe – she was directly beneath His Majesty's bedchamber; she must not do anything to disturb him – toward Count Lucien's carriage. Its lanterns gleamed on the polished black and white marble. The eight bay horses snorted and champed their bits. A footman swung the carriage door closed and leapt up behind.

'Hup!' the driver said. The carriage rolled forward, the horses' iron shoes ringing on the cobblestones.

'Wait!' Marie-Josèphe called softly. 'Please wait!'

Count Lucien leaned from the window. 'Guillaume, stop,' he said. The carriage halted. The footman jumped down again and opened the carriage door. Count Lucien stood to speak with Marie-Josèphe.

'Count Lucien – I'm so sorry, I don't mean any ingratitude, thank you for the harpsichord, it's beautiful, but – it's out of tune, and I cannot find the key.'

'M. Coupillet has been instructed to tune it for you in the morning.'

'M. Coupillet!' she exclaimed, dismayed.

'He will do exactly as you instruct him,' Count Lucien said, as if giving her a gift.

'I'm grateful, sir, but . . . I'd prefer a harpsichord key to M. Coupillet.'

He smiled. 'It shall be as you wish. Will it wait till morning?'

'Yes, sir – otherwise I'll wake my brother with the twanging!'

He chuckled.

'Thank you, sir.'

'You're welcome, mademoiselle.'

Monsieur's carriage, bright with gilt and lanterns, rattled across the cobbles, passed through the gateway to the Place d'Armes, and disappeared down the Avenue de Paris.

'Are you going to Paris with Monsieur?' She envied the men their freedom; she wished to see Paris with a longing both unsophisticated and obvious. She wished she had kept her silence; her curiosity was ill-bred and impertinent.

'I am going home,' Count Lucien said.

'I thought you lived here. Near His Majesty. In the chateau.'

'In the courtiers' rat warren?' Count Lucien said. 'No. I seldom stay in my apartment here. I require all the comfort I can find, Mlle de la Croix. Comfort is not to be found in the chateau of Versailles.'

'Lucien, come inside, you're abusing yourself with the night air.' The Marquise de la Fère leaned forward and put her hand on Count Lucien's shoulder, a gesture of concern and affection. The carriage-lantern cast harsh shadows over her pox-scarred complexion. She drew a silk scarf across her damaged beauty.

Count Lucien turned to her. Marie-Josèphe could not make out what he said, but his voice was flirtatious, and equally affectionate. The marquise laughed softly, let the scarf fall, and stroked Count Lucien's cheek.

'Good evening, Mlle de la Croix,' the marquise said.

'Good evening, Mme de la Fère.' Marie-Josèphe stammered a little with shock and surprise.

'Good night, Mlle de la Croix.' Count Lucien bowed and withdrew. The carriage rumbled away.

Marie-Josèphe returned to her tiny apartment. Now she understood what Madame, what the chevalier, had meant when they referred to Mme de la Fère as 'Mme Present' and to Mlle de Valentinois as 'Mlle

Past,' and she supposed they must have good reason to refer to the exquisite Mlle d'Armagnac as 'Mlle Future,' though she appeared to Marie-Josèphe already to be fully occupied with Lotte's brother.

I suppose I should not be surprised to see Count Lucien with a lover, she thought. *Why should he be any better than Chartres? He is an atheist, after all.*

Once more she had misunderstood him, misunderstood what everyone had told her about him. Madame had told her, without quite saying so, that Count Lucien was a rake. The Chevalier de Lorraine had warned her as well. She had no right to be disappointed in Count Lucien.

I wonder, she thought, *if Mlle d'Armagnac will be the lover of both Chartres and Count Lucien? I wonder if they know they're rivals?*

In Yves' sitting room, she spread the tapestry over the harpsichord. At the tiny desk by the window, she laid out a sheet of drawing paper and a sheet of music paper. She thought, *If only I could draw with one hand and write music with the other!*

She chose the drawing paper. The drawing for His Majesty's medal would require less time. Besides, she had no idea what direction the cantata should take. She would wait; once she had tuned the beautiful harpsichord, playing it might inspire her.

She looked through the dissection sketches and set them aside. They informed her technique but crushed her inspiration. No illustration of dead creature, flayed skin, exposed bone and muscle, would fulfill Count Lucien's request. His Majesty's medal must represent the sea monster alive, ferocious, a suitable, dangerous prey of the Most Christian King.

She tried to imagine what the male sea monster must have looked like in life, but instead she sketched its face as she had seen it, haloed by broken glass and bits of gilded lead. Only when she had finished did she understand why her brother had burned her first rendition of this drawing. The sea monster looked like a dead god with a gargoyle face, a demon Christ crowned with thorns of glass.

No wonder past generations thought sea monsters the spawn of Satan, Marie-Josèphe said to herself. She shivered, and slipped the drawing to the bottom of her box.

She imagined the female monster swimming in the sea, leaping like a dolphin, singing like a nightingale. She imagined it ruthless as a kraken. She drew it free, with waves caressing its tails.

In the guttering illumination of the candle flame, the drawing trembled at the edge of life. The creature cried out, not with fury or fear, but with fierce joy.

Marie-Josèphe gasped and wrenched herself upright. Her body quivered with an intense, terrifying pleasure.

Outside, a low bank of fog glowed in the darkness, filling the gardens so the marble statues walked on clouds and the sea monster's tent floated like an island. A warbling melody filled the night. Shadows cavorted among the orange trees.

Is that Chartres, and his lover? Marie-Josèphe wondered. *Or an incubus and a succubus?*

The shadows turned to her. Naked and alluring, they beckoned. They promised joy and pleasure in return for her submission. She shivered, distressed at the power of their temptation. She could not think of them as evil.

Marie-Josèphe blinked sleep from her eyes, unable to distinguish between imagination and dream.

The sea monster's song remained. Marie-Josèphe opened the window. Cold damp night air poured in with the delicate melody. She snatched up a pen and transcribed the refrain.

Hours later, after the moon had set, false dawn turned the groundmist brilliant silver.

The sea monster fell silent. The shadows disappeared. The pen slipped from Marie-Josèphe's cramped fingers. She gathered up the sheets of paper that had fallen to the floor all around her, the drawings and the score for the cantata. Shivering, exhausted, her eyes and her hands aching, she pulled the window shut and huddled within the chevalier's luxurious cape.

Chapter 14

Lucien laid his hand along the side of Juliette's face, to remember the last touch of her warmth, her bawdy humour, her wit, the slight irregularities of her skin that were as dear to him as her brown eyes, her long silk-straight hair defying its intricate arrangements and fashionable curls.

She turned her head, shy, even now, of her marred skin.

'I will miss you,' he said.

'And I, you.' She bent to kiss him. 'But I will always cherish our time together.'

He handed her into his carriage, and watched as it drove away into the dawn.

Zelis bowed; Lucien clambered into the saddle and turned the mare toward the chateau. She walked through the beautiful autumn morning; she pranced, rudely switching her tail. He allowed her to trot. He spoke; she sprang into a gallop.

Lucien let Zelis run, but even the pleasure of her speed and her spirit could not banish the sadness of saying goodbye to the Marquise de la Fère.

Zelis galloped along the Avenue de Paris. Lucien coaxed the mare to a more sedate pace. Visitors filled the approaches to the chateau; he did not care to ride over His Majesty's subjects.

Juliette and I will remember our last night together, Lucien thought, *and the caresses we exchanged. I will not think of tonight, of my empty bed. I will think of a suitable wedding present, a proper token of my deep esteem for her. And I will anticipate Mlle d'Armagnac.*

Zelis swivelled her ears toward the coaches, toward the children, toward the pavillions selling ice cream or renting out pot-metal swords. She had seen all these things a thousand times. On the battle-field or on a hunt she was the most valiant of mounts, steady, watchful, and brave. At other times, boredom made her flighty and fanciful,

201

ready to shy wildly at a fallen branch. Yet she would canter without flinching past the explosion of a cock pheasant into flight.

Lucien kept a light touch on the reins, reminding the Arabian of his presence and his attention. She might frolic, but he would not be unseated, not with his leg nearly healed, not in the view of the merchants and gentlemen, the housewives and ladies of Paris. They were all above the class of people to whom he threw the King's alms; nevertheless, they knew him, or knew of him. They bowed to him as he passed; he tipped his hat.

Lucien would not allow himself to regret Juliette's decision. She would have stayed, but he could not promise what she wished. Each time the impairments of his body twisted him into a knot of pain, or, worse, when he was stricken at a time when he could neither acknowledge the pain nor do anything to quench it, he renewed his vow never to marry, never to father a child.

In the passageway beneath the north wing of the chateau, Marie-Josèphe took Zachi's reins from Jacques and climbed the mounting steps. Though Zachi stood stock-still as Marie-Josèphe slid into the saddle, the mare collected herself, ready with her whole being to fly through the gardens and across the forest. She switched her black tail like a flag.

Such a shame, such a waste, Marie-Josèphe thought, *to ride such a beautiful horse only back and forth from the chateau.* Jacques handed up her drawing box.

The ring of hooves on cobblestones echoed against the walls. Count Lucien rode toward her.

'Good morning, Mlle de la Croix,' he said.

'Good morning, Count Lucien,' Marie-Josèphe replied coolly. 'I trust you found your comfort last night.'

'I was very comfortable indeed, Mlle de la Croix. Thank you for your concern.'

Faced with his perfect civility, Marie-Josèphe chided herself for her common behaviour. It was not her place to judge Count Lucien's liaisons or his sins. He had done nothing to earn her ire except tell her the truth. She was embarrassed. She could not even apologise, for he had refused to take offense.

202

Hoping to redeem herself, she opened the drawing box and gave Count Lucien the sea monster sketches. He looked at them, raising one fair eyebrow.

'Are they adequate?' she asked.

'That isn't for me to say. The King must decide.'

'I thought them rather good,' she said with some asperity.

'They are excellent,' he said. 'I never doubted they would be. Whether they're suitable – the King must decide.'

'Thank you for your opinion.' Marie-Josèphe smiled. 'And for the harpsichord key, which arrived free of any encumbrance.' A footman, not M. Coupillet, had delivered it. 'And for the wonderful harpsichord.' The instrument enhanced her playing well beyond her true ability.

Zachi arched her neck and struck at the cobbles with her forefoot. The iron shoe rang on stone, filling the passageway with echoes.

'She wants to run,' Marie-Josèphe said.

'She wants to race. It's bred in her blood. Tomorrow, or the next day, she may run – His Majesty invites you to join his hunt.'

'That would be wonderful!' Marie-Josèphe exclaimed. 'That is to say, His Majesty's invitation honours me, and I accept with gratitude.'

After His Majesty's awakening, while His Majesty was performing his devotions, Lucien spent an hour reading reports and petitions, then walked through the State Apartments.

Wax or paint or new gold leaf shone from every surface. The King's sunburst glowed from doors and wall panels. Gold and yellow flowers decorated every candle-stand and table, continuing the theme of the flowers in the gardens. At dusk, servants would whisk away the flowers and replace them with branching candelabra and new tapers.

At Carrousel, the visiting monarchs would understand that France, Louis the Great, had lost nothing in magnificence or power, despite the wars.

Lucien entered the chamber given over to the construction of His Majesty's Carrousel costume. The royal harness-makers busied themselves around a great stuffed warhorse.

His Majesty stood on a low platform, wearing only his shirt and his stockings. The royal tailor and the royal wigmaker and the royal shoemaker backed away from His Majesty, bowing, carrying his costume to their workbenches.

'M. de Chrétien, good day to you, a moment please,' His Majesty said. 'My sons, my nephew, let me see you. And where is my brother?'

They hurried to him, Monseigneur the Grand Dauphin in the costume of an American, Maine in Persian dress, and Chartres robed as an Egyptian. The Persian and Egyptian costumes amused Lucien, for they looked like nothing he had ever seen in Persia or Egypt. Maine's Persian coat was quite handsome; his turban of silver gauze set it off nicely. The velvet fabric copied the designs of a prayer rug. Like all his clothes, the coat disguised his twisted back; a lift in one shoe lengthened his short leg.

His Majesty might laugh, Lucien thought, *but Mme de Maintenon would surely be horrified to know that her favourite stepson wears religious symbols of Islam.*

He had no intention of informing her of the situation, and he hoped the few who might know the meaning would have the mother wit to hold their silence.

M. du Maine pivoted before his father, and bowed, theatrically touching his forehead and his heart. His Majesty nodded his approval.

Monsieur rushed into the room. Attendants bustled to strip him and costume him. Lorraine strolled in, perfectly composed, smoking a cigar. He bowed to His Majesty, joined Monsieur to watch the fitting, and put out the smoke just quickly enough to avoid any suspicion of insolence.

Chartres showed off his costume to his uncle. He wore a long robe of pleated linen, a girdle of silver and sapphires, a wide jewelled silver collar, and silver sandals. Cobra and vulture decorated his headdress.

His lovers will enjoy the robe, Lucien thought, *as it is very near transparent.*
'Very good, Chartres.'

Maine and Chartres, natural rivals, matched each other in magnificence. *They might have been friends*, Lucien thought, *if they had been born to different families, if they were not kept suspicious of each other, if they were not always in doubt of their places.*

Monseigneur turned uncomfortably before his father, in his leather shirt and leggings, and a breechclout of fur as thick as a codpiece. Gold fringe tied with feathers and beads hung nearly to the floor. He wore a fantastic headdress: a frame of bent reeds, painted gold, covered with pompoms, egret feathers, and bunches of lace.

The American fashion suited him badly; he possessed neither the figure to set off the style nor the dignity to present it. He was a decade older than Maine and fifteen years older than Chartres; his costume would have looked quite fine on either of them.

'Monseigneur's costume misses something,' His Majesty said. The tailors clustered round, holding up drifts of lace, more gold fringe, a cape of iridescent feathers.

'Emeralds,' His Majesty said.

One of the apprentices whispered to the royal tailor.

'I beg your pardon, Your Majesty,' the royal tailor said, 'but the wild Americans are not known to use emeralds.'

'Emeralds. Nothing better. Along the seams and the hems, and sewn into the fur. A string of emeralds set in yellow gold to tie around Monseigneur's forehead.'

'Yes, Your Majesty,' the royal tailor said, with a ferocious glare at his apprentice.

'Will that meet with your approval, Monseigneur?' Neither His Majesty's voice nor his expression showed any hint of amusement.

Mademoiselle Choin may approve the breechclout, Lucien thought, *when she undresses Monseigneur and finds emeralds hidden in his fur. But Monseigneur le grand dauphin is anything but happy.*

'Yes, Sire,' Monseigneur said.

'And my brother, how does your costume progress?'

Monsieur tottered forward.

'The shoemaker has put heels on the toes of my shoes, sir,' Monsieur said mournfully. 'I fear they must be redone.'

'I have it on excellent authority that yours are true Japanese sandals,' His Majesty said. 'Made in the traditional style.'

Monsieur hiked up the skirts of layers of embroidered and fancifully dyed kimono. Underneath them all, he wore wide white silk

205

pantaloons. He stood on sandals like small wooden platforms, gilded, attached to his feet with gold leather straps and golden buckles.

'How am I to ride at Carrousel, in this footgear?' Monsieur said. 'The robes are exquisite, do you not think so, sir? But the sandals—!'

Monsieur's wigmaker appeared behind him, whisked off his perruke, and settled a new wig on his head. The hair was jet black, straight, and lacquered into a complex topknot. It left his neck and shoulders oddly bare.

'Your saddlemaker will solve the problem of the footgear, I have no doubt of it,' His Majesty said. 'I agree, I commend you on the choice of your robes.'

Monsieur pulled aside the lapels of successive layers. 'This one is embroidered with gold. This one is a weave of silver threads. And this one, true Oriental silk, the technique requires a year for each colour.' Minuscule twisted spots of colour formed a complex pattern on the silk of the under-robe. 'The artisans who create them commit ritual suicide after completing one, for their eyes will no longer bear the task.'

'Indeed, is that true?'

'Why, sir, I have it on the best authority of my silk importer,' Monsieur said.

The wigmaker brought a mirror and held it for him. Monsieur turned this way and that, inspecting the lacquered wig. The armourer brought a long, recurved bow and an ivory quiver of wicked hunting arrows.

'This mirror is too small,' Monsieur said.

Servants carried in a full-length mirror.

'You are the very image of a Japanese warrior, dear brother,' His Majesty said.

'It misses something, sir,' Monsieur said. 'I shall have no hat – are you certain the Japanese warriors wear no hat? – and my hair will be naked. It wants ornament, such as the golden pins.'

'Those are ladies' ornaments,' His Majesty said.

His expression quizzical, Monsieur waited for an answer that applied to him.

'I have given them to my daughter. Your daughter-in-law.'

'She's borrowed my jewels often enough,' Monsieur said. 'And as often as not never returned them.'

'The hair ornaments are Chinese. You must not adulterate your costume.' His Majesty considered. 'Japanese warriors are said to wear helmets. You shall have a helmet, of plumes and golden scales.'

'Thank you, sir,' Monsieur said, somewhat mollified.

Smiling, His Majesty turned to Lucien. 'M. de Chrétien! Is your costume finished?'

'Yes, Your Majesty.'

'I trust you did not skimp. It must be magnificent – though not more magnificent than mine.'

'I hope it will please you, Sire.'

'It is finished very quickly.'

'It took less time to create, Sire – being smaller.'

His Majesty laughed, then nodded at the roll of papers in Lucien's hand. 'What do you have for me?'

Lucien presented Mlle de la Croix's drawings to the King. Louis' likeness would grace the medal's face. In the old fashion, but appropriate for Carrousel, he appeared as a mounted youth in Roman armour, gazing into the farthest distance. A sea monster cavorted on the reverse drawing. Its grotesque face expressed joy; its tails whipped spume from the waves.

'I had expected the hunt – the captured creature,' His Majesty said. 'But this is quite extraordinary. Chrétien, have it struck. Deliver one, with my compliments, to—'

Under the eye of governors and nursemaid, Bourgogne, Anjou, and Berri marched in, wearing versions of His Majesty's costume. The little boys lined up before the King and saluted, fists to their chests.

'My Roman legions!' His Majesty exclaimed. 'I am most pleased.'

Berri brandished his Roman sword.

'Our fencing lesson, M. de Chrétien, if you please!'

Lucien bowed. 'Certainly, Your Highness.'

'You may have M. de Chrétien later,' His Majesty said. 'Now he is advising me.' He dismissed his heirs. 'What was I saying?'

'Your Majesty wished me to reserve a medal – for Mlle de la Croix, perhaps?'

'For my sister-in-law, for her collection. You suggest that Mlle de la Croix should have one as well?'

'Yes, Your Majesty. For her, and her brother, too, of course.'

'Have they a medal collection?'

'I doubt it sincerely, Your Majesty. The family is penniless.'

'That will change.'

'In that case,' Lucien said, understanding His Majesty's intentions, 'a medal from Your Majesty, commemorating the brother's capture of the monster and the sister's depiction of it – a mark of Your Majesty's favour – will begin the repair of their fortunes.'

Louis looked again at his own likeness.

'Unlike Bernini, Mlle de la Croix understands how a rider sits a horse. Does she wish to join the hunt?'

'She is pleased to accept, Your Majesty.'

'And does she flatter you, as she flatters me?'

'Why, Your Majesty – she flatters neither of us.'

'Chrétien, you fancy her, I do believe!' He laughed. 'But what of Mme de la Fère?'

'Mme de la Fère tired of widowhood. She has accepted an offer of marriage.'

'Without your counter-offer?'

'I don't intend to marry, as Mme de la Fère understands.'

'You tell your lovers, but I wonder how many of them hope to change your mind?'

'They cannot, Sire, but I hope that's the only way in which I might disappoint them. I honour Mme de la Fère. We part as friends.'

'And Mlle de la Croix?' His Majesty said, ignoring Lucien's diversion.

'She is devoted to your service, Your Majesty, and to advancing her brother's work. She wishes for scientific instruments.'

'Scientific instruments? I suppose she must occupy her time somehow, until she's married – she needs a husband. She's a devout young woman. She prays in church, instead of sleeping or ogling fashions.

She is well-regarded by Mme de Maintenon as well as by Madame my brother's wife.'

'Then she is remarkable, Sire.'

'Who shall she marry, Chrétien? I must pick someone worthy of my love for her father and mother. Some might object to her lack of connections, but I will make up for them. Perhaps I should desire you to change your mind.'

'I hope you will not, Sire.' Lucien spoke lightly, despite his alarm.

His Majesty sighed. 'My court is sadly lacking in other suitable candidates. She would prefer someone with passion, I feel sure, and who else fits that description? It was different in my youth.'

His Majesty might prefer someone with passion, but what Mlle de la Croix desired in a husband, if indeed she desired a husband at all, Lucien did not know. How much of her character had the convent formed? How much of her natural desire had been frightened out of her?

Lucien kept his own counsel.

Fountains played and whispered on every pool; flowers in all shades of gold and yellow burst from silver pots along the edges of the pathways. The gardens were filled with visitors. People had already gathered at the sea monster's open tent; they stood around the cage, pointing and laughing.

Marie-Josèphe hoped no one important would appear at today's dissection. No member of court had any reason to attend, in His Majesty's absence. For that, Marie-Josèphe was grateful. She looked so plain and ordinary today. Odelette, in full health again, attended Lotte in Marie-Josèphe's place, so Marie-Josèphe's hair remained appallingly undressed. She wore not a bit of lace or ribbon; she did not dare put on another beauty-patch.

As if in compensation, her monthlies had slowed to a fraction of their usual flux. The change worried her, but it was such a relief and she feared physicians so, she put it out of her mind.

Humming the refrain of the sea monster's cantata, she entered the tent, made her way through the crowd of visitors, entered the cage, and locked the door behind her.

The sea monster lurched up against the fountain's rim, reaching toward the barrel of live fish. The spectators shouted with amazement.

'Wait, be patient.' Marie-Josèphe scooped the net through the sea water and carried her wriggling prey over the edge of the fountain and down the wooden steps.

What shall I train it to do? she wondered. The creature was remarkably quick to understand her commands.

'Sea monster! Fishhhh! Ask for a fishhhh!'

The sea monster swam back and forth before the steps, diving and flicking her tail, plunging up from the bottom and leaping halfway out of the water, splashing Marie-Josèphe with drops of brackish water.

The sea monster sang the cantata's refrain.

'What a clever sea monster! I know you can sing, but now you must speak. Say fishhhh.'

'Fishhhh!' the sea monster cried, snarling.

'Oh, excellent sea monster.'

Marie-Josèphe flung a fish. The sea monster snatched it from the air and crunched it neatly with sharp snaps of her teeth. The visitors applauded.

'Now you must come closer, you must take the fish from my hand.'

The sea monster swam to her and took the fish. She held the fish captive between the translucent webs of her long-fingered hand. The sea monster stared straight at Marie-Josèphe, her eyes deep gold.

Deliberately, slowly, she opened her hand and let the live fish free.

'Aren't you hungry, sea monster?'

One fish remained in the net. Marie-Josèphe dipped the net into the pool.

The sea monster moaned. Her hand crept forward, past the net, and touched Marie-Josèphe's fingers. Marie-Josèphe stayed still as the sharp claws dimpled her skin, though the sea monster's strength frightened her.

The sea monster released Marie-Josèphe's hand. Though the marks of her claws remained, she had not broken Marie-Josèphe's skin, or even scratched her.

The fish wriggled and splashed. The sea monster snorted and plucked the fish from the net, as Marie-Josèphe had shown her only once.

'Can you leap, will you play?' Marie-Josèphe said, speaking to herself more than to the creature. 'If you entertained the King, he might spare you.' She gave the sea monster another fish.

'Fishhh!'

'You are very clever, but His Majesty already has parrots.'

The sea monster splashed away, arched her back, and sank slowly head first into the water. She waved her webbed toes in the air. Marie-Josèphe laughed along with the visitors. Then the sea monster parted her double tail, exposing her female parts, opening the pink skin like a flower.

Spectators tittered and whispered.

Marie-Josèphe slapped the water.

'No!' she said severely as the sea monster splashed down and surfaced. *You're only a beast*, she thought, *but even a beast might offend Pope Innocent — or Mme de Maintenon*. She remembered, blushing, the time at Saint-Cyr when an adolescent puppy, confused by its animal urges, had mistaken Mme de Maintenon's ankle for a bitch. Mme de Maintenon had shaken her foot so hard that the poor silly dog, its tongue hanging out, its eyes glazed with its cravings, spun across the room and fetched up against the doorpost.

The sea monster swam to her, singing and snarling, splashing her hand on the water as Marie-Josèphe had done.

'Never mind,' Marie-Josèphe whispered. 'I know you don't understand. I know you don't mean anything by it.'

Back in Martinique, an old man who lived on the beach used to play with the dolphins. He threw them an inflated pig-bladder and they returned it to him, passing it from one to another as if they were playing tennis.

'Could you play tennis, sea monster?'

The sea monster spat and dove.

The cage door clanged; Yves descended the stairs in one long stride. The sea monster vanished beneath the water, leaving barely a ripple.

211

'Good morning,' Yves said.

'Isn't it a glorious day?'

'It is glorious. Your sea monster looks much healthier. Practically sleek.' He smiled at her. 'I knew that if anyone could persuade it to feed, you could.'

'She begins to obey me. And to speak.'

'Yes, like a parrot, I know.' Yves glanced away, troubled. 'Don't become too fond of the beast.' He sat on the edge of the fountain. 'Don't make it your pet. I can't bear to think of your heart broken out of fondness for it.'

'Such a waste!' Marie-Josèphe exclaimed. 'Her kind is so rare . . . Can't you—'

'My net caught the sea monster's destiny. There's no appeal.'

The sea monster, swimming slowly closer, flicked droplets at Marie-Josèphe's skirt.

Yves offered Marie-Josèphe his hand; she took it. The sea monster hissed and flung a handful of water at them both. It splashed across Marie-Josèphe's neck and shoulder, soaking her cravat.

'Oh—!' She brushed at the water, managing to sweep away the droplets before they stained her riding habit.

'Fishhhh!' the sea monster snarled.

Marie-Josèphe scooped a whole netful of fish from the barrel and freed them into the fountain. The sea monster chased them, diving with a great splash of her tails.

Marie-Josèphe's hand cramped and her pen flew from her fingers, spattering ink across her sketch. The pageboy lunged to catch the quill, but it fluttered to the laboratory floor and stained the planking with a black blob. The boy snatched it up.

'Yves, a moment, please.'

Stiff and pale, her brother straightened from sectioning the sea monster's brain. 'What's the matter?'

The page brought a fresh quill. Marie-Josèphe massaged her palm. The spasm eased.

'Nothing. Please continue.'

Yves looked around. Long shadows dimmed to dusk as the sun set. Servants moved through the tent, lighting candles and lanterns, lowering the sides of the tent against the evening breeze. The duke de Chartres sat beside the portrait of the King; the rest of the audience, all visitors, remained standing.

Yves stretched, arching his back. He squeezed shut his eyes, bloodshot from the reek of preserving spirits.

'By your leave, M. de Chartres, I'll continue tomorrow,' Yves said, 'when my sister has light enough to draw.' He placed the brain in a jar and shrouded the sea monster's carcass. Servants brought ice and sawdust.

The page-boy pinned Marie-Josèphe's final sketch to the display frame. The sequence of drawings led from a full view of the sea monster's grotesque face, through skin, layers of muscle, odd facial cavities, to its skull and its heavily convoluted brain.

Chartres jumped up and peered closely at the sketches with his good eye, holding a candle so close that Marie-Josèphe feared he would set the paper on fire.

'Remarkable,' he said. 'A remarkable day. Remarkable sights. Father de la Croix, observing your work is a privilege.'

'Thank you, sir.'

'How strange,' Marie-Josèphe said, looking at her sketches as a progression, from the intact face with its swollen resonance cavities, through skin and muscle, to bone, each layer less grotesque, more familiar.

'What's strange?' Yves said.

'The skull. It looks human. The face muscles—'

'Nonsense. When have you ever seen a human skull? I never dissected a cadaver till I was at university.'

'At the convent. The relic. They brought out the saint's bones on her feast day.'

'It's the skull of a beast,' Yves said. 'Look at the teeth.' He pointed to the prominent canines.

'I grant you the teeth.'

'It's like a monkey skull,' Chartres said. 'An example of God's

213

humour, no doubt, like the form of many orchids—' He bowed to Marie-Josèphe. 'If you'll forgive me for mentioning the similarity to—'

'I beg your pardon, sir,' Yves said. 'My sister's natural delicacy . . .'

Chartres grinned.

'The creature's very little like a monkey,' Marie-Josèphe said quickly. 'I have dissected a monkey.'

'Don't you think teeth are trivial, Father?' Chartres said. 'After all, we lose them so easily. When we look at the female monster's skull, no doubt her teeth will be much smaller.'

'Her teeth are equally large and sharp, sir,' Marie-Josèphe said.

'Your imagination is overwrought,' Yves said.

'Now that she mentions it,' Chartres said, 'this does look rather like a human skull.'

'Have you had much occasion to study the human skull, M. de Chartres?' Yves asked.

'I have, Father. On the battlefield, in the rain and the mud, the horses' hooves dig up old graves, from old battles. I found a skull, I kept it in my tent the whole of the summer. Not only did I study it, I spoke to it. I asked if it had fought with Charlemagne, or St. Louis.'

'Did it answer?' Yves asked.

'A dead skull, answer?' Chartres asked quizzically. He tapped his fingernail on the edge of the paper. 'But it looked very like this.'

'I shall mention your observation in my notes,' Yves said. 'Which I must hurry along and write.'

'I'll walk with you,' Chartres said. 'You'll see my point before we reach the chateau.'

Chartres paused to salute the portrait of his uncle; Yves followed suit. The two men departed together, deep in philosophical discussion. Marie-Josèphe curtsied to the painting and set about straightening Yves' equipment, under His Majesty's eye. When the servants came to take His Majesty's picture reverently away, Marie-Josèphe felt obscurely comforted.

Chapter 15

The Venetian boat glided along the Grand Canal, poled by a gondolier singing an incomprehensible Italian folk song. In the bow of the gondola, Marie-Josèphe trailed her hand in the water. Silver water lilies bearing lighted candles spun past, swirling.

Lorraine had claimed the next seat in the gondola. Madame and Lotte occupied the central bench, while Monsieur sat aft at the gondolier's feet.

Ahead of the gondola, His Majesty's miniature galleon raced his galley. The gondolier had resigned himself to last place as soon as they left the bank. His passengers were entirely content with his singing.

The overseer screamed at the convict rowers. He lashed their backs. The galley plunged into the lead.

'Hardly a fair race.' Lorraine gazed at Marie-Josèphe. The candlelight, and the light of the waxing moon, flattered his handsome face. 'A whip against the barest breeze.' He slipped his hand around Marie-Josèphe's ankle. She moved her foot; he gently restrained it.

There's no harm in it, Marie-Josèphe thought. *His touch pleases me. Yves would not like me to allow it, but Yves allows himself his own pleasures, riding in the galleon with the King and the Pope, reliving the sea monster hunt.*

'Why must they race?' Marie-Josèphe said. 'The poor men—'

'They're only convicts,' Lorraine said. 'Prisoners of war, or murderers—'

'Surely not!'

'Who else would suffer such treatment? My dear, His Majesty races so he may lose his bet with King James. Then James will have money for another week or two at Versailles.'

'His Majesty is magnanimous,' Marie-Josèphe said.

Lorraine moved his hand above her ankle to her calf.

Monsieur gazed at Lorraine. Despite the shadows of candlelight,

215

despite his powder and diamond patches, distress showed plain in his face. Marie-Josèphe wondered if perhaps the friends had argued.

The galley reached the man-made island that floated where the arms of the Grand Canal crossed. A cheer went up from the English King's party.

'You are looking particularly splendid this evening,' Lorraine said.

'Thank you, sir,' she said. 'It's entirely thanks to you.' She stroked the peacock feather in her hair. 'Odelette had no time for my hair. Mademoiselle needed her – and Mary of Modena particularly requested her attendance. I'm so proud of her success! But if not for your peacock, my hair would be—'

'What a fortunate peacock.' He closed his eyes, and opened them; his long eyelashes brushed against his cheeks.

The gondolier, a fine tenor, held a high note till the bow of his boat touched the island. Marie-Josèphe applauded him; he bowed. Lorraine tossed him a gold piece. The passengers disembarked onto the heavy planks of the island. Lorraine took Marie-Josèphe's arm and helped her onto the platform. Nearby, in the galley, the rowers gasped for breath. Loincloths and chains hid their nakedness. They glistened with sweat and blood. Lorraine hurried her past them, out of hearing of their groans as their salty sweat stung deep welts.

A fairyland of delicate gold archways and tall spires distracted the guests. Sprays of crystal dispersed the light of a thousand candles in colours across drifts and wreaths of flowers. The chamber orchestra's music filled the perfumed air. The island was wonderful. Yesterday it had not even existed.

'You must have some wine,' Lorraine said.

At the edge of the island, sprites walked on water, carrying trays of wine and baskets of sweets. The supports of the island lay just beneath the Canal's surface, invisible bridges for the servants in their costumes. Lorraine fetched Marie-Josèphe a glass of wine.

'Is this your third? Or fourth?'

Marie-Josèphe laughed. 'Oh, sir – I've lost count.'

They passed beneath an arbour. Moss lay soft under their feet. Lotte plucked a strawberry from the trailing vines and ate half. Red juice shining on her mouth, she gave the other half to Marie-Josèphe.

She crushed its sweetness between her teeth. Lotte brushed her fingertip across Marie-Josèphe's lips.

'You wear hardly any powder or rouge,' she said. 'There, now your lips aren't quite so pale.' She picked another strawberry and gave it to her mother. Madame embraced her daughter and ate the strawberry. The arbours hung heavy with fruit and sweets tied with gold thread.

'Come along, my dear.'

Monsieur took Lorraine's free arm. Lorraine bent to kiss Monsieur quickly on the lips.

'Rumour says, our friends plan games in a hidden bower.' Monsieur's manner excluded Marie-Josèphe; his troubled gaze hesitated on her face, then returned to Lorraine. 'You must allow me retribution, after what you did to me last night.'

'It will be my entire pleasure – to gamble with you, Monsieur.' Lorraine's manner grew formal, and he bowed.

Monsieur and his family and Marie-Josèphe all followed Lorraine's lead in saluting His Majesty. The King approached, smiling, accompanied by Mme de Maintenon, M. du Maine, Mme de Chartres, and her friend Mlle d'Armagnac. Mme de Chartres wore a towering fontanges, but Mlle d'Armagnac went against the mode in an even more extreme fashion than Marie-Josèphe. She wore as a headdress a great fan of peacock feathers.

Marie-Josèphe wondered where Count Lucien had got to; she always expected to see him, when she saw the King.

'Good evening, my brother,' Louis said.

'Good evening, sir.' Monsieur and the King smiled at each other, despite the ceremony with which they always spoke.

'Mlle de la Croix.' His Majesty raised her gently. 'The image of your mother! Ah, my dear, how glad I am that you are safe in France.'

'Thank you, Your Majesty.' She returned his smile. Despite the loss of his upper teeth, he maintained the charisma of his youth, and added to it the refinement of age. He patted Marie-Josèphe's cheek.

'Your floating island is delightful,' Monsieur said.

'A pleasant little thing, is it not? Brother, I require your knowledge. Who's the most passionate man at my gathering tonight?'

Monsieur hesitated, but his glance touched Lorraine.

217

'Chrétien has declined to be entered in the race,' the King said.

'Why, Your Majesty? Because he won't go to sea?' Lorraine's gesture encompassed the floating island.

His Majesty chuckled. 'No, no, perhaps because it would be an unfair competition. M. du Maine is passionate – aren't you, dear boy?' The King patted his natural son's shoulder. 'But you reserve your passion for your wife!'

'I must suggest Father de la Croix,' Mme Lucifer said.

'No, no, no, he's eliminated on any number of grounds. Besides, he must dedicate his passion to God.'

Monsieur finally added a word to the conversation. 'You shall choose, sir, as your decision must be correct.'

'I know who you'd choose, if your natural modesty didn't restrain you.' Louis spoke without irony. 'Your advice is most valuable. Now, come along, I must give over to James my command of the ocean.'

As Mme de Maintenon passed, she glared with an expression of ferocious resentment, leaving Marie-Josèphe confused, hurt, and startled. Always before, Mme de Maintenon had treated her with the intention of kindness.

His Majesty led the way to the open centre of the island. His guests gathered, their costumes as bright as the candles. The chamber orchestra played, and a wide expanse of gleaming parquet lay ready for the dance. Pope Innocent and his Cardinals, in shining white and brilliant red, challenged the jewels and gold lace of the courtiers. Yves wore only black, but his presence drew the eye. Odelette attended Queen Mary, bearing her handkerchief on a velvet cushion.

Louis and James met in the centre of the dancing floor. Louis crowned James with a diadem and presented him with the trident of Poseidon. An exquisite rope of pearls, at least three armspans long, twined around the sea-god's weapon.

'You bested me,' His Majesty said. 'And in my own boat!' He laughed.

'Next time I'll command a wind from the sky, so the race will be closer.' James laughed, too, and adorned Mary of Modena with the pearls. He could not reach over her fontanges, it was so tall. Instead, he poured the pearls across her bosom and looped them over her bare pale shoulders.

His Majesty took his seat before the orchestra. A little sea-nymph, in golden scales, ran up to place a cushion for his foot. The King invited his royal guests to join him, and the rest of the courtiers gathered behind.

Marie-Josèphe's mind wandered from the play and its balletic interludes, for it retold ancient history: the Fronde, the civil war. Her attention drifted from the music. She fancied she could hear the sea monster's singing.

Before her, Madame nodded, jerked awake, nodded again. Her chin sank toward her ample breasts. In a moment she would begin to snore. Marie-Josèphe laid her hand on Madame's shoulder. The duchess d'Orléans snuffled once, snapped awake, and sat up straight in her chair. Marie-Josèphe smiled fondly and tried again to follow the action on stage. A dancer represented the young King, triumphing though his uncle Gaston roused a large faction of France's aristocracy against him. The coup d'état failed.

Marie-Josèphe wished she had seen His Majesty dance. When he was younger, his performances as the sun, as Apollo, as Orpheus or Mars, formed part of his legend. He had not taken part in ballets for decades.

The entertainment ended. His Majesty's guests expressed their appreciation, and His Majesty accepted their gratitude.

The Grand Master of Ceremonies, who had paid handsomely to hold the position for the quarter, approached Madame. He bowed to her, then turned to Marie-Josèphe.

'The King requests your attendance, Mlle de la Croix.'

Marie-Josèphe sketched a quick and startled curtsy to Madame, slipped out of the crowd of courtiers, and hurried after the marquis.

His Majesty sat in his armchair, listening to the music, one fine leg outstretched, the other resting on its cushion. Marie-Josèphe dropped to the floor in a rustle of silk and lace. She felt improperly dressed, with her hair so simply arranged.

His Majesty bent forward, lifted her chin, and gazed into her face with his beautiful dark blue eyes.

'The image,' he said, as he always said, 'the very image of your mother. She dressed her hair in just such a manner – no towers, no apartments for mice!'

219

His Majesty rose, drawing Marie-Josèphe to her feet.

'Let us dance.' The King escorted her into the music, into the dance's intricate patterns. Before all the court, Marie-Josèphe danced with the King.

She could hardly breathe. Her cheeks flushed and her sight blurred. His Majesty's touch, his friendly gaze, his favour, combined to make her feel faint.

'You dance as exquisitely as you play, Mlle de la Croix,' Louis said. 'As your mother did.'

'She was very beautiful and very talented, Your Majesty,' Marie-Josèphe said. 'Much more than I.'

'We all remember her well,' Louis said.

For Marie-Josèphe, her parents existed in a halo of golden tropical light, her mother wise and kind, her father absent-minded and good humoured, until the dreadful week when she had lost them both.

'My old friends and enemies, my protegés and advisers are passing,' the King said. 'Queen Christina. Le Brun, Le Vau, evil old Louvois. Molière and Lully. La Grande Mademoiselle . . . sometimes, do you know, I even miss old Mazarin, that tyrant.' The King sighed. 'I miss M. and Mme de la Croix.'

'I miss them too, Sire. Terribly. Only God could have saved my mother, she was so ill. She died so quickly.'

'God was tempted, and He took her. But He does not allow His angels to suffer.'

She did *suffer*, Marie-Josèphe thought. Her fury at God and the physicians flared bright from its embers. *She suffered dreadfully, and I hate God so much that I do not know why He has not struck me with lightning into Hell.*

During a turn in the dance she brushed away a tear, hoping His Majesty would not notice. How could he help but notice? But he was too much a gentleman to comment.

'I think they would not have died, if—'

'If I had not sent them to Martinique?'

'Oh, no, Your Majesty! It was the physicians – the surgeons . . . Your commission honoured our family.' Marie-Josèphe curbed the uncharitable thought: *if you missed them so, Sire, why didn't you call my family back to France?*

'Your father was honourable, indeed,' His Majesty said. 'Only Henri de la Croix could increase his poverty while holding a colonial governorship.'

'Father lingered,' she whispered. 'I thought he would recover. But they bled him—'

The King's gaze focussed blankly beyond her shoulder.

I've said too much, she thought. He has important concerns, I mustn't trouble him with my grief and my anger.

'Those times are returning,' the King said. 'The times of youth and glory. Your brother will bring them to me.'

'I—I hope so, Your Majesty.'

She blinked away her tears, made herself smile, and concentrated on the perfect pattern of the dance. She feared what might happen when His Majesty realised Yves could not help him to live forever.

'I must find you a worthy husband,' he said offhand.

'I cannot marry, Your Majesty. I have neither connections nor dowry.'

'You must want a husband!'

'Oh, yes, Sire! A husband, children—'

'And scientific instruments?' He chuckled.

'If my husband allowed it.' She blushed, wondering who had been making fun of her to the King. 'But I see no way of achieving such a dream.'

'Did your father never tell you—? I suppose he would not. I promised, at your birth, that you would be properly dowered.'

The music's final flourish ended. His Majesty bowed graciously. The applause of His Majesty's court raked Marie-Josèphe like wildfire. She gathered her wits, fell into a deep curtsy, and kissed his hand. He lifted her to her feet. Like the perfect gentleman he was, he conducted her to the edge of the dancing floor, where Monsieur and the Chevalier stood whispering.

'You will dance the next dance with Mlle de la Croix,' he said to the Chevalier de Lorraine, and put her hand in his.

Marie-Josèphe ran up the stairs to her room, ecstatic. The candle flickered in her hand. She cupped her fingers around the flame to

221

shield it. She hoped Odelette had returned from attending Mary of Modena; she hoped Yves had returned from attending Pope Innocent. She hoped they were both still awake. She wanted to tell them the King's wonderful news. She might tell Odelette about her long walk with Lorraine, crossing the water on the clever secret bridges, strolling beside the Grand Canal in the moonlight. She thought she would not tell Yves, not quite yet, though Lorraine had gone beyond the bounds of gallantry only once or twice.

Muffled voices disturbed the quiet. Marie-Josèphe smiled. *Odelette and Yves have both returned*, she thought, *and Yves has done something to aggravate Odelette. We might as well be back in Martinique. The three of us together, with Odelette abusing my brother because he's left his linen in a pile on the floor.*

She opened the door to her room.

She could not make out what she was seeing. The light was dim. Beyond that, she did not believe what was happening.

A nobleman writhed on her bed, scrabbling beneath the bed-clothes, his hat upside-down on the rug and tangled with his coat. His breeches twisted around his knees. His shirt hiked up, exposing his naked buttocks. One of his shoes flew from his foot and clattered to the floor.

'You want me.' Desperation thickened the familiar voice. 'I know you want me.'

'Please—'

Marie-Josèphe bolted forward and grasped the young man's shoulder. Odelette clutched his arms, her fine dark hands clenching, fighting.

'Go away,' said Philippe, duke de Chartres. 'Can't you see we're busy?'

'Leave her alone!' Marie-Josèphe cried. 'How dare you!' His lace shirt tore in her hands.

'Mlle de la Croix!'

Astonished, flustered, Chartres leaped from the bed and fumbled to cover himself. Odelette sat up, her blue-black hair spilling around her shoulders, her eyes pure black in the candlelight, her complexion suffused with heat.

222

'How dare you, sir! How do you come to assault my servant!'

'I thought—I meant to—' His hair stood out in wild ringlets. 'I thought she was you!'

He smiled into her silence. Odelette burst into tears.

Chartres bowed to her. 'Though I would certainly enjoy an hour in your company.'

Odelette flung herself around and sobbed into her pillow.

'I believe you do not dislike me,' Chartres said.

He held out his hand. Marie-Josèphe slapped him hard.

'How dare you think I'd welcome the attentions of a married man – of any man not my husband!'

Marie-Josèphe pushed past Chartres. She sat next to Odelette and gathered her into her arms.

'If you intended to drive me away,' Chartres said, 'you might as well have pelted me with roses.'

'Leave us, sir.'

'You tempted me, mademoiselle, and now you wrong me.' Chartres gathered up his plumed hat, his gold-laced coat, his high-heeled shoe.

The door slammed.

'Oh, my dear, are you all right? Did he hurt you? I swear I never gave him reason to think I – or you—'

Odelette sobbed and pushed her away, more violently than Marie-Josèphe had pushed Chartres.

'Why did you interfere? Why did you stop him?'

'What?' Marie-Josèphe asked, baffled.

'He might have got a bastard on me, he'd acknowledge me, he'd buy me and free me and take me home – my royal husband!' She cried out in anger and grief and drew her knees to her chest and buried her face and wrapped her arms over her head.

Marie-Josèphe stroked her hair until her sobs eased.

'He can never marry you. He's already married.'

'That only matters in your world – not in mine!'

Marie-Josèphe bit her lip. She knew only what Odelette's mother had told them both, about Turkey. Odelette saw it as a paradise, but Marie-Josèphe did not.

223

'He'd never acknowledge you. Or any child you bore him.'

'He would! He must! He has other bastards!'

'But he thinks of you as a servant. He'd command me to turn you away – turn you out – you *and* your baby!'

Odelette raised her head, glaring with such fury that Marie-Josèphe drew back in astonishment.

'I am a *princess*!' Odelette cried. 'Slave or no, I am a princess. My family is a thousand years older than Bourbons – or any Frenchman. My family ruled when the Romans skewered these barbarians on their spears!'

'I know.' Marie-Josèphe dared to hold her.

Odelette huddled against her, shivering with despair, crying with rage.

'I know,' Marie-Josèphe said again. 'But he wouldn't acknowledge you. He wouldn't take you to Constantinople. I'd never turn you out, but if he applied to the King and the King banished you, I could never stop him.'

She stroked Odelette's long hair. It tumbled down her back and pooled on the bed behind her.

'I'll free you,' Marie-Josèphe said.

Odelette drew away and looked into her face. 'She said you never would.'

'Who?'

'The nun. The mother superior. Whenever I did her hair, when her lovers would come—'

'Her lovers!'

'She did have lovers, I don't care if no one believes it.'

'I believe you,' Marie-Josèphe said. 'I'm astonished, but I believe you.'

'—she said you would never give me my freedom. She said you refused to give me up.'

'The sisters persuaded me it was a dreadful sin to own a slave—'

'It is,' Odelette said severely.

'Yes. But they never wanted me to free you. They wanted me to sell you, to give the money to the convent.' She held Odelette's hands and kissed them. 'I feared to do that, dear Odelette. They never let me speak to you, I never knew what you wanted, and I thought – though

224

sometimes I wondered – no matter how dreadful it is here, it could be so much worse—'

'It was never dreadful at the convent,' Odelette said. 'I dressed their hair. I would rather embroider the linen of nuns than wash your brother's stockings . . .'

Tears ran down Marie-Josèphe's cheeks, tears of shock at Chartres' actions, relief at Odelette's revelation, and, if she admitted it, of self-pity, because for Marie-Josèphe the convent had been terrible.

'No wonder Mademoiselle and Queen Mary steal you away from me,' she said, trying to smile. 'But that doesn't matter now. I refused to sell you—'

'I'm glad of that,' Odelette said. 'I shouldn't be a slave. I'll never be a slave except to you.'

'You'll never be a slave to anyone,' Marie-Josèphe declared. 'You are free. We shall be as sisters.'

Odelette said nothing.

'I'll ask—' Marie-Josèphe hesitated. She doubted her own judg-ment, for she had trusted Chartres. 'I'll ask Count Lucien.' Count Lucien, though a dangerous freethinker, at least was honest. 'He'll know how to go about it – what papers you want – but from this moment you are free. You are my sister.'

'Yes,' Odelette said.

'I promise you.'

'Why have you waited so long?'

'You never asked it of me before.' Marie-Josèphe dashed the tears from her eyes with the back of her hand. She took Odelette by the shoulders. 'What was the difference in our station? We lived in the same house, we ate the same food, if you washed my brother's stock-ings, I washed his shirt! I never thought of you as slave or free.'

'You cannot understand,' Odelette said.

'No, I cannot. Until the sisters plagued me about my sin, I never thought of it, and for that I beg your forgiveness. But, dear Odelette, afterwards I *did* think, and I thought, if I free you, the convent will put you out in the street with nothing. No resources, no protector, no family. I had nothing to give you!'

'I can make my own way,' Odelette said angrily.

'And you shall, if you wish. But, think, sister, our fortunes are improving. If you wait, only a while, I'm convinced, if you stay with me, you'll share in them. You'll go into the world better than a lady's maid. You might go to Turkey – if you truly wish to go to Turkey, which you have never seen—'

'As you had never seen France,' Odelette said, 'but here you are.'

'That's entirely different,' Marie-Josèphe said.

'How, Mlle Marie?'

'Perhaps it isn't different after all, Mlle Odelette. But if you do go home to Turkey, would it not be better to return rich and well-attended, as suits your true station, rather than as a maidservant, or a gypsy?'

'That would be better,' Odelette said. 'But . . . I cannot wait too long.'

'I hope you won't have to,' Marie-Josèphe said. 'Now, come, go back to sleep if you can. I'll lock the door.'

'Let me help you undress.'

'Only help me with my gown, I have a little work to do still.'

First Odelette must have something to wear, for Chartres had rent her threadbare shift beyond repair. In the wardrobe, Marie-Josèphe's shift with the turned hems lay on top of a new one, of heavy warm flannel with three lace ruffles.

'Where did this come from?'

'Queen Mary. You may wear it. I shall take your old one.'

'It's yours, you shall wear it.'

Marie-Josèphe helped Odelette into the new nightshirt, gratefully accepted her sister's help in getting out of her gown and shoes and stays, and tucked her sister back into bed. She used the chaise percée and splashed cold water on her face and hands.

When she washed away the dried blood between her legs, she real-ised her bleeding had stopped, days early. Worried, she tried to gather her courage, to overcome her terror of submitting to the medical arts. For a moment she resolved to speak to a physician.

But she had so many other, more important things to worry about, so many things to do. The physicians here were so grand, she should not waste their time with female complaints. And, in truth, she could only feel grateful for being spared more mess, more inconvenience. To be safe, she put on a clean towel, and soaked the bloody one in a basin of cold water.

I wonder if the sea monster bleeds? She answered her own question: *That's ridiculous. Animals don't bleed. They're free of the sin of Eve. Besides, if the sea monster bled like a woman, she would be in terrible danger from sharks.*

She fetched Lorraine's cloak. His musky perfume tickled her nose, as the curl of his perruke tickled her cheek when he bent down to whisper to her. She curled in the chair by Odelette's bed, her music score in her lap, her bare feet tucked under the warm cloak. Candle-light flickered across the pages.

I thought the score was perfect, she said to herself, *but the sea monster is so sad, so frightened in her captivity* . . .

Odelette slipped her hand from beneath the covers, reaching for Marie-Josèphe, holding her fingers tight. Marie-Josèphe left her hand in Odelette's even after her sister had fallen asleep. She revised the score, turning the pages awkwardly, one-handed. She dozed.

She gasped awake, frightened by the pleasure that invaded her body. The sheaf of music paper spilled to the floor.

The burnt-out candle, its smoke pungent, left her room without a breath of light. A song crept around her, as cold as night air. The sea monster swam through the window, as if the glass were transparent to material flesh. She hovered above Marie-Josèphe, upside-down, her hair streaming around her and toward the ceiling.

Shivering, entranced, Marie-Josèphe thought, *This is a dream. I can do as I like. Nothing, no one, can stop me.*

She stood, and raised up her hands to the sea monster.

The song hesitated; the sea monster vanished. Marie-Josèphe hurried to the window. The tent loomed at the bottom of the garden, the white silk glowing eerily. Gardeners' torches flickered in the North Quincunx and the Star and reflected from the Mirror Fountain. The creak of the gears of the orange-tree carts pierced the soft murmuring quiet of the gardens of Versailles.

Singing again, the sea monster appeared, bright as sunlight. Other sea monsters followed, swimming in the air, circling, caressing each other, creating a whirlwind, a whirlpool.

Marie-Josèphe stepped toward the window, expecting to pass through the panes, like the sea monsters. She bumped her nose painfully.

How strange, she thought. *In a dream I must be able to pass through the window and swim in the air like the sea monsters. I cannot; my imagination fails me. If I open the window and step out, I would fall. Everyone says that a dreamer who falls instead of flying must die.*

She ran down the stairs, hugging the cloak tight against the surprised glances of the servants. They were not used to seeing members of court an hour before dawn. For some courtiers, the hour before dawn was the only time they ever slept.

Beyond the terrace, the gravel cut her feet. She dreamed herself on Zachi's back. She dreamed herself a pair of stout shoes. Nothing happened. The gravel felt sharper. She ran down the stairs and stepped onto the Green Carpet. The grass was cold and wet, but it did not cut her. The candles verging the Carpet had burned to puddles of wax and smoking wicks.

The radiant sea monsters led her to the tent. The guard slept, lulled by the sea monster's song.

Inside the tent, inside the cage, inside the fountain, the sea monster splashed furiously with both her tails. A waterfall of luminescence erupted around her.

She sang.

Marie-Josèphe sat on the rim of the Fountain.

'If this were my dream,' she said, 'if this were your dream, you wouldn't be imprisoned.'

The sea monster cried. A male sea monster — the sea monster whose body Yves was dissecting, brought back to life by the song — swam around the ceiling of the tent. Marie-Josèphe closed her eyes, but the image remained, fashioned in her mind by the singing, swimming in front of her as plain as anything real.

'I see your songs,' Marie-Josèphe said. 'And you understand what I say. Don't you? Do you speak? Do you speak in words?'

'Fishhh,' the sea monster said, and then she sang.

A tiny fish, its edges made harsh by the rasp of the sea monster's voice, flitted across her vision. The song described the fish itself, and

228

its surroundings, the sound of its swimming, the taste of its flesh. The sea monsters spoke not in words, but in images, interconnections, associations.

Marie-Josèphe hummed the fish's melody. An indistinct image wavered before her and vanished. 'Oh, sea monster, my song must be only a blur in your ears. I'll do better, I promise. Sea monster, what's your name?'

The sea monster sang a complicated melody. The song described the sea monster, and it hinted, as well, at joy, and brashness, and youthful wisdom.

'How beautiful! It's perfect.'

The sea monster swam to her. She trailed a glowing wake. The luminescence flowed down her shoulders and along her hair. The sea monster rested her elbows on the lowest step and gazed at Marie-Josèphe. Her whispered song formed shapes and scenes.

Marie-Josèphe ran to the laboratory, snatched scraps of paper and charcoal, and hurried back to the sea monster. She sketched the songs, not in words or notes but rough scribbled pictures. Her eyes filled with tears; sometimes her tears smudged the paper. But the scenes remained clear, for she heard them.

In her song, the sea monster swam alone. Filth and algae dimmed the fountain's clarity. Litter and coins covered the bottom of the fountain.

The sea monster's song turned the water sapphire. The trash and the coins transmuted to white sand and living shells. Bright iridescent fish flitted past, changing colour all together from blue to silver as they turned.

A strange sea monster swam through the tropical sea. She was older than the captured creature, her skin a darker mahogany, her hair a lighter green, her tails dappled with silver. She was pregnant.

She swam through swiftly shoaling water to a white beach, an isolated island in the expanse of the ocean. The sea monster struggled onto the sand, rolling in the warmth of it, nesting in it, pillowing her belly.

Marie-Josèphe's sea monster writhed onto the beach beside the pregnant monster. The male sea monster followed, and another. They surrounded the mother sea monster, grooming her hair, rubbing her back, stroking her belly.

The mother sea monster moaned, and wailed, and her body tensed; the aunt and uncle sea monsters supported her so she lay reclining. Marie-Josèphe watched the birth with dread and fascination. It was difficult, painful for the mother, more like the birth of a baby than like the easy births of animals. But finally the wizened baby sea monster lay against its mother's breast. She held it, crooned to it, and let it suckle while her family washed it with warm sea water and unfolded its wrinkled, webbed toes.

Days passed; it grew; in the shallows of the island, it splashed and played with its mother and its aunts and their friends. Its mother nursed it; Marie-Josèphe's and Yves' sea monsters fed the mother with fish and beche-de-mer, clams and whelks and bits of seaweed for garnish.

The sea monsters taught the baby to swim; they taught it to love the sea. The took it underwater, showing it when to breathe and how to hold its breath, showing it the wonders of the ocean, warning it of the dangers. A shark glided by, hungrily eying the baby, wary of the adults, and vanished into distant blue. Dolphins sped past, replying to the sea monsters' songs with the percussion of their clicks and squeaks. The sea monsters swam between the tentacles of a huge tame octopus that lived within the skeleton of a Spanish galleon. The sea monsters played with gold pieces and jewellery fit for kings and emperors, dropped the riches unheeded on the sea bottom, and swam away.

At times of great danger, or during hurricanes too wild to play in, the sea monsters sank beneath the waves, exhaling great clouds of bubbles, and grew very still. They ceased rising to the surface. They lay with their eyes closed, their mouths open, and every little while their chests heaved as if they were breathing water.

After the baby sea monster had learned how to sleep safely at the bottom of the sea, the little family group swam away from the birth island. They took turns carrying the child, and disappeared into the depths.

The scenes shuddered. The captive sea monster's voice failed, in a hoarse croak, and the visions with it.

Sunrise dimmed the glowing water.

Shivering with cold and understanding, Marie-Josèphe gripped

230

the uneven stack of paper that documented what she had heard and envisioned. The last bit of charcoal fell onto the planks, hitting as quietly as a drift of ash.

'You've shown me your life,' Marie-Josèphe said. 'Your life, your family—'

The sea monster sang again.

Yves appeared before Marie-Josèphe, as he had appeared in apparition, standing silent and cold, bleeding. In distress, Marie-Josèphe covered her eyes. The image still hovered before her, cupped in the palms of her hands. She covered her ears. The image of her wounded brother blurred, and disappeared.

The sea monster sang to her, in images unrelated to any words, *I offered your brother the fate he visited upon my friend, but I could not frighten you by threatening to rip him open from pulse to balls.*

The tiger burned bright in the dawn, and vanished.

The sea monster sang to her, *I sang a warning against the predator, for I feared it would smell your blood, as sharks smell blood from a great distance. I sang until you must be safe, or dead, and until my throat hurt from crying. But you are fearless, and I could not make you my ally by warning you.*

The whirlwind of sea monsters streamed around the peak of the cage, sleekly stroking mates and friends, sighing their pleasure.

I abandoned fear, the sea monster cried, *and sang to you of love and passion, and finally, you heard me, and listened.*

'Sea monster—' Marie-Josèphe whispered.

The sea monster groaned harshly and clambered up the steps. Marie-Josèphe held her, stopped her. The drawings spilled onto the ground.

'Don't, please, stop.'

The sea monster cried. Her claws could have ripped Marie-Josèphe cruelly, but she remained quiet.

'I can't free you,' Marie-Josèphe said. 'Where would you go? The sea's too far, even the river's too far. You belong to His Majesty. My brother would be ruined if you escaped.'

The sea monster snarled, baring her teeth, before she flung herself into the fountain, sending up a great angry splash.

Marie-Josèphe began to cry. 'Oh, sea monster, sea *woman*!'

Chapter 16

Marie-Josèphe stumbled up the Green Carpet, anxious to leave the gardens before anyone saw her running bedraggled and dew-damp and barefoot. She wished she had Zachi to ride. She could hardly feel her toes. She clutched the sheaf of sketches, shielding her dangerous new knowledge beneath the Chevalier's warm cape. The sea woman's despair stalked her like a beast.

Upstairs, she peeked into Yves' room. He snored softly. His cassock, shirt, and boots lay in an untidy path from doorway to bed. She put her sketches on his desk, shook him till he sat up mumbling that he was awake, changed her mind about the drawings, and hid them away.

If I tell Yves about the sea woman, how can he believe me? she thought. *But if I show him . . . if I show everyone . . .*

Odelette returned, carrying a tray of bread and chocolate. In a new morning dress of sprigged muslin and lace, she glowed with health and beauty.

'I'll stay with you.' Odelette's expression was sombre. She put the tray on the table near the window.

Marie-Josèphe, distracted and distressed, could not think what she was talking about, could not think where the dress could have come from. Then she remembered: Chartres' assault; her own promise; Mary of Modena's favour.

'But only until the family fortunes are repaired, or until I may return home unashamed. I'll make my own fortune, if I can. I'll no longer serve you – but I will help you, if you request it, because, Mlle Marie, you know nothing of fashion. No one may ever again call me a slave.'

'I accept your terms, Mlle Odelette, and I'll be grateful for your help.' Marie-Josèphe kissed her cheek. Odelette embraced her and leaned her forehead on Marie-Josèphe's shoulder. She began to tremble; she drew back abruptly. Her dark eyes glistened.

'When you go, I'll miss you as my sister,' Marie-Josèphe said. 'Nevertheless, I'll do everything I can to speed your independence.'

Self-possessed again, Odelette gave an elegant bow of her head. She sat at the breakfast table. Marie-Josèphe joined her, sitting in the window-seat. Marie-Josèphe poured chocolate for them both. Hercules followed, miaowing; Marie-Josèphe gave him a saucer of warm milk.

'Do I smell chocolate?' Yves strolled in. He ran his hands through his hair. It fell into curls as graceful as any perruke. He glanced at Odelette. 'Where am I to sit?'

'You may bring yourself a chair,' Odelette said, perfectly composed. 'You're strong and fit.'

He frowned. 'Enough — I'm hungry. Let me have my place, Odelette.'

'My name is not Odelette. My name is Haleeda.'

Yves laughed. 'Haleeda! Next you'll tell me you've become a Mahometan!'

'Indeed I have.'

'I've given Mlle Haleeda her freedom, and adopted her as our sister.'

'What!'

'I freed her.'

'On a whim? She's our only possession of value.'

'She belonged to me — I'll free her if I wish.'

'In five years, when you're of age, you may free her.'

'I gave her my word. She is free. She is our sister.'

He shrugged. 'I'll sign no papers to that effect.' To Haleeda he said, 'Never fear there's a question of my selling you — but we cannot live at court without a servant.'

Odelette — Haleeda — rose from table so quickly that the chair crashed over. She fled to Marie-Josèphe's bedroom.

'Yves, how could you!'

He righted the chair, sat down, and poured the chocolate.

'I? I'm guilty only of protecting our station.'

He dipped his bread into his chocolate and ate the sweet and soggy mass, wiping his chin with his hand.

'It isn't right to own another human being.' *Or to keep one imprisoned in a cage*, she thought.

'Nonsense. Who have you been talking to? What other dangerous ideas have you adopted?'

She did not dare to speak of the sea woman now. She took Yves' hand. 'Don't be angry – you have the King's favour. He's promised me a dowry – a husband! You can afford to be magnanimous. Our sister—'

Yves flung down his soggy bread. 'A dowry? A dowry! The King never mentioned your marriage to me.'

'I thought you'd be pleased,' she said.

'I don't like these changes in you,' he said. 'You say your greatest wish is to assist me in my work, but—'

'How can I assist you, locked away in a convent—'

'You must live somewhere while I travel—'

'—forbidden to study, accused of—'

'—and Versailles is no place for a maiden.'

'If I were married, I wouldn't be a maiden.'

'Perhaps,' Yves said, 'if you returned to Saint-Cyr . . .'

Marie-Josèphe struggled to remain calm. If she showed her brother how terrified she was of his suggestion, he would think she had gone mad. Perhaps he would be right.

'Mme de Maintenon ordered all the instructresses to take holy orders. That's why I had to leave.'

'Go back. Give yourself to God.'

'I'll never take the veil!'

The heavy clash and clink of gold interrupted them. Magnificent in outrage, Haleeda flung down a handful of louis d'or. The coins rolled and bounced across the carpet, clattered onto the planks, rattled to a stop in the corner.

'I shall buy myself. If that isn't enough, I can get more.'

Haughty as any court lady, Haleeda wore a new grand habit of midnight-blue silk. A long rope of lustrous pearls twined through her blue-black hair.

'Where did this come from?' Yves asked. 'Where did you get that dress, that jewellry?'

'From Mademoiselle – from Mlle d'Armagnac – from Mme du Maine – and from Queen Mary!'

Yves gathered up the coins. 'I'll consider your plea . . . after you correct your errors of religion.'

Marie-Josèphe snatched the coins and pressed them into Haleeda's hands. 'Your prizes are yours, and your freedom.'

'I mean what I say!' Yves stormed from the apartment.

'Yves never meant it,' Marie-Josèphe said. 'He—'

'He was affected by that devil, who believes all Turks should be slaves. That Christian devil, the Pope.'

Lucien toiled up the Queen's staircase. His back hurt. He would rather be out riding, but he must listen to the marquis de Dangeau read his journal of the King's activities, and record His Majesty's approval.

The musketeer bowed to him and opened the door to Mme de Maintenon's apartment.

His Majesty sat quietly speaking to his wife, who nodded to him as she bent over a tapestry. Lucien avoided looking at the tapestry; he did not care to see more heretics burning.

'M. de Chrétien,' His Majesty said. 'Good day to you. Quentin, a glass of wine for M. de Chrétien.'

Lucien bowed to the King, grateful for the courtesy his sovereign showed him.

'And set out a goblet for M. de—'

A fracas outside the apartment doors interrupted the valet. Quentin hurried to silence the disturbance.

'That cannot be M. de Dangeau!' His Majesty exclaimed.

'Monsieur, you may not enter,' Quentin said. 'His Majesty is with his council—'

'With his mistress, you mean! Let me pass.'

Monsieur forced himself past the guard. Quentin, double Monsieur's size and strength, moustache bristling, barred Monsieur's way. Behind Monsieur, at the top of the stairs, M. de Dangeau hesitated, watched horrified for but a moment, then backed cautiously away and disappeared.

'Let my brother pass,' His Majesty said to Quentin, who answered only to the King.

'Sir, you must stop this farce!' Monsieur stamped in, as flustered and fancy as an angry circus pony.

'Farce, brother?'

'Why must I hear from common gossip that my intimate friend is to marry a colonial upstart?'

'Perhaps because your "intimate friend" did not choose to tell you,' Mme de Maintenon said.

'You watched me give her to him—'

'For a dance!'

'—and you made no objection, dear brother.'

'Dear brother!' Orléans' voice trembled dangerously close to shouting. 'How can I be your dear brother? You plan to steal all I care about, my only comfort, my only pleasure! In front of me, in my very sight, you give his hand to—to—'

Lucien wished himself elsewhere. Observing this ugly scene would do him no good.

M. de Dangeau is a fortunate gentleman, Lucien thought, shocked by Monsieur's outburst. *He receives a reward for being five minutes late.*

'But you approve of Mlle de la Croix,' His Majesty said. 'She's a member of your household, after all.'

'My wife's household! I cannot blame Mlle de la Croix – she's an innocent in this! You planned it! You threw them together, to steal Lorraine's affections from me!'

'I gave him to you,' Louis said, his expression dark. 'I will take him back if I wish. I will give him to another, if it pleases me.'

'He'll never leave me – he'll defy you – I'll—'

'Philippe!' Louis leapt to his feet and shook his brother by the shoulders.

Monsieur gaped, astonished. Lucien had never heard His Majesty address his brother by his given name; perhaps Monsieur never had, either.

'I thought only of your protection, dear brother. I love you. If Lorraine marries—'

'I don't need your protection.'

'Do you not?'

'And Lorraine doesn't need a wife!'

'She will shield him – and you – from accusations—'

'He has any mistress he likes. I don't mind!'

No one contradicted him, though everyone in the room had witnessed Lorraine's taunting him, paying public attention to each new mistress; everyone in the room had witnessed Monsieur's spells of bitter jealousy and despair.

'Do not force a wife on him. He's the only one who loves me.'

Mme de Maintenon rose. 'Love!' she cried. 'How can you call that love? Your behaviour – disgraceful, sinful! His Majesty protects you continually. If you weren't Monsieur, you would have been burned, and your paramour with you!'

Monsieur flung up his arms, pushing his brother away. He glared at Mme de Maintenon with hatred and despair.

'And you!' Monsieur cried. 'You want to give her my lover so she won't take yours!'

Mme de Maintenon collapsed. Taken aback, Louis turned to her. 'Madame, it isn't true!'

'Don't deny you're tempted, sir,' Monsieur said. 'By her beauty, her intelligence, her innocence. Do you believe she can replenish your youth?'

'Go away, brother,' Louis said.

'Willingly! Give me back my cavalry. Lorraine and I will fight your war, like Alexander and Hephaestion. Perhaps I'll be killed, like Patroklos—'

'Have the dignity to compare yourself to Achilleus!'

'—and you'll be rid of me—'

'No. It's impossible.'

'You give me nothing to do, you block my son from any share of glory, and now—'

'Get out!' His Majesty shouted.

Monsieur bolted. He flung open the door himself, moaning with despair.

'How can he accuse me of treachery?' His Majesty cried. 'How can I save him? How can I help him?'

He wept. His tears splashed on the intricate parquet. He caught his breath; he fought for control. His keening grew louder; it filled the room with grief.

'Come to me, my dear,' his wife whispered. 'Come to me.'

The King fell to his knees and buried his head in Mme de Maintenon's bosom. She held him, crooning. She glared at Lucien.

Without waiting for His Majesty's leave, Lucien bowed, backed away, and fled.

Marie-Josèphe rode Zachi past the marble statues overlooking the Green Carpet. Grateful for a moment's peace, she looked into each serene stone face, wishing for their calmness.

The orators would never hesitate to speak of the sea woman, she thought, *and no one would hesitate to believe them. Roman gods and orators would never feel guilty about skipping Mass; they would set out on adventures, they would win righteous battles, and never think twice about arguing with their brothers or failing to attend Mademoiselle.*

Haleeda will arrange Lotte's hair, Marie-Josèphe said to herself, *and Duke Charles will compliment her, and she will never notice my absence.*

At the bottom of the garden, a line of visitors snaked onto the Green Carpet, filing into the tent, crowding around the Fountain of Apollo, applauding the sea woman.

She shouldn't be on display, like an animal in the Menagerie! Marie-Josèphe thought. *It's beneath her dignity! And I'm responsible – I taught her the foolish tricks.*

Marie-Josèphe had no authority to close the tent.

Zachi tossed her head and pranced, asking to gallop, asking to run until her mane flew in the wind and Lorraine's cloak swept back like wings.

'No, my charger,' Marie-Josèphe whispered. 'We must keep to a stately pace. We might trample someone, if we swooped down to steal the sea woman away.'

She wondered if the sea woman could ride, if perhaps she rode great whales through the ocean. If she could . . .

Marie-Josèphe dismissed the wild idea. She would never get the

238

sea woman past the guards. Double-burdened, Zachi could not out-race even a cold-blooded horse. She might try, and break her heart.

'It would be to no avail,' Marie-Josèphe said, 'for the rescue could not succeed. Yves would never forgive me, for the sake of his work. Count Lucien would never forgive me, for the sake of His Majesty. And I'd never forgive myself, for the sake of you.'

'What time to return, mamselle?' Jacques held the stairs and helped her dismount.

'I cannot say.' She patted Zachi's sleek neck and her soft muzzle; she breathed into her flaring nostrils. 'I'll send for her.'

'You're a wonder, mademoiselle,' said one musketeer, 'training the sea monster to entertain the visitors.'

'Shame it's for such a short time,' said the other.

Marie-Josèphe hurried to the cage. The sea woman swam back and forth, around and around, tantalising the spectators.

The sea woman vanished. The pool stilled.

The surface roiled. The sea woman burst from the water in a rush of spray. Her naked body gleamed. She leaped completely over Triton, flipping her tails – her webbed feet – at the top of her arch. She arrowed down, vanishing without a splash or ripple.

The spectators applauded. 'Throw it a fish!'

'Make it leap again!'

Marie-Josèphe ignored the demands.

I will not ask the sea woman to perform like a trick dog, she thought. She sang the sea woman's name; the sea woman trilled, creating curtains of light and sound that glowed and hissed like the northern lights. Marie-Josèphe walked between them. All oblivious to the coruscating shimmer, the visitors waited for their entertainment.

'Guard,' Marie-Josèphe said, 'kindly call the lackeys, to pour the fish-barrel into the Fountain.'

'Give the fish to—'

She gave him a haughty look. He bowed.

The lackeys tilted the barrel. Sea water and live fish gushed over the rim of the fountain. With a shriek of pleasure, the sea woman burst through the river of sea-water. Terrified, the lackeys dropped the barrel; it tumbled into the fountain. The sea woman dove to evade it. The servants fled, ignoring the curses of the musketeers.

The visitors laughed and applauded. They might as well have been watching an Italian comedy. Her back to the rabble, Marie-Josèphe scowled.

'Now you've got no fish to throw to the monster!' a visitor shouted. 'We want to see the sea monster!'

'Throw the monster a fish!'

'She's no monster!' No one heard her. Water rushed; the sea woman leapt, flung a fish, and splashed flamboyantly. The fish flew through the air, between the bars of the cage, and hit the visitor in the chest. Water spattered Marie-Josèphe's face and her riding habit. Waves surged over her feet, soaking her shoes.

Delighted, the visitors laughed. A child scampered forward and snatched up the fish and flung the flopping creature back through the bars. The sea woman leapt again, caught it, and ate it in two bites. The tail vanished last. The child laughed; the sea woman trilled at her.

'The sea monster wishes to train us!' said the child's mother. All the crowd and the musketeers joined her laughter. The sea woman flipped her tails and vanished.

The floating barrel bobbed. The sea woman pushed it around the fountain. She made it turn and spin; she rode the spin upward and launched herself, flying into a dive. Her audience applauded.

'Stop it!' Marie-Josèphe cried, humiliated for the sea woman, furious. No one paid the least attention.

'Mlle de la Croix, control yourself, I beg you.'

Count Lucien stood by the Fountain, frowning, leaning lightly on his walking stick.

'Make them stop, please, Count Lucien.'

'What are they doing, that upsets you so?'

'Teasing her – baiting her, like a bear!'

'I doubt you've ever seen a bear-baiting, for this is nothing like. Your sea monster plays for them, as she plays for you.'

'It isn't fitting.'

Count Lucien chuckled.

'Please don't laugh at me.'

240

'I had no intention of doing so. On the contrary, I'm sad for you, if you don't know the pleasure play can bring. To people as well as to animals.'

'She isn't—'

The barrel bumped up against the platform, interrupting Marie-Josèphe, thudding loudly again and again. Water splashed on Marie-Josèphe's shoes.

Marie-Josèphe knelt and plunged her hands into the water. The sea woman left off battering the barrel and swam to her, sleeking past her fingers.

With one short burst of song, the sea woman sketched her life. She caught her food, she swam through bright coral reefs in tropical seas. In the north, she capered among inverted iceberg mountains. She traced the depths with an exploration of sound. She played with the children of her family. She swam among the tentacles of a tame giant octopus with her friend – her friend, the man of the sea who lay dead and flayed on the dissection table. She and her friend made love, love for pleasure's sinful sake with no thought of procreation, in the illumination of the octopus' spark-spotted skin. When desperate danger threatened, the sea woman sank into the lightless depths and nearly ceased breathing. Ever, and always, the touch and the songs of other sea people surrounded her.

'I only thought of your fear,' Marie-Josèphe whispered. 'I didn't think of how bored you must be. How lonely.' She sat with her wet feet on the water-level platform, her elbows on her knees and her chin on her fists.

The visitors grew impatient. 'Make it leap! Make it scream and laugh!'

'Sing your story again,' Marie-Josèphe whispered to the sea woman. 'So they can hear it.' She rose and spoke to the visitors. 'The sea woman tires of leaping, but she'll tell you a story.'

The sea woman sang, not the story of her life, but a story from her people's history. Surprised, apprehensive, Marie-Josèphe described the images with inadequate words.

'Four hundreds and three thousands of years ago, the people of the sea first met the people of the land.'

241

An entrancing ship, its sail painted with octopuses and fish, glided graceful as an albatross. The sea people watched, unafraid, curious. Handsome, narrow-waisted youths – boys and girls alike, their hair curled in ringlets – threw off their short belted kilts and dove from the ship to meet the people of the sea. They played and sang together. The people of the land were like no others Marie-Josèphe had ever seen or heard of, exotic and dark-eyed and unimaginably lovely, graceful as the wind.

We gave them songs, they gave us stories, the sea woman sang, *that cannot be taken, only given. We met as friends.*

The sea people accompanied the ship to an island, gold in the shimmering heat of the sapphire-blue Mediterranean. The ship glided into a harbour. A stone palace spread across a cliff. At the harbourside, bare-breasted women in bell-shaped skirts, their hair dressed with gold, led the way to greet their visitors. The children threw flowers into the water; the sea people twisted the blossoms into their hair.

'The sea people entered the chief city of the land of Atlantis,' Marie-Josèphe said. 'We rode in pools painted with dolphins and squids. The sea people and the people of the land exchanged shells and flowers.'

The song changed. The melody grew dark, the harmonics threatening. Marie-Josèphe fell silent as an immense explosion wracked the ground and whipped a hot wind across the island. Burning cinders and molten stones rained down. Ash rolled over the sea-people's chariots.

The eruption ended. The city was destroyed.

We searched for our friends, the sea woman sang. *We saw them no more. They were the first of us to perish when we met the people of land.*

'That is all,' Marie-Josèphe said, leaving the sea people as they accepted flowers in the lost city of Atlantis. The visitors applauded.

The sea woman snarled and splashed her angrily, demanding an explanation.

'How could I tell them—?'

You must always finish the story, the sea woman sang. *Promise, or I'll tell no more. You must always finish the story.*

'Very well,' Marie-Josèphe said. 'I promise. From now on, no matter what, I'll finish the story.'

'Tell another!' the visitors shouted. 'Yes, another story!'

A servant pushed through the crowd, hurrying to Count Lucien, handing him a note. The count read it, then tramped to the area between the cage and the line of applauding visitors. His limp had nearly gone.

'Guests of His Majesty,' he said. His pleasant voice, barely raised, filled the tent. The visitors fell silent, respectful of the King's representative. 'His Majesty asks that you leave the sea monster for today.'

Without objection, without complaint, the visitors filed out. The men bowed to Count Lucien; the women curtsied. Even the little ones, delighted to face an adult at their own level, offered him childish salutes, which he returned as graciously as he recognised their parents.

The sea woman surfaced, making a rude sound, spraying water. She asked Marie-Josèphe where all the people of land were going, and what she was to do for amusement.

Marie-Josèphe leaned over the top stair. 'Count Lucien! Count Lucien, you were right,' she said. 'She'd rather play, and tease the visitors – I was wrong to ask you to send them away.'

'I didn't send them away to please you, Mlle de la Croix,' Count Lucien said.

'Of course you wouldn't send them away to please me.' Bone-weariness caught her. She sank onto the lowest step. 'I'd never think such a thing.' The musketeers lowered the sides of the tent, closing in the silence.

Count Lucien climbed onto the rim of the fountain. 'Are you quite all right, Mlle de la Croix?'

'Yes, sir.' And yet she did not move.

Count Lucien handed her his flask. She drank the pungent calvados gratefully.

The sea woman glided to her and hovered at her feet, one webbed hand on each of Marie-Josèphe's ankles. The sea woman poked and prodded with her sharp nails, exploring Marie-Josèphe's shoes, her stockings, singing to ask, *what is this strange second skin grown by the people of land?*

The spirits drove back Marie-Josèphe's exhaustion. She rolled down her stocking so the sea woman could touch her skin. The sea woman's swimming webs were as smooth and fine as China silk. She stroked Marie-Josèphe's leg, probing her shoe. She clucked her tongue against the roof of her mouth, her face turned toward Marie-Josèphe's foot though her eyelids drooped shut. She sank into the water, drawing Marie-Josèphe's foot with her, to look at it with her voice.

'Wait, sea woman! I cannot afford to ruin these shoes.' Marie-Josèphe bared her foot. 'Now you may look at my feet however you like.'

The cold fountain water rose above Marie-Josèphe's ankle. The sea woman submerged. Her voice tickled Marie-Josèphe's toes.

Marie-Josèphe giggled. 'May I look at your foot?'

Without lifting her head or body from the water, the sea woman slid one foot over the edge of the platform. Her hips and knees were far more limber than the joints of a land human. Marie-Josèphe stroked the sea woman's instep, and the sea woman wriggled her clawed toes. Warmth radiated from the rough skin of her legs.

'Mlle de la Croix, I believe you've had enough calvados.' Count Lucien retrieved his flask. 'The scholars of the Academy of Sciences will not like to see you unclad.'

'The Academy!' Marie-Josèphe exclaimed. Yves had said not a word about the honour. She snatched her foot from the sea woman's hands, startling her so she surfaced, snorting.

Marie-Josèphe saw an opportunity, but she had no time to plan. She sang the sea woman's name.

'Sea woman, dive, breathe underwater. If you value your life, don't come up until I beg you to return.'

The sea woman whistled in distress, kicked hard, and dove backward in a long graceful curve. Bubbles rushed from her mouth and nose. She breathed out the last of her air and lay on the bottom of the pool, quiet as death.

Outside the tent, footsteps crunched on gravel.

Marie-Josèphe scooped up her shoe and stocking and ran to the laboratory, her left shoe tapping on the planks, her bare right foot

244

silent. She reached her place by the dissection table just in time to conceal her bare foot and her shoe and stocking beneath her skirt.

Footmen ceremoniously positioned the King's portrait. Yves entered the tent, leading a half-dozen dark-clad scholars and their students. He barely nodded to Marie-Josèphe. The scholars bowed to the portrait and to Count Lucien; they gathered around the dissection table. Count Lucien's groom brought a step-stool for him to stand on.

Yves uncovered the body of the sea woman's friend and spoke expansively, in Latin, before the King's philosophers. 'Natural philosophy proves the sea monsters are natural creatures, albeit ugly ones, like dugongs and sea-cows.'

He had saved an arm to dissect for the gentlemen of the Academy. He cut it, exposing sinews, bones, joints.

In the silence of the sea woman's languor, Marie-Josèphe documented the work. She drew with difficulty. Now that she knew the truth she saw the human features of the dead man. The long fine bones of his fingers reminded her of Count Lucien's beautiful hands.

Yves put down his knife. Marie-Josèphe laid down her charcoal and flexed her cramped hand. A student displayed her final drawing.

The gentlemen of the Academy questioned Yves about his hunt, his work, the King's patronage.

'The creatures have large lungs, as one would expect, similar to those of the slower sea mammals. I've observed one to remain underwater for ten or twelve minutes.' He moved quickly to the body's other organs. 'The heart—'

He never mentioned the anomalous lobe of the lung.

'Nothing remains to be learned from the monster's carcass,' Yves said. 'I shall of course compare female to male, inasmuch as the female's fate allows, though we gain little knowledge from the imperfect female copy of any creature.'

'Remarkable work, M. de la Croix,' said the senior scholar, also speaking Latin. 'Let us observe the living sea monster for a moment, if you please.'

'Call the sea monster, sister.' Yves left off speaking Latin, as if he had no idea Marie-Josèphe understood it.

Hurrying ahead, a little awkward with one bare foot, Marie-Josèphe entered the cage. She locked the door, put the key into her pocket, and sat composed on the fountain's rim with her hands folded in her lap.

How strange it feels, she thought, *to do nothing. I cannot remember the last time I sat without drawing or needlework or copying or prayer.*

Yves tried the locked gate. 'Open the gate.'

'I cannot.' Marie-Josèphe replied in Latin.

Pretending nothing was amiss, the gentlemen peered into the murky water, straining for a glimpse of the sea woman.

Yves frowned. 'Come now. Command the creature to leap for the gentlemen. And let me in, immediately.'

'She's displaying her ability to breathe underwater.'

'The young lady has mistaken your creature for a fish,' said the senior scholar. The other natural philosophers chuckled. 'M. de la Croix, your assistant has addled her mind by straining it with the Classics.'

Glowering, Yves rattled the gate.

If she had gained nothing else at the convent – and she had gained very little – she had learned to face wrath and contempt with tranquility. But facing Yves' displeasure took all her strength.

'Her lungs possess an anomalous lobe, unique to the sea people,' Marie-Josèphe said, still speaking Latin.

Yves stiffened. 'Your comments are of no interest.'

He believes I'll tell the secret, Marie-Josèphe thought. *The false secret.*

'She hasn't surfaced since you arrived,' she said. 'The lobe allows the sea people to breathe underwater. To breathe from the water.'

'Come out of there immediately.' Yves' voice rose.

'She intends to remain submerged until she proves it.'

'Does this anomalous lobe exist, Father de la Croix?'

Yves hesitated. 'It does.'

'Why did you not mention it?' the gentleman asked.

'I shall write a paper about it. As I've not fully studied it, I didn't wish to pass on erroneous conclusions.'

'Admirable restraint.'

'Thank you.'

246

'A glimpse of the sea monster, while it still lives, would please us all.'

Yves snatched up a pike and thrust it through the bars, but the sea woman floated out of reach.

'Mlle de la Croix,' Count Lucien said in a courteous voice, 'will you open the gate?'

'I cannot, Count Lucien. I beg your forgiveness. I wouldn't resist your direction, but this is a matter of the life or death of the sea woman.'

'Is she dying?'

'She's saving her life. She'll wake at her King's command.'

Chapter 17

The sea woman lay at the bottom of the pool, aware of the dirty water, the fish schooling past, the voices of the men of land. Bright sunlight warned her that she could not dive deep enough to fall into a proper trance. She maintained the languor as best she could, because the land woman had asked it of her. Every little while she gasped water into her lungs, then expelled it gradually.

The land woman was the first being she had dared to trust since her capture, the first being perceptive enough to understand her. She would trust her as long as she dared.

She lay very still, gilded by phosphorescence.

The sea woman drifted supine at the bottom of the pool, her eyes open and staring. Her long green hair floated around her. Underwater, she gasped as if for air.

The King arrived.

Marie-Josèphe rose and curtsied. Count Lucien, Yves, and the gentlemen from the Academy bowed. His Majesty struggled from his wheeled chair. His gout lamed him terribly; he put one arm around Lorraine and leaned his other hand on Count Lucien's shoulder. Monsieur followed, carrying His Majesty's walking staff, chasing Lorraine with his gaze. M. Boursin shambled nervously in with the rest of the entourage. The white lace at his collar and cuffs accentuated his prominent Adam's apple, his bony wrists and skeletal hands. He carried an old book.

'Is it dead?' he muttered. 'If it's spoiled, I'll be ruined. If it's dead, I'll kill myself! It was fat enough yesterday – I should have butchered it then!'

Count Lucien beckoned to an artisan, who apprehensively attacked the lock with a file. Metal rasped on metal.

His Majesty reached the cage and peered inside. 'Have you killed my sea monster, Mlle de la Croix?'

'No, Your Majesty.' Marie-Josèphe's calm was as unshakeable as the King's.

'Has it drowned itself?' He raised his voice above the racket of the file. Metal shavings fell to the ground.

'No, Your Majesty.'

Count Lucien touched the artisan's shoulder. The man stopped filing while His Majesty spoke.

'What is it doing?'

The artisan filed at the lock.

'She's breathing underwater, Sire.'

The artisan stopped —'Why is she doing this?'

—and started.

'Because I asked her, Your Majesty.'

The artisan stopped just long enough for His Majesty to speak, then redoubled his efforts at the lock.

'You've trained her well.'

'I never trained her at all, Sire.'

'She obeyed you,' Yves said. 'Like a dog.'

'She's demonstrating the function of the unique lobe of her lung. It isn't—' She hesitated. She kept the false secret. 'It only allows her to breathe underwater.'

'How do you know the true function of this organ?'

'Your Majesty, the sea woman told me.'

Lorraine laughed, a short hard bark quickly suppressed. The artisan stopped, filed hard, stopped again.

'Sea woman?' His Majesty exclaimed. 'Do you mean to say the sea monster speaks?'

'Marie-Josèphe, enough! I forbid you—' Yves fell silent, like the artisan, when His Majesty held up one hand.

'Answer me, Mlle de la Croix.'

'Yes, Your Majesty. I understand her. She understands me.' The artisan sawed at the lock again. 'She isn't a monster. She speaks, she's intelligent. She's a woman, she's human, like me, like all of us.'

249

'Your Majesty, please forgive my sister – I am entirely to blame, I've permitted her to tax herself—'

'Will it awaken and return to the surface?'

'She will do as you command, Your Majesty,' Marie-Josèphe said. 'As will I.'

'Stop that noise.' The artisan left off filing and backed away, bowing. 'Mlle de la Croix,' His Majesty said, 'be so kind as to open the gate.'

She descended, fitted the key in the keyhole, and turned it. The lock fell apart; the gate opened.

Leaning on Count Lucien and Lorraine, His Majesty made his way to the fountain's rim.

'She understands. I'll show you.' Marie-Josèphe descended the stairs to the platform. She patted the water. 'Sea woman! His Majesty bids you return!' She sang the sea woman's name.

The sea woman stretched languorously. She opened her eyes. With an abrupt and powerful kick, she ascended. At the surface, she coughed and spat out a great deal of water. She breathed with a great gasp, blew the spent breath out, and gasped again. The swellings on her forehead and cheeks expanded and deflated, making her face grotesque.

'It's alive!' M. Boursin whispered.

'What is this thing, Mlle de la Croix,' His Majesty said, 'if not a monster?'

'She's a woman. She's intelligent—'

'It's no more intelligent than a parrot,' Yves said.

'This vision of ugliness, a woman?'

'Look at the skull of the sea-woman's mate, Sire. Look at his bones, look at his hands. Listen to the sea woman and I'll tell you what she says.'

'The monster's nothing like a man,' Yves said. 'Look at its grotesque face, the joints of its legs – the concealment of its parts, if Your Majesty will forgive my mentioning the subject.'

'A dog, a parrot, a creature!' His Majesty exclaimed. 'But certainly not a woman!' He turned away.

The shock of failure overcame Marie-Josèphe, as cold and

250

suffocating as if she had fallen into the sea woman's prison. The sea woman, swimming back and forth at her feet, understood the King's refusal. She shrieked and spat.

'M. Boursin,' His Majesty said. 'Your plans, if you please.'

'Your Majesty, I've discovered perfection!' M. Boursin joined His Majesty inside the cage. He opened his shabby old book and displayed it for the King.

'Excellent, M. Boursin. I am pleased.'

'Be so kind as to throw it a fish, Mlle de la Croix, make it leap, so I may estimate it.' M. Boursin gazed greedily at the sea woman; Marie-Josèphe gazed with disbelief at M. Boursin and the King.

The sea woman spattered droplets at them with sharp flicks of her webbed toes.

'Your Majesty, the Church deems it a fish, suitable for Fridays. But its flesh is said to be succulent as meat. If I butcher it now, Your Majesty, I might make a dish – a little dish, for Your Majesty alone, perhaps a paté – for your supper alone, so you need not wait for mid-night feast.'

'That is most thoughtful of you, M. Boursin.'

'And with the rest of the flesh, I'll recreate Charlemagne's ban-quet, it will be my masterpiece!' He leaned precariously over the rim of the fountain, glancing from the book to the sea woman and back.

He displayed the book to the Academicians, to Yves, to Marie-Josèphe.

A sea woman lay on her belly on a huge platter, her back unnatu-rally arched and her knees bent; her webbed feet nearly brushed the top of her head. She held a dead sturgeon as if it were suckling at her swollen breasts.

'I'll fatten its teats with shrimp and scallops. I'll stuff its body with baked oysters. I'll dress its hair with golden caviar! What a shame the male died, what a shame I can't prepare two! I must butcher this one soon.'

In the woodcut, the roasted sea woman stared with eyes wide open and empty.

Marie-Josèphe screamed.

'I'll need a Caspian sturgeon . . . Why, Mlle de la Croix, don't be alarmed, the creature is grotesque, but I can almost make it beautiful!'

'Close your book, M. Boursin,' said Count Lucien.

Lorraine took the stairs in one leap and snatched Marie-Josèphe into his arms, holding her, muffling her sobs against his chest.

'What's the matter?' M. Boursin said. 'Mlle de la Croix, don't you like seafood?'

'Where's my smelling bottle?' Monsieur said. 'I put it in my pocket – Did I leave it in my muff . . . ?'

'Your Majesty,' Yves said, 'I beg your forgiveness, my sister has forever been tender-hearted. She's made a pet of the monster . . .'

Marie-Josèphe huddled against Lorraine, trembling terribly, fighting to control her sobs.

'Here it is!' Monsieur said.

A pungent explosion in her nostrils sent her into a fit of sneezing. Tears blurred her vision.

'May I take it, Your Majesty? The meat must hang, Your Majesty, or it will taste gamy, Your Majesty.'

'The creature is a fish,' Count Lucien said.

'A fish, M. de Chrétien?'

'If the sea monster isn't human,' Count Lucien said, 'then it's a beast. M. Boursin himself brought to Your Majesty's attention that the Church has judged sea monsters to be fish. If M. Boursin kills it today, its flesh will be rotten before Your Majesty's banquet.'

'But—' M. Boursin said.

'M. de Chrétien is correct,' His Majesty said.

'But—'

'No more, M. Boursin! You may not butcher the creature today! M. de Chrétien, if you please, arrange for Dr. Fagon to attend Mlle de la Croix.' The King remained perfectly calm, perfectly in control.

'Yes, Your Majesty.' Count Lucien departed.

Lorraine swept Marie-Josèphe up in his arms. His musky scent overpowered the sharp sweetness of Monsieur's swooning compound.

'My deepest apologies, Sire,' Yves said. 'I overtaxed her – her natural sympathy – a shock—'

Lorraine pushed past courtiers and Academicians alike, carrying

Marie-Josèphe from the tent. Sunlight spread over her face like hot wine. Zelis' hoofbeats struck a rhythm in the distance; Count Lucien rode away toward the chateau.

'Let me down,' Marie-Josèphe whispered. 'Call Count Lucien back, please, I don't want to see Dr. Fagon.'

'Shh, shh.' Lorraine embraced her more strongly.

His Majesty climbed into his wheeled chair and sat at his ease while his deaf-mutes pushed him away.

'Be easy, mademoiselle. Dr. Fagon will set you right.'

Lorraine laid Marie-Josèphe on her bed. Haleeda jumped from the window-seat, dropping the lace and wires of Queen Mary's new fontanges.

'Mlle Marie, what's happened?'

Yves sat beside Marie-Josèphe.

Lorraine said, 'The surgeon will be here soon.'

'That's what I fear!' Marie-Josèphe whispered.

Haleeda sponged her face.

'You know the creature's to be butchered,' Yves said. 'How could you become so attached to it? This is just like your lamb, when you begged Papa not to kill it—'

'Don't task me with what I did as a child,' Marie-Josèphe said. 'I'm not a child any longer.'

'Your behaviour—'

'I'm attached to the sea woman as I'm attached to you, as I'm attached to Mlle Haleeda – I beg for her life because she is a thinking, reasoning person, a being with a soul, and because I do not wish my King to be a cannibal—'

Dr. Fagon cleared his throat. Marie-Josèphe fell silent.

'You're speaking nonsense,' Yves said.

Dr. Fagon and Dr. Félix entered Marie-Josèphe's room without asking her consent. Marie-Josèphe thought wildly that her apartment was becoming as crowded as one of His Majesty's evening entertainments.

'His Majesty is right to be concerned with your well-being,' the first physician said.

253

'I'm perfectly well, sir.' Her voice was steady, but she was trembling. She felt cold and light-headed.

'Hush, you are pallid and hysterical.' Fagon bent over her and peered into her eyes. 'What happened?

'She received a shock,' Lorraine said. 'She fainted.'

'Nonsense,' Haleeda said. 'Fainted!'

'Be silent!' Dr Félix said.

'She's only tired,' Haleeda said, outraged. 'She's hardly slept since M. Yves returned.'

'No one spoke to you.' Dr Félix swung around toward her so violently that Haleeda flinched.

'Sir!' Yves said. 'The King's favour doesn't allow you to abuse members of my household.'

'Don't touch her!' Marie-Josèphe said. 'Don't touch me!'

'Marie-Josèphe, let him examine you,' Yves said.

Haleeda flung herself across Marie-Josèphe. Marie-Josèphe buried her face against her sister's shoulder, grateful and terrified.

Dr. Félix and Lorraine pulled Haleeda up. She struggled and keened. Félix propelled her toward Yves.

'Take your servant away,' Fagon said. 'We cannot work with two hysterical women in the room!'

Yves held Haleeda so she could not move from his side.

'Brother—' Haleeda cried.

'Take this madwoman away,' Fagon said. 'I shall send the barber to bleed her, as well.'

'It's for your own good, sister,' Yves said, 'I'm sure it is.' He backed out of Marie-Josèphe's room, into his dressing room, taking Haleeda with him.

'Yves, don't let them – please – remember Papa—' Fear overtook Marie-Josèphe, for she was lost.

Félix held her face between his powerful hands. Fagon forced her mouth open. His fingers tasted of blood and dirt. She could not scream. He poured a bitter draught down her throat. She gagged and struggled.

'Sir,' Dr. Fagon said to Lorraine, 'will you condescend to help, for His Majesty's sake?'

'I'll help for my own sake, for she's mine.' Lorraine pinioned Marie-Josèphe's arms with his hard hands.

'I never fainted, I never faint.' She turned her head away from Dr. Fagon's dirty fingers. 'I assure you, sir—'

'I shall bleed her,' Dr. Félix said. 'Bloodletting will calm her mind.'

Marie-Josèphe fought, terrified, but she could not overcome the strength of all three men. She tried to bite.

'Don't struggle so. We're acting for your benefit.'

Her scream came out as a strangled cry. Kneeling on the bed beside her, Lorraine covered her with his musky scent. He pressed her shoulders down with all his weight. The long locks of his perruke tumbled around his face and curled at Marie-Josèphe's throat. She kicked. Someone held her feet, one bare, one shod.

'Show some courage,' Lorraine said. 'Make His Majesty proud of your fortitude – not ashamed of your cowardice.'

Félix pushed her sleeve above her elbow and held her wrist tight. He took up his blade. The sharp steel pierced the soft skin of her inner arm. Hot blood flowed through pain, its scent cutting through Lorraine's heavy perfume. She moaned. Her blood gushed into the bowl, spattering her riding habit and the bedclothes. Bright flecks stained the lace spilling from Dr. Fagon's sleeves.

Smiling, gazing into her eyes, Lorraine held Marie-Josèphe down.

Lucien limped along the narrow, dim corridor, ignoring the faded pain of his wounded leg and the stronger, nearly constant ache in his back. He disliked the attic of the chateau. He disliked its shabbiness, its smell, its memories. As a child, a page, he had lived in the Queen's apartments. After the Moroccan embassy, returned to the King's good graces, he had lived in the town of Versailles until the builders finished his own country lodge. He had lived here in the courtiers' warren only during the most miserable months of his life, when he was alienated from His Majesty.

Mlle de la Croix's door opened. Dr. Fagon, Dr. Félix, and Lorraine stepped into the hallway. Mlle de la Croix's cry of despair dissolved into a whimper. Lucien frowned. He judged character well;

he did not often mistake courage. He had considered her stalwart, if impetuous.

Lucien nodded to Fagon and Félix; he returned Lorraine's cool bow. Félix rubbed his thumb over the back of his hand, smearing drops of blood to faint streaks.

'I have cured her hysteria,' Félix said.

'His Majesty will be glad to hear it. He's fond of the young lady and her family.'

'And of her golden hair and her white bosom,' Lorraine said.

Lucien replied with a conventional compliment. 'No one could fail to admire her.'

Though Mlle de la Croix was entirely innocent, rumours of a liaison with the King could work only to her benefit. Lucien wished His Majesty would in fact form such a liaison. His connection with Mme de Maintenon, drawing him deep into piety, did little to sustain his vital spirit.

'She may require another bloodletting tomorrow, to augment the cure.' Fagon tilted the basin. Liquid blood moved beneath the clotted skin.

Félix probed the blood with his finger, breaking the elastic surface. Fagon righted the basin as the blood flowed over the edge and stained the carpet.

'Her blood is far too thick, as you must observe,' Fagon said, 'but I shall balance her bodily humours.' He chuckled. 'Though she may bite my finger off!'

'She tried to bite me, too,' Lorraine said as they walked away. 'The minx.' He chuckled. 'Like a trapped animal. But she has quite trapped my heart.'

All alone, Mlle de la Croix lay crying in a tangle of bedclothes and bloody lint, her face hidden in the crook of her elbow. She heard or felt Lucien standing beside her. She reached weakly toward him.

'Dear God, please, no more—'

She touched his arm, fumbling. A bloodstain widened on the bandage. Lucien took her hand.

'Oh!' She drew away, shocked and startled. Her hair fell in damp untidy strands around her drained face. 'Forgive me . . . I thought you were my brother.'

'I will call him.'

'No—! I don't want to see him.'

'Do you feel better? Calmer? Cured of delusions?'

'I don't see delusions! I can talk with the sea woman! You must believe me, sir – if you don't, why did you take such a risk on her behalf?'

'His Majesty does as he pleases,' Count Lucien said. 'I only offered him the rationale.'

'Is that the only reason you spoke?'

Lucien did not reply.

'Very well,' she whispered. 'You care for nothing but His Majesty. You spoke because you know he mustn't murder the sea woman – he mustn't risk his immortal soul!'

'Sleep,' Lucien said, preferring not to continue a conversation that took this direction. 'Dr. Fagon will return in the morning.'

'Do you want me to die of bleeding, like my father?'

Her voice fell to a horrified whisper. Lucien regretted dismissing her courage, for everyone he had ever known possessed a secret terror. As far as Lucien was concerned, fearing physicians was perfectly rational.

'Do you hate me?' she whispered.

'Of course I do not hate you.'

'Don't let him bleed me again,' she said. 'Please.'

'You do ask too much of me.' If the King ordered Mlle de la Croix to be bled, Lucien could do nothing to stop it. He devoted himself to carrying out Louis' wishes, not to hindering them.

'Please. Please promise me.' She struggled up, clutching his hand with awful desperation. Fear and pain had leached the intelligence from her face. 'Please help me. I have great need of a friend.'

'I'll do what I can.'

'Give me your word.'

'Very well,' he said, against his better judgment, but moved by her fear. 'I give you my word.'

She collapsed, still holding his hand, trembling. She closed her eyes. Her agitation calmed; her fingers relaxed.

Lucien sighed, and smoothed her sweat-darkened hair.

Marie-Josèphe drifted, awake, asleep, aware of Count Lucien, comforted by his promise, aware of the denizens of her imagination, afraid to see them in her dreams. She feared sleep, but she shrank from waking.

When she woke, moonlight spilled through the window, pooling on the floor like molten silver. Count Lucien had gone. Haleeda slept beside her, holding her, a welcome warmth. Dr Félix must have forgotten his threat to bleed Marie-Josèphe's sister; Haleeda's arms bore neither wound nor bandage. Yves dozed, slumped over a sheaf of papers. He would have a terrible crick in his neck in the morning.

Yves and Haleeda must have undressed her, for she wore only her blood-spattered shift. She hoped Haleeda had asked Count Lucien to withdraw; she hoped she had not been unclothed before the King's adviser. She was no royal lady, to be dressed by tailors and observed by men at the most intimate times of her life.

She sat up, weak and light-headed.

Yves woke. 'Sister – are you recovered?'

'How could you let him bleed me?'

'It was for your own good.'

He had found her sketches. He flicked through them, his face impassive.

'The sea woman told me that story,' Marie-Josèphe said. 'The true story of the hunt. You caught three sea people. Not two. They struggled. The sailors killed one—'

'Hush,' he said. 'I told you the story.'

'You never did. They killed one. They ate his flesh. You ate—'

'—the flesh of an animal! It was delicious. Why shouldn't I eat it?'

'You claim to love truth! But when you hear it, you deny it. Please believe me. Yves, my dear brother, what's changed so, that you have no faith in me?'

Her agitation woke Haleeda. 'Mlle Marie?' She pushed herself up

258

on her elbow, blinking sleepily. Marie-Josèphe took her hand, desperate for her comfort.

'The sea monsters are beasts, created for the use of man,' Yves said. He sat next to her on her bed. 'You should retire from court. Too much attention has distracted you. In a convent, you'd be safe from this agitation of your spirits.'

'No.'

'You'd be happy, back in the convent.'

'She'd never be happy there!' Haleeda cried.

'For five years, I read no books,' Marie-Josèphe said. 'The sisters said knowledge would corrupt me, like Eve.' She had tried to forgive her brother his awful decision, but she could not let him repeat it. 'I heard no music. The sisters forbade it. They said, "Women must be silent in the house of God. The Pope demands it". I did without books, without studying – I had no choice! I couldn't stop my thoughts, my questions, though I couldn't speak them. Mathematics—!' Her laugh was wild and angry. 'They said I was writing spells! I heard music that was never there, I could never stop it, no matter how I prayed and fasted. I called myself a madwoman, a sinner . . .' She looked into his face. 'M. Newton replied to my letter – but they burned it, unopened, before me. How could you send me there, where every moment tortured me? I thought you loved me—'

'I wanted you to be safe.' His beautiful eyes filled with sudden tears. He put his arms around her, relenting, hugging her protectively. 'And now, I've asked too much of you – the work is too difficult.'

'I love the work!' she cried. 'I do it gladly. I do it well, and I'm not a fool. You must listen to me!'

'I have the obligation to guide you. Your affection for the sea monster is unnatural.'

'My affection for her has nothing to do with what she told me. You know her stories are true.'

He knelt beside her bed. He took her arm.

'Pray with me,' he said.

Prayer will comfort and sustain me, Marie-Josèphe thought.

Marie-Josèphe slipped to the floor and knelt. She folded her hands, bowed her head, and waited for the welcome embrace of God's presence.

'Odelette, join us, pray for Marie-Josèphe's recovery.'

'I will not!' Haleeda said. 'I'll never pray like a Christian again, for I am a free woman, and a Mahometan, and my name is Haleeda!' Hugging herself for warmth, she turned her back and stared into the moonlit gardens.

'Dear God,' Marie-Josèphe whispered. 'Dear God . . .'

Does God have a plan for my suffering? she wondered. *But my suffering is nothing, compared to the martyrs – compared to the despair of the sea woman. Other people undergo bleeding without a second thought. I should submit to it bravely.*

Instead, she had forced Lorraine to behave in a way that destroyed his high opinion of him. She no longer cared what Lorraine thought. She had diminished herself in Count Lucien's estimation, which mattered to her a great deal.

'Dear God,' Marie-Josèphe whispered. 'Dear God, please speak to me, please direct me. Tell me what is right and proper for me to do.'

She begged, she even dared to hope, for a reply. But in the face of her entreaties, God remained silent.

Chapter 18

Moonlight flooded through the window and pooled on the floor. Marie-Josèphe slipped out of bed. She stood still; a dizzy weakness passed.

Haleeda slept soundly; Yves was gone. Shivering, Marie-Josèphe slung Lorraine's cloak over her shoulders and crept into the dressing room. She held herself up by leaning against the wall, by grasping the doorjamb.

Lorraine's perfume surrounded her. Her stomach clenched. She flung down the cloak and struggled not to vomit. She would never wear the cloak again, no matter how soft and warm it was. She would burn it, if she had a fire.

She opened the window and gazed into the night. The moon, two days from full, loomed over the sea woman's prison. Marie-Josèphe tried to sing, but she could only whisper.

Yet the sea woman heard her, and replied.

She's still alive, Marie-Josèphe thought. *Bless Count Lucien—*

Marie-Josèphe snatched up her pen. A new scene for the cantata poured from the sea woman's song. The pen sprayed tiny grace-notes above the staff. The candle puddled and drowned.

She wrote the last few notes and waved the page in the air to dry the ink. The cantata was complete.

Marie-Josèphe drew the tapestry from the harpsichord and flung it around her shoulders. She opened the keyboard.

In the shadowy dawn, tears running down her face, she played the story of the sea people's tragedy.

Lucien attended the King's awakening, but his thoughts were elsewhere. While Dr. Fagon did his work, Lucien blotted the perspiration from His Majesty's forehead. He bowed to His Majesty when the

King led the procession to Mass, but Lucien did not follow. A church was the one place where he would not follow his King.

'Dr. Fagon.'

Lucien and the First Physician were alone in His Majesty's bedroom. The doctor looked up from studying the results of His Majesty's regular purge.

'M. de Chrétien,' he said, bowing.

Count Lucien returned Fagon's salutation with a nod.

'Mlle de la Croix is better, I trust? I shall look in on her later.' Fagon shook his head with disapproval. 'No wonder she broke down, with all her unwomanly tasks. Someone should speak to her brother. I've planned an extensive course of bloodletting.'

'That will not be necessary,' Lucien said.

'I beg your pardon?' Fagon exclaimed.

'You'll let no more blood from Mlle de la Croix.'

'Sir, are you instructing me in my profession?'

'I'm instructing you that she wants no more treatment, and I'm instructing you to respect her wishes.'

Lucien spoke quietly. Dr. Fagon was well aware of Lucien's influence with His Majesty, the favour the King showed him and the peril of ignoring him.

Fagon spread his hands. 'If His Majesty commands—'

'It is unlikely in the extreme that His Majesty would observe your treatment.'

'It is *likely* in the extreme that His Majesty's spies will observe!'

'No one need be present who might betray you. Can you not trust M. Félix?'

Fagon considered, then bowed again. 'I shall observe your instructions, subject only—'

Lucien raised one eyebrow.

'—only to His Majesty's presence.'

Lucien bowed in return. He could not ask Dr. Fagon to defy the King's orders, in the King's presence. He hoped Mlle de la Croix would not ask it of him.

★

The harpsichord traced the story of the sea monster hunt. When Marie-Josèphe began the cantata, she thought the story altogether heroic. With every revision, it had become more tragic.

She closed the keyboard and gazed at the smooth wood. She was spent.

Somehow, somehow, I must make His Majesty see what he's doing, she thought. *He loves music. If he would only listen to the sea woman, he might see what I see, he might understand her.*

The door of the dressing room opened. Startled, Marie-Josèphe looked up. She expected no one. Her sister had gone to attend Mary of Modena; Yves had gone to attend the King's awakening.

Gazing at her ardently, Lorraine stood in the doorway between her bedroom and Yves' dressing room. Dark circles under his eyes marred his beauty.

'Do you enter a lady's room without invitation, sir, or chaperone?'

'What need have we of chaperones, my dear? We needed none on the Grand Canal.'

His velvet cloak, sadly wrinkled and salt-stained, lay in a heap in the corner. He retrieved it and shook it out.

'You've had your use out of my cloak, I see.'

'You may have it back.'

He held its collar to his face. 'Your perfume scents it. Your perfume, your sweat, the secrets of your body . . .'

She turned away, embarrassed, flustered.

'May I have not even a smile? The King offers me as a sacrifice to your beauty, but you break my heart. I lay my finest garment at your feet – but it is nothing!' He flung the cloak to the floor. 'I destroy myself with worry about you—' He stroked one finger across his cheek, beneath the dark circle.

'You destroy yourself,' Marie-Josèphe said drily, 'by revelling all night in Paris.'

Lorraine laughed, delighted. 'Dr. Fagon did you good! You are yourself – and cured of your fantasies, I trust.' He leaned on the harpsichord, gazing soulfully at her.

'You helped Dr. Fagon steal my strength. If the sea woman dies, I'll never recover it.'

263

'When she's gone, you'll find another cause to occupy your mind. And your heart. A husband. A lover.' He moved nearer, feigning interest in the musical score.

'It isn't proper for you to be here, sir.'

Behind her, he pressed against her back. His scent smothered her. He laid his hands on her shoulders, slipped his fingers beneath her hair, beneath her shift, cupped his hands around her breasts. His hands were hot on her skin. She froze, with shock and cold and outrage.

'Mlle de la Croix,' Count Lucien said from the doorway. 'I see that you are protected from surgeons.'

His voice broke her paralysis. Count Lucien bowed and disappeared. Marie-Josèphe broke from Lorraine's grasp.

'Count Lucien! ' She ran after him. He limped toward the stairs. 'I—the Chevalier—it wasn't—'

'It wasn't?' Count Lucien said. 'That's a shame.'

'A – a shame?'

Count Lucien faced her, leaning on his walking stick, gazing up quizzically.

'His Majesty himself favours the match. Lorraine belongs to an illustrious family, but he is perpetually in need of money. You will have a generous dowry from His Majesty. An alliance between you and Lorraine will repair both your fortunes.'

'I have no amorous feelings for the Chevalier de Lorraine.'

'What has that to do with marriage?'

'I scorn him!'

'Against the King's will?'

'I'll never marry him!' Marie-Josèphe shivered, seeing Lorraine's intense blue eyes above her, while the surgeon's blade slashed her. She slipped her right hand beneath her left sleeve. The bandage was wet with blood.

'Perhaps you should tell that to Monsieur.'

'Why would I tell His Majesty's brother?'

'Why are you telling me?'

'Because I have – because I wish you to think well of me.'

'I think well enough of you.'

Lorraine slammed the door of Marie-Josèphe's room and sauntered toward them. His cloak swept from one shoulder.

'The jester and the wild Carib maiden,' he said, laughing. 'What a combination!'

Count Lucien stepped forward, holding his cane at his side as if it were a sword. If they fought, Lorraine would surely wound or kill him. Lorraine wore a real sword, while Count Lucien carried only his dirk.

'You are very rude, sir!' Marie-Josèphe said.

Lorraine laughed. 'Chrétien, is she your protector?'

'Apparently she is. I trust yours is as valiant.'

'I have a sovereign who forbids duelling. I choose to obey him – in *all* things.' He stalked past them and descended the stairs.

'I'm so sorry.' Marie-Josèphe leaned against the wall. 'I spoke out of turn.'

A handsbreadth of edged steel gleamed between the staff and the handle of Count Lucien's walking-stick. Count Lucien pushed and twisted the handle; the sword cane *clicked*; the blade disappeared.

'Lorraine is quite right,' Count Lucien said. 'His Majesty forbade duelling. No doubt you've saved my head.'

'You're making fun of me, sir—'

'On the contrary.'

'—when I hope for your regard.'

'My regard, and more,' Count Lucien said. 'For your own happiness, you must set your sights elsewhere.'

Marie-Josèphe returned to her room, pressing through the ruins of all her fine plans. She refused to think about what Count Lucien had said. She returned to the harpsichord, to the one thing that had gone right. She gathered together the score of the sea woman's cantata.

I've done justice to her music, Marie-Josèphe thought. *When His Majesty hears it, and I tell him who it belongs to, he must believe what I say about her.*

She still felt light-headed, but she no longer feared she would faint. She carried the score through the chateau to the musicians' room. She peeked in, hoping to find M. Minoret, the King's strict music master of the third quarter, or M. de la Lande, the charming master of the fourth quarter. For His Majesty's celebration, all four chapel masters and all the King's musicians gathered at Versailles. His Majesty's guests were never without music.

Master Domenico Scarlatti sat alone at the harpsichord. Marie-Josèphe waited, enjoying the unfamiliar music, till he finished with a cascade of embellishments, stopped, looked out at the beautiful day. He sighed heavily. Staring out the window, he fingered variations one-handed.

'Démonico.'

'Signorina Maria!' He jumped up. He sat down, despondent. 'I'm not to rise for two whole hours.'

'I won't interrupt.' She embraced him. 'That was lovely.'

'I'm not supposed to play it.' He played another variation. 'Only what Papa has planned for the King.'

'Is it your own?'

'Did you like it?'

'Very much.'

'Thank you,' he said shyly.

'You'll be able to play whatever you like, when you're older,' she said. 'I doubt anyone could stop you!'

He grinned. 'In two years – when I'm eight?'

'Perhaps in two years – when you're ten.'

'What's that? His Majesty's cantata? Can I see?'

He paged through it, jerking his head to its rhythms, humming an occasional note, fingering with his free hand.

'Oh, it's wonderful! It's ever so much better—' He stopped, embarrassed. 'I mean—that is—'

'Than what I played at St Cyr?'

'Forgive me, Signorina Maria, but, yes, ever so much better.'

'You said you liked the other songs.'

'I, that is, they were pretty, but I – I wanted you to like me so you'd marry me. When I grow up.'

'Oh, Démonico.' She smiled, amused through her distress, but she could not humiliate him by telling him their stations were impossibly distant. 'I'm far too old for you, I'll be an old lady before you're ready to marry.'

'I wouldn't care – and M. Coupillet is an old man!'

'No, he isn't.' Then she understood: Domenico was jealous. 'He *is* selfish and mean – who would want him?'

'*I'm* not selfish, and I'm not mean—'

'Of course you aren't!'

'—and even though I love you, your cantata is wonderful! Your other songs *were* very pretty, but—'

'—I hadn't practiced or played or composed a song in many years. I wasn't allowed.'

'That is horrible,' he whispered.

'It was,' she said.

'How will you ever catch up?'

'I never will, Démonico,' she said, 'but that time's past, stolen, and I must stop feeling sorry about it. The sea woman gave me this music as her gift, it's entirely to her credit if it has any quality.' She wondered if it did have any quality, if Domenico saw excellence in it because he loved her. She wondered whether her unpracticed talents had debased the song of the sea woman's life.

M. Coupillet strode into the practice room, followed by a group of sunburned string players wiping their brows, blinking in the dim room, and calling for wine and beer.

Domenico leaned closer, conspiratorially. 'M. Coupillet said you'd never finish. He said you couldn't.'

'Did he!' she exclaimed, then relented. 'After all, he was nearly right.'

Domenico bent over the keyboard as if he had never paused in his practice. He played Marie-Josèphe's cantata.

'The varnish on my viola melted, I swear to God,' said one of the younger musicians. 'Next time I have to follow the King around the garden in the sun without a hat, I'll use my oldest instrument.'

'Michel wants to put a hat on his viola,' said another of the musicians, laughing.

'I'll use my newest strings,' said a third musician, looking ruefully at the broken string on his violin.

'Your broken string was the fault of that plump little princess,' said Michel. 'Under those silver petticoats, I'll wager she's bleeding like—'

267

M. Coupillet stamped his director's baton on the floor. 'Enough, Michel. You've blasphemed, insulted the King, and spoken lewdly, all in the space of a minute. And in front of M. Scarlatti's little arithmetic teacher.'

'I beg your pardon, mamselle.' Michel the viola player bowed to her and turned his attention to a cup of wine and a slice of bread and cheese.

'What do you want, Mlle de la Croix?' M. Coupillet asked. 'Why are you here? To beg relief from composing His Majesty's cantata?'

'It's finished,' she said. She could hardly listen to him, because she was listening to Domenico. When he played, the music sounded as she imagined it.

M. Coupillet waited. When she neither replied nor gave him the music, he thumped his baton on the floor again, startling her, snatching her attention back.

'You must give me the score,' he said.

'But Domenico is—' She stopped, amazed. The score lay on the seat beside Domenico; he played from memory.

Marie-Josèphe reluctantly gave M. Coupillet the pages. He weighed them in his hand; he riffled through them.

'What *is* this? An opera? Do you think you're Mlle de la Guerre? You – an amateur, a woman! – you give me an opera to conduct? Worthless! Hopeless!' He tried to tear the sheaf in half, but it was too thick; his hand slipped and he ripped only the first half-dozen pages. He wrenched it with both hands, like a dog shaking a rat, and flung the whole thing down. The score spilled across the polished parquet.

'Sir!' She stooped to gather the torn, rumpled sheets.

'Incompetence! It's dreadful.' He waved his baton toward Domenico. 'You think to match yourself against genius such as Signor Alessandro Scarlatti!'

Domenico's shoulders shook from laughter, but his hands never faltered, playing the piece M. Coupillet took for his father's.

'Signor Scarlatti admired it!'

'What do you expect? He's *Italian* – Signor Alessandro admires your white bosom, your—'

'You insult me on every level, sir!' She tried to leave, but M. Coupillet barred her way.

'His Majesty asked you for a song – a few minutes of music!' M. Coupillet said. '*You* insult me – you insult *him* – with this, this bloated abortion.' He emphasised his words by thumping his baton. 'You charmed him with your coquettish ways, but your charm won't distract him from your arrogant failure.'

'You're unfair, sir.'

'Am I? I should have had this commission – he never would have noticed you if not for my embellishments—'

'Little Domenico's embellishments, if you please, M. Coupillet. It's contemptible enough for you to steal my accomplishments, but to steal a child's—'

'A child? A child!' He shook his baton toward Domenico. 'I have it on good authority, the boy's a midget of thirty years!'

'I'm six!' Domenico shouted, and kept on playing.

Marie-Josèphe burst out laughing, but her sense of the absurd only infuriated M. Coupillet the more.

'Do you dare to laugh at me? Am I insufficiently grand? I, who brought you to His Majesty's attention?'

'Through no desire of your own, sir!'

'Desire? How dare you mention desire? You flirt with the Neapolitan, you flirt with the King, you even flirt with dwarves and sodomites, but you ignore and despise me—'

'Good-bye, sir.'

Still he would not let her pass.

'Do you imagine I noticed you for your music? For your amateurish compositions and your fumble-fingered playing? I do not say you would not have been adequate – adequate, no more – if you'd devoted yourself to the art, but you've wasted whatever talent you ever had, and it's just as well! Women play by rote! Women play as if they were still in the schoolroom! And as for the compositions of women – women should be silent! Women are good for only one thing, and you're such a fool you don't even know what it is.'

A fleck of spittle, foaming, collected at the corner of his mouth. He loomed over her, shouting.

She clutched the untidy pile of paper. 'Let me pass.' She meant her voice to freeze him, but her words revealed her vulnerability. Across the room, the young musicians stood in uncomfortable silence, their backs turned, as afraid as Marie-Josèphe of their master.

'Give me the score,' he said. 'I'll condescend to carve a song out of it, but you must show me some gratitude – and His Majesty must know the credit is mine.'

'No, sir. I won't insult His Majesty with my inferior female music.' Coupillet moved aside. His bow was a taunt, an insult.

'Do you wish to go? Yes, go! You'll fail without my help. I'll explain to His Majesty how you neglected his commission!'

Marie-Josèphe rode Zachi toward the Fountain of Apollo, holding tight to her drawing box and the score inside it. She dared not return to the musicians' room. Perhaps she could find Domenico when he had finished his practice.

Do I have reason to find him? she wondered. *He's only a little boy, prodigy or not, how can he judge the music? Besides, M. Coupillet will surely forbid him to play it. I should have let M. Coupillet pick out a few measures, and then I wouldn't be utterly humiliated in front of the King.*

In truth, she could not bear the thought of letting M. Coupillet alter the sea woman's music.

In the Fountain of Apollo, the sea woman sang and leaped for the entertainment of the visitors. Marie-Josèphe put aside all her own worries and humiliations. They were trivial compared to the sea woman's peril.

She pushed through the crowd to the cage, where a bright flock of noblewomen sat watching the sea woman. Mme Lucifer smoked a small black cigar and whispered to Mlle d'Armagnac, whose hair was hidden beneath an iridescent headdress of peacock feathers.

When Mlle d'Armagnac saw Marie-Josèphe, she rose to her feet. All the other ladies followed her lead. Baffled, Marie-Josèphe curtsied to them.

She knelt at the edge of the fountain and sang the sea woman's name. 'Sea woman, will you tell these people of land a story?'

The sea woman swam to the foot of the stairs. She lifted her arms; Marie-Josèphe slipped her fingers into the sea woman's webbed hands.

The sea woman snorted; the swellings on her face rippled. She drew Marie-Josèphe's left hand toward her, forcing Marie-Josèphe to stoop. She prodded the bandage and nibbled at the knot that held it. The pressure increased the throbbing.

'Please, don't.' Marie-Josèphe pulled her hand away. 'You're hurting me.'

A group of noblemen entered, laughing and pushing their way past the visitors. Lorraine led half a dozen young men to the front of the audience. They bowed with exaggerated courtesy to the ladies and to His Majesty's portrait; they threw themselves into their chairs, lounging and slouching and smoking. Marie-Josèphe turned away from Lorraine, away from Chartres.

'Please, sea woman,' Marie-Josèphe said. 'A story?'

Madame arrived, with Lotte; Count Lucien accompanied them. Marie-Josèphe rose and curtsied. She smiled shyly, tentatively, at Count Lucien, hoping he would forgive her for her foolishness this morning. He nodded to her in a gentlemanly fashion. Madame's presence – or was it Count Lucien's? – brought the men to proper behaviour.

The sea woman began her tale in a melodious whisper.

'She will tell you a story,' Marie-Josèphe said.

'The ocean cradled the sea people for a thousand hundred years. We lived in peace with the men of land.'

Marie-Josèphe found herself in the midst of the story. The sea surrounded her, cool on her bare skin. She continued to speak, to sing, to tell the story, but her audience vanished and the people of the sea surrounded her. She swam, and sang; she caught fish and ate them raw; laughing, she played with sea-children among the spark-speckled tentacles of a giant octopus.

'Then the men of land discovered good sport in pursuing us from their ships . . .'

A strange sound raked the water. She and her family surfaced into the sunlight. Curious and unafraid, ready to welcome the land people

271

as they had greeted the Minoans, the sea people swam toward the dragon-prowed ship floating on the waves.

'They sailed into our waters . . .'

A great net soared over the sea people, fell among them, and captured one of her brothers and two of her sisters. Men of land leaned over the side of the ship, laughing and shouting. They landed the sea people, ignoring their cries.

'They raided the sea people.'

With sails and long oars, the Northmen set their ship in motion. The free sea people followed, horrified. The screams of their friends echoed through the wooden sides of the ship, filling the sea with pain.

'And they tortured us.'

The Northmen tied the sea man to their dragon prow. His screams warned them of rocks and reefs. Sometimes they aimed their figurehead toward the rocks, and laughed at his cries.

'They used the sea women against their will, as no woman wishes to be used.'

The Northmen threw the sea women overboard. They floated, limp, bruised, bleeding from secret places.

'The sea people—' Marie-Josèphe choked on tears. 'Please, sea woman, please, no more.'

You must finish, the sea woman sang. *You promised to finish the story*.

Marie-Josèphe continued. 'The sea people comforted the injured sea women. But just out of the sight of the eyes, sleek and deadly shapes appeared. Hunting sharks surrounded the group, scenting the blood, moving in to attack.

'The sea people turned outward to defend themselves, circling their injured friends and their children for protection. They sang a song of description and warning into the sea, so other families would hear it and beware the men of land and their marauding ships.'

Yves stared at Marie-Josèphe, shocked. He had arrived, with Dr. Fagon, while the story surrounded her, filling her sight. Marie-Josèphe stammered out the end of the tale; she covered her face with her hands, hiding her tears. Her heart thrashed wildly, driven by horror on the sea woman's behalf, fear and embarrassment on her own.

The visitors and most of the courtiers applauded, cheering as they would for the greatest drama of Racine.

'There, there, my dear,' Madame said softly. The Princess Palatine embraced Marie-Josèphe, holding her gently against her ample bosom, stroking her hair. Lotte joined them, patting Marie-Josèphe's hand.

'What a tragic story! How imaginative you are!'

'Overwrought melodrama,' Lorraine said.

'You're too harsh, sir,' Chartres said mildly.

'Come along, child,' Madame said. 'We'll ride with the King's hunt. The fresh air will have you well in no time.'

'Fagon,' Lorraine said, 'you should bleed her again.'

Marie-Josèphe started, ready to fly to Zachi, ready to run. Lorraine laughed, her first true enemy.

Count Lucien cleared his throat.

'Letting blood is not,' Fagon said nervously, 'is not indicated, at this time.'

Chapter 19

In the midst of a chaos of horses and dogs, carriages and shouting, Zachi stepped delicately across the paving stones of the courtyard. Marie-Josèphe stroked the mare's sleek red-gold neck.

'Do you know my frailties, dear Zachi?' she whispered. *I'm only tired*, she thought, though her feverish despair resembled no exhaustion she had ever felt.

Zachi swivelled one fine ear, then pricked both ears forward and arched her neck. Her walk was as smooth as still water.

Shouting, beating their leopard-spotted ponies' sides with their heels, the young princes clattered across the paving stones. A half-grown hound bayed and scrabbled to chase them. Its leash, fastened to the collar of an experienced old bitch, strangled it back. The bitch growled; the pup cowered. The King's hunt assembled, fifty horses and riders, a dozen open caleches. The stallions snorted and reared; the courtiers preened as proudly.

Horse sweat, human sweat, dung, smoke, and perfume mingled with the scent of orange blossoms and the cool sharp air of September. The sky glowed blue.

Monsieur and the Chevalier de Lorraine rode out on matched black Spanish chargers. Monsieur's diamond patches glittered against his powdered skin, his new coat gleamed with gold lace, and white plumes spilled nearly to the cantle of his saddle. He cocked his hat in the most stylish manner. Lorraine, impossibly elegant in his embroidered blue coat, sported a new diamond ring, displayed over his glove on his forefinger.

Marie-Josèphe hoped she could avoid him in the crowd.

'Unusual to see Monsieur riding astride,' the Duke du Maine said. His heavy hunter shouldered up beside Zachi.

'He has a beautiful seat, sir,' Marie-Josèphe said. 'See how his horse responds to him.'

'He wishes he could put that bridle on Lorraine, and make him admire his seat.' Maine chuckled.

Marie-Josèphe could make no sense of Maine's comment, except the insulting tone.

'I have heard he led bravely,' Marie-Josèphe said. 'Riding at the head of his company in battle.'

'Not until he'd spent two hours before his mirror. He must have taken four hours, to get himself up today.' Maine's horse moved closer. Maine's knee brushed against Marie-Josèphe's leg. Zachi flattened her ears and nipped at the horse. Marie-Josèphe did not correct her.

'Monsieur has been kindness itself to me, sir,' she said. 'And Madame, and Mademoiselle – I wouldn't like to hear them spoken of with disrespect.'

Maine turned toward her. The motion straightened the unevenness of his shoulders. The shadow of his wide plumed hat accentuated his intense beauty, the beauty of his father the King as a young man.

'Madame should have been born a man, and Monsieur a woman.'

Leaving Marie-Josèphe shocked to speechlessness by the poison in his voice, Maine stabbed his spurs into his horse's flanks and galloped away.

'Mlle de la Croix!' Madame, in the shabby riding habit that she wore when her position did not require court dress, trotted toward her on a substantial chestnut horse.

'Good day, Madame.' Marie-Josèphe smiled; Madame's happiness radiated, overcoming Marie-Josèphe's distress like the sun overwhelming clouds: she was outside, on horseback, on a perfect September day. Madame's complexion was high, her cheeks red, her eyes bright.

Madame smiled fondly back at Marie-Josèphe. 'Mademoiselle and I were terribly distressed when you were taken ill. You look a little feverish, my dear. Shall I send my physician to you?'

'I'm quite recovered, Madame, please don't trouble your physician.' Marie-Josèphe tugged her sleeve, making sure it covered the bandage and hid the red streaks.

'Are you fit to ride?'

'I wouldn't miss the King's hunt for anything!' She hoped His Majesty did not rescind his invitation the moment he saw her. 'Zachi

275

will take care of me.' She stroked the bay Arab's neck again; she never tired of touching the soft warmth of the Arabian's skin, and the hard power beneath it.

'M. de Chrétien's horses are swift and sure-footed,' Madame said. 'Too small for me!' She laughed, then gazed quizzically at Marie-Josèphe. 'I've not known M. de Chrétien to lend his horses, in the past, even to his intimates.'

'It's for my brother's convenience, to better serve His Majesty,' Marie-Josèphe said. 'But it is kind of him to let me ride her on the hunt, for my own pleasure.'

'My dear, you deserve a bit of pleasure – I think you do nothing but work.'

'Yet I've been remiss in my duties to you and to Mademoiselle. Please forgive me.'

'Your brother needs you while he serves the King, I'm resigned to that. We cannot do without you for long, though, remember,' Madame said. 'And Mademoiselle cannot do without your Odelette at all – they've invented six new hairstyles this morning alone, and will think of a dozen more while we hunt.'

'My sister Haleeda is a wonder, Madame, it's true.'

'Your – sister?' Madame arched both eyebrows. 'Haleeda?'

'My adopted sister, who is now free, who uses her true name, and who shares any good fortune I might encounter.'

Madame considered. 'A magnanimous decision, and a proper one. It isn't quite . . . acceptable . . . for you to own a slave.'

'I've recently come to realise it, Madame. Please remember, I'm an ignorant colonial girl.'

Madame chuckled, then grew serious. 'I wonder, my dear, if it's necessary to raise her to the status of your sister. Your servant, perhaps, would be more suitable.'

'That's impossible, Madame, as I cannot pay a servant.'

Madame's sceptical expression doubted the seriousness of Marie-Josèphe's reply. A clatter of hooves and the shrieks of youthful voices distracted her. The Grandsons of France galloped across the courtyard for a third time, laughing, shouting encouragement to their invisible cavalry troops. As aloof as a desert sheik, Zachi ignored the commotion. Madame's horse shied; she laughed and calmed it.

'Those boys.' Madame shook her head with disapproval. 'They'll lame their ponies, galloping about on stone. And Berri is too bold for his own good.'

Monsieur rode toward them, flanked by Lorraine and Chartres. Marie-Josèphe looked wildly for a place to flee from Monsieur's friend and Monsieur's son.

Chartres favoured her with his wild-eyed grin as if he had not offended her, as if she had never taken him to task. Monsieur gave her a strangely pitying glance, touched Lorraine's arm and bent toward him to whisper. She wondered why they always whispered.

Chartres, Marie-Josèphe thought, *I can manage, but I wish I could avoid M. de Lorraine.*

'My wild island maiden!' Lorraine said.

'I am not your maiden, sir,' Marie-Josèphe said coldly, 'and your jest does not amuse me.'

Lorraine chuckled. 'I will change your mind.'

'Her mind is made up, sir,' Monsieur said with unusual sharpness.

Suddenly the young princes pulled their ponies to a halt. They took off their hats. All the courtiers quickly joined them, lining up on either side of the Gate of Honour. Marie-Josèphe found herself with Madame on her right, a solid presence, and Chartres on her left, unpredictable. Chartres and Monsieur separated her from Lorraine.

She calmed herself. *Chartres cannot insult me, Lorraine cannot abuse me*, she thought, *surely not, not in front of so many people, in front of Madame and Monsieur.*

Her fondness for Monsieur and Madame increased with her gratitude. She felt safe with them. She wondered again what Maine had meant by his slander upon Monsieur; she wondered if he had meant his comment as a threat to his uncle, to his sister Madame Lucifer's father-in-law.

His Majesty's open hunting caleche drove through the gilded gate, drawn by four spotted Chinese horses with two postillion riders.

Innocent sat beside the King on the gold-embroidered cushions; Mme de Maintenon and Yves faced them. His Majesty faced forward, Yves backward. Gun-bearers, houndsmen, and bodyguards followed.

As His Majesty passed, nodding to his court, the riders all saluted him and the men doffed their hats. Marie-Josèphe bowed as best she could riding sidesaddle. She suppressed a giggle, wishing she knew how to make Zachi bow. Perhaps Count Lucien would show her.

Count Lucien, polished, elegant, mounted on Zelis, rode at His Majesty's shoulder. Zachi flared her nostrils at the sight of her stablemate Zelis, and Zelis pricked her ears and snorted, but both mares were too well-mannered to whinny. Marie-Josèphe bowed to the King, and then to Count Lucien, shy after all that had happened. He tipped his hat politely.

A sharp pinch stabbed the upper curve of Marie-Josèphe's bottom. She gasped, stifling an outcry. She slapped the spot, hoping to kill or drive off the horsefly before it bit her again, or bit Zachi.

Her palm smacked not a horsefly, but fingers.

Chartres withdrew his hand, smiling at her, laughing silently at her shocked expression. He put his stung fingers to his mouth, sucking them, then kissing the spot she had slapped. She glared at him; she backed Zachi a few steps so she would be behind him. She carried no whip; a whip would be an insult to the horse she rode. No doubt it was for the best, for it would be a terrible scandal if she struck the King's nephew with a riding crop.

To Marie-Josèphe's relief, Chartres wheeled about and followed Monsieur and Lorraine in His Majesty's wake.

'Did you see?' Madame said. 'Did you notice?'

'What, Madame?' Marie-Josèphe exclaimed, equally afraid that Madame had observed her son's behaviour, and fearing she would believe Marie-Josèphe invited it.

'His Majesty. His perruke.'

'It's very beautiful,' Marie-Josèphe said.

'It's brown!' Madame exclaimed.

'Brown?'

'Brown! Dark brown, to be sure, but brown nevertheless, lighter, ever so much lighter than he's been accustomed to wear for so many years.'

Madame joined the riders following the King; Marie-Josèphe rode after her, baffled by Madame's joy.

'Do you think, Mlle de la Croix, that his coat is rather gold-coloured, than brown?'

'I suppose, Madame, that one might call it dark gold.'

'I thought so!'

Ahead of Madame, courtiers jostled for position, gradually supplanting the musketeers protecting the King and the Swiss Guards watching over Pope Innocent. No one succeeded in supplanting Count Lucien, at His Majesty's right, for he was too watchful and Zelis too bold. Monsieur and Lorraine took over the place next to Yves, on the left of His Majesty's caleche.

'Mlle de la Croix,' Madame said softly, 'forgive me if I intrude, but I'm somewhat responsible for your place at court—'

'I'm very grateful for your protection, Madame.'

'I believed you were fond of M. de Lorraine.'

'I believed so, too, Madame.'

'It would be a good match.'

'It will never be a match.'

'Have you quarrelled?'

'No, Madame.'

'And yet—'

'He revealed his true nature to me, Madame—'

'He told you—?' Madame's voice rose.

'I asked him – I begged him – not to let Dr. Fagon bleed me. Yet he held me for the lancet – and he smiled when I cried.'

'Oh, my dear—'

'Count Lucien would never have behaved in such a base way.' Marie-Josèphe blinked back tears, not wanting to cry in front of Madame, not wanting to spoil the beautiful day with tears and horrible memories. 'Lorraine pretended to be my friend, Madame, but . . . he is pitiless.'

Madame squeezed Marie-Josèphe's hand. 'I hoped, with His

Majesty's influence, your goodness, he might – ah, never mind. I am sorry for myself, but glad for you.'

Marie-Josèphe kissed Madame's hand. Madame smiled, but tears filled her eyes. She glanced toward her husband and Lorraine.

'I wish he would love someone worthy of him,' she said softly.

'Lorraine?' Marie-Josèphe exclaimed, shocked that Madame would insult her so bluntly.

'Not Lorraine!' Madame said. 'Lorraine is a fool not to honour your regard.' She sighed. 'Not Lorraine. Monsieur. My husband.'

'But, Madame! You're worthy of him – you're worthy of anyone.'

'Dear child,' Madame said. 'Dear child. You're as sweet as your mother was, no wonder the King loves you.'

'Does he, Madame?' Marie-Josèphe asked, neither expecting nor receiving a reply.

Lucien rode easily beside His Majesty's hunting caleche. The exquisite day banished troubles as the sun and the breeze banished Versailles' usual miasmatic damp. Zelis pranced, showing off the fine arch of her dappled neck, the banner of her black tail. The exercise of riding eased the pain in Lucien's back. He had, necessarily, spent too much time of late on sedentary court functions, and too little time making love. Mlle Future – Lucien was well aware of the nicknames his lovers had at court – showed a reluctance to become Mlle Present that was unfamiliar in Lucien's experience.

And yet you have not pressed your suit, Lucien said to himself.

Lucien found, to his astonishment, that his interest in Mlle d'Armagnac had waned before it ever waxed to fullness. She was beautiful, but her conversation carried no hint of originality. She flirted, which was enjoyable. She had already bragged of being his mistress, which was impertinent, not least to Juliette, as well as being untrue. Lucien was faithful after his own fashion, to one woman at a time.

His Majesty's caleche passed between the rows of saluting courtiers. Today's hunt was larger than usual, joined as it was by guests. His Majesty wished to entertain his guests with a unique hunt, and to provide his kitchens with enough game to feed all his court and his company.

The postillions urged the caleche horses into a trot; they stepped out along the wide grassy path toward the forest of Versailles. Drumming rumbled in the distance. A horn blared, commanding the attention of the hounds. A gyrfalcon shrieked; its wings pounded the air with a soft and powerful rhythm. It settled onto the falconer's glove, its talons scratching the thick leather.

The caleche passed Monsieur's household. Monsieur bared his head in respect for his brother, and his friend Lorraine bowed with every appearance of goodwill. Ignoring Mme de Maintenon utterly, Madame gazed upon the King with wistful joy. As Lucien tipped his hat to Mlle de la Croix, Chartres pinched Mlle de la Croix's bottom, and grinned mischievously.

Chartres could shock even Lucien, who cultivated the image of being unshockable. His Majesty did not see what had happened, which was fortunate. Mlle de la Croix, though she flinched with surprise, kept her presence and her place. Instead of bolting into His Majesty's path, she slapped Chartres soundly. Chartres snatched back his hand.

You are fortunate she has no claws, foolish prince, Lucien thought, *or you'd count only to nine on your fingers*.

Monsieur's family fell in behind His Majesty's caleche, and the rest of Louis' court followed. All the princes, the grandsons of His Majesty, his nephew, and his illegitimate sons and daughters galloped in a pack, jostling for position, never forgetting their rivalries for a moment.

The caleche entered the forest; the hunting party moved from the pleasant warmth of the sun to the pleasant coolness of the shade. The horses stepped silently on the new-laid sod. Drums echoed through the gold-green light.

The caleche horses cantered along the forest road. Zelis flicked one ear. The mare wished to gallop, to run. Lucien held her in gently, for they must not outrun the King's conveyance.

If Mlle de la Croix would free herself, Lucien thought, *I wager she'd be quite magnificent*. He laughed to himself, then sobered, for her piety

281

enslaved her. Her signs of affection troubled him; the match would be disastrous.

Zachi offered to outdistance every other horse and rider. Marie-Josèphe asked for moderation with her hands, her voice; the mare settled, and cantered behind the princes. The rutted road of a few days before was transformed to smooth grass.

Grateful for the horse's good manners, and reserving a small part of her attention for Chartres and Lorraine, Marie-Josèphe tried to put aside her worry for the sea woman. She enjoyed the wind on her face, the freshness of the day, the sunlight and shadow dappling the world.

The caleche broke through the forest into a wide meadow. The sun's heat rose around her like a tropical sea, bringing with it the scent of crushed grass. The caleche stopped. The hunting party ranged itself to either side, and the gun-bearers brought the hunting-pieces.

Drums and beating-sticks coalesced into a ring of noise. Zachi arched her neck, snorted, pranced in place. She wished to join her sister-mare Zelis. Marie-Josèphe would gladly have let her. She hoped to speak to Count Lucien, to make up, somehow, for her inexcusable behaviour. But Count Lucien rode near His Majesty. Marie-Josèphe had no leave to approach the King, not even to speak to her brother.

A bearer handed a gun to Count Lucien, who inspected it and handed it to His Majesty. Pope Innocent and Mme de Maintenon remained empty-handed, but Yves accepted a fowling-piece.

Yves was a dreadful shot, when we were children, Marie-Josèphe thought. *I hope he has improved – or more creatures than rabbits will be in danger today!*

The sea woman returned to her thoughts. Marie-Josèphe could not glory in her own taste of freedom, when her friend swam round and round in the filthy brackish water, trapped, she who had been used to swimming in the clean deep sea, any distance, any direction, governed solely by her will. Only His Majesty could restore her to her home and her family.

'Mlle de la Croix—'

Marie-Josèphe started. So intent had she been on the sea woman's peril that she had forgotten her own.

'—you must give me a token to carry, like a knight of old.'

282

Chartres plucked at a bit of her lace, smiling, his wild eye giving him a rakish look. The breeze ruffled the long white plumes in his hat.

The Duke of Berwick rode beside him, which astonished Marie-Josèphe. Madame would surely disapprove of her son's associating with a bastard, even James Fitzjames, the King of England's natural son.

'Let my friend Chartres be your champion, do,' Berwick said. He spoke with a heavy accent, but he did not lisp like his father, and he was very handsome.

'I have no token, sir,' Marie-Josèphe said.

'Come now, you must – an earring, a handkerchief, a lacing from your corset—'

'A ruffle from your petticoat,' Lorraine said from her other side.

The men on their larger horses pinned her between them. Zachi liked this no more than Marie-Josèphe. She flattened her ears and stamped one hind foot.

'If I give you my handkerchief, sir, I will not have one, and my mother would be ashamed to see me.'

The drumming neared, a wall of sound.

The ground thundered as the ancient aurochs, freed from the menagerie, lumbered from the forest. The hunting party cried out in amazement and appreciation of the exotic creature.

The aurochs plowed the earth with its hooves; it ripped leaves to shreds with the points of its long horns. It bellowed and tossed its head, glaring about it with age-dimmed eyes. The other hunters held their fire, in respect of their King's right to take the huge bull.

His Majesty aimed. The aurochs drank the air with wide wet nostrils. As if scenting the danger of gunpowder, it lowered its head and charged the royal caleche.

His Majesty fired.

The aurochs thundered toward him. Its wound pumped blood straight from its heart.

'Your mother is dead, Mlle de la Croix,' Lorraine said.

'You are cruel, sir.'

Count Lucien calmly handed His Majesty another loaded gun. With equal assurance, His Majesty aimed, and fired.

The aurochs stumbled, recovered, and plunged on.

Even Chartres hesitated with astonishment, but the game Lorraine led was too tempting. He leaned from his saddle and snatched at Marie-Josèphe's petticoat lace.

His Majesty aimed, and fired a third time.

The aurochs lurched and fell, crashing to the earth before His Majesty, running as it lay. It spattered blood all around, on the ground, on the caleche, on His Majesty's dark gold coat. When it died, the hunters cheered His Majesty's elegant shooting.

'You are missing your hunt, sir.' Marie-Josèphe slapped Chartres' hand away; this time she meant to hurt him.

The forest trembled like a creature alive. Camels shambled from it, and stags raced out, too many to count. Rabbits scampered headlong after them. A fox rushed into the meadow, its tail bushed with fright. Freed by His Majesty's first kill, the hunters fired, volley after volley as the bearers handed them newly loaded guns. The camels bellowed, fell to their knees, and toppled over dead. Stags screamed and fell. Rabbits plunged over their bodies, then tumbled, shattered, across the grass.

Madame, in her scarlet livery, aimed and fired with intense calm. The fox leaped into the air, its shriek piercing the cacophony of guns and drums, and fell dead at her horse's feet.

'His Majesty's hunt bores me, mademoiselle,' Chartres said. 'I've found another that I like better.'

Chartres plucked the lace at her throat. Marie-Josèphe backed Zachi, but Lorraine blocked their way. The lace ripped. Lorraine pulled one of the pins from her hair.

Arabian oryxes burst from the forest. The hunting party redoubled their fire. As if felled by a single shot, the antelopes tumbled forward in a tangle of slender legs and slender spiral horns, robbed of their grace by death. Screaming murder, iridescent peacocks flapped and lumbered onto the hunting field, scrambling among the dead stags, over the rabbits in their death-throes.

Gunsmoke roiled up and hid the forest, while the roar of gunfire drowned out the noise of the beaters. The breeze stirred the powder-smoke like thick fog.

Marie-Josèphe urged Zachi forward. Berwick's charger stepped in front of her. Chartres snatched at the lace again, tearing it from her throat. Lorraine tugged at the lace of her sleeve, dragging it against the painful cut of Dr. Fagon's lancet.

A cloud of terrified grouse erupted from the underbrush, flapping wildly, so frightened they flew into danger instead of running to safety. Berwick's horse shied, startling Lorraine's and Chartres' mounts.

Gyrfalcons screeched and arrowed toward their prey. Their claws hit the plump birds with the soft thud of crushed wings.

Marie-Josèphe touched Zachi's mouth with the reins. The Arabian rushed backwards, reared and spun and leaped into a gallop. Chartres and Berwick and Lorraine pounded down the trail after her. Zachi sped past gamesmen opening wicker baskets, flinging a score of gobbling dindon from America into the air. Zachi never wavered when the stout brown birds erupted, into the range of the hunters' guns.

Hoofbeats echoed so close that Marie-Josèphe feared to look back; she urged Zachi on. Chartres, the lightest of the three men, grasped the hem of Marie-Josèphe's habit and nearly unseated her, but she tightened her right leg around the saddle-crook and shouted for Zachi to run, to flee.

Zachi ran, joyous and sure-footed, skimming over the path, outdistancing the larger horses. The hoofbeats and snorts fell behind. The laughter of the pursuers turned to irritation, then to anger. Marie-Josèphe leaned as close to Zachi's neck as the sidesaddle allowed.

Zachi outdistanced the horses, the riders, the clamour of the hunt. Marie-Josèphe rode alone. She sat back; Zachi slowed her headlong run. The mare cantered, then trotted, then walked, along the main branch of a tangle of manicured trails, flicking her ears as Marie-Josèphe spoke.

'No horse can outdistance you,' Marie-Josèphe said. 'No horse can even keep up with you. You are magnificent, and when I must return you, I'll grieve, but I could never afford to keep you as Count Lucien can – as you deserve.'

As if she had summoned him by speaking his name, Count Lucien appeared from a side trail.

'If you continue this habit of speaking to animals, Mlle de la Croix,' Count Lucien said, 'you'll earn a reputation you won't enjoy.'

Zelis stopped before Zachi; the two mares blew into each other's nostrils. Marie-Josèphe fantasied that they told each other what had happened, and Count Lucien understood them.

'A reputation as a witch might aid me now,' she said. 'I beg your pardon, of course I didn't mean that.'

'You're missing His Majesty's hunt.'

'As are you.'

'I took a brace of grouse; I don't eat as much as some men.'

Marie-Josèphe's outrage boiled over. 'Those wretched boys!' she cried. 'That wretched Lorraine!' Her hair hung wild around her face; her lace was ruined; her left arm ached fiercely. She bunched up her hair in her uninjured right hand; she dropped it; she fumbled at her torn cravat. She burst into tears of anger and frustration.

Humiliated, she turned away from Count Lucien.

'What you must think of me!' she said. 'You see me only when I'm begging for your help, or crying like a child, or making a fool of myself—'

'Hardly that.' He rode closer. 'Hold still.'

She shivered at his touch, thinking, wildly, *Chartres pursued me but Chrétien caught me, they both believe I—*

'I am a dangerous man, but you'll never be in danger from me. Be easy.' Count Lucien's voice gentled her.

He tied her hair back with his own ribbon, letting his chestnut perruke fall free around his shoulders.

'I liked Chartres,' Marie-Josèphe whispered. 'A sweet boy – I thought! What did I do, to make him behave so?'

'He behaved so because he wished to, and because he can indulge his wishes,' Count Lucien said. 'It had nothing to do with you, except that you appeared in his sights like an antelope.'

Marie-Josèphe stroked Zachi's shoulder. 'But I escaped, because you surround me with afrits to watch me.'

'Zachi is only a horse,' Count Lucien said. 'A remarkably swift horse, but only a horse, after all.'

286

He guided Zelis to Zachi's left, where he straightened Marie-Josèphe's cravat and arranged it like a steenkirk, fastening its end to her hunting jacket with his own diamond pin.

'I'll be in the forefront of fashion,' Marie-Josèphe said.

'At its very zenith.'

Marie-Josèphe gathered the reins in her right hand. Swelling and waves of pain made her left hand useless. She nestled it in her lap.

'What is wrong?'

'Nothing.'

'You are flushed with fever.'

'With the wind. With escape—'

Count Lucien took her hand. She pulled away.

'Truly, nothing—'

'Be still!' Count Lucien said sharply. He exposed her wrist. His fair complexion paled to chalk white.

The red streaks had turned ugly purple. Dried blood stuck the bandage to her skin. Her arm throbbed. She thought, *Though he's an officer, he doesn't like the sight of blood*.

'I'll send to my lodge for M. de Baatz's salve. It's infallible for wounds and fever. It saved my life this summer.'

'I'm very grateful to you, sir.'

'Can you ride back, or shall I fetch a carriage?'

'I can ride.' She was ashamed to admit she feared being left alone. 'I'm very strong, I never get sick.'

'Good. If you ride, no one will be tempted to send for Fagon.'

To avoid Dr. Fagon, Marie-Josèphe thought, *I'd ride to the Atlantic — I'd ride the Silk Road to the Pacific. At the shore, Zachi will turn into a sea horse, the sea woman will magically meet us, and we'll all swim to Martinique.*

'M. de Chrétien,' she said, 'I don't have delusions.'

'Why are you telling me this?'

'When I thought I saw Yves in the garden, bleeding – when I fled from the tiger that wasn't there – it was the sea monster, as I thought she was then. It was the sea woman, showing me how to hear her. Teaching me to recount her stories.'

'Hard lessons.'

287

'Effective ones. As you heard—'

'Yes,' Count Lucien said. 'It was extraordinary.'

They passed the trampled, bloody hunting meadow. Dogs growled over offal; servants gutted the catch and loaded it onto carts. Powder smoke thickened the air. The scent of blood and fear dizzied Marie-Josèphe. Her cheeks burned. She sought to distract herself from the fever, from the throbbing of her arm.

'May I ask you something, Count Lucien?'

'Certainly.'

'Madame said something I didn't understand. She said, "I wish Monsieur would love someone worthy of him". How can such a great princess consider herself unworthy?'

'You misunderstood her,' Count Lucien said. 'She meant he loves Lorraine.'

'Lorraine?'

'Monsieur,' Count Lucien said carefully, 'has been passionately attached to M. de Lorraine these many years.'

Marie-Josèphe considered. 'Do you mean, like Achilleus and Patroklos?'

'Rather, like Alexander and Hephaestion.'

'I didn't know—'

'It isn't much spoken of, being so dangerous.'

'—anyone in the modern age was like Alexander. I thought passionate love between men was as mythical as centaurs – did you say, dangerous?'

'Without His Majesty's protection, Orléans and Lorraine might both be burned.'

'Burned! For love?'

'For sodomy.'

'What is sodomy?'

'Passionate love between men,' he said. 'Or between women.'

She shook her head, confused.

'Physical love,' Count Lucien said. 'Sex.'

'Between men?' Marie-Josèphe asked, amazed. 'Between women!'

'Yes.'

'But why?' she exclaimed. She asked nothing about how, because she had little notion of the how, between a man and a woman, and she was not supposed to possess such knowledge.

'Because your Church forbids it.'

'I mean, why would they want to, without the promise of children—'

'For love. For passion. For pleasure.'

She laughed outright. 'Oh, nonsense!'

'You're laughing at me, Mlle de la Croix. Do you know more of sex than I do?'

'I know what the nuns told me.'

'They know nothing of sex at all.'

'They know it's a sin, a plague upon the human race, a curse for women, a trial for men, to remind us of Eve's sin in the Garden of Eden.'

'That is the nonsense.'

'What have I said to make you so angry?'

'You? Nothing. But your teachers make me angry. They have corrupted your intelligence with lies.'

'Why would they lie?'

'That has always puzzled me,' Count Lucien said. 'Perhaps you should ask Pope Innocent – but I doubt he'd tell you the truth either.'

'Will you?'

'If you wish.'

She hesitated. She had always sought the truth, in all other ways.

'I've always been told,' she said, 'that modest young women should know nothing of intimate matters.'

'You've been told to restrict yourself in all manner of ways – your studies, your music, your intelligence—'

'I wish you to tell me!'

'The truth,' Count Lucien said. 'Passionate love – sexual love – is the greatest pleasure one can experience. It dispels sadness. It banishes pain. It's like the finest wine, like the morning of a day of perfect weather, like the most beautiful music, like riding free forever. And it's like none of those things.'

Count Lucien's voice – could it only be his voice? – made her pulse

289

race with the excitement of danger and forbidden sins. Her arm throbbed, but at the same time a mysterious string of ecstasy tightened, its note rising toward the music of the spheres. Marie-Josèphe caught her breath.

'Enough, please.' Her voice shook. Her body trembled with the same pleasure that had awakened her to the sea woman's song.

'As you prefer.'

Riding in the cool forest shade, she regained her composure. 'Count Lucien, if M. de Lorraine loves men – what does he want with me?'

'M. de Lorraine does not so much love men, or women, as himself and his own interest.'

'Why didn't anyone tell me? Warn me?'

'Perhaps because you didn't ask.'

'I always asked questions, when I was a child.' She met his transparent grey gaze. 'I delighted in asking.'

'You may ask me whatever you like, Mlle de la Croix, and if I know the answer I will tell you.'

Zachi snorted. Undergrowth crackled nearby.

'There she is, our lost Mlle de la Croix!'

Lorraine, Chartres, and Berwick burst out of the forest, whipping their lathered horses. Chartres forced his mount ahead of the others.

'I thought you'd been eaten by a bear!' Chartres cried. He aimed for Marie-Josèphe, but found himself separated from her by Zelis and Count Lucien. His horse tossed its head. Bloody foam flew from the bit.

'Bears are shy,' Marie-Josèphe said. 'They'll never harm you, unless you provoke them. Unlike other predators.'

'The provocation is so delightful,' Chartres said. 'I may die of a broken heart.'

Berwick and Lorraine spurred their powerful, exhausted horses up close behind Zachi and Zelis.

'Mind her heels,' Count Lucien said, for Zelis laid her ears flat back in irritation. Lorraine and Berwick forced their stallions to lag a step or two.

'What an animal!' Berwick exclaimed. 'I've never seen such speed as this bay possesses. Mlle de la Croix, you must sell the creature to me.'

'I must not, sir, as Zachi isn't mine.'

'Is it the King's horse? He'll give it to me, I'm his cousin.'

The relationship was more intricate, but Marie-Josèphe could not remember exactly what it was; it was, as well, complicated by Berwick's bastardy.

'Berwick,' Chartres said with condescension, 'these petit horses all belong to Chrétien.'

Lorraine guffawed. 'Who else would they belong to?'

'It may be too small, but it's marvellously swift. Monarch will cover her. Their issue will win every race—'

'That's impossible, M. de Berwick,' Count Lucien said. 'You may send a mare to my stud in Finisterre, if you covet a foal with some qualities of the desert Arabian.'

'No, no, that won't do, your stud on my mare? Absurd.'

'Somehow,' Lorraine said, 'he would manage.'

'M. de Lorraine, M. de Berwick,' Chartres said severely, 'you are in the presence of a lady.'

Marie-Josèphe almost burst out laughing at Chartres' hypocrisy, but she feared the men would take her for an hysteric. This time, they would not be so far wrong.

'I beg your pardon, miss,' Berwick said offhand, mixing his languages, never taking his attention from Count Lucien. 'Chrétien, you must sell me this bay mare!'

'Must I?'

'I'll give you ten thousand louis!'

'Do you mistake me, sir, for a horse-trader?'

The French aristocracy did not engage in trade. Count Lucien's voice contained no anger, but from that moment Marie-Josèphe never doubted he was a dangerous man.

'Not at all, not at all!' Berwick strove to retract the insult. 'But an arrangement between noblemen, an exchange—'

'I do not part with these horses. They were a gift. Were Zachi to bear a foal from any sire but her own desert breed, her bloodline would never be pure again.'

'Ridiculous!'

'The sheik believed it. I choose to respect his beliefs. I will not part with the mares: I gave my word.'

291

'Your word!' Berwick exclaimed. 'You gave your word to a Mahometan? No Christian need keep such a promise!'

Even Chartres and Lorraine flinched. Marie-Josèphe stared at Berwick in shock.

'No doubt that's true,' Count Lucien said coldly. 'But I am not a Christian.'

Berwick laughed. No one joined in his hilarity. He retreated into an uncomfortable silence.

'Let us return to the hunt.' Count Lucien impelled Zelis forward with sudden urgency.

Marie-Josèphe spoke to Zachi, freeing her to run. The two Arabians galloped together, outdistancing the three stallions that Zachi had raced to exhaustion.

Marie-Josèphe followed Count Lucien through the straggled hunting party. The huntsmen and gun-bearers bowed him past; the courtiers on horseback gave way for His Majesty's adviser. He approached His Majesty's caleche, where Mme de Maintenon spoke intently to His Majesty and His Holiness. Her animation enlivened her, as if she were in her favourite place, Saint-Cyr, instructing her beloved students. Monsieur spoke flirtatiously to Yves, who valiantly attended to Mme de Maintenon's discourse without snubbing Monsieur.

Madame rode behind the King, chatting and laughing with her ladies, who rode in a caleche and wore grand habit.

'Do you ride with Madame,' Count Lucien said. 'Chartres cannot misbehave too badly in her sight, or the formidable lady will turn him over her knee, and Lorraine as well.'

Marie-Josèphe wished it were true; she wished Count Lucien would ride beside her back to the chateau.

'Thank you,' she said. 'You must attend His Majesty—'

'I must send for M. de Baatz's salve,' Count Lucien said. 'Return to your apartment, rest – I'll have the salve brought to you.'

'I cannot. The sea woman is alone—'

'Someone else can feed her.'

'—and lonely. If I don't tend to her, I'll arouse comment – they'll think I'm ill!'

'The Fountain of Apollo, then.' He tipped his hat courteously, rode ahead, paused to send a musketeer galloping off toward the chateau, then allowed Zelis to take him briskly to his place at His Majesty's side.

Marie-Josèphe hoped Count Lucien's salve would soothe her arm. The purple streaks stretched across her palm.

I mustn't let anyone else see, she thought as she joined Madame, *or they'll send for Dr. Fagon . . .*

'Mlle de la Croix!' Madame said smiling. 'There you are, my dear. Did you see my fox?'

The hunt might have taken place a year ago, for all she recalled of it. She had forgotten the fox. Free of Chartres and Lorraine, relatively safe in the company of Madame and His Majesty, she felt weary and feverish.

'Yes, Madame, of course, your fox.'

'I'll present him to His Majesty.' A servant in Madame's livery ran toward the caleche carrying the limp scrap of red fur. 'But His Majesty will return him to me. His pelt will make a lovely tippet. I dispatched him with a single shot, so the fur will hardly be damaged at all.'

The servant handed the fox to a huntsman, who presented it to Yves, who offered it to His Majesty. Pope Innocent drew back from the bloody carcass. His Majesty touched the dead fox; his reply returned by a route as circuitous as the fox's arrival.

Madame's servant dodged between horses and stopped at Marie-Josèphe's side.

'His Majesty asks Madame to attend him.'

'Madame,' Marie-Josèphe said, 'His Majesty—'

As Marie-Josèphe spoke, Madame advanced like a cavalry officer. Marie-Josèphe followed in her substantial wake. Count Lucien surrendered his place in respect of the Princess Palatine; only Madame separated Marie-Josèphe from the King.

Lorraine, Chartres, and Berwick rode their lathered horses out of the forest. They rejoined the hunting party, riding up next to Monsieur.

Lorraine tipped his hat to Marie-Josèphe. She ignored him. Between Madame and Count Lucien, she did feel safe. Monsieur brushed his fingertips across Lorraine's hand, a possessive gesture that Marie-Josèphe now understood, as she understood Pope Innocent's frown. She felt sorry to have caused Monsieur concern and jealousy.

I suppose, she thought, *I cannot tell him he has nothing to fear from me. It would be kind, but it would be the height of arrogance.*

'Good afternoon, Madame,' His Majesty said. 'You shot excellently well.'

'Your Majesty, it's my greatest joy to ride with you.' Madame's voice and words grew tender, much different from her usual bluff comments, when she spoke to the King.

'You've won the prize.' His Majesty unfastened a collar from the dead fox's throat, bringing away a handful of light, a wide bracelet of gold and diamonds. He fastened the bracelet around Madame's wrist.

'Your Majesty,' Madame said, breathless. 'I am overwhelmed.' She admired the sparking rainbow facets and showed the bracelet to Marie-Josèphe.

'It's beautiful, Madame,' Marie-Josèphe said sincerely. 'The most beautiful bracelet I've ever seen.'

Madame glowed in His Majesty's attention; she even nodded to Mme de Maintenon with a smile very different from her usual exquisitely polite coolness. Taken aback, Mme de Maintenon hesitated, then nodded in return.

'I have a prize for you, as well,' the King said to Mme de Maintenon. 'Close your eyes and put out your hands.'

'Oh, Sire—'

'Come, come, come!' He bullied her cheerfully.

Mme de Maintenon obeyed her husband. The King opened a black velvet bag and poured out a magnificent parure of diamonds and sapphires: earrings, brooch, and bracelet. The jewellery gleaming in her palms, Mme de Maintenon sat obstinately motionless, her eyes tightly closed.

His Majesty's cheer faded. 'You may open your eyes.'

Mme de Maintenon barely glanced at the ornaments. 'How beautiful – of course I cannot in good conscience wear them.' She pressed the jewels into His Holiness' hands. 'Sell them, and give the proceeds to the poor.'

'Your charity is legendary.' His Holiness handed the parure to Yves, who took it with the same reserve with which he had handled the dead fox.

Louis remained impassive. Madame was not so stoic.

'I could never part with a present from Your Majesty,' she said. 'I'm far too selfish and worldly. I shall wear my bracelet to Carrousel.'

His Majesty nodded to Madame.

Even his smallest action is splendid, Marie-Josèphe thought, and dared to hope for her friend.

'I should sell it to pay my servants,' Madame whispered to Marie-Josèphe, 'but I shall wear it — if Monsieur doesn't insist on borrowing it!'

'I would have liked to see you wear my gift, if but once,' His Majesty said to Mme de Maintenon. He did not raise his voice; neither did he make any attempt to keep the conversation confidential. Monsieur suddenly turned to Lorraine and began a spirited discussion; similarly, Madame displayed the intricate clasp of her new bracelet to Marie-Josèphe. Everyone pretended to be unaware of the exchange between the King and his wife. Even His Holiness looked politely away, asking Yves about some nearby bird or leaf or insect.

The King has no private moments, Marie-Josèphe said to herself. *It must make no difference to him, whether he speaks in front of a few noblemen serving at his awakening, or in front of his whole court.*

'Sire, I'm a plain old woman. I'd look foolish in a young bride's baubles.'

'You're always beautiful to me,' His Majesty said.

'My only beauty is my good work, which I dedicate to you, who rule by the grace of God.'

Louis, called in his youth Dieudonné, God-given, shook his head. 'That's true, yet I'm still a man, who desired to give his wife a gift.'

An uncomfortable silence fell between the King and Mme de Maintenon.

Monsieur's sudden giggle interrupted it. 'The sea monster?' he cried. 'The sea monster told bawdy tales?'

'Indeed it did, and Mlle de la Croix translated them for us.'

Lorraine looked past Monsieur, past Yves and His Majesty, past

Madame. He smiled his devastating smile at Marie-Josèphe, but he had robbed himself of its power over her.

'Do you tell your story again, Mlle de la Croix,' Lorraine said easily, 'for Monsieur and for His Majesty.'

'It isn't my story, sir.' She did not plan the rude chill in her voice, but she could not regret it. 'It belongs to—'

'I forbid you to repeat it,' Yves said.

'—the sea woman.'

'It's entirely improper, Monsieur,' Lorraine said. 'About Northern raiders – and bestiality with sea monsters.'

'Would that not be rather cold – and slimy?' Monsieur shuddered theatrically. 'I would prefer – but, my dear, you know what I prefer.'

'It was not about bestiality,' Count Lucien said. 'It was about murder, rape – and betrayal.'

'To be sure, M. de Chrétien, it was.' To Marie-Josèphe, Lorraine said, 'Your story gains in excitement – coming from your lips. Barbarians ravaging gargoyles—'

'Sir!' Mme de Maintenon's flushed cheeks were the only colour about her. 'Consider in whose presence you are speaking!'

Curiosity vanished from His Holiness' expression, replaced by offended virtue.

'Mlle de la Croix,' His Majesty said, 'teach the sea monster tricks, if it amuses you, but govern this delusion about her nature. Your mother would never have invented such appalling stories.'

Silence fell. Monsieur stopped chuckling.

'Your Majesty—'

Lorraine interrupted her. 'She thinks Your Royal Highness is a cannibal.'

'And govern your tongue as well.'

'I never believed any such thing, Sire,' Marie-Josèphe exclaimed, horrified. She had only wished to protect him from such an accusation. 'Never!'

'Forgive my sister,' Yves said. 'She has not yet recovered from her illness.'

With a persistence driven by fever, Marie-Josèphe continued.

'Your Majesty, please spare her life. She's a woman with a soul, like yours or mine. If you kill her, you'll commit a mortal sin!'

'I would entertain His Holiness' views on mortal sin,' the King said. 'I might entertain even your brother's. But I hardly think I need listen to yours.'

'Do you call His Majesty a murderer?' Lorraine said, his voice as soft as oiled silk.

'It is neither murder,' His Holiness said, 'nor against any commandment, to kill a beast. God put beasts on Earth for the use of man. You must not task yourself with moral philosophy, Mlle de la Croix. It's too demanding for the minds of women.' He made a gesture of dismissal. 'Dabble in your natural philosophy, or better yet take up cooking.'

'Natural philosophy proves the sea woman is human!' Marie-Josèphe cried.

Louis shook his head. 'Dr. Fagon assured me you were cured of your hysteria.'

Count Lucien placed his hand on Marie-Josèphe's wrist, startling her, stopping her protest.

'Your Majesty,' Count Lucien said.

Both Mme de Maintenon and Innocent pointedly ignored him, but His Majesty responded with open curiosity.

'Your advice, M. de Chrétien?'

'Consider, Sire, if Mlle de la Croix is correct.'

'Ridiculous,' said Innocent.

'She's proved the sea monster understands her.'

'That is true,' His Majesty admitted. 'However, I am led to believe her cat understands her. Am I to give M. Hercules a place at court?'

His courtiers dared to titter at his joke.

'You are fortunate to live in the modern age.' Innocent gazed on Marie-Josèphe with concern and suspicion. 'In times past, a woman who spoke to animals – to demons – risked the stake.'

The courtiers stopped laughing. Yves paled. 'Your Holiness, my sister has made a pet of the monster. She doesn't realise—'

'Be easy in your mind, my son,' Innocent said to Yves. 'I don't accuse your sister of being possessed. I do suspect she may be mad, mistaking beasts for people.'

'As the Church mistook beasts for demons,' Count Lucien said.

Innocent glared. 'There was no mistake about it – they were products of demonic possession. The Inquisition drove out the satanic influence.'

'Their status changed once – why not again? What remains to be proven,' Count Lucien said to His Majesty, 'is whether the creature speaks a human language and therefore is not a creature. This is a scientific age. If I understand what Father de la Croix has said of science – he will correct my errors, I trust – science demands proof. Allow Mlle de la Croix to prove her contention.'

His Majesty's gaze searched Count Lucien's face. Finally, impassively, he said, 'I will see.'

Chapter 20

Marie-Josèphe entered the sea woman's prison. She hesitated, swaying dizzily. Murk clouded the pool. Marie-Josèphe sat down before her equilibrium deserted her. Her arm throbbed.

She whispered the sea woman's name. 'His Majesty will hear me on your behalf. You must tell him a story I could never make up. A story to move him. A story to charm him to our cause.'

The sea woman growled her contempt for the King. She would fight the toothless one for her freedom. The land woman must throw him into the fountain, where the sea woman could sing at him until his heart stopped and his bowels turned to water.

'Don't say such things! What if someone else learned to understand you?'

The sea woman swam to her. Her whispered song created loneliness and despair. Slow ripples spread outward along her path. Marie-Josèphe plunged her hand beneath the surface, hoping the cool water might soothe the ache. The ripples she created met the sea woman's wake; their interaction entranced her for a moment.

The sea woman grasped Marie-Josèphe's swollen hand. Her nostrils flared. Marie-Josèphe gasped; the pain of the touch broke through her feverish distraction.

'Let me go, please, you're hurting me.'

The sea woman refused to release her. Her eyes gleamed dark gold. She sniffed and licked Marie-Josèphe's swollen palm. Following the angry purple streaks, she pushed at the sleeve of Marie-Josèphe's hunting habit and exposed the bandage. She hummed with worry, then changed the key to reassurance. She nibbled at the bandage; with her long pointed webbed fingers she untied the bloody linen. The water had soaked it loose. She exposed the angry wound.

Outside the tent, horses galloped near and pulled up. Men spoke;

Count Lucien entered, his distinctive footsteps uneven, punctuated with the tap of his sword-cane.

The sea woman kissed Marie-Josèphe's arm, tonguing the incision, drooling profusely on the wound. The scab cracked and bled. Marie-Josèphe felt sick.

'What is she doing?' Count Lucien spoke quietly, but the tension in his voice startled Marie-Josèphe. The sea woman released her and submerged in the pool.

'I don't know,' Marie-Josèphe said. 'She didn't tell me.'

The sea woman fled. The small man of land, in his complicated outer skin, did not behave cruelly, like the one who covered himself with black. The small man intrigued her more than he frightened her, yet still she feared him. If he were the land-woman's particular friend, she might trust him more. But the land woman had not yet chosen him.

Alone beneath the surface, she cried. She hoped she had helped the land woman. Had she kissed her sick arm sufficiently? She hoped so. She was afraid to tell her ally what she was doing, afraid to say she could help, for if the men of land discovered what she had done, what she could do, they would cut out her tongue and take it away with them. One of them would wear it around his neck on a string of seaweed, like the sailors did. They were such fools, they terrified her.

I'm always afraid, she thought. *Ever since the net, ever since the galleon, I've been afraid, though I was never afraid in my life before!*

The fear made her angry. If the land woman died of her wounds, the sea woman would be all alone with no ally at all to help her escape. She must escape.

Lucien let Marie-Josèphe's arm bleed.

'Make it stop,' she said, near panic.

'I will. In a moment. The blood will—' He stopped, unwilling to frighten her further with talk of bleeding out the poison. 'I will. One moment.' He took off his gloves and dug in his saddlebag for lint, bandage, spirits of wine.

'This will hurt.' He poured the spirits over the wound. It diluted the thick blood and flowed in pink streams down Marie-Josèphe's arm. Marie-Josèphe neither cried out nor flinched. Lucien pressed a wad of lint onto the open incision. He brought out the small silver casket containing what remained of M. de Baatz's salve. He had used most of it on Chartres' wound and his own. He had not yet been home to Brittany to replenish his supply.

If only Papa would give me the recipe, Lucien thought. *If only he'll bequeath it to me, or even to Guy, instead of letting the secret be lost.*

'This will soothe you,' he said. As soon as the bleeding ceased, he spread the thick black salve across the wound. He used it all. A wound as corrupt as this could kill a powerful young soldier; even with the salve, Lucien feared gangrene. He dressed the wound and bandaged it.

'There, you see, the swelling's less already.' Lucien hoped he was not deceiving himself. He smiled, grasping for certainty. 'That will see you well in a day or two.'

'Thank you, Count Lucien.' She laid her unwounded hand over his. 'How many times have you rescued me, today alone? Do you know, you are the only one ever to rescue me.'

Lucien bowed over her hand. He withdrew and put his gloves back on, tempting as it was to leave his hand within her tantalising touch, to let her warmth soothe his joints, which always ached.

'Many people find Versailles to be full of quicksand and fevers,' he said.

'You rescued me from Saint-Cyr as well,' she said. 'Am I wrong in believing that?'

'I did direct the change,' he said.

'As well as my release from the convent on Martinique – and my sister Haleeda's?'

'Yes, at His Majesty's desire.'

'Allow me to thank you,' she said, 'even if your only thought was to oblige the King.'

'It was entirely my pleasure,' Lucien said.

'Count Lucien,' she said hesitantly, 'might I beg you for your assistance in a matter that obliges only me?'

'It would be entirely my pleasure to offer my assistance.'

She explained her wish to free her slave, whom she called sister. Lucien agreed to arrange for the papers, though he warned her that only her brother's signature would put them into force. He wondered if she would persuade him to follow her will in the matter, for Yves de la Croix's courtly manner hid a powerful streak of obstinacy.

'Thank you, sir.' Marie-Josèphe laid her hand on his in a gentle touch of gratitude.

Yves hurried into the tent, flung open the cage door, and plunged down the fountain stairs in a single stride. Marie-Josèphe drew her hand from Lucien's and jerked her sleeve over the bandage.

'For the love of God, Sister, why are you doing this?'

'To save the sea woman. To save His Majesty's soul.'

He flung up his arms in exasperation. 'You risk my work and the King's favour, to save a pet. If Innocent believes the beast is your familiar – you risk your life.'

The guards pulled aside the tent curtains.

His Majesty arrived.

Marie-Josèphe rose, composing herself. 'Sea woman,' she whispered, begging her to approach.

The court of Versailles arranged itself in order of rank and precedence. Madame caught Marie-Josèphe's gaze and gave her a smile part encouragement, part dread. Lotte, her hair perfectly, elaborately dressed, blew her a kiss. Even Monsieur, arm-in-arm with Lorraine, offered her a friendly nod. Lorraine gazed at her with hooded, satisfied eyes.

Once the courtiers had taken their places, the sentries allowed visitors into the tent. Outside, a broadsheet-seller hawked copies of the sea woman's first story, the visit to Atlantis, illustrated with drawings of sea monsters writhing together in the waves.

His Majesty and Pope Innocent, the two most powerful men in the world, entered the cage to observe His Majesty's captive.

Marie-Josèphe curtsied, hoping respect would make amends for her hunting clothes, her torn lace, her dishevelled hair. The other courtiers had changed into court habit. Innocent wore a robe of incandescent white. His Majesty had donned a magnificent coat of gold velvet, with gold lace and diamonds, and a brown perruke adorned with gold powder.

The sea woman floated beside the statue of Apollo. She snorted, engorging the whorls on her face with air.

She dove, disappeared, and resurfaced like an explosion, leaping from the water, spinning, landing flat with an enormous splash. Pope Innocent stepped back so quickly that he would have lost his balance if Yves had not caught his elbow. His Majesty never moved, though droplets beaded on his coat like tiny pearls.

The sea woman trilled and snarled, spat water, and vanished.

'Ill-trained beast,' Innocent said.

'She said—'

'Hush!' Yves said.

'Let your sister speak, Father de la Croix. What did the creature say?'

'The sea woman said . . . "The white one is as ugly as an eel". I beg your forgiveness, Your Holiness, but the sea people think we're all ugly, because of our smooth faces.'

'Only your innocence saves you from insolence,' Louis said.

'Innocence is no excuse for such presumption,' said the Pope.

'I mean no insult, Your Majesty, Your Holiness. Nor does the sea woman—'

'Do you not?'

'I speak for her. Her name is—' She sang the sea woman's name. His Majesty listened, his eyes half closed. Marie-Josèphe wished for him to open his mind, to see what she could hear. 'She doesn't know our customs.'

'Do you, Mlle de la Croix?' the King said.

'Our custom,' Innocent said, 'is to eat the flesh of sea monsters. God put sea monsters – and all beasts – on Earth for the use of man, as He put women on Earth to submit to men. I look forward to savouring sea monster flesh.'

'I shall hear what the monster – what Mlle de la Croix has to say.'

Faint with relief, Marie-Josèphe fell to her knees before the King. She grasped his hand and kissed it.

'Thank you, Your Majesty.'

He extricated his hand from her grasp; he brushed his fingertips across her hair. He left the cage and settled in his armchair, Pope Innocent at his right hand.

Could I make the sea woman sound more diplomatic? Marie-Josèphe wondered. No: I'd tangle myself in lies. Besides, she'd correct me herself.

The sea woman waited. Floating at the platform in the scummy water, she kicked the surface to tan foam with her double tail. She slithered up the stairs and lay exposed and vulnerable on the rim of the fountain. She snarled.

Marie-Josèphe bent to kiss her gnarled forehead. The sea woman grabbed her left hand and buried her face in her palm, sniffing her skin, touching it with her tongue, in a crude and flagrant parody of the kiss Marie-Josèphe offered the King. Like Louis, Marie-Josèphe twisted her hand away. She settled her drawing box.

The sea woman cried out a surge of anger like a tidal wave

'No, sea woman, please,' Marie-Josèphe whispered, 'this might be your last chance, it's a story they want, tell a tale of sea creatures, of great storms, of Atlantis—'

The sea woman murmured, promising a story, an extraordinary, glorious story, if only Marie-Josèphe would interpret.

Marie-Josèphe faced His Majesty and sought to turn the sea woman's images into words.

'Why did you murder my friend and slash him to pieces?'

Yves' face paled to gray beneath his tan.

'If you want to see inside him, you should touch him with your voice.'

The sketch formed as if the sea woman had burned it into the paper. The sea man, alive, joyful, dove through the waves, his bones and organs a clean clear shadow within him.

'Why did you kill my best sweet friend, who shared the touch of . . .' Paralysed with embarrassment, Marie-Josèphe struggled for a description she could say in front of the King. 'Who shared the touch of our secret places?'

Marie-Josèphe saw before her the broken body of the sea man, drifting into dark depths. The sea woman swam beside him, weeping, her tears mingling with the water.

'You did not respect his life,' Marie-Josèphe said. 'You do not respect his death.'

The sea woman swam beside the body of her friend, braiding her hair with his, dark green with light.

'After you killed him, you should have taken him properly into the sea.'

She sank deeper into the darkness with her dead friend. Marie-Josèphe's tears blurred her vision, blurred her sketch. The song's images remained clear. She feared the sea woman planned to die.

The sea woman's friend sank into a darkness swirled with light. Luminescent sea creatures shone like stars in the night sky. The sea woman cut the lock of her friend's hair with a shell blade.

In the fountain, the sea woman fingered the tangled light-green hair knotted to her darker hair.

'He gave me a token, a pretty thing, a shiny stone, to tie into my hair. I would return it to him.'

The sea woman's song faded; the image of her friend's body disappeared, falling through darkness and beyond the pinpoint lights and glowing ribbons. The images disappeared entirely. Marie-Josèphe bent her head and wiped her tears on her sleeve. The true world returned to her sight.

Her heart sank, for His Majesty frowned and His Holiness glared and Yves looked ready to faint, while the nobles whispered to each other, appalled. But the audience of commoners sighed and wept with pity. Count Lucien, behind His Majesty, stared at the floor. The curls of his perruke hid his face.

'That is all,' Marie-Josèphe whispered.

'Pagan ritual,' His Holiness said. 'Did you learn these things from wild men, Mlle de la Croix?'

His Majesty rose. 'Doesn't the sea monster wish to keep this love token?'

Lorraine laughed at His Majesty's witticism, enjoying Marie-Josèphe's anguish. Monsieur chuckled briefly, but with more distress than amusement.

The sea woman sang a melody of heartbreaking beauty, a distillation of love and grief.

'I would send it with him,' Marie-Josèphe sang, following the melody. 'Send it into the depths with him, to acknowledge that I, too, will die.'

'Does she not,' His Majesty said carefully, 'claim to be immortal?'

'No, Your Majesty.'

'We are all immortal in the love of God,' His Holiness said. 'Does your sea monster believe in the Resurrection? In God's everlasting life?'

'Life itself is everlasting,' Marie-Josèphe sang, in harmony. 'People live, people create new life, people die. People never come back.'

His Holiness made a sound of utter disgust. 'Your games have passed beyond amusement, Mlle de la Croix – even beyond pagan belief. You tread the edge of heresy!'

'I didn't invent the story, Your Holiness,' Marie-Josèphe said. 'Please, please believe me. The sea woman told it. She doesn't understand heresy—'

'You should,' Innocent said.

'But she could understand God!' Marie-Josèphe exclaimed. 'She could, if Your Holiness taught her. You could give Our Saviour to the people of the sea—'

'Be silent!' His Holiness said. 'Convert beasts?'

'She thinks Jesus on the Mount should have preached to loaves and fishes instead of to people.'

No one laughed at Lorraine's observation; Count Lucien gave him a glare of perfect animosity.

'Where's the token?' Louis ignored both Lorraine and Count Lucien. 'The token she wishes to give to her mate?'

The sea woman snarled. Marie-Josèphe winced, shocked by the reply: shocked, but not surprised. She hesitated, hoping in vain that she would not have to lie.

'Your Majesty, someone took it.'

'Who?'

'One – one of the sailors.'

The sea woman protested, thrashing her tails, splashing Marie-Josèphe's back with cold fetid water.

'Your Majesty, isn't this proof that she talks to me? I have no other way of knowing about her token.'

'Dear foolish child,' Louis said, 'I have no way of knowing the token ever existed.' He gazed at her sadly. His next words, she knew, would be a death sentence.

'Don't kill it,' a visitor whispered from the back of the tent. Other commoners took up the refrain: Don't kill it, don't kill it. His Majesty's brow clouded. Marie-Josèphe wanted to cry to the visitors, Don't you know, His Majesty cannot be cajoled or threatened? With all goodwill, the spectators only made things worse. A musketeer strode toward the disturbance; the whispers stopped.

'You're most clever,' His Majesty said to Marie-Josèphe, 'trying to save your pet by making it into Scheherazade.'

His Majesty's courtiers laughed, all but Count Lucien.

'One Thousand and One Ocean Nights, by Scheherazade the Sea Monster!' Chartres cried.

The sea woman clambered past Marie-Josèphe, dragging herself to the top of the stairs. She glared at the King.

'Shhhhrrrzzzzaaddddd,' she snarled.

'The clever Mlle de la Croix has taught it to talk!' Lorraine exclaimed. 'Though not as well as a parrot.'

Monsieur laughed. 'Sherzad the parrot!'

'The myth requires—' His Majesty said.

The laughter ended.

'—that I allow it to live for another day.'

In amazement, in desperate gratitude, Marie-Josèphe flung herself at the King's feet and kissed the cold hard diamonds at the hem of his coat. He brushed his fingertips over her hair.

His Majesty left the tent, walking as strongly as if he had never been afflicted with gout. Innocent and his attendants accompanied him. The courtiers followed. The visitors cheered His Majesty as if their protests had had something to do with his decision.

'Let us have another sea monster story, mamselle!' shouted one of the spectators when His Majesty had left.

Cries of approval and agreement surrounded her in an opaque cloud of noise. They threatened to overwhelm her. Count Lucien grasped Marie-Josèphe's elbow.

'Are you quite well?'

She was too faint with exhaustion and relief to get to her feet. Count Lucien pushed her sleeve above her wrist. The swelling had vanished, and the streaks had receded.

Marie-Josèphe drew back, for his touch made her tremble.

'Will he spare her?' she whispered.

'I cannot say. This is a reprieve.'

'A day . . .'

'Anything can happen in a day.'

Yves slipped away from the other courtiers. Agitation gripped him. If anyone saw him, they would surely send him to the madhouse. His eyes must be staring, white-rimmed; his hair must be wild as a hermit's. He gripped the ring in his pocket. The gold burned patterns into his flesh.

He left the Green Carpet, where the courtiers attending the King were likely to see him. He strode past the Obelisk, up the hill, into the Star Garden.

He ran, his heart pounding, through the Circle.

He stumbled, panting, into the chapel. It was, of course, deserted. At the altar, before the image of the Crucifixion, he fell. He shuddered, holding back sobs till his chest and his throat ached with unshed tears. The world spun around him as if he were drunk. He lost all track of time.

Lying prone, his burning hand pressed to the cool marble floor, Yves de la Croix prayed.

Chapter 21

Sherzad sang.

The sea woman's images spun around Marie-Josèphe, a water-spout of mirages. Sea people sunbathed on a small sandy island. The sea stretched around it without interruption. The sea people, safe and happy, played with their family's new child. The baby's hand had begun to grow its webs, her toenails to thicken and withdraw into claws. Her hair was as soft as spume. She hummed and babbled, creating large amorphous pictures. Her mama, her sisters and brothers and cousins, her aunts and uncles, exclaimed with wonder and approval.

'On our birth islands, we are vulnerable, but we believed ourselves safe.'

Marie-Josèphe interpreted as well as she could, from a language with no words. She sketched rapidly as she spoke. The charcoal scribbles did no justice to the beauty of Sherzad's songs, but they documented the story. Servants took the finished sketches, displayed them, pinned them up.

'We were not safe.'

A galleon appeared on the horizon. A cross blazed from its flag. Sherzad's song broke into discord. The galleon's cannons thrust through its gunports.

'The ships of the men of land sought us.'

The galleon came about, presenting its broadside to the tiny birth island. The cannons fired in a horrible rolling roar. Sherzad screamed in grief and pain. Men stormed the island with pikes and nets.

'They called us devils. They killed and captured us, for the glory of your god.'

Lucien heard again the sound of battle in the sea woman's songs. He heard the screams of dying men and horses. Exhilaration took him like strong wine; despair overcame it. Sherzad's song brought back Steenkirk, and Neerwinden.

309

'They took us to the mainland, to cities, they imprisoned us and tortured us, they killed us slowly.'

In Marie-Josèphe's sketch, an Inquisitor shattered a man of the sea on the rack. In the background, a human figure burned at the stake.

Lucien heard again the catcalls of his youth, the other pages at court tormenting him: 'Dwarf, dwarf! Your papa is a devil and your mama is a witch!'

They never stopped, until he earned the King's esteem.

'The men of land went truly mad. They killed us, they killed their own people. The Church sought evidence of fornication between women and the sea demons. What it sought, it found. It condemned any woman with a dwarf child, for the child was pure proof of congress with the devil.

'The sea people knew the men of land as enemies.'

Marie-Josèphe stared in horror at her sketch: a woman broken on the wheel and thrown into the sea, her dwarf child holding tight, sinking with her, drowning. The servant took the drawing away before she could stop him.

The servant displayed the illustration. While the rest of the audience was still applauding the pathos of Marie-Josèphe's story, the servant reached Lucien. He tried to hurry past, but Lucien caught his wrist, made him stop, and took the sketch from him.

Lucien thought: *Not long since, that woman could have been my mother. That child would have been me.*

The sea monster left off its singing.

'That is all.' Marie-Josèphe's voice shook. She turned to the sea woman. 'How could you?'

The sea monster shrieked, splashed backwards, and flung water everywhere. She laughed maniacally, laughed as no beast could laugh. If Lucien had doubted Marie-Josèphe de la Croix before, now he believed everything she had ever claimed about the being, and more.

At the edge of anger, Lucien rose and left the tent. He did not care to lose his temper in public.

Lucien sat by the Reflecting Pool. If he plunged into the water he might cool his fury.

If I plunge into the water, he said to himself, *I might also drown. I prefer to remain angry*.

'Count Lucien!' Mlle de la Croix ran toward him, pale with dismay. 'I'm sorry, I'm so sorry, I didn't mean – how could Sherzad be so cruel?'

'Have the courage to claim your own revenge.'

'My revenge? For what?'

'You offered, and I declined.'

'And I'm acting the rejected flirt? Sir, you wrong me.'

Lucien's anger erupted. 'What do you expect from a dwarf, ugly, misshapen—'

'Count Lucien, I love you.'

'That is your misfortune.'

'Your spirit is beautiful. You allowed me to see your kindness, and . . .' She hesitated. 'Do you understand what I said? I love you.'

'Many women love me. I'm a generous man, and a knowledgeable lover.'

'You are arrogant, sir.'

'I have told you that I am. I have reason to be. I possess a title of the sword, the title of the companions of Charlemagne, a title already ancient when these upstart dukes and marquises were created. I enjoy the trust of the King. I'm heir to vast lands and great wealth—'

'I don't care about that!' Marie-Josèphe said. 'If you weren't Lucien de Barenton, Count de Chrétien, I'd feel the same.'

'Ah. If I were a starving peasant, beaten because I couldn't pay my taxes, my hovel pillaged by the soldiers of my own King – you'd love me?'

'You're an *atheist*, and I love you.'

Lucien's sense of the ridiculous evaporated his anger. He laughed. When he regained control of himself, he said, 'Mlle de la Croix, if I were a peasant, I'd have been sold to gypsies in my cradle . . . or drowned, like the child in Sherzad's story.'

'Surely, no, not now. Not you.'

'Mlle de la Croix, you want a husband.'

'Yes, Count Lucien,' she said softly.

'I'll never marry. I'll never bring a child into this life.'

311

'But your life is wonderful. The King loves you, everyone respects you—'

'Pain torments me,' he said, telling her what he never admitted to anyone, except a lover.

'Every life bears pain.'

'You have no idea what you're saying,' he said, irritated by her ignorant assurance. 'I am in pain every moment of my existence. Except when I love a woman—' He hesitated, then began again. 'When I love a woman, especially if I loved a woman, how could I pass my affliction to her children? You want a husband, you want children. I will never marry, and I will never father a child.'

'God gives us little choice in that matter,' she said. 'If we choose love.'

He laughed at her. 'No god has anything to do with it. Even the most unimaginative lover can trouble to wrap his member in a baudruche. We have one way to make a child, a thousand ways to love.' He said again, 'I will never marry,'

'Why are you saying this to me?' she cried. 'Why not say, I have no affection for you, I cannot return your love?'

'Because I promised to tell you the truth, if I knew it.'

She fell silent with hope and confusion.

'Do you still want me?' Lucien asked. 'As your lover?'

'I . . . It isn't right, Count Lucien, I can't—' She blushed and stammered; she spread her hands in supplication. 'The Church says—My brother wouldn't—'

'I'm perfectly indifferent to the wishes of the church or to the demands of your brother. What do you want?'

She answered his question, if obscurely. 'If you marry, your children might be – they might not—'

'My father is a dwarf. He retired, crippled—'

His father had ridden beside Louis XIII; valiant, renowned, he had ridden in the service of the child-King Louis XIV during the civil war.

Lucien's father no longer rode.

'I am my father's image,' Lucien said.

'Rumour says—'

'Rumour lies.'

'Many people believe it.'

'Louis has enough misshapen children without counting me among his brood. Besides, he acknowledges his bastards.'

She sank down before him and grasped his hands.

'I didn't make up Sherzad's story, I didn't conspire with her to hurt you. I heard the story as you did, as she sang it. If I'd known what she planned, I would have made up a story. I'd never willingly cause you pain. I beg you, please believe me.'

'I believe you,' he said gently. 'But I can't give you what you wish for. If you love me, I'll break your heart. If you defy His Majesty for the sea woman's sake, the King will break your heart. Or worse.'

'But Sherzad is human. As human as you or I.'

'Yes,' Lucien said. 'Yes, I believe it. Only a human could be so cruel.'

'I'm so sorry—'

'Not cruel to me,' he said. 'Cruel to you.'

Footsteps drew Yves from his fugue, the footsteps and the fear they struck in him. Few members of the court of Versailles visited the chapel unless His Majesty was in attendance. Yves could not face His Majesty. He raised himself on his elbow, stiff from the chill of the marble.

'There you are.' Marie-Josèphe's voice chilled him.

Yves noticed what he should have seen long before: her exhaustion, her despair, her love for him, her disappointment.

'I was worried.' She sat on the confessional bench. 'Forgive me.'

He opened his mouth to reply, to chastise her—

'Forgive me, Father, for I have sinned.'

Yves climbed to his feet. 'It isn't proper for you—for me—'

'You promised to hear confession. You promised His Holiness.'

She folded her hands in her lap and sat with preternatural stillness. As a child, she could sit in the woods till she became invisible to the birds and the creatures. She would never move until he overcame his terror and heard her confession.

He sat beside her. He stared at his hands. 'How did you sin, my child?'

'I lied to my King.'

'That never bothered you before!' he exclaimed.

'About the sea woman.'

If she had made up everything about the sea monster, then how could she also know – but it did not matter.

'I thank God that you've repented,' he said, relieved. 'Go and sin—'

'I'm not finished!' Marie-Josèphe said. She looked straight at him. 'No sailor took Sherzad's token! You know it, but you said nothing. She said, "The dark man took it. The dark man, the man in black robes".' She drew a deep, shaky breath. 'The man who is my brother.'

'You saw the ring – you guessed—'

'I've never seen it. You took it while she fainted, after you forced seaweed and dead fish down her throat—'

'It did speak to you—' Yves whispered.

'I couldn't say to the King, My brother is a common thief. So I lied! I lied, and my lie may kill Sherzad!'

Yves pulled the ruby ring, the gold ring with the shiny stone, from his pocket.

'I'm sorry,' he said. 'I'm sorry, I didn't know . . .'

He fled the chapel.

He flew down the hill to the Fountain, leaving Marie-Josèphe struggling to keep up. He pushed his way through the visitors, flung open the cage door, and ran down the stairs. His breath tore his throat.

Oblivious to the spectators, Yves stepped off the platform. The water rose up around him, soaking his cassock. He waded toward Apollo.

'Sea woman! Sherzad!'

The sea woman surfaced beneath Triton. She spat at Yves and snarled.

'Forgive me, I didn't know, I didn't understand – I didn't believe . . .'

The sea woman watched him, submerged but for the top of her head and her eyes.

Marie-Josèphe hurried to the Fountain. Yves turned to her.

'Tell her – I thought nothing of taking her ring. I thought, how strange to find rubies tangled in an animal's hair—'

'Tell her yourself,' Marie-Josèphe said, out of breath. 'But you frighten her, so be gentle.'

'I captured you,' Yves said. 'I allowed your friend to die, and now I've sentenced you to death as well. I didn't understand. I'm sorry. I didn't know. I'm sorry, for the love of God, please forgive me.' He held out the ring, offering it to her.

Sherzad swam slowly closer, keening.

Outside the tent, draft horses stamped impatiently, jingling their harness. Their driver waited for his cargo, to take it to the sea.

Marie-Josèphe sat on the rim of the Fountain of Apollo, holding Sherzad's hand, stroking her coarse dark hair. The sea woman lay on the steps, bracing herself on the stone rim; she leaned against Marie-Josèphe, dripping fetid water, her naked body warming Marie-Josèphe's side. She pressed her cheek into Marie-Josèphe's palm, wetting it with her tears. Marie-Josèphe held her close, wishing she could comfort her. The song of Sherzad's mourning pierced her skin like tiny knives.

Yves spread a silk handkerchief over the man of the sea's ruined face, and wrapped the canvas shroud around him. With his own hands he helped three servants lift Sherzad's friend. They placed him in the coffin. Yves folded the canvas around him. The servants carried the coffin to the cage, so Sherzad could look on her friend one final time.

The sea woman fell silent. Though she would not touch her friend with her voice, she placed her webbed hand onto his chest. Her fingers trembled.

'He received no last rites,' Yves said. 'I was with him, but I gave him no last rites . . .'

'Never mind,' Marie-Josèphe said. 'The sea people aren't Christians. They have no god.'

'I could have saved him,' Yves said. 'If I'd known . . . I will save Sherzad, I'll save her people.'

'Give Sherzad her ring.'

Sherzad plucked the ring from Yves' palm with extended claws.

'I will bury your friend at sea,' Yves said. 'I promise it.'

315

Sherzad whispered, *I want to go, I want to acknowledge his death and contemplate my life.*

Yves shook his head.

'Dear Sherzad,' Marie-Josèphe said, 'I'm so sorry, it isn't possible.' Sherzad's grief made Marie-Josèphe want to weep, but how could she indulge her own sorrow in the face of the sea woman's loss?

Sherzad freed one of her friend's last straggled locks from beneath the kerchief; she knotted the ring into his hair.

She bent over the coffin, her long hair shadowing her face. Marie-Josèphe put her arm around Sherzad's shoulders, but the sea woman shrugged her off, slid down the stairs, and submerged without a sound.

'Was he her husband, whom I allowed to die?'

'Her friend, her lover, not her husband,' Marie-Josèphe said. 'The sea folk don't marry, they make love for pleasure, and on Midsummer Day they mate—'

'I know it! I predicted it, I found it, I saw it – I should have known no mere beasts could behave with such depravity. Perhaps they're demons, after all—'

'The Church says they aren't. And isn't the Church infallible?'

Yves flinched at the anger and sarcasm in her voice.

Yves helped the servants move the coffin back to its supports. They fitted its lid. Yves set the nails himself. He helped them carry the coffin to the freight-wagon, gave the driver a gold coin, and sent the wagon off on the road to Le Havre.

At the sea woman's tent, Lucien asked Zelis to bow; he dismounted carefully. Pain edged his spine, creeping up on him like a tiger as the day went on. He regretted Juliette's departure desperately, but he could not ask her to return.

You're a fool, he said to himself, *to be so respectful of Mlle de la Croix's scruples.*

He was far too proud to entice her into his bed – even if she were of a mind to be enticed – with promises he would not keep: promises of marriage, assurances of saving the sea woman's life. If Marie-Josèphe did not want him for friendship, for love, for the pleasure they could give each other, he did not want her either.

316

But he would not delude himself; he liked her, he enjoyed talking with her, he sympathised with her dilemma.

He entered the tent, glad to have good news to give her.

'Hello, Count Lucien.' Marie-Josèphe turned her gaze away from a faint ripple that marked the course of the sea woman. She smiled at him, sadly, shyly. She showed him her arm. 'Your salve did its work. Thank you.'

He took her hand, for no other reason than to touch her. Monsieur's lotions had softened her work-roughened hands – the lotions, and her release from scrubbing the stone floors of a convent – but ink stained her fingers.

'I'm happy to see you recovered.' The heat that touched his face had nothing to do with Mlle de la Croix, only with the wine.

'Are you well? You seem a little—'

Lucien chuckled.

Mlle de la Croix blushed as furiously as when they first had met, when she thought she caused him offense with everything she said.

'Never mind,' she said, 'it's none of my business why you're drunk this early in the evening.'

'I'm drunk this early in the evening, Mlle de la Croix, because I'm not making love this early in the evening.'

Is she more perceptive than the rest of His Majesty's court, he wondered, *who never notice when I dull the ache in my back with wine instead of ecstasy? Or is she the only person brave or ignorant enough to comment?*

She glanced away; she only thought she had embarrassed him, while he had certainly embarrassed her. He regretted it, and his sense of humour failed him.

A curl of her hair slipped over her shoulder, caressing her. He almost touched the lock of hair; if she had been any other woman at court, and he had been moved to touch her hair, he would have done so, and things might have progressed from there. But Marie-Josèphe had made her wishes known already. Lucien reined himself in more violently than he would ever check one of his horses.

'Do you not think,' Marie-Josèphe said, still looking across the Fountain, 'you would serve yourself better if you embraced your

317

suffering? Do you not think your suffering would benefit your spiritual health?'

'I do not,' Lucien said. 'I avoid suffering whenever possible and with whatever means come to hand.'

'The Church exalts suffering.'

'Did scrubbing floors in silent unhappiness do you any good? Does this prison elevate your friend Sherzad? Suffering only makes one miserable.'

'I can't argue with you about my religion, sir. You'll draw me into danger, for you're much cleverer than I.'

'I never argue about religion, Mlle de la Croix, but I may, on occasion, make a statement of common sense.'

She made no reply. Her shoulders slumped with weariness and despair. No dry witticism could ease her fear, but his news might give her a moment's respite.

'His Majesty requests—' he said.

'M. de Chrétien!' Marie-Josèphe's brother strode into the tent. 'I have something for you to do.'

'Yves, don't interrupt Count Lucien.'

'What is it, Father de la Croix?' Lucien spoke courteously, though he did not much like the form of the request. No one commanded him, except the King.

Yves explained, and made his request. 'The coffin is on the way to Le Havre. Can you have it sent to sea? Sent to sea and buried there?'

Lucien's voice grew chill. 'You have taken it upon yourself to dispose of His Majesty's sea monster.'

'To give the man of the sea a decent burial. His Majesty wouldn't deny—'

'Count Lucien, you believe the sea people are—'

Brother's and sister's protests collided.

'Why will you not understand this?' Lucien said, doubly provoked. 'It doesn't matter what I believe. His Majesty has not ruled the sea monsters to be men.'

'I promised Sherzad's friend a sea burial,' Yves said.

'You had no right to make such a promise.' Lucien, furious, never raised his voice. 'You certainly have no right to tell me to carry it out.'

318

Yves shook his head, confused. 'But, M. de Chrétien, you told me, whatever I needed—'

'To satisfy His Majesty's will!' Lucien exclaimed. 'Not your own.'

'His Majesty cares nothing for the dead creature,' Yves said. 'Only what I can discover about—'

Lucien raised his hand sharply; Yves fell silent.

'Mlle de la Croix,' he said, 'you yourself begged His Majesty to study the sea monster's skull. His Majesty has condescended to do so.'

Marie-Josèphe made a sound of despair, and buried her face in her hands.

'The wagon's only an hour gone,' Yves said. 'We can fetch it back.'

'His Majesty wishes to inspect the skull now.'

'I've put you in a terrible position,' Marie-Josèphe said. 'I beg your pardon – will you forgive me?'

'My forgiveness cannot solve this dilemma,' Lucien said.

'Tell the King,' Yves said, 'that I must prepare the skull, so it will not offend—'

'Do you suggest that I lie to His Majesty?' Lucien blew out his breath in exasperation. 'I regret, Father de la Croix, Mlle de la Croix, that I cannot consider such a thing.'

Chapter 22

The gardens of the chateau blazed with light. Visitors filled the paths, seeking the best vantage point from which to observe the fireworks over the Grand Canal. In the state apartments, a crowd of His Majesty's courtiers and royal guests devoured a light collation.

The Queen's side of the chateau was deserted.

Marie-Josèphe and Yves followed Count Lucien up the Queen's Staircase. Marie-Josèphe dreaded what was to come.

I'm estranged from Count Lucien's affections, she thought. *No, not from his affections — I never possessed his affections — but I hoped I had earned his regard. I cannot blame him, but, oh, how I regret it.*

She and Yves had taken advantage of him. Time and again he had taken their part, and they had returned his courtesy by endangering his position with the King.

Marie-Josèphe felt more alone than she ever had in her life. Count Lucien was angry at her. Sherzad hardly trusted her. And her brother . . . Yves strode along beside her, grim and silent, guilty and distressed. By proving to him the humanity of the sea monster, she put him in danger of losing his vocation and his passion.

When he sent me to the convent, Marie-Josèphe thought, *I could believe that if he knew what he had sent me to, he would relent. I had the company of my memory of him. Now I have nothing. Count Lucien is right. Suffering only makes one miserable.*

And if that is true, Marie-Josèphe thought, *is he right about pleasure, as well?*

She should feel guilty, she should regret her lack of faith, but she only felt betrayed and unhappy.

Marie-Josèphe trudged along the corridors, between lavish tapestries, orange trees, a profusion of flowers and candles, on a pilgrimage to beg forgiveness.

I could ride Zachi through these halls, Marie-Josèphe thought wildly.

320

She could gallop across the parquet, she could clatter down the Staircase of the Ambassadors, or leap over the balcony like Pegasus; we could flee into the gardens, into the forest, and disappear.

Then she thought, *I wonder if I'll ever ride Zachi again.*

The sentry allowed them to pass into the apartment of Mme de Maintenon.

His Majesty and His Holiness sat together near the open window. Mme de Maintenon, in her curtained chair, bent over an embroidery of gold thread on scarlet satin. Marie-Josèphe glanced toward her, hoping for her sympathy, for the kindness the marquise had shown her at Saint-Cyr. Mme de Maintenon never looked up. Marie-Josèphe shivered.

It's only the cold, she thought. *Poor Mme de Maintenon, with her rheumatism.*

Count Lucien bowed. 'Your Majesty.'

'M. de Chrétien.'

Marie-Josèphe curtsied to the King; she knelt to kiss Innocent's ring. His hand was cool, the ring cold against her lips. His Holiness extended his hand toward Count Lucien, who regarded him in stony silence. Marie-Josèphe curtsied to Mme de Maintenon, but the marquise neglected to acknowledge her greeting.

'Mlle de la Croix,' His Majesty said. 'What has possessed you?'

'I'm sorry, Your Majesty. I never meant to offend you.'

'You asked me to determine the truth,' His Majesty said. 'I have condescended to try – and now I find you've disposed of the evidence. How can I know you haven't made everything up?'

'I'd be a fool to do so, Sire! I'm not a fool. I felt such pity for Sherzad, I never thought—'

'Pity – for a beast!' Innocent exclaimed. He turned his attention to Yves, his expression concerned. 'Your association with the creature troubles me. You're being led into serious error.'

'I'm searching for God's truth,' Yves said.

'Do you think you know God's truth better than I do?' His Holiness asked, affronted.

'No, Your Holiness, of course not – I only seek knowledge of His will through His material creations.'

'You shall study His Word,' His Holiness said. 'Not the utterances of demons.'

'Demons lie!' Marie-Josèphe cried. 'Sherzad's said nothing but the truth.'

'The truth isn't for you to determine, Mlle de la Croix,' His Holiness said.

'What has she said, that's false? She's told us ugly truths. But they are truths.'

'You would have done better to follow my predecessor's order. Women should remain silent and obedient.'

'Even women have souls. Sherzad is a woman. Killing her would be a mortal sin.'

'Do not lecture me on sin.'

Silence fell and deepened; the only sound was the faint *shussh* of Mme de Maintenon's silk passing through the tapestry.

'I believe my sister is right, Your Majesty. Your Holiness.'

'Do you?' His Holiness said. 'Have you discussed souls with this creature? Have you discussed Christian faith? Have you converted it?'

'No, Your Holiness.'

'Then on what evidence do you believe your sister correct and the Church in error?'

'Not in error!' Yves exclaimed. 'I believe God put me in the position of witnessing a miracle. I believe He has raised the sea monsters toward humanity. '

'The creature is grotesque,' His Holiness said. 'There's nothing of humanity about it.'

'Sherzad is less grotesque than I,' Count Lucien said, his voice like a rose: perfect, beautiful, hiding thorns. 'And I am human . . . Of course, I am very rich.'

Marie-Josèphe wanted to run to Lucien, to embrace him, to deny his description of himself, for he was splendid.

Innocent rose from his chair and turned on Lucien in a fury.

'You deny the existence of God! Perhaps the Grand Inquisitor was right after all. Perhaps you and the monsters are the spawn of demonic fornication.'

322

'My father and my mother would be offended to hear it,' Lucien said calmly.

'Chrétien, enough of your atheistic wit,' His Majesty said.

'Chrétien!' His Holiness spat out a word he would ordinarily speak with reverence. 'Even your name is a mockery!'

'Then it mocks Charlemagne, who gave it to my family for our service to him.'

'Cousin,' Louis said to Innocent, 'M. de Chrétien enjoys my protection for his beliefs – even for his lack of beliefs.'

'Your Majesty,' Marie-Josèphe said, 'you're the Most Christian King. Champion the sea folk – their conversion would add to your glory!'

'This is only a tactic, to save your pet,' Louis said.

'It's true I can't bear to think of her being killed,' Marie-Josèphe said. 'But I truly believe she's a woman. Sire, if you eat her flesh, you'll endanger your immortal soul.'

Louis leaned back in his chair, weary and old beneath his bright chestnut perruke.

'Marie-Josèphe, dear child,' he said, 'I've ruled for fifty years. Compared to what I've done for the glory of France, cannibalism's a small sin.'

Marie-Josèphe was too shocked to reply.

'Give me the sea monster, cousin,' Innocent said. 'You must.'

'Must I?'

'It must be studied. It's dangerous. If Father de la Croix is in error, then the creature is a demon, and it must be exorcised. But perhaps Father de la Croix is correct, and we've witnessed a miracle of creation. If that is true, the creature must be brought to God. Converted from its pagan wildness, for the glory of God.'

'I'll give you my baboon,' His Majesty said. 'You have as much chance of converting it.'

Affronted, His Holiness rose. 'You will forgive me,' he said, 'if I take my leave. I'm an old man. Your opposition exhausts me. Father de la Croix, attend me.'

He swept out of the apartment.

'Please excuse me, Your Majesty,' Yves said. 'Please forgive me—'

'Go,' His Majesty said. 'Leave me in peace.'

Yves bowed to His Majesty and hurried after Innocent.

Marie-Josèphe's nails cut into her palms. Tears stung her eyes. The faint melody of Sherzad's song crept through the open window, her grief carried by the cold breeze.

'You shouldn't provoke our holy cousin, M. de Chrétien,' His Majesty said.

'Pardon my bad manners, Your Majesty. Your holy man surprises me with his revulsion.'

'What do you care for holy men?'

'Nothing, Sire. Yet I'm always surprised when they turn out to be hypocrites.'

'I require him as an ally. France requires His Holiness, his armies – and his treasury.'

'If you allowed it, you would get more loyalty from the Protestants—'

Mme de Maintenon jerked her head up, glaring at Lucien; His Majesty replied with cold fury.

'Don't provoke me, Chrétien. How fortunate that you're only an atheist – and not a Protestant.'

Lucien did not reply. Marie-Josèphe ached for him. She wondered if the King's basilisk glare might turn them both to stone.

'Your Majesty,' she asked timidly, 'is the treasury in great need?'

'The kingdom faces many challenges,' His Majesty said. 'It will survive – without the help of heretics.' His glare softened, with sadness. 'Challenges would be easier to face if the people I favour, the people I love, didn't oppose me, task me, and destroy my peace. You may withdraw. I do not wish to see you again tonight.'

Marie-Josèphe expected Count Lucien to bid her goodnight – or farewell – outside Mme de Maintenon's apartment, but instead, he walked with her to the narrow attic staircase.

'You needn't come any farther, Count Lucien,' Marie-Josèphe said. 'Thank you for your courtesy.'

'I'll show you to your room.' He accompanied her up the stairs, to the dark, dingy attic. He did not belong in such dim places, but in the

324

sun, magnificent in blue and gold, riding his grey Zelis, at the side of his King.

'Why won't he listen?' Marie-Josèphe cried.

'He does listen,' Lucien said. 'He listens, but he keeps his own counsel.'

'Your love for him blinds you.'

'My love for him helps me understand him,' Lucien said. 'You Christians – your claim to love everyone means you love no one.'

'That isn't fair!'

'Of course not – as your holy father proclaims, I'm far from fair.'

'Count Lucien—' Marie-Josèphe's voice faltered. 'You're fair to me.' She meant it in all senses of the word. But she could not continue, for she was not strong enough to resist what might come of her declaration.

She opened her door. Her room was empty; she wondered, worried, where Haleeda might be. Dressing Lotte's hair, carrying Mademoiselle's handkerchief, standing with the Queen of England, waiting for the fireworks.

Will Lotte wonder where I am? Marie-Josèphe thought. *Will Haleeda? It doesn't matter. I don't care about the entertainments.*

'I lived in this attic, when I was a youth,' Lucien said. 'I hated it – so much I almost welcomed being sent away from court.'

He slipped past her, hoisted himself onto the window seat – Hercules leaped from curled sleep, hissing – and climbed out the window.

'Count Lucien!' Marie-Josèphe ran to the window.

He stood between a pair of sculpted musicians, gazing down the length of the garden, past the fountains, past Sherzad's prison, to the forest.

'Come back in, you'll fall—'

'The attic was hot, it was stuffy – when I couldn't bear it any longer, I came out here.'

'I wish it were hot.'

'The evening is balmy, and the sky is beautiful.'

The view was neither spectacular nor severe, but it was beautiful: crowded garden paths bordered with candles that flickered behind

325

oiled paper, the Grand Canal leading away from Sherzad's glowing tent, geometric perfection arrayed against the green expanse of the distant forest. The highest, westernmost clouds reflected the last sliver of the setting sun.

Count Lucien sought out depressions in the stone side of the chateau: handholds, toeholds.

'I haven't climbed to the roof since I was a youth. Will you come with me?'

'In those clothes? In these clothes?'

He shrugged out of his coat and his gold-embroidered waistcoat and tossed them onto the window seat. He kicked off his shoes and removed his perruke. His fair hair, an astonishing white gold, gleamed in the faint light.

Count Lucien and Hercules eyed each other; Hercules kneaded the cushion, careless of his claws. Count Lucien placed his new perruke safely on the head of the musician who graced Marie-Josèphe's window.

Marie-Josèphe laughed. 'He could attend His Majesty's entertainment, if he wished.' She sighed. 'I can't climb to the roof.'

'Why not?'

'Stays. Slippery shoes. What will you think of me, if I climb to the roof in my shift?'

'I'll think you want to climb to the roof. Decide, quickly, if you please – when everyone gathers on the terrace for the fireworks, I won't be standing here bareheaded for His Majesty to see.'

She collected her breath, and her nerve. 'If you will unlace me.'

She took off the coat of her riding habit; she took off her shoes and stockings. She turned her back to the window; Count Lucien untied her laces with a touch both gentle and sure.

Barefoot and in her shift, she faced the window and the twilight.

'Come out,' Count Lucien said. 'It isn't so dangerous.'

She took his hand and crept onto the ledge beside him. She clutched the statue of a lutenist, her hand on the musician's bare breast. No one would mistake her for one of the statues, for she had on too many clothes.

Count Lucien scrambled up the wall, showing her old and

326

well-used hand and foot-holds. From the roof, he reached down to help her.

Voices drifted upward. Guests streamed out of the chateau, onto the terrace. Marie-Josèphe shrank behind the musician.

'Hurry!'

She stole after him, partly hidden by the statue as she climbed. In an exhilarating moment she was over the edge and sitting on the low-pitched roof.

'You're right, Count Lucien,' she said. 'The view is much better from here. But if His Majesty found out—!' She drew her knees up under her shift and hugged her arms around them. The roof tiles gathered the day's warmth.

'His Majesty spent a good deal of time on these roofs, when he was a youth.'

'Why?'

'To visit his paramours – and the parlourmaids.'

Marie-Josèphe gave him a startled glance.

'You're in no danger of seduction, Mlle de la Croix. The roof is an adequate seat, but an uncomfortable bed. I've told you—'

'That I'm in no danger from you. I trust you, sir.'

'—I've told you, I require all the comfort I can find.'

'Do you have any calvados?'

'I left my flask in my coat.'

'Too bad,' Marie-Josèphe said.

'I do recommend sobriety on some occasions.'

'Such as?'

'Climbing to the roof of a chateau.'

She laughed. In the midst of the laughter she felt like bursting into tears.

'And perhaps sobriety's best when you lose your temper. I'm sorry my brother and I caused you such annoyance today,' she said. 'But . . . you were very severe with Yves.'

'He spoke to me like a servant! How did he – how did you – expect me to reply? Mlle de la Croix, you have no idea how severe I can be. If you're fortunate, you'll never see me lose my temper – when I'm sober.'

'I'm so sorry we offended you—'

'He offended me. You only requested that I accomplish the impossible.'

'That doesn't offend you?'

'To be thought a miracle worker?' Count Lucien smiled, and Marie-Josèphe considered herself forgiven.

'Will you forgive Sherzad for causing you pain?' As soon as she had spoken, she wished she had not, but she could not call back her words. She tried to soften them. 'I know she never meant—'

Count Lucien turned to her abruptly, silencing her with a gesture. 'Her story gave me understanding,' he said, 'as I have no doubt she intended. You must believe that it makes no difference.'

'Only the King's belief matters.'

'Yes.'

'It would cost him nothing to free her.'

'Nothing?' Lucien exclaimed. 'Immortality?'

'She cannot bestow immortality, Count Lucien, I promise you. Only God can do that.'

Count Lucien gazed down across the gardens, sombre.

'I'm sorry,' Marie-Josèphe said.

'I hoped—' Count Lucien shook his head. 'What will happen, when he dies—'

'We all must die. He'd kill her for nothing.'

'No. He has public reasons to dominate the sea monsters. It adds to his glory and his power. It demonstrates the vitality of France.'

'What a great deal to ask of one small sea monster! Should she win the war, end the famine and fill the treasury as well?'

'If she could do that by living instead of by dying,' Count Lucien said, 'then His Majesty might free her.'

The moon, nearly full, blossomed over the roof of the chateau behind them. A ragged cloud passed across its face, fragmenting its silver light like falling petals. The shards of silver fell gleaming across Count Lucien's head and shoulders, across his short hair, so blond, so fair, the colour of white gold. The moonlight traced his profile, the arch of his eyebrow.

Lucien turned toward Marie-Josèphe, wondering why she had gasped.

'You aren't His Majesty's son!'

'So I've assured you,' Lucien replied.

'You're the son of—'

'I am my father's son.' Lucien spoke sharply, trying to distract her from her dangerous insight.

'—the queen!' she exclaimed. 'Queen Marie Thérèse! You have her fair hair, her grey eyes – she loved you—'

Very few people had ever divined the truth of Lucien's parentage, or, if they had, they had the sense to remain silent about it.

'The greater love she bore was to my father.' Lucien could not lie to Marie-Josèphe de la Croix. 'And my father loved his Queen. He responded to her grave unhappiness. He loves his King. He gave the King his respect and his friendship. The queen is dead and beyond reproach, but my father is alive: if you shout your suspicion to the world, you accuse him of treason, and me of—'

'I'll never speak of it again,' she said.

They sat together in silence. Below them, the gardens filled with people: His Majesty's royal guests, the court, His Majesty's subjects. Clouds gathered above the park, blocking out the moonlight.

'How was it possible?' Marie-Josèphe whispered.

Lucien smiled. Despite the risks of knowledge, he appreciated the recomplications. 'My birth was worthy of a Molière farce. And indeed M. Molière considered a play on the subject: A noblewoman – he did not quite dare to make her the Queen – bears the child of her noble dwarf lover, who – in the midst of a dozen court observers! – exchanges his infant son for the newborn daughter of the queen's jester's mistress, and spirits the boy away to his gracious wife, so they may claim him as their own, while a convent fosters the changeling and the true child returns to his true mother as her page, like any noble youth—'

'What a remarkable tangle,' Marie-Josèphe said.

'Yes.'

'Molière never wrote his play.'

'Too dangerous.'

'That never stopped M. Molière.'

'He was fearless when confronted by censors and prisons, it's true,'

329

Lucien said. 'It isn't so easy to be fearless when confronted by my father.'

'Your father challenged him?'

'Challenge a commoner? Certainly not. He offered to have lackeys beat him senseless for insulting the Queen. M. Molière rather lost his sense of humour about the situation.'

'Poor M. Molière.'

'Poor M. Molière indeed, he could have been the downfall of my family. And of His Majesty's family, if Monseigneur's birth were also called into question.'

'It's true that Monseigneur doesn't quite resemble—'

'Please do not insult the late Queen in my presence.'

'I beg your pardon. But why such complexity? Why not simply spirit you away?'

Amazed that she could be so intelligent and yet so naive, Lucien said, 'Because the daughter of a queen and a commoner is not much threat. The son of a queen and a companion of Charlemagne might challenge the throne of France as well as Spain.'

She nodded her understanding. 'What of your sister?'

'I have no sister. Do you mean the changeling?'

'Yes.'

'She's content, she says, in her convent; she possesses all the piety my family lacks. Her true parents were Spanish, of course, members of Her Majesty's retinue.'

'Doesn't she want to live in the world?'

'Perhaps not,' Lucien said, 'for she too is a dwarf. And a Moor, with a Christian vocation. She's respected where she is. France is her home. Where would she go? To the Spanish court as her true father's successor? She could speak truths to their pathetic king, but he'd never hear her.'

'Is this why you've decided not to have children?'

'Because they might be snatched away and put on the throne of Spain?' Lucien laughed. 'A horrible fate. No, I told you why I'll never father a child. Why do you think there's any other reason?'

'What of the future of your house? And your ancient title?'

'My younger brother will carry it on.'

'Your brother! Does he——'

'Resemble me? Not in any way.'

'——come to court?'

'Not if I can keep him from it.'

'Why not?'

Lucien sighed. 'My brother's a fool.'

'I cannot believe it!'

'Don't misunderstand me. Guy is perfectly amiable. He's good-hearted. But as for wit, or intelligence – he has neither. He allows himself to be drawn into mischief, thinking only that it will be good fun.'

'And yet you give him the future of your family.'

'I found him a good wife,' Lucien said. 'She's of excellent origin and no little fortune. She isn't her own first cousin. Even better, she isn't Guy's first cousin. She's fond of Guy and she manages the family well. Her children are a joy. When my nephew comes of age, I'll grant him the title comte de Chrétien. He won't disgrace it.'

'Will your nephew have your spirit?'

'He'll have my mother's spirit – and my brother's strong back.'

'What of——' Marie-Josèphe said hesitantly. 'What of the woman you call mother? Your father's wife? Did she hate you terribly?'

'I honour and love her. She's my mother, as her husband is my brother's father.'

'In the eyes of the law, but——?'

'In the line of inheritance, which is the important thing. We're both acknowledged, and legitimate, and cherished. She treats me graciously, as my father treats her son. She and my father are dearest lovers. Unlike most husbands and wives, they aren't unfaithful to each other for their pleasure or their love. Only for their children.'

'Who is your brother's father?'

'That isn't my secret to tell,' Lucien replied. 'You must ask me some other question.'

She thought for a moment. 'How did you come to leave court? I can hardly imagine you anywhere else.'

'I didn't leave willingly. I left in disgrace.'

'I cannot believe it!'

331

'Do you see in me no potential for disobedience?'

Marie-Josèphe laughed. 'You'd disobey any order, you ignore all convention! But, displease the King? Never.'

'Youthful foolishness. I was barely fifteen.'

He had never told anyone the truth, that he took the blame for his brother's foolishness. He was the eldest, after all; it was his responsibility to help Guy find his place in His Majesty's court. At that he had failed. Guy bore the worst punishment; His Majesty never exiled him, but Lucien sent him home to Brittany and refused all his entreaties for a second invitation to Versailles.

'His Majesty's punishment worked to my great advantage,' he said. 'He sent me with his embassy to Morocco. To learn diplomacy, he said. We travelled through Arabia, Egypt, the Levant.'

'The greatest mathematicians in the world lived in Arabia,' Marie-Josèphe said. 'Until M. Newton.'

'I didn't have the honour of meeting Arabic mathematicians,' Lucien said. 'But I met sheiks and warriors and holy men. I rode with the Bedouins. My sword was forged in Damascus. I lived in a hareem.'

'A hareem – but how?'

'On our journey, we all fell ill, with a dreadful flux – I'll spare you the details.'

'I know the details.'

'I am sorry to hear it. The Sultan took us into his household. A less brave and ethical man would have put us out to die. Some of us did die, but his altruism saved most of us. His physicians watched over the grown men. The women of the household cared for the boys, the pages, for in the house of a devout Mahometan, the men live in one part of the house, the women and girls in another. Young boys live in the women's quarters until they reach a certain age and develop a certain attention.

'As a youth,' Lucien said with dry directness, 'I was rather small. In the chaos of illness and darkness and death, I was mistaken for a page of ten, rather than a young man of fifteen. No one in the embassy could say it was a mistake and call me back. We were too sick. I came to my senses all unaware, wondering if a god really did exist—'

'Of course He does!'

'Then He is Allah, and He brought me into His garden to mock my disbelief. I awoke in the women's quarters.'

'They made short work of putting you out, I'm certain.'

'No — how could they? I'd be killed, or worse. The women — the Sultan's wives, his daughters, his brothers' wives, his sons' wives — would be disgraced. They could be divorced. Or stoned to death.'

'How did you escape?'

'I did not. I stayed until the last day of the embassy, when I crept out over the rooftops and joined the caravan home. The women kept my secret. I became their secret. They were women of intelligence and kindness and passion, locked away from the world, kept at the mercy of men's whims.'

'And you were a youth of a certain age and attention.'

'Indeed I was.'

'Tempted into sin. At the mercy of their whims.'

Lucien laughed. 'I hadn't thought of it that way. I honour their mercy and their whims. They awakened me. Before that time, I'd never lived for a moment when my body didn't pain me.'

'You're no better than their husbands, who imprisoned them!' Marie-Josèphe cried. 'You took your pleasure from them and placed them in danger.'

'I took nothing. Ours was an exchange of gifts. My gifts were clumsy and ill-made to begin with, I admit, but they were sincere, and my beloved friends were patient. I learned nothing of diplomacy during those months. Instead, I learned the art of rapture. I learned how to give it and how to receive it. I learned how much more it's worth when it's both given and received.'

Lucien fell silent. Marie-Josèphe tried to make herself feel disgusted and offended, as she knew she should, but his story moved her.

How much I would have cherished a secret friend, in the convent, she thought. *Not a man! Not for . . . not for rapture. For affection, for conversation, for friendship, for all the things forbidden me because they would distract from the love of God. If a pagan, a heretic, had appeared in my cell and begged for asylum, I would have hidden her and protected her.*

'If you lived in rapture, why are you sad?' she demanded, for

Lucien stared across the water with a far-away and melancholy expression.

Lucien remained silent for so long, she thought he would not reply.

'The amiable Sultan's eldest son, the crown prince . . . He took a young wife, that is, a new concubine . . . She was fourteen, homesick, but she could never go home – she'd been enslaved and sold. She had been used to liberty . . . Her gaze was like a trapped bird. We became friends.'

He stopped to govern his voice.

'She had as little experience as I. Her sister wives could tell her what to do to please her husband, when he demanded her presence and compelled her first submission. They could have told him how to please her, even when he claimed her virginity. But he never listened to their wisdom. He took her. He forced her. He raped her.'

Lucien rubbed his hand across his forehead, hiding his eyes from the memory.

'But, he was her husband,' Marie-Josèphe said as gently as she could. 'He couldn't rape—'

'Don't preach your ignorance to me.'

'I beg your pardon.'

'By their law – by your law – he couldn't rape her. What she surrendered to was rape, all the worse because she couldn't resist, she couldn't object, she couldn't refuse. Should we have comforted her by saying, Your husband acted within the law?'

'It's God's will, M. de Chrétien, for women to suffer.' Marie-Josèphe hoped that explaining properly might bring Count Lucien to belief. 'If she were a Christian, she would have understood and submitted willingly.'

'I cannot fathom why you accept such arrant lunacy.' He spoke quietly. 'If she were a Christian, you'd consign her to hell, for she killed herself.'

Recovering from her dismay, Marie-Josèphe whispered, 'I am so sorry. I'm sorry for your friend's pain, for your grief, and for my inexcusable condescension.' She took his hand. He turned away, hiding his bright tears, but he permitted her touch.

334

A rocket blazed across the sky.

Fireworks burst in a great floating carpet from the Grand Canal to the chateau. A hundred colours painted patterns in the sky. The roof tiles trembled with the noise. In the midst of the roar of rockets, the spectators cheered.

A burst of blue and gold formed a great expanding sphere. Small red rockets streaked over it. The low clouds reflected the light of the fireworks, an eerie, distorted mirror. The explosions formed a solid presence.

Gunpowder smoke hovered, pungent and gritty. Lucien lay back on the warm tiles and gazed into the sky.

'Is this what war is like?' Marie-Josèphe asked.

'Not in the least. It lacks the mud, the discomfort, the fear. It lacks the screams of dying men and disembowelled horses. It lacks severed limbs, and death. It lacks the exhilaration, and the glory.'

The fireworks continued, embroidering the sky with needles of colour and light. A golden letter 'L' and its mirror image, surrounded by flowers and starbursts, brightened the gardens to day.

Marie-Josèphe leaped up, climbed over the edge of the roof, and disappeared. Startled, Lucien followed her. In her room, she struggled into her clothes. Standing on the window seat, the cat glaring at him slit-eyed from the shadows, Lucien said, 'May I help you?'

'I heard Sherzad,' Marie-Josèphe said.

Lucien buttoned her dress, distracted from her words by the touch of her hair falling over her shoulders.

'I didn't think – she must be so frightened!' She pulled on her shoes and ran away before Lucien had retrieved his perruke from the lutenist. He put it on, thinking, *You never should have revealed yourself to her without it.*

Sherzad swam in the centre of the fountain. She screamed a challenge. The explosions assaulted her. The roof of the tent lit up with the light of bombs and guns, Greek fire and mortars, all the weapons that had been arrayed against the people of the sea for so many generations.

She screamed again, shrieking with fury and grief.

Marie-Josèphe ran into the tent.

The Fountain gleamed with unearthly light. Apollo's horses struck sparks from their hooves. Sherzad thrashed, sending up a fountain of luminescent water. With each blast of rockets, the shining intensified in waves.

In a moment Marie-Josèphe was on the platform, covering her ears against the explosions, against Sherzad's screams. She called out softly, reaching to Sherzad through the sea woman's fear and anger, through the dense fabric of sound.

Sherzad moaned and swam to her. Glowing ripples marked her path. Marie-Josèphe held her hands and gazed into her eyes. Sherzad touched her with her voice.

'I'm so sorry, dear Sherzad,' Marie-Josèphe said. 'I've never seen fireworks, not like this, I had no idea – it's all right, it isn't war, it isn't the guns and the mortars. You needn't fight, you needn't be afraid. The men of land do this for play.'

Labouring up onto the platform, Sherzad lay in Marie-Josèphe's arms, reassured and comforted. Her body shone as if lit from within. Marie-Josèphe stroked her long coarse glowing hair, combing out all the tangles except the knotted lock of her dead friend's hair.

She did not untangle the remembrance knot, but she stroked it thoughtfully. Light covered her hands.

'Sherzad,' Marie-Josèphe said, 'where did your friend get the ruby ring?'

Chapter 23

$\mathcal{S}$unday morning, when the King walked to Mass with his family, Marie-Josèphe plunged through the crowd of petitioners and flung herself at his feet. She said nothing, but held a letter out to him in both hands. She feared he would not take it. She dared to look at him. He gazed at her, impassive, showing neither annoyance at her presence nor satisfaction at her submission.

He took the letter.

Lucien felt ridiculous, standing in the Marble Courtyard with red and white ribbons sewn to his hunting coat and breeches and falling around his feet. *If it were spring*, he thought, *I could play the Maypole*.

'More ribbons, M. de Chrétien,' His Majesty said. 'Your horse must be accustomed to the motion.' Louis wore a coat similarly decorated.

'My horse is accustomed to the chaos of war, Your Majesty,' Lucien said. 'Zelis won't jibe at a few fancy banners.'

Zelis stood by the courtyard stairs, tied by nothing more than her reins dropped to the ground, as the King's Carrousel team galloped their mounts across the Place d'Armes, ribbons flapping from their wrists and shoulders and knees. The spotted Chinese horses bucked and squealed when the ribbons blew around their flanks. Their eyes showed white with fear or excitement. Nearby, the King's master of horse tried to calm His Majesty's snorting mount. It wanted to join its stablemates in playing at fear.

'More ribbons,' His Majesty said.

The royal tailor tacked more ribbons to Lucien's good velvet hunting coat.

His Majesty handed Lucien a folded piece of paper.

Lucien opened Marie-Josèphe's letter. He knew what it said. He had recommended its simplicity:

' "Your Majesty: Sherzad offers you her ransom: a great treasure ship".'

'Explain this, if you please, M. de Chrétien,' said the King.

'The sea people play among the wrecks, Your Majesty,' Lucien replied. 'They use gold pieces and jewels as decoration. As toys for their children, who dandle pearl necklaces and drop them as they swim – for they can always find more.'

'Mlle de la Croix says this to save the life of the sea monster. Enough ribbons!' The tailor backed away, bowing.

'Yes. But I believe it's true.'

'And do you believe the sea monster's stories as well?'

'I believe Mlle de la Croix accurately describes what the sea woman sings to her.'

'There's no proof.'

Lucien drew Sherzad's ruby ring from his pocket and offered it to His Majesty. He had taken the ring from the retrieved coffin of the dead sea monster.

'Sherzad carried this when she was captured.'

'How do I know this?'

'Because I say it's true,' Lucien said, in a tone he had never before used to the King. He bowed stiffly. 'May I withdraw, Your Majesty?'

'Certainly not. The team misses you in the patterns.'

Lucien left the Marble Courtyard and spoke to Zelis; she bowed for him to mount.

The Arabian strode across the cobblestones of the Ministers' Courtyard, trotted onto the hard-packed dirt of the Place d'Armes, and cantered into position in His Majesty's Carrousel team. The ribbons waved wildly behind Lucien, their ends chattering in the wind of his speed. His Majesty rode out, his horse prancing nervously, his ribbons flowing and bouncing in time with the curls of his copper-coloured perruke. He took his place in the centre.

Shoulder to shoulder, His Majesty's team crossed the Place d'Armes at a dignified walk. The line split, the horses wheeling past each other, sixteen to one side, sixteen to the other, at the trot. His Majesty led the first line, the duke de Bourgogne led the second, mirroring the pattern of the first. The two lines split into four, the new

338

lines led by Anjou and Berri on their spotted ponies in a double mirror image. At the canter, the four lines performed an intricate drill.

From the four quarters of the Place d'Armes, the four lines of horses turned inward, leapt to the gallop, and ran headlong toward each other. In the centre of the Place, the horses passed head-to-tail, close enough to touch, racing through a dangerous crosshatch at top speed.

The four lines interlaced into two; the two lines faced each other. The riders bowed, Bourgogne to His Majesty, Berri to Anjou. Lucien's counterpart was Berwick; they saluted stiffly. The two lines wheeled again, melded again, and came to a halt shoulder to shoulder facing the King.

'Excellently done.' His Majesty accepted their salutes.

Provoked as he was by the King's questioning his candour, Lucien still found His Majesty's presence moving.

His Majesty wheeled his tall spotted horse and led his team from the field. The other riders jogged toward the stables, but His Majesty turned aside.

'Attend me, M. de Chrétien,' he said.

Lucien followed the King through the gardens and down the slope toward the Fountain of Apollo. He drew his dirk from his belt and used its point to sever the threads holding the ribbons to his coat wherever he could reach.

Beneath the tent, the sea woman's mournful singing filled the hot, humid air. Father de la Croix waited in his laboratory, paler and more ascetic than ever. Mlle de la Croix conversed in whispers of melody with the sea woman. Servants set down a carved wooden frame and settled the painted globe of the world within it.

'Dismiss them, M. de Chrétien,' His Majesty said, 'and fetch Mlle de la Croix.'

Sherzad growled and muttered and submerged herself in the murk. Marie-Josèphe recognised Lucien's footsteps on the planks behind her.

He can no longer appear as if by magic, she said to herself. *I always know when he's near . . .*

'His Majesty will see you.'

'Thank you,' Marie-Josèphe said. 'I am so grateful—'

'No more gratitude,' Lucien said. 'This concerns us both.'

Marie-Josèphe gave Sherzad one last encouraging caress, rolled up the damp, crumpled sea chart, and followed Lucien to the laboratory. The wet hems of her gown and petticoats slapped her ankles. She had dressed carefully, in the grand habit that bared her shoulders, and revealed a decolletage she thought dangerously daring, though her gown was modest compared to what the princesses wore.

The King raised her from her curtsy. He was alone with brother, sister, and Lucien. Marie-Josèphe faced him, looking him almost straight in the eye. She thought, with a shock: *He isn't so much taller than I. I thought him as tall as Lorraine – taller! – but it was an illusion of his high shoes and his wig, an effect of his power.*

'My relentless Mlle de la Croix,' His Majesty said. 'Explain yourself.' Red and white ribbons, like those on the back of Lucien's coat, covered his coat and breeches.

Marie-Josèphe spread the chart on the laboratory table. Sherzad had puzzled over it, unable to comprehend the purpose of a drawing that was, in her view, horribly and dangerously inaccurate. *What is the point*, she had asked, when Marie-Josèphe finally succeeded in explaining it to her, *of showing only the edge of the sea?*

The sea woman sang. The long underwater slopes and sea-cliffs and treacherous rocks formed in Marie-Josèphe's vision, a ghostly presence around her brother and Count Lucien and the King.

'Here.' Marie-Josèphe traced a spot on the chart, pointing out a group of jagged rocks in a cove near Le Havre. 'A galleon sank here. The rocks hold it, and its treasure spills out.'

'Your Majesty's flagship could reach the wreck in a few hours,' Lucien said.

'M. de Chrétien,' His Majesty said, his impassive voice warming with a hint of humour and fondness, 'you will not even sail on the Grand Canal. Who are you to give anyone advice about navigation?'

'I beg your pardon, Your Majesty.'

'However, you're right. If the treasure exists. Has the creature played here – so close to shore?'

'She knows it from a story her family tells.' Marie-Josèphe

340

hesitated, then plunged ahead. 'The sea folk like to tell stories of ships that almost reached land.'

'How long ago?'

'I don't know, Your Majesty. Sherzad's grand-aunts visited it.'

'Two generations! The wreck could be dispersed, the treasure lost.'

'It's a small risk, a small investment, Your Majesty,' Lucien said. 'The sea woman's life gives you treasure. Her death gives you a morsel of meat.'

'That morsel represents a feast as great as any of Charlemagne's,' His Majesty said. 'And the chance of immortality.'

'Your Majesty, I beg you to believe me, it's a myth,' Marie-Josèphe said. 'Sherzad cannot give you immortality.'

His Majesty turned to Yves. 'You are silent, Father de la Croix.'

'Yes, Your Majesty.'

Marie-Josèphe willed her brother to say what he must know, that Sherzad could not convey immortality upon anyone, even Louis le Grand or Pope Innocent.

'I wish you to speak, Father de la Croix.'

Yves' silence stretched on; he did not meet Marie-Josèphe's gaze. He took a long, weary breath.

'Your Majesty, I have no proof one way or the other. I cannot gather evidence without killing the sea monster – or capturing more of the creatures, if any still live.'

'Dear brother,' Marie-Josèphe said, in despair, 'no matter what you do not know – you do know Sherzad is human.'

'Sire,' Lucien said, 'you may always take the sea woman's life.'

'Are you asking me to spare it?'

'I'm offering my counsel, which in the past Your Majesty has condescended to request.'

'M. Boursin begs for time to prepare the monster's flesh. I shall give him one day, though he will spoil my peace with complaints. You may have until midnight of Carrousel, midnight tomorrow, to find the treasure.'

'And if Sherzad finds it – you'll spare her life?'

His Majesty offered no conciliation. 'I will see.'

*

341

Marie-Josèphe hurried to the Fountain of Apollo and Sherzad. The sea woman swam slowly to her, drifting without energy. Needing comfort herself, Marie-Josèphe comforted Sherzad.

'Count Lucien has sent his fastest racehorse with His Majesty's orders,' she said. 'The ship will sail – it will find your treasure. And you'll be free.'

Sherzad leaned against Marie-Josèphe's knee.

At home, she sang to Marie-Josèphe, *we could shout our wishes into the sea. Everyone would hear. But if you shout into the wind, your voice disappears.*

Marie-Josèphe laughed sadly. 'You have the truth of it, sister.'

Swim with me, Sherzad sang. *I am dying, friend, I need the touch of other people to sustain me.*

'I cannot,' Marie-Josèphe whispered. 'I'm so sorry, dear Sherzad, it's impossible.'

The musketeers opened the tent and allowed the visitors to enter. They clustered around the cage, calling to Sherzad, whistling, stretching their hands through the bars to attract her attention.

A footman brought His Majesty's portrait and settled it in his armchair.

'We must tell another story,' Marie-Josèphe said to Sherzad. 'A cheerful story, please, Sherzad.'

Lorraine, Chartres, and the duke of Berwick strolled in. They sat in the front row, bowing with exaggerated courtesy to His Majesty's picture. Marie-Josèphe pretended they were not there, even when they whispered together, laughed, and insulted her with significant glances.

If they come one step toward me, she thought, *I'll slam the cage door in their faces!*

'We've come for a story, Mlle de la Croix!' Chartres exclaimed.

Marie-Josèphe ignored him, a dangerous discourtesy. She stretched her hand to Sherzad, who enclosed her fingers with the silk-soft swimming webs, then broke away and swam across the pool at a hazardous speed. She leaped, soaring out of the water, arcing over Triton's trumpet.

'Sherzad, stop, be careful!'

Lorraine laughed. 'Make her do that again!'

'No!' Marie-Josèphe cried, too distressed, too furious to pretend Lorraine did not exist. 'She hasn't enough room in this tiny cage.'

'His Majesty gives the sea monster more space than he gives his courtiers.'

Sherzad swam back to her, leaping again, coming down perilously close to the platform. Her gold eyes shone with wild rage and desperation.

'Brava!' cried Lorraine.

'If you please, Mlle de la Croix,' Chartres said, 'give us our story.'

Sherzad swam across the pool, turned at the last instant, and swam across again. The prison tormented her. She dove to the inlet and struggled with the grating. It never moved. The fountain contained nothing she could use as a tool or a pry, for the bits of metal littering its bottom were all soft and useless; the gray metal and the sun-coloured metal alike bent in her hands.

Marie-Josèphe called to her; Sherzad ignored her. She swam back and forth, as fast and as hard as she could in the small space, not nearly as fast as she could swim in the open ocean. She keened and cried into the murky water. A fish swam past. She snatched it and ripped it to bits. Scales flickered and floated away.

She leaped. With her powerful legs she propelled her body entirely out of the water. She let herself fall with a great splash. Water washed over the steps and gushed above the stone rim, soaking Marie-Josèphe's feet. Marie-Josèphe drew back with a cry of dismay. Sherzad could not understand why she never wanted to keep her feet wet.

Beyond the bars of the cage, the land people in their strange chaotic coverings gathered to listen to her. Most stood – Sherzad wondered how they could bear the pain of standing – but a few sat. Marie-Josèphe had tried to explain why this was; she had begged Sherzad to lower her eyes when the toothless man looked at her. Sherzad found no reason to do so.

The toothless man's picture sat in his place today. The people of land made pictures with colours on surfaces, poor flat representations of their subjects. They should set someone to sing the image of absent guests.

Sherzad leaped again. The land people exclaimed and slapped their hands together. She leaped again, and again they covered her with a wave of meaningless noise. Meaningless to her, but significant to them, their way of showing interest or approval.

The small man came into the tent. Sherzad snarled and dove. She no longer hoped to trust him. He had smeared that nasty black stuff on Marie-Josèphe's arm. Did he want to kill her? She would claw him if she got the chance, for trying to hurt Marie-Josèphe. She wished she could warn her friend, but she would have to explain how Marie-Josèphe came to be healed. She did not dare.

All the land people suddenly stood up. The man in white, with the gold cross, came into the tent. All the land people bowed until he sat beside the picture of the toothless one. Marie-Josèphe ran out and knelt and kissed his hand. The action puzzled Sherzad, for the man in white responded to the kiss without pleasure, and Marie-Josèphe gained no pleasure from kissing him.

Marie-Josèphe returned to the Fountain and sang, begging Sherzad to tell a story. Sherzad leaped again, testing the reaction of the land people. She landed dangerously near the rim of the Fountain, splashing hard. The land people made a considerable noise.

Sherzad swam to the steps and clambered over the sharp corners to lie on the rim beside Marie-Josèphe.

'Dear Sherzad, you frighten me so when you leap like that . . .'

Sherzad turned her attention to the man in white. Now and again she found some kindness in his face, though he wore the gold cross that terrified Sherzad's heart.

Can I draw him to my cause? Sherzad wondered. *Or is his attachment to murdering us too strong?*

Marie-Josèphe spoke, like a child, for her untrained voice produced single notes. Sherzad replied with a trill of harmonies, fixed her gaze upon the Pope, and began.

She sang of her kind's first encounter with the golden cross.

'The people of the sea gained some respite by fleeing, by choosing

344

birth islands far out in the middle of the ocean, by removing themselves to great mats of seaweed too dense for ships to traverse.

'They did not move their mating place. Its indigo depths lay between treacherous shallows. All the families gathered there, on a single day each year, then dispersed again. Surely the men of land could not find them.

'One year, a great storm preceded Midsummer's Day. The sea people gloried in it, riding the immense waves, diving through the spume, submerging, when the weather became too violent, to drift into lethargy and sleep. When the storm broke, the sea people rose to the surface and swam in the bright hot sun. Leaving the adolescents in charge of the children, the adults gathered for their mating.'

Marie-Josèphe stopped singing, stopped speaking. Sherzad gripped her wrist, pricking her with her sharp claws, snarling in disgust at her cowardice. *Tell them*, she said, *you must tell them. How will they know we are people, if they don't believe we feel joy?*

'The mating haze crept over them. They crowded together, swimming in a contracting circle; they created a great whirlpool with their delight. They swam against each other, sliding and touching, arousing themselves, arousing each other, losing themselves in their ecstasy.'

Marie-Josèphe faced the Pope squarely and spoke as Sherzad sang.

'In the midst of the haze, a lost ship staggered toward the mating orgy, its sails tattered from the storm. Among the rips and tears of the galleon's mainsail, painted in sunlight, a cross burned.

'The men of land spied the people of the sea in their mating haze. The ship pitched toward the gathering. The men of land were jealous of the sea people's pleasure, rapturous and terrified at their discovery of such a mass of demons. Their ship plunged into the orgy, through clusters of joyous sea people unaware of the ship's presence.

'The ship crushed sea people, who did not even try to escape. The sailors flung casks over the side, screaming, Demons! demons!

'The casks exploded, blowing splinters, nails, fragments of chain across the waves. The sea folk came to themselves as their pleasure turned to agony and their blood swirled in the water. The whirlpool, cut by the ship, vanished into the depths. Panicked youths saw their families die before them, as they held the terrified, crying babies.'

The Pope stared stonily at Sherzad. No kindness came into his face; he showed no more pity than the priest who stood in the lost ship's stern, holding up a cross of the sunlight metal, proclaiming his responsibility for the devastation of wounded and dying sea folk.

'I am the Hammer of Demons, the scourge of Lucifer,' Marie-Josèphe sang.

The Pope rose. Sherzad loosed Marie-Josèphe's wrist. Marie-Josèphe clutched the bars of the cage to steady herself. The spectators burst into applause at the pathos and tragedy of the story.

'I didn't make it up,' Marie-Josèphe whispered. 'How could I make it up?'

'I must have the creature in my keeping,' the Pope said.

Chapter 24

The gold sunbursts, the gilded candle-stands covered with fresh flowers, the scent of orange blossoms and heavy perfume, the elaborate hangings and the exquisite paintings oppressed Marie-Josèphe. Following Madame and Lotte, she hesitated at the entryway of Apollo's salon. The press of courtiers forced her into the room, and the crowd held her immobile.

The usher knocked his staff against the floor.

'His Majesty the King.'

All the men removed their flamboyant hats. The courtiers made way for their monarch. Marie-Josèphe remained with Madame and Lotte, too close to the front of the crowd and too much in public view to have any chance of creeping out, of fleeing to Sherzad. Sherzad's voice whispered to her, but she could not tell if she heard it truly, or only imagined it in the crush and noise and smell and heat.

This must be the first time I've been too warm at Versailles, she thought.

She peeked over Lotte's shoulder. In all other directions, the fanciful headdresses of the women and the high, leonine periwigs of the men blocked her view.

Everyone bowed. Before she dropped into a curtsy, Marie-Josèphe caught a glimpse of the King. He had replaced his copper perruke with one of bright blond. The shining curls contrasted elegantly with His Majesty's dark blue eyes. White plumes cascaded from his hat. Gold embroidery and rubies covered the flame-coloured velvet of his coat. He wore old-fashioned red satin petticoat-breeches, and shoes with diamond buckles and high scarlet heels.

'He's a young man again,' Madame whispered into Lotte's ear. 'Exactly as he was when he was young!' Her voice quavered. 'So brilliant – so fair—' Her eyes filled with tears.

Emotion nearly overcame Madame, who made unremitting fun of court ladies because they acted younger than their age, who made

347

unremitting fun of herself for never bothering to fight the changes of growing older. The portly duchess wrapped her hand around Lotte's arm. At Lotte's glance, Marie-Josèphe moved up beside Madame. She slipped her hand beneath Madame's elbow to support her.

'Let us take you to your room, Mama,' Lotte said.

'No!' Madame whispered. 'The King would not like us to leave.' She straightened up, trembling, maintaining the illusion of her usual stolid self.

His Majesty mounted his throne. His sons and grandsons took their proper positions.

'His Holiness Pope Innocent of Rome.'

Innocent entered the room, in shining white, surrounded by his cardinals. Yves followed, bearing an elaborate monstrance of silver and crystal. The monstrance carried within its sculpted starburst its holy burden of the Body of Christ. Yves placed the monstrance before Louis' throne. The crystal windows magnified the Host.

'We welcome the consummation of our treaty,' Innocent said.

'As do I, cousin,' Louis said.

The usher thumped the floor again. 'His Majesty James of England and Her Majesty Queen Mary.'

James entered, Mary of Modena on his arm. They wore white velvet covered all over with pearls, gifts of His Majesty. Marie-Josèphe clapped her hand over her mouth to keep from laughing aloud at the Queen's fantastical headdress. She detected the hand of Haleeda, and she thought, *I must find a way to return my sister to her home – or Queen Mary will surely kidnap her off to the cold island of England!*

'Cousin,' James said, hardly lisping at all, 'I've caused a gift to be made for you.'

The Queen's half-starved little Irish slaves hurried in, struggling under the weight of an enormous picture frame of carven, gilded wood. White silk covered the painting. Louis leaned forward eagerly, caught himself, and sat back at his ease, making it appear that he had only shifted his position on his throne. He loved the paintings of the great masters; among his most prized possessions were paintings by Titian, gifts from Italy. If James had brought him another, it was purchased with Louis' own money, but no matter.

James whipped the white silk away and revealed a larger than life image – a flattering image – of James himself in ermine robe and the crown jewels of England.

'So we shall always be near,' James said.

'Allied in the campaign against the heretics,' Mary said.

His Majesty nodded his appreciation to James, to Mary. The young slaves lugged the painting aside and held it upright, where it could watch the proceedings. James placed himself where he could see the portrait.

'His Majesty the Shah of Persia.'

What a conundrum this must be for the Introducer of Ambassadors! Marie-Josèphe thought. *How can he know what rules to follow, what precedence to set? Perhaps His Majesty made up new rules for this concentration of royalty.*

Resplendent in gold robes of Eastern design and a tiered golden crown, the Shah strode into the throne room. He touched his forehead, his heart. Louis nodded courteously. The Shah's viziers and attendants followed, in silk robes and white turbans, the servants carrying rolled-up carpets. They laid magnificent Persian rugs out before His Majesty, one after another, one on top of another, fifty of them, each more intricate, more magnificent, larger than the rest, till the pile stood waist-high. The topmost carpet covered the others, its corners and sides draping to the floor, as if it were risen from the ground, a magic carpet from the stories of Scheherazade.

The Shah spoke; his vizier translated.

'A token of our esteem and love for our ally, Louis the Great, King of Christendom.'

The usher rapped his staff. 'The Prince of Nippon.'

The prince was a small and elegant man with straight black hair intricately arranged and lacquered. A dozen men in lacquered red armour accompanied him. He wore layers of silken kimono in autumn colours and patterns, very full white trousers, and a pair of curved swords. While the clothing of the French courtiers emphasised and increased their height, the robes of the prince widened his shoulders and his body.

'I bring greetings from Shogun Tsunayoshi in the name of

Higashiyama-tennou the Emperor, the greatest monarch of the East, as you are the greatest monarch of the West.'

His attendants carried chests of black and red lacquer, painted with golden dragons. The chests contained fifty bolts of patterned silk, fifty kimono of exquisite colour and pattern, and fifty jade figurines on silken cords, each jade creature so lifelike that the puppy might leap from the prince's hand and scamper around the floor, the frog might croak and leap into the reflecting pond. Jade curves interconnected and intertwined; it was impossible to imagine how anyone had carved them.

Finally the prince took from beneath his outer robe a long narrow box of red lacquer, utterly plain.

'The greatest treasure, from our finest artist.' He knelt and placed the box on a small lacquer table carried in by two of his attendants. Reverently, he drew out a scroll and unrolled it. The backing and border were of fine silk with a subtle pattern, but the scroll was nothing more than white paper marked with three scribbles of black ink. The prince held the scroll as if it were a relic or the original parchment of Scripture. The courtiers whispered; Madame said to Lotte, 'Why, when the Siamese came, even their gifts were better than that one!'

His Majesty nodded to the prince without giving any hint that he might be disappointed or insulted.

'Our allies the War Chiefs of the Huron.'

Two wild Americans walked in, an elder and a younger man, side by side, wearing beaded deerskin, massive steel knives, and hats from Paris. They did not remove their hats, and no one corrected them. They never bowed; they never smiled, though Marie-Josèphe fancied she saw the younger man's lips twitch with laughter. Lines of pain and age marked the older man's face, for he had lived through the destruction of his village, his family, his people. The remnants of his band were the allies of the French in the same way as James and his court in exile.

Two servants carried a birchbark canoe to the King and placed it at his feet. The younger Huron unrolled a shirt of fringed white deerskin sewn with porcupine quills in striking geometric patterns.

His Majesty smiled. 'You sent me beaded swaddling clothes when I was a child. It's fitting that you give me a beaded shirt now that I'm an old man.'

The older chief unwrapped a smaller leather parcel and brought out a pipe decorated with long, golden-brown, white-tipped feathers.

'We bring the peace pipe,' the younger chief said in perfect French, 'to celebrate our alliance.'

They laid the gifts at His Majesty's feet.

'Her Highness the Queen of Nubia!'

The Queen of Nubia, her skin and hair and eyes the colour of ebony, was the most beautiful woman Marie-Josèphe had ever seen. A million tiny beads of gold and lapis lazuli formed her headdress, clinking together in soft music. Her pleated linen robe was fine and sheer as silk, translucent, outlining and revealing her body. Only her wide gold necklace and girdle preserved her modesty, covering her breasts and her sex. She entered the throne room reclining on a litter carried by eight large dark men, followed by four young women, almost as beautiful as she, waving fans. Four more of her attendants led her gift into the throne room. The courtiers murmured in surprise, for they had never known horses to climb the stairs of the chateau, nor ever seen such strange striped horses as these, harnessed four abreast to a hunting chariot. Scenes of oryx and cheetah glowed in the colours of precious stones on its golden sides. Handsful of carnelian, turquoise, and lapis had been crushed to give the colours their unearthly intensities.

Snarls reverberated through the room. Marie-Josèphe caught her breath, certain that Sherzad had shrieked so loudly everyone could hear her. Then the courtiers near the door gasped and shouted and surged backwards.

Six cheetahs stalked across the floor, their claws clicking and scratching on the parquet, their spotted gold coats more striking than any metal. Each wore a collar paved with a different precious stone, fastened to two leashes, for two huntsmen held each beast.

Everyone drew back except Madame, and by necessity Marie-Josèphe and Lotte, for Madame was fascinated by the creatures.

351

'Your prowess at the hunt is renowned,' the Queen said. 'I bring you a hunting chariot and the greatest chasers in the world, cheetahs from the plains of my homeland.'

'Your gift is as extraordinary as your beauty, great queen,' His Majesty said.

The treaty ceremony began.

Marie-Josèphe glanced down. Count Lucien slipped into place beside her.

'The ship has sailed,' he said softly. 'Do not hope too much.'

'I have no other choice but hope,' Marie-Josèphe said. Under cover of the reading of the treaty between Louis and Innocent, a long drone of Latin, she whispered, 'Count Lucien, why did you come to my defence? To Sherzad's defence?'

'You have the truth of the matter. Butchering a sea monster cannot benefit His Majesty. Ransoming a sea woman can.'

'Is that your only reason?'

Without replying, Lucien turned away to watch his sovereign resign some of his authority to the Church of Rome.

Marie-Josèphe rode Zachi along the path beside the Green Carpet. Visitors picnicked on the grass. His Majesty's courtiers had deserted the gardens to prepare themselves for Carrousel. Hidden quartets filled the air with music. The pumps shrieked and groaned, a background to the cheerful tunes, to the rain of the fountains.

A heavy wagon rumbled into the music and the beauty and stopped beside the Fountain of Apollo. A half-dozen men jumped out, carrying staffs. The chevalier de Lorraine dismounted from his tall horse and led the way into the tent.

Marie-Josèphe urged Zachi into a run. At the tent, she dropped her drawing box, scrambled down, and left Zachi standing.

'Sir! Stop! In His Majesty's name!'

Lorraine turned back from Yves' laboratory. 'Where is the key to the cage, if you please, Mlle de la Croix?'

'It isn't time! It's only noon! His Majesty promised—!'

'Calm yourself. His Majesty orders the sea monster to perform for his guests.' He rattled the bars of the cage. 'Leap, sea monster!'

'No!'

Sherzad leaped high, splashing down dangerously close to the edge of the fountain.

'She can't leap properly – there isn't room – as you see, you needn't prod her!' She stood between the men and the cage, trying to think of a protest that would stop them.

'His Majesty commands her to perform her acrobatics in the Grand Canal.'

Though Sherzad would welcome the change, Marie-Josèphe could not quiet her suspicions. 'Why do you supervise the change, instead of Count Lucien?'

'Perhaps M. de Chrétien has more important duties – or perhaps he's lost His Majesty's favour.'

'Why did His Majesty – why didn't you call for me to explain to Sherzad?' She gestured toward the armed men. 'You didn't need—'

'I suggested it, of course,' Lorraine said. 'As a gift for you – I never called for you because you flee on the fastest horse in the kingdom when I try to speak to you.'

'I have good reason!'

'Shall I tell His Majesty that his sea monster refuses his commands?'

'No,' Marie-Josèphe said. 'But put away the staves. If you don't frighten her, she might agree to lie quiet in the sling.'

She unlocked the cage and ran to Sherzad, who hovered nervously, whistling and humming questions. Marie-Josèphe explained what would happen.

The men lowered the sling into the water. Sherzad circled it nervously, fearfully. She still carried on her body the marks of the net that had captured her.

'Please trust me, dear Sherzad,' Marie-Josèphe said. 'The Grand Canal is so much bigger – so much cleaner!'

Sherzad touched the sling. As she hesitantly swam into it, Marie-Josèphe thought, *She trusts me – but by what measure should I trust M. de Lorraine? This may be a ploy to take her to M. Boursin.*

But if they wished to kill her, they could spear her or shoot her as she swam.

Marie-Josèphe had no choice. She urged Sherzad into the sling. Otherwise the men would beat her and net her.

Her heart pounding with trepidation, Marie-Josèphe walked beside Sherzad, holding her hand. Unrestrained, Sherzad fidgeted and sang in anticipation. If Lorraine betrayed her, nothing would stop her from defending herself.

M. Boursin ran, ungainly, down the Green Carpet.

'Oh, excellent, excellent,' he cried. 'May I butcher it now? Follow me, quickly—'

'No!' Marie-Josèphe cried. 'She has until midnight!' She turned on Lorraine in a fury. Sherzad screamed. Her claws ripped the sling with a high harsh tear. 'You lied—'

'I didn't, calm yourself, mademoiselle!' Lorraine stopped Boursin with a gesture. 'Stand back, sir.'

'Be easy, Sherzad, everything will be all right.' The sea woman calmed to a tremble beneath Marie-Josèphe's hands. Marie-Josèphe reproached herself for her suspicion.

Boursin followed frantically. 'You're going to loose it? What possesses you?'

'It's the King's wish,' Marie-Josèphe said. 'He's promised Sherzad her life – find something else to cook!'

'His Majesty promised me a thousand louis!' M. Boursin said. 'If my presentation surpasses Charlemagne's banquet.'

'Sherzad promised him more – for her freedom.'

'Perhaps His Majesty wants both,' M. Boursin said. 'Treasure and meat!'

Frightened by Sherzad's agitation, the workmen hurried the short distance to the Grand Canal and lowered the ruined sling to its bank. Sherzad cried out and struggled and splashed gracelessly into the water.

'It will run itself down,' Boursin said. 'It will be lean and stringy – if the banquet isn't perfect, I'll kill myself!'

'Leap, sea monster!' Lorraine shouted.

Sherzad flicked her tails, splashing water over Lorraine's polished boots. She dove and disappeared.

'It had better not bruise its flesh,' Boursin said.

'Go away,' Lorraine said to Boursin. 'It may bruise itself all it wants, but it had better not climb out.'

'She has nowhere to go,' Marie-Josèphe said. 'She cannot walk, she can only swim.'

Marie-Josèphe leaned over the canal, searching for Sherzad. M. Boursin searched with her, but an angry glare from Lorraine sent him backing away.

'Midnight,' he said. 'At midnight you must be here to deliver the creature to me.'

'Not till after midnight.'

'At one minute past!'

Boursin clambered on board the wagon with the workmen and the slings and nets and staves. He drove away, leaving Marie-Josèphe alone with Lorraine.

'Does it comfort you?' Lorraine asked, smiling his charming smile. 'Are you grateful for this one last taste of freedom for your pet?'

Marie-Josèphe snatched her hand furiously from his touch.

'You're beneath contempt! My friend is in deadly peril, and you – you—'

He laughed, nonchalant in the face of her fury. 'You shouldn't provoke me, mademoiselle. Someday you might find me your only ally.'

He swung up on his horse and cantered away. The surface of the Grand Canal lay flat and still.

Sherzad luxuriated in the flow of clean cold water, in the space around her. She did not even mind the tastelessness of fresh water, after so many days of living in filth. She hummed and whistled, listening to the shape of her surroundings, all long sharp edges and regular curves, nothing growing but bits of algae and the broken stems of water plants struggling to reach the surface before being slashed away or uprooted. The keels of small boats projected through the surface into Sherzad's domain.

She swam into the faint confused current, looking for the underwater river.

*

Zachi whickered softly.

Zelis galloped toward Marie-Josèphe. The mare stopped, hooves scattering gravel; Count Lucien slid from her back. When he hurried, as now, he was awkward. No wonder he preferred to ride, no wonder he did not dance, at the court of the Sun King, that prized grace so highly.

'Mlle de la Croix.' He showed her a tiny silver message capsule. 'From the carrier pigeons.'

'They've found the treasure ship—?'

'The location. The ship – not yet.'

'Don't tell Sherzad,' Marie-Josèphe said.

'Very well.'

Sherzad whispered to her.

'Why is she out of her cage?'

'His Majesty— Lorraine said, His Majesty ordered her to the Grand Canal so she could leap for his guests.'

Count Lucien said nothing. Marie-Josèphe said nothing. Count Lucien walked away, no longer hurrying, leaning, Marie-Josèphe thought, more heavily than usual on his sword cane. She wanted to call him back, she wanted to reassure him: His Majesty had conceived a whim, and Lorraine happened to be nearby to carry it out.

Whatever she wished, it was not her place to claim such intimacy with Count Lucien. She had already declined his terms.

She knelt on the bank and adopted a cheerful demeanour. When Sherzad surfaced before her, Marie-Josèphe bent to kiss her forehead.

Sherzad's skin felt strange, cooler and rougher than normal. One of her claws was broken, and an ugly ulcer disfigured the curve of her shoulder. Her hair was tangled and dull, but her eyes gleamed wild.

'Dear Sherzad, what happened, what's wrong?'

In Sherzad's song, the sea woman fought her way past the iron gratings and out of the canal, swam along an underwater stream, and gained her freedom in the sea.

'Oh, my sweet, did you believe the Grand Canal is a river? It isn't, it only connects to the aqueduct. Don't despair. The ship will find the treasure. His Majesty will keep his promise.' Marie-Josèphe touched the inflamed skin around the ulcer. 'How did this happen?'

Sherzad flinched and snarled, complaining of the filth in the fountain.

'Count Lucien—!' She hoped to stop him before he rode away. But he had not mounted Zelis. The two horses, unbridled, cropped the manicured grass beside the Queen's Boulevard. Count Lucien came away from the horses, carrying saddlebags and a rolled-up rug.

'May Sherzad beg the use of your salve?' Marie-Josèphe asked. 'She's hurt herself.'

Sherzad's snarl refused Sieur de Baatz's salve.

'It saved my life! No, now, don't lick the wound, you'll only make it worse.'

'I have none,' Lucien said. 'I've sent to Brittany, to my father, for more.' He unrolled the red Persian rug onto the grass. 'Sea woman, may I look at your injury?'

Sherzad slipped from Marie-Josèphe's grasp and hovered just out of reach.

'My charm eludes her,' Lucien said.

'She's frightened. She's in despair. She tempted them, Count Lucien – she lured them into releasing her here, she planned an escape. How I wish she'd succeeded!'

'You wouldn't like to witness His Majesty's wrath if she escaped.'

'I don't care!'

'You should.'

Lucien sat on the rug, his legs straight out in front of him. He pulled off his gloves. The tendons and muscles of his hands moved and flexed. His fingernails were perfectly manicured. He opened his saddlebag and drew out a bottle of wine and two silver goblets.

'Marie-Josèphe,' he said, intent, 'His Majesty's power is absolute. It overcomes any impediment to his will.'

'What could he do?' she exclaimed.

Lucien jammed a bottle-screw into the cork and twisted it hard. 'He could bleed you again. He could accuse you of witchcraft. A word to M. Bontemps sends you to the Bastille.' Lucien jerked out the cork and filled the goblets. 'He could give you to the Inquisitors—'

'He wouldn't—'

'Or he could banish you to a convent.'

357

'Please, don't.'

'As he's banished lovers.' He handed her a goblet.

'Are you trying to frighten me?'

'Yes.'

'For my own good, as my brother restricts me and Dr. Fagon bleeds me and Lorraine persecutes me!'

'You've said you love truth: The truth is, you oppose His Majesty at great peril. Would you rather I lied?'

Marie-Josèphe drank, too unhappy to savour the wine. Everyone she thought she could trust had lied to her, except Count Lucien.

'I could not bear it if you did,' she said.

'I swore I'd never put you in danger,' Lucien said. 'Lies are dangerous.' He took bread and cheese and meat pastries and fruit from the saddlebag. 'But we've had enough difficult truths. Let us play at being carefree peasants. No intrigue, no etiquette, no court—'

'No money, no food, no shelter,' Marie-Josèphe said.

'Another difficult truth,' Lucien said. 'We'll play at being courtiers on a picnic.' He drank a long draught of his wine and refilled their glasses. He reached into his pocket, drew out a heavy folded piece of parchment, and handed it to Marie-Josèphe. She unfolded it and read it and glanced at him with gratitude.

'Sir, I'm so grateful—'

'It was but a moment's effort,' he said. 'The decree of manumission for your sister means nothing if your brother withholds his signature.'

'He will give it,' she said.

When Sherzad decided she was in no danger of having M. de Baatz's salve inflicted upon her, she swam closer, asking curious questions.

'Would you like to try our food?' Marie-Josèphe offered Sherzad a piece of bread. Sherzad tasted it and spat it out, pronouncing it fit for fish-food. She liked cheese even less, rejecting it even for fish. Marie-Josèphe handed the sea woman her goblet.

Sherzad sniffed. She thrust her mouth and chin into the goblet and upended it, drinking as the red wine spilled out over her throat and her breasts like blood.

358

'Do show her how to drink, Mlle de la Croix,' Count Lucien said. 'This is excellent wine. I don't mind if she guzzles it, but I wouldn't have it wasted.'

Sherzad did better on her second attempt, draining the goblet and demanding more.

'No, it's your first time,' Marie-Josèphe said. 'It will make you silly, if you aren't careful . . . All right, just a little.' She and Sherzad shared a goblet of wine. Sherzad sang, comparing the effects of drinking wine to those of eating a certain luminescent creature from the deep, deep sea.

Sherzad leaned on the bank of the canal, humming and whistling softly. She took Marie-Josèphe's hand and pressed it against her cheek, against her lips. She pushed the sleeve away from the lancet wound. The cut had nearly healed, and the inflammation had disappeared.

'Do you see? Count Lucien cured it.'

Sherzad snorted, slid into the water, and swam away. Sunlight gilded her.

A little drunk herself, Marie-Josèphe lay back on the rug, supported on her elbows.

The tent stood over the Fountain of Apollo, its sides open to the breeze. Within the cage of Sherzad's late prison, Apollo and his chariot drove widdershins. Marie-Josèphe scowled at the statue.

'Why do you frown?' Count Lucien chided her gently. 'I planned a moment to ease your worries.'

'Apollo is driving the wrong way.' She drew a path across the sky, from sunrise to sunset. 'He should follow the sun, not oppose it.'

'He faces the King,' Count Lucien said.

'The world follows rules that have nothing to do with kings.' Marie-Josèphe picked up an apple and let it drop to the carpet, picked it up, dropped it again. 'The laws of motion, the laws of optics, the motion of the planets – gravity. M. Newton proved it. His Majesty might command this apple, Defy nature's law, do not fall! He might command all he likes. Nevertheless, it would fall.'

Count Lucien watched her quizzically.

'I am investigating the nature of gravity,' Marie-Josèphe said haughtily. 'As M. Newton did.' She took a bite of the apple. It crunched between her teeth, juicy and tart.

'If he has already done it,' Count Lucien said, 'can you not leave these dangerous questions to him?'

Marie-Josèphe leaned toward him eagerly. 'M. Newton discovered what gravity does – but he himself admitted he doesn't know what it is. It would be wonderful, I think, to discover its nature. Is it a force? Is it the hand of God?' She spread her arms as wide as she could reach. 'M. Newton made his discoveries by studying the planets – the largest things we know. Perhaps one should look at the smallest things!' She brought her hands close together. 'Something causes the attraction. If distance attenuates it, might proximity concentrate it? Perhaps one could see it. If I had the use of Mynheer van Leeuwenhoek's microscope—'

'If it's there to be seen,' Count Lucien said, 'why has Mynheer van Leeuwenhoek not seen it?'

'Because he wasn't looking for it.' Suddenly shy – she had never confessed her ambition to anyone else – Marie-Josèphe spread her hands, releasing everything she had said. 'Pay no attention—'

'Have you no faith in my philosophical inclinations, Mlle de la Croix?' Count Lucien said mildly. 'Am I incapable of understanding your theories?'

'I don't yet understand them myself, sir.' Marie-Josèphe glanced away, chastened. 'They require time and work. I have too little of the former and too much of the latter.'

Unwilling to say more about her unlikely dreams, Marie-Josèphe rose and fetched her drawing box from where it had fallen when she confronted the Chevalier. She searched beneath the remnants of her musical score for a fresh sheet of paper. The ripped pages fell onto the Persian rug. Marie-Josèphe gathered them up.

'What is that?' Count Lucien asked.

'His Majesty's cantata. My wretched composition.'

'It doesn't satisfy you?'

'I thought – thanks to Sherzad – I had achieved something beyond my ability,' she said. 'Now I don't know what to think.' She offered him a page of the score. 'See for yourself.'

He waved it off. 'I haven't the talent to imagine a piece from its written notes.'

'M. Coupillet says I'm an amateur, a woman and he says the piece is too long . . . In that he's quite right.'

'How does that make it wretched?'

The melody soared in Marie-Josèphe's mind, melding with the song Sherzad sang from halfway down the Grand Canal.

'He hardly looked at it!' she exclaimed. 'He said he wouldn't direct it, he said women cannot – and he demanded, and I refused—'

'His Majesty admired—'

'Is His Majesty any different from the others?' Marie-Josèphe cried. 'Does he want the music, or does he want my – my particular gratitude?'

'You've many reasons to be grateful to him—'

Marie-Josèphe bit back an angry response, an angry denial.

'—but has he demanded your . . . particular gratitude?'

'He's been chivalry itself,' Marie-Josèphe said, embarrassed. 'What I said was unworthy of him.'

'Even his detractors—'

'Detractors? Of His Majesty? In France?' Marie-Josèphe exclaimed.

Nonplussed, Lucien fell silent. He chuckled. 'Everyone agrees His Majesty possesses superlative judgment of music. If your piece is too long, shorten it. Ask the aid of young master Scarlatti, who is too young yet to be concerned with any woman's particular gratitude.'

'You underestimate Master Démonico. I did show it to him. He admired it. When he plays it, oh, it sounds . . . but Master Démonico plays celestial music for his finger-practice.' Marie-Josèphe scribbled a note to Domenico, sent it away with a servant, then squared the pages of the score and returned them to her drawing box. 'Thank you for your good advice, Count Lucien. I'm glad you don't reserve it for the King alone.'

'You may show me your gratitude—'

Marie-Josèphe looked up sharply.

'—by playing the composition for me,' Lucien said easily.

'Master Domenico's skill—'

'—is extraordinary. I admit it. I'd rather hear the music from your hands.'

'It is very long.'

'So much the better.'

He poured more wine and looked out over the Grand Canal. They sat together in companionable silence and finished their picnic.

Marie-Josèphe sipped her wine and nibbled one last pastry. The servant, out of breath, returned with an answer to her note, a page bearing Domenico's brave attempt at courtly language in his scrawled childish handwriting: 'Signorina Maria must not worry another single moment, I fancied she would wish me to play her composition, because everything having HIS MAJESTY's glory as its end is marvelously exciting; and when the desire to please Signorina Maria is joined to it, what further aim could one have?'

Marie-Josèphe showed the note to Count Lucien, folded it, and slipped it into her bodice, amused by Domenico's response and grateful for it.

The sun was halfway through the sky.

'I must go,' Count Lucien said. 'I must prepare for Carrousel.'

'And I must attend Mademoiselle.' Marie-Josèphe picked up a stick of charcoal. 'But, please, sit still a moment. Let me draw your hands.'

'They are hardly my best feature,' he said. 'I might at least have had dainty hands and feet.'

'Your hands are beautiful.' She sketched, but his rings distracted from the lines. She took his hand, amazed at her boldness – *I must be drunker than I thought!* she said to herself – and removed one of his rings. The warmth of his fingers caressed her palm. He might as well have caressed her face, her breasts, for heat flushed across her cheeks and her throat.

He submitted to her whim until she touched the sapphire ring set in gold, the one he always wore.

'I never take it off,' he said. 'His Majesty gave it to me when I returned to court.'

'Very well,' Marie-Josèphe said, disappointed, for her will could never compete with the King's. She put his other rings back on his fingers. She closed the drawing box on the music score, and on the unfinished drawing of Count Lucien's hands.

Chapter 25

Along line of open carriages drew up around the eastern end of the Grand Canal. His Majesty graciously hosted His Holiness; they rode alone in a carriage magnificently gilded, its sides and wheel-spokes studded with diamonds. It occupied the central spot, with the best view. The royal family and other visiting monarchs flanked the King's carriage. His Majesty's courtiers arranged themselves in the second row. Servants hurried among the fantastic carriages, offering wine and pastries, fruit and cheese.

Marie-Josèphe rode in Monsieur's coach, squeezed between Madame and Mademoiselle, facing Monsieur and the chevalier de Lorraine. She wished desperately that she were riding Zachi, her afrit. She would gallop away to the pigeon loft and wait for news from the galleon.

In the next coach, with his wife Mme Lucifer, Chartres lounged lazily, exchanging languorous glances with young ladies of the court. He ignored Mlle d'Armagnac and her peacock feathers. Marie-Josèphe supposed he had found another mistress. Chartres noticed Marie-Josèphe's coldness no more than he responded to Mlle d'Armagnac's wistful sighs; he had not even noticed, or if he noticed he had not mentioned, that Marie-Josèphe no longer visited his observatory, she never looked into his compound microscope, she never borrowed his beautiful slide rule.

Marie-Josèphe's coldness to Lorraine provoked him. With every jog of the carriage, he moved his feet closer to hers, till the soles of her shoes pressed back against the riser of the carriage seat. He rubbed his toe against her ankle. At the same time, he whispered to Monsieur and casually slipped his fingers beneath Monsieur's gold-embroidered coat to caress Monsieur's thigh.

Madame left off admiring her new diamond bracelet.

'Your feet are too big, M. le chevalier,' Madame said. 'Kindly give

363

us a bit of room.' She rapped his knee sharply with her fan. Marie-Josèphe's love for Madame brought the tears she was fighting close to spilling over. She bit her lip to keep from crying.

'Madame, you wound me – my feet are renowned for their daintiness.' Lorraine drew his feet away from Marie-Josèphe's ankles. 'Perhaps you have my feet confused with another part of my body.'

'Yes, indeed,' said Madame, affronted. 'Your tongue, I have no doubt.'

Monsieur gave his wife a glance of amused disbelief. Lorraine for once was speechless. Lotte trembled with laughter repressed as forcibly as Marie-Josèphe's tears. Blushing, Marie-Josèphe suddenly suspected what Lotte was laughing at, and why she could not laugh aloud. Madame, who serenely feigned ignorance of any second meaning to her comment, would not like to know that Mademoiselle understood it.

'Look at Queen Mary!' Lotte said. She pointed to the carriage of James and Mary, next to His Majesty's. 'She's a pirate, that woman! Can't you make dear Haleeda give me a few more minutes of her time?'

'If Mme la Reine tries to stand up,' Madame said drily, 'she will topple over.'

Mary of Modena wore a headdress impossible in its height and grandiosity. Ribbons and lace spilled down her back and fluttered from wires an armslength above her head. If she were riding in a closed coach it would never fit.

'Mlle Haleeda chooses her own commissions,' Marie-Josèphe said apologetically to Lotte. Her brother might refuse to sign the papers, but Marie-Josèphe considered her sister free in name if not in fact.

'Madame the Queen,' Lotte said, 'is more generous with her rewards—'

'Generous with His Majesty's money!' Madame said.

Haleeda rode in the Queen's carriage, bearing her handkerchief. Marie-Josèphe, astonished, could not choose between delight for her sister's triumph and terror for her risk.

I should be delighted and terrified, Marie-Josèphe thought, *for triumph carries risk as certainly as failure.*

The footman placed the steps. Marie-Josèphe climbed from Monsieur's carriage and hurried to the bank of the Grand Canal.

'Sherzad!' she called. She sang to the sea woman. For long minutes she feared Sherzad would not come to her, but finally the sea woman's tails flicked a spray of water at her feet.

'Sherzad, will you leap for His Majesty?'

Sherzad swam, rolling over and over, her hair streaming around her. Two hundred paces from the end of the canal, she turned and swam toward His Majesty's coach, speeding at a terrific rate. She leaped, surging from the water. She landed with a tremendous splash. Amazed, the guests exclaimed and applauded.

Marie-Josèphe found Count Lucien, mounted on Zelis and attending His Majesty. She searched for reassurance, for a nod to say the galleon had found Sherzad's treasure. He met her gaze; grave, he shook his head.

Sherzad leaped and spun in the air, her dark skin catching the evening light. She splashed down, spattering His Majesty.

'Again!' His Majesty exclaimed.

Sherzad leaped again, turning end for end, silhouetted against the sinking red sun and the mass of scarlet and yellow and orange clouds. She dove into the water without a ripple. The sunset reflected from the Grand Canal, turning it into a golden road.

'Again!' His Majesty exclaimed.

Instead of leaping, Sherzad swam to the bank and struggled up, leaning her elbows on the stone rim.

She sang to the King, spilling the beauty of her story and the desperation of her plea into the air between them. Marie-Josèphe listened – watched – with her eyes closed to blot out the canal, the court, the gilded carriages, and her friend Sherzad imprisoned.

Should I interpret? she wondered. *Should I tell His Majesty of Sherzad's family, the beauty and the freedom of the sea, the adventures, her grief for her dead lover?*

Sherzad's song compelled sympathy without words.

Marie-Josèphe opened her eyes. His Majesty tapped his fingers impatiently.

'Make her leap, Mlle de la Croix.'

'I cannot, Your Majesty. I can only beg it of her.'

'Leap, sea monster! I command you.'

Sherzad snorted, slid underwater, and vanished.

Marie-Josèphe ran to His Majesty's carriage and flung herself to the ground beside it. On her knees she reached into the open carriage and touched the King's shoe.

'She begs you to release her, Sire. I beg you. Please. Please.'

'The ransom saves her. She proposed the agreement.'

'A few more hours—'

His Majesty drew his foot from Marie-Josèphe's hand.

'May I withdraw, Your Majesty?'

'Certainly not. I've invited you to Carrousel. I expect you to attend it.' He rapped on the side of the coach. 'Drive on.'

Yves hardened his heart against the sea woman's pleas and his sister's supplication. Midnight would bring Sherzad's doom. He could not save the creature, he could not save his sister from grief, or from her own stubborn folly. He could only save himself.

I can please the King, he thought, *and the King will order me to continue my work. I can anger the King, and lose his aegis, and spend the next year, the next ten years, the rest of my life, in a cell in a monastery reading treatises on morality.*

If he had doubted it before, he now knew that Louis the Great, the Most Christian King, possessed more worldly power than any other man, more worldly power than the Prince of Rome. No matter that his influence had declined with war and famine, no matter that neither his Carrousel nor his sea monster would restore his youth. Louis in decline remained superior to any other prince's summit.

Yves thought, *If I could make His Majesty immortal – or if he believed I made him immortal . . .*

The carriages drew up in front of the chateau, in the Ministers' Courtyard, facing the Marble Courtyard.

The Marble Courtyard was transformed for a performance. The sea-machine rolled waves of blue and gold across the back of the stage, while layers of clouds hung above it. Thousands of candles turned the dusk to daylight. Draperies of sky-blue velvet concealed the doors and windows of the chateau. M. de la Lande conducted a lively tune.

'Where's M. Coupillet?' Marie-Josèphe whispered.

'Didn't you hear?' Lotte said. 'Such a scandal – His Majesty dismissed him.'

'But he wasn't – he didn't—' Marie-Josèphe thought, guiltily, *He offended me, but I didn't mean him to be humiliated, I didn't mean him to be banished, I should never have told Count Lucien—*

'He persuaded M. Desmarest to write grands motets, then took credit for the music! His Majesty could never forgive such a thing.'

Marie-Josèphe's guilt subsided, to be replaced by embarrassment. *Silly fool*, she thought, *to think an insult to you might earn retribution.*

The chamber orchestra's music turned ominous, then gave way to the brilliant notes of young master Domenico Scarlatti's harpsichord, playing Marie-Josèphe's score as the background for the ballet.

Marie-Josèphe caught her breath.

Domenico's technique did justice to Sherzad's music. *Démonico is wonderful!* she thought. He played from memory: the score remained in her drawing-box.

Marie-Josèphe closed her eyes. The Inquisition advanced ominously on the sea people.

The audience gasped. Beside her, Lotte shivered deliciously. Marie-Josèphe opened her eyes.

An awful monster leaped from the rolling waves. The demon danced across the stage. It resembled Sherzad, Sherzad made to look horrible, her face all protruding fangs and long ears and twisted goat-horns, bloody lips and great red eyes. Painted sea monsters dove among the waves as the dancer cavorted.

A golden chariot descended from the clouds. Tritons appeared, sounding a fanfare with their trumpets. The horses of Apollo stepped like clockwork across the stage, pranced in place as the sun god descended, and sank out of sight beneath the waves.

The harpsichord sang with a joyous, victorious air, the theme of Sherzad's freedom.

His breast shining with a gold sunburst radiating diamonds, Apollo

367

confronted the sea monster. The short sword gave small protection against the sharp talons of the creature; like knives, the talons scored Apollo's small round shield. Yet as the combatants danced, the sea monster gradually yielded to Apollo's will, cringing before him, embracing his knees, bowing its head in willing submission to collar and chain.

That isn't what Sherzad sang! Marie-Josèphe cried to herself. Despite the ballet, Sherzad's song telling Sherzad's story thrilled her; the music existed for anyone who would take the trouble to see it.

Apollo led the sea monster across the stage. In the shadows beside the harpsichord, a tenor rose to sing, accompanied by Domenico's sublime technique.

Apollo, god of the sun,
Your flight creates the dawn.
Your might conquers the sea,
Your light gilds the waves,
The creatures of the ocean
Surrender to your glory!

The music ended. Tenor, Apollo, and Domenico bowed to His Majesty, while the sea monster prostrated itself on the stage. His Majesty nodded and smiled, accepting their representation of his triumph. Around him, royalty and aristocracy, cardinals and bishops applauded him. He took their tribute as his due.

'What a wonderful performance!' Madame exclaimed. 'What lovely music! Did Signor Scarlatti compose it?'

'Sherzad composed it, Madame,' Marie-Josèphe said.

'The sea monster!' Madame laughed. 'You composed it yourself – how talented you are!'

'Marie-Josèphe, dear heart, don't cry,' Lotte whispered.

Count Lucien rode Zelis to Cardinal Ottoboni's carriage. He bade Yves dismount and attend his King.

Yves bowed to His Majesty and kissed Innocent's ring.

'Your success pleases me, Father de la Croix.'

'Your Majesty. I—'

Yves glanced at Marie-Josèphe, but she could not possibly hear what he was about to say. Perhaps she would never forgive him for the choice he had made.

'Your Majesty, Your Holiness,' he whispered, so no one else could hear. 'I've proved — proved the effect of the sea monster's strange organ. It is . . . as you hoped.'

His Majesty remained as impassive as the practice of fifty years of rule could make him. Innocent reacted with dismay.

'Cousin,' he said to Louis, 'consider. If this is true — what does God mean us to do? The Church must examine the creature. I must have it.'

'I will see,' His Majesty said. 'M. de Chrétien, if you please.'

Yves glanced up, into the clear grey gaze of Count Lucien. The count regarded him with utter contempt. He had heard what Yves said, and he knew it for a falsehood.

Yves looked away. Count Lucien could do nothing; he was as ignorant of natural philosophy as all the courtiers; he could not prove Yves lied.

Count Lucien handed the King a flat square box of exotic wood inlaid with a coruscation of mother-of-pearl. His Majesty opened it. On black velvet, a gold disk bore a representation of His Majesty in Roman armor, riding bareback on a charger, his hair flying in the wind. His Majesty lifted the medal. It twisted on its heavy chain, turning to reveal an incised portrait, Marie-Josèphe's drawing of Sherzad, leaping joyously through the waves.

Yves realised what he had done.

He stumbled, his legs weak. Catching the side of the carriage, Yves kept his feet. He tried to raise his head. Short of breath, he stared at the ground, at the sparkling wheels, thinking, *I could fling myself beneath them. How else can I do penance for my deceitful words, but by casting myself into hell? I'll never have to face Marie-Josèphe when she understands what I've done, never hear the sea woman's death scream, never see His Majesty's disappointment, when he dies . . .*

His Majesty placed the medal around his neck. The audience murmured its approval. Yves raised his head, tears running cold down his face. His Majesty smiled.

369

'You show a charming and modest sensibility, Father de la Croix,' His Majesty said. 'Come. Ride with me.'

Yves climbed into the carriage, as weak as if he had been felled by a tropical fever. He sat beside His Majesty, wiping his tears on his sleeve, forcing himself not to throw himself at the King's feet, confess his dishonesty, and destroy himself as well as the sea woman.

The carriages looped around, clattered through the gateway, and conveyed their passengers to the Place d'Armes. An enormous grandstand surrounded the parade ground. Velvet cushions softened the gold-painted wood; great sprays of flowers brightened every corner. Lavender, strewn on the steps, perfumed the air. Servants stood by to conduct His Majesty's guests to their seats, to serve them a modest repast, to present each guest with a silver goblet commemorating Carrousel. Jugglers and troubadours and trobairitz strolled past, playing and singing.

Cardinal Ottoboni and the rest of His Holiness' delegation conducted Pope Innocent to his place of honour in the royal box. A footman opened His Majesty's carriage.

'Take your place in the royal box, Father de la Croix,' His Majesty said. 'And cheer for my team.'

'Yes, Your Majesty.' Yves stepped down.

'I'm proud of you,' Louis said. 'Very proud, my son.'

Yves turned back, bewildered. 'Your Majesty—?'

'Your mother would forgive me for telling you now,' His Majesty said. 'She would not have me acknowledge you while her husband was alive.'

His carriage grumbled away across the hard-packed earth. The Princes of the Blood and the other favoured courtiers galloped after, to prepare for the competition.

His Majesty's son? How could it be?

Yves followed the servant blindly to the grandstand.

It explains so much, Yves thought. *Our family's exile to Martinique. The King's attention. My rise at court . . .*

The servant showed him to the royal box. Yves collapsed on the bench, torn among elation, grief, and guilt.

'Father de la Croix,' said Mme Lucifer. 'How kind of you to keep us company, when all the other men desert us and give us no place in their games.'

She slipped her hand across his knee, casually, as if only to support herself while she leaned close to inspect his medal. Madame and Mademoiselle sat nearby, with Marie-Josèphe in attendance. Yves could not meet his sister's eye.

I cannot bear it, he thought.

But he must. Mme Lucifer and Mlle d'Armagnac pressed him close between them, crushing him with their touch, their voices, their perfume.

'Are you here to make a sinner of me?' whispered Mme Lucifer, his half-sister.

While Lucien rushed into his Carrousel costume and checked Zelis' decorated harness, Jacques ran away to the pigeon loft and returned downcast.

'No message, sir.'

Lucien nodded. He had hoped for news of the treasure, but he had not expected it. He hurried to the stableyard. In a silken pavilion, the King prepared for the games.

'M. de Chrétien. I approve of your costume.'

'Thank you, Your Majesty.'

The Roman teams of the past always wore red trimmed with white, rubies set off with diamonds. Lucien disliked bright red; it flattered neither his fair complexion nor his light eyes. In general he preferred auburn, blue, or gold; he even used blue silk ribbons to tie his baudruches.

For Carrousel, he had indulged himself with a tunic of cloth-of-gold beneath the red leather armour, knowing the King might command him to change it at the last minute.

'Your Majesty, you've done me the honour of offering me a favour.'

'Right now, M. de Chrétien?'

'Tomorrow I will not want it, Sire.'

His Majesty's voice grew wary. 'If it is in my power.'

'I ask for the life of the sea—'

371

'Do not!' His Majesty cried. He spoke again, in a normal tone. 'Do not ask the impossible of me.'

'You have, on occasion, asked the impossible of me.'

'Don't reproach me, either,' His Majesty said. 'Don't you value my life, Chrétien?'

'More than my own, Sire. As you know well.'

'Mlle de la Croix leads you to this folly. Talking monsters, secret treasures! I never thought to see you – you! – baffled by a woman. You should have taken her—'

'I do not take women, Sire,' Lucien said, offended.

'You're too scrupulous by half. One could mistake you for a Christian.'

Lucien bit back his reply. Responding to the insult would not benefit him, or Marie-Josèphe, or the sea woman.

'Your Majesty, Mlle de la Croix' opinion is common sense – and unlike her brother's, it's disinterested.'

'You'd have me believe my own blood lies to me.'

'Would this be unique in your experience, Your Majesty?'

If Louis expected the revelation of Yves' parentage to surprise Lucien, he would be disappointed; but the King must be aware it was not much of a secret. Except, of course, to Yves and Marie-Josèphe de la Croix.

Louis drew himself up angrily, suddenly burst out laughing, stopped, and regained his dignity.

'I value your candour, Chrétien.'

'I don't say Yves de la Croix is a liar,' Lucien said. 'I do say he has good reason to deceive himself.'

'And Marie-Josèphe de la Croix has none?'

'What reason? The brother wins your favour. The sister risks your ire.'

'I cannot give up the sea monster,' Louis said. 'I will not. Don't ask me for the creature's life, so you and I may remain friends.'

Lucien bowed. *I've done my best*, he thought. *I cannot do more.*

He had not expected to succeed, and though he hated to fail, he was surprised not to be disappointed.

He was angry.

★

Marie-Josèphe gulped wine from her silver goblet. As soon as the servant refilled it, she drained it again.

A week ago, she thought, *the gift of a silver goblet from the King would have pleased me beyond all measure. Only a week!* She waved away the servant and put the goblet on the floor. Getting a little drunk might benefit her courage, but getting very drunk would impede her.

Trumpets sounded a fanfare; drums announced the beginning of Carrousel. The jugglers and singers ran from the parade ground. Torches flared, hundreds bursting into flame simultaneously, filling the air with smoke and pitch, illuminating the Place d'Armes with harsh light and long shadows. The full moon hung huge and orange in the eastern sky, opposing the sun.

Sherzad had only a few hours to live.

The Carrousel teams galloped onto the practice field.

His Majesty, as Augustus Caesar, Emperor of Ancient Rome, led the procession, riding the tallest spotted Chinese horse. Its red leather harness sparkled with an encrustation of rubies and diamonds; its crest exploded in pompoms of red and white feathers. Every buckle and fastening on saddle and bridle, breastcollar and crupper, glinted gold. Red and white ribbons fluttered from the horse's mane and tail.

The King wore a tunic paved with diamonds, while rubies nearly covered the lambrequins of the skirt and sleeves of his red leather armour. Silver ribbons, studded with diamonds, fastened his high-heeled red sandals. Gold dust adorned his bright blond perruke. A fantastic headdress of white ostrich plumes fastened with enormous rubies arched over his head; the plumes cascaded to his horse's rump. He carried a round Roman shield. His device, the sun in beaten gold, dispersed clouds of burnished silver.

The grandsons rode at His Majesty's right, each in a variation of His Majesty's costume, each on a spotted Chinese horse: His Majesty on a warhorse, Bourgogne on a cavalry charger, Anjou on a palfrey, Berri on a pony. The rest of the Roman team rode dapple greys.

Lucien rode immediately behind the King. His shield bore the full moon, shining with the light of the sun.

The teams circled the parade ground at a gallop. Riding his black Spanish charger, Monsieur carried a mirrored shield, to reflect the rays of his brother the Sun King. Lorraine rode beside him, on his matched black stallion. Together, in Japanese robes, lacquered armour, and fanciful helmets, they led their team two abreast.

M. du Maine's following, in turbans and voluminous desert robes, rode red-gold bays. Silk tassels of all colours trimmed their silver bridles. M. du Maine carried a branch of the laurel tree, sacred to the sun.

Chartres led his band of ancient warriors, in their translucent Egyptian linen. He carried a tall sheaf of sunflowers that whipped in the wind, shedding yellow petals. His band of chestnuts challenged Maine's bays, until the two troops raced head to head, running up on the heels of Monsieur's team.

Emeralds studded Monseigneur's leather leggings and gleamed in the fur of his breechclout. The cloak of iridescent feathers fluttered from his shoulders. The Grand Dauphin carried a leather shield edged with egret plumes and painted with a silver eagle, its eyes turned to the golden sun.

Monseigneur's war party crossed the parade ground in a wild bright chaos of feathers and jewels, leather fringe and beads, fur and ribbons. Each rider vied with all the others in extravagance and colour; no rider had matched his horse to any other: piebald galloped next to skewbald, paint next to claybank. The Huron war chiefs rode with his group, as exotic as all the others in borrowed body-armour, lace, and their plumed Parisian hats.

In the grandstand, the Prince of Japan looked as if he wished he were part of Carrousel, while the Shah of Persia looked as if he were glad he was not. The Queen of Nubia lounged upon cushions, protected from the moonlight by an awning of black silk held by her handmaidens.

Each team rode its pattern. Monsieur, Chartres, and Maine strove for speed and precision, while Monseigneur's band – to the astonishment and delight of the audience – excelled at feats of daring and bravado, standing upright on their saddles at the gallop, swooping down to snatch golden hoops from the ground.

The moon rose halfway to its zenith. The galleon had sent no further news.

In His Majesty's Roman cavalry, Lucien rode Zelis into the Place d'Armes.

As in their practice, the Roman troop split into two lines, into four, mirroring, double-mirroring the design.

The riders turned inward from the corners of the parade ground and urged their horses to a dead run. All four lines of horses galloped straight for the centre of the field, straight toward each other. The audience cried out in anticipation, and fell silent in apprehension.

Lucien raced after the King, holding Zelis in her place.

A moment's hesitation, a moment's change of speed, would explode the manoeuvre, crashing it into a pandemonium of screaming horses and fallen riders, a disaster as brutal as war. After such a collision – a collision involving the King and three of his four legitimate heirs – no one would think of the sea woman. She might disappear . . .

Lucien could not bring himself to sabotage the drill.

Zelis raced through the pattern, performing it cleanly. The four lines melded to two, to one; the horses pranced toward the aristocracy's side of the grandstand. The audience screamed and cheered and threw their flowers to the ground before their King.

The King rode to the foot of the grandstand. His subjects bowed; even the visiting monarchs rose in salute. At his signal, a line of baggage-wagons rolled onto the parade-ground. Ribbons festooned wagons and draft horses.

'Cousins, I bring you tokens of my esteem.'

He spoke to James and Mary of England. The footmen on the first wagon pulled a white silk cover from a painting twice the size of the portrait James had given Louis. The image of Louis, riding bareback in Roman armour, gazed majestically upon his exiled cousin.

'So we shall never be parted.'

'For our most distant cousin, come from his island fortress—'

The second wagon bore an enormous tapestry, rolled like a scroll. The footmen wound it on its rollers, displaying to Japan its entire length in sections. Twice as tall as a man, a hundred paces long, it documented His Majesty's triumphs, guarded over by the gods of classical Rome.

'—a tapestry from the Gobelin manufactory, the finest in the world.'

Three wagons glittered and sparkled and chimed with a trio of crystal chandeliers, which the King presented to the Queen of Nubia.

'To illuminate your palace . . . though your beauty outshines their light.'

The Shah of Persia's gift required ten wagons, each carrying several enormous mirrors mounted in baroque frames.

'Mirrors of French manufacture, the finest and clearest, for your hareem. And for our allies in New France—'

A single wagon sufficed, but the gift to the Huron war chiefs was the most costly of all. Two mannequins, made to look like wild Americans by the feathers in their perrukes, displayed suits, with hats and gloves and shoes to match, of white velvet covered with diamonds.

'—suits made to our own pattern.'

Finally, His Majesty addressed Pope Innocent.

'And for our holy cousin of Rome . . .'

Two wagons rolled forward. Behind panels of patterned silk, an animal shrieked.

'Exotic creatures.'

Hope flashed through Lucien's heart. He did not wish Pope Innocent's inquisitors on any being, much less on the sea woman. Being butchered and cooked by M. Boursin might be more merciful, but being imprisoned by the Church was a postponement of death. It contained the possibility, however remote, of reprieve.

'One wild man.'

The footmen whipped away the panels. In the first wagon, a baboon screamed and bared its fangs and rattled its cage and shat copiously through the bars.

'Two serpents, to remind us of the Garden, the fruit of knowledge, and our sins.'

Two immense anacondas twined about each other, weighing down the branches of an orange tree.

'And three great steeds, to carry the message of Holy Mother Church.'

The three Grandsons of France rode forward, dismounted, led their spotted horses to the foot of the grandstand, and knelt before His Holiness. Bourgogne and Anjou performed their duty stoically, but when the Pope's Swiss Guard took the reins of his pony, the duke de Berri burst into tears.

Innocent's disappointment could not match Lucien's, but Lucien had to conceal his.

'Bless you, children,' Innocent said to the princes. He rose to reply to the King. In a voice grave enough for a funeral oratory, he said, 'Cousin, I will pray . . . for your soul.'

Louis wheeled his horse and galloped from the parade ground. His teams clattered after him, ribbons streaming, jewels glittering, harness chiming with gold, leaving behind the steeds, the serpents, and the wild man.

I can endure this no longer, Lucien thought. The knowledge dismayed him, and freed him.

Chapter 26

Marie-Josèphe slipped away from Lotte and Madame, losing herself in the crowd. She must creep unseen to the west side of the chateau and into the garden, where she could bribe away or steal one of the gardeners' mule-carts.

She wished she were riding Zachi. Then she could lead the cart instead of driving it, and put less burden on the mule. But if she took Zachi, she would implicate Count Lucien.

Count Lucien rode in front of her, barring her way. In the moonlight he gleamed with rubies and diamonds.

'You shouldn't leave supper before the King.' He nodded toward the courtyard, where the strains of a merry dance intertwined with the fragrance of meat and wine and honey.

'It's nearly midnight. Sherzad has no other friend to be with her when she dies.'

With a sharp gesture, Count Lucien flicked away her false explanation.

'You have no intention of letting her die,' he said. 'This will mean your downfall.'

'I have no choice. There's no word from the treasure ship—'

'An hour ago, there was not. Now? I shall find out.'

Boldly, she took his hand. 'How is it that you always appear when I am thinking about you?'

'It is because you think about me all the time.'

'Sir—!'

'As I think of you.' He bent down and kissed her fingers. He turned her hand over, gently, delicately, and kissed her palm.

He wheeled Zelis around and galloped into the shadows.

★

Supper was laid out under the moon in the Ministers' Courtyard. The meal was light, only fourteen courses, to leave the guests a fine appetite for the last event of Carrousel, tomorrow's banquet.

'Do escort us to supper, Father Yves,' Mme de Chartres said softly. Her hand on Yves' thigh traced out all the reasons her husband referred to her as Mme Lucifer. 'My husband has deserted me to polish the dust from his serpent.'

Her comment shocked Yves until he realised she meant the cobra on the headdress of Chartres' costume. Then he wondered if she did mean the cobra. She held his right arm, Mlle d'Armagnac his left, and they led him to the courtyard. Trestle tables covered the cobblestones, candelabra lit the tables, and servants offered food and wine.

'How charming, a picnic,' Mme Lucifer said in a derisive tone. 'Tomorrow we'll be spared the rabble – even the Gallery of Mirrors has its limits.'

'Let us look at your medal.' Mlle d'Armagnac and Mme Lucifer moved closer. Mlle d'Armagnac inspected the medal. The chain pulled at his neck.

Mme de Chartres was much shorter than he. If he looked at her at all, he could not help looking at her bare bosom. Her breasts pressed against his ribs, her hand tested the buttons of his cassock, her belly rubbed his sex. Yves and Mme Lucifer might as well be naked for everyone to see.

'Madame, pardon me—'

'Of course – if you stop struggling.'

'You know who I am – a priest—'

'What does that matter?'

'—and your brother!'

Mlle d'Armagnac handed the medal to Mme Lucifer. Both women laughed and pulled at the chain around his neck. 'Father Yves, why torment yourself? No one else bothers! Your sister gives her favours to M. le Chevalier—'

'That isn't true!'

'—and the notorious M. de Chrétien—'

'Do not insult my sister, madame!' *Is it an insult*, he thought wildly, *to speak the truth? I should have saved her, I should have sent her back to the convent, I never should have allowed her to come to Versailles!*

'—and even the King. You're so scrupulous!' Holding his tether, she plunged her other hand beneath his cassock.

He tore away before she grasped him. The opening of his cassock trapped her, forcing her to stumble after him.

'You're His Majesty's natural son—'

'—so your sister must be his natural daughter!'

Mme Lucifer snatched her hand free. Mlle d'Armagnac burst into laughter. They followed him like Furies.

'You cannot deny it,' Mme Lucifer said. 'Everyone knows the King puts on these fetes only for his mistresses.'

Stumbling around, trying to flee, Yves came face to face with Pope Innocent and all his cardinals. His Holiness' stormy expression turned thunderous.

'Your Holiness, I—I—'

'Go to the chapel, my son,' Pope Innocent said. 'Meditate on the subject of sin.'

'Father de la Croix!'

His Majesty strode toward Yves. His Carrousel teams followed him, a cavalry imagined from all the most exotic times and places of the world. The King, in costume, glittered with millions of livres' worth of diamonds and rubies. The white plumes of his crest draped down his shoulders and back like a cloak. The first time he appeared as Augustus Caesar, he had been twenty-eight. He looked that young again.

His Majesty took Yves by the shoulders and embraced him, in the full view of all his cavalry, all his courtiers, all the visiting monarchs, all the Princes of the Church.

'Come stand at my right hand, my son.'

'To the chapel,' Innocent repeated. 'Meditate – and consider particularly the sin of pride.'

Yves took one step toward His Majesty.

Yves saw, beyond the gate of the courtyard, Marie-Josèphe standing at the shoulder of a gray horse, looking up at the Count de

380

Chrétien – *She would hardly look up at him under any other circumstances!* Yves thought, then thought of another situation in which she would – and touching his hand. Chrétien raised her hand to his lips. He let her go, prolonging the touch as a lover would. He rode into the darkness. Marie-Josèphe hurried away and disappeared.

'Father de la Croix!' Pope Innocent said.

'Come along,' His Majesty said. 'Have some supper. I like a man with a hearty appetite.'

'I – forgive me, Your Majesty,' Yves said. 'I must obey His Holiness.'

He fled from the courtyard.

Marie-Josèphe tried to slip into shadows. Footsteps followed her. It was impossible to hide behind an orange tree while wearing a grand habit. Her pursuer strode toward her, grim-faced.

Her brother grasped her shoulders, his eyes wild, his hair awry, his cassock ripped open. The sea monster medal hung heavy on his chest, tangled with his crucifix.

'Yves—?'

'This liaison will be your ruin!' he cried.

'This – liaison?'

'Has he bewitched you?'

'Who? What are you talking about? You don't believe in witchcraft!'

'That scheming atheist—'

'Count Lucien has offered you nothing but wisdom! How can you speak so cruelly of him?'

'He's a despoiler of women—'

'And he's offered me only kindness! I admire him—'

'—and he'll despoil you, if he hasn't already!'

'—and I love him. If he'd take me, I'd have him!'

'You are like our mother – a wanton—'

'How dare you?' Marie-Josèphe exclaimed. 'Our mother? Have you lost your mind?'

'Have you lost your virtue? Our mother did – the King had her, he got me upon her, and you—'

'Yves, you're ridiculous.'

He stopped raving, hope in his eyes. If he were not so distraught, she would have laughed at him.

'Mama and Papa were in Martinique two years before I was born – did the King, unacknowledged, creep over the Atlantic to Fort de France?'

'But I was born in France.'

'Yes,' Marie-Josèphe said.

'The King acknowledged me.' Yves broke down crying. 'He revealed my bastardy, before His Holiness, before everyone. And Mme Lucifer said you were Chrétien's lover, and the King's natural daughter, and . . . and . . .'

'What? Tell me.'

'And the King's mistress.'

'Count Lucien treats me with complete respect. His Majesty has never offered me an improper word or gesture.' She embraced Yves with sudden sympathy. 'Oh, Yves, dear brother, this explains so much, I'm so sorry for you.'

She tried not to laugh: *So that's why the ladies rose for me*, she thought, *and why Mlle d'Armagnac copied my peacock feather!*

She smoothed Yves' hair, comforting him. 'When have I had time to be anyone's mistress?'

At the bottom of the garden, Sherzad sang of loneliness and of despair.

'I must hurry,' Marie-Josèphe said. 'Sherzad's calling me. Go back, accept His Majesty's accolades.'

The rumble of wagon wheels approached.

'I'll go with you,' Yves said. 'I'll give Sherzad last rites—'

'She doesn't want you!' Marie-Josèphe cried, desperate to make him go, to send him out of peril. 'She isn't a Christian, she doesn't want—'

Count Lucien drove a baggage wagon past the Orangerie, incongruous in Roman armour, plumed hat, and white deerskin gloves.

'Count Lucien!' Marie-Josèphe ran after the wagon.

'Whoa!' The cart-horses stopped.

'Any news of the treasure ship?'

382

'Marie-Josèphe,' Lucien said patiently, 'would I be driving this ugly wagon if I had good news?'

She scrambled up beside him, awkward in her elaborate skirts. Yves grabbed her arm.

'In the name of God, what are you doing?'

'Yves, go back to the King. Lucien, please, hurry.'

He chirruped. The cart horses lunged forward.

'I am so grateful to you,' Marie-Josèphe said. 'Somehow we must save Sherzad's life – and His Majesty's soul.'

'I'm an *atheist*,' Lucien said. 'I have no business saving anyone's soul.'

Marie-Josèphe laughed. She could not help it. 'Lucien, I love you, I love you without limit or boundaries.'

Driving with one hand, Lucien slipped his fingers around hers.

The wagon shuddered. Startled and frightened, Marie-Josèphe turned. Half in, half out of the wagon bed, Yves clutched the sides and pulled himself in.

'Go back to the chateau!' Marie-Josèphe cried.

'If I do,' Yves said, 'I'll never atone for betraying Sherzad.'

The full moon hung in the sky, a handsbreadth from its zenith. Marie-Josèphe sang to Sherzad, telling her, *Swim to the far end of the Grand Canal, we must go far from M. Boursin, he must not see you climbing into the wagon.*

Sherzad replied, her song full of hope and excitement. Propelling herself along the Grand Canal, she outpaced the galloping horses.

M. Boursin would appear at the east end of the Grand Canal one minute after midnight. He might wait a moment for Marie-Josèphe to appear, to bid the sea woman to surrender herself. At two minutes after midnight, he would sound the alarm to the guards. He would tell the King.

Marie-Josèphe looked back. The chateau glowed on its hilltop, brilliant with light.

A line of torches snaked along the path.

'Hurry,' Marie-Josèphe whispered.

Lucien wheeled the horses around the gravel track.

'Take the reins,' Lucien said. 'Yves and I will—'

Sherzad clambered onto the bank at the western end of the Canal. Clumsy, agitated, she writhed toward the wagon. The cart-horses spooked and snorted and reared. The wagon lurched. Lucien rose, bracing himself, speaking softly to the powerful draft horses, bringing them to a nervous, sweating standstill.

'You must steady the horses,' Marie-Josèphe said. 'I'll calm Sherzad.' She climbed down and ran to the sea woman. 'Be easy, sweet Sherzad, be still, we'll help you.'

In a frenzy, Sherzad fought Marie-Josèphe and her brother, struggling toward the wagon as if she were still in her own element. Her claw grazed Marie-Josèphe from shoulder to breast. Sherzad slipped away, crashed to the ground, gasped, moaned. Marie-Josèphe knelt beside her.

'Sherzad, listen, listen to me.' She took Sherzad's webbed hands. She sang, showing Sherzad what she hoped would happen. The horses stamped and snorted. Lucien soothed them with his voice and held them in check.

Sherzad sobbed and lay still. Marie-Josèphe and Yves lifted her into the wagon. So lithe and quick in the water, she was graceless on land. They sat on either side of her in the splintery wagon-bed, bracing her so she would not fall.

Lucien loosed the reins gradually, letting the horses walk, jog, canter, run, without jolting his passengers from the wagon. Terrified, the sea woman clutched Marie-Josèphe around the waist. She squirmed up beside her and kissed the deep bleeding scratch, humming regret.

'Never mind, Sherzad. Never mind.'

'And now?' Lucien shouted over the rumble of the wheels.

'The sea.'

'If we can reach it. Do you then have a plan for yourself?'

'I didn't think beyond – I couldn't . . .' She slipped her hand into her bodice and drew out a knotted handkerchief. 'I have a few livres – as I didn't have to bribe anyone to get a wagon. It will buy us bread – and fish.'

Lucien chuckled. He laughed. Marie-Josèphe opened her mouth to protest, then she began to laugh as well.

Rubies and diamonds covered Lucien's armour. The fugitives were magnificently wealthy.

They were, as well, instantly identifiable and impossible to disguise.

The wagon rumbled through luminous darkness; the full moon gleamed on the mist.

'We might go to Brittany,' Lucien said.

'We might take passage on a ship. We could go home to Martinique.'

'I'll take my chances with the King's guard,' Lucien said, 'before I'll ever willingly get on another ship.'

Marie-Josèphe knew, Lucien must know, they had little more chance of hiring a ship than of escaping to Brittany.

Sherzad raised her head, her nostrils flaring; she slid from Marie-Josèphe's arms and shrugged off Yves' grasp and clambered up to lean on the jolting wagon seat. She gasped the wind in over her tongue, expelling the air in a hiss of satisfaction. The cart-horses plunged into a dead run.

'Easy, easy.' The horses breathed in rough snorts; Lucien slowed them. 'We have a long way to go.'

The full moon sank past midnight. The harness rubbed the horses' sweat to foam.

'Look,' Yves said.

Far behind, the road turned into a river of light, a rushing brilliant flood.

'The King,' Lucien said.

'We'll never reach the sea,' Yves said.

'We had little chance of reaching the sea.'

'We've thrown our lives away on a hopeless task——?'

'Sherzad, the Seine will lead you home,' Marie-Josèphe said, 'but you must swim as fast as you can, you must hide underwater whenever you hear men, or horses, or dogs.'

Sherzad understood. She sang a song of farewell to Marie-Josèphe; she laid her head against Marie-Josèphe's shoulder and kissed the slash she had made across her breast. Marie-Josèphe's blood smeared her cheek.

Lucien urged the labouring horses up a low rise. The lanterns and torches of their pursuers surged closer, penetrating the hollow with a spear of light.

'Lucien, can we hide? Leave the road, let them pass——?'

'Not enough cover. Too much moonlight.'

The wagon crested the rise. A curve of the Seine gleamed through luminous grey mist. Sherzad smelled the water. She sang, impatient and wild. The tiring horses fled her voice. The wagon bumped down the switchback slope.

'A few minutes,' Marie-Josèphe said. 'Only a few minutes and you'll be free.'

The jewelled riders crested the hill. Their lanterns flung their shadows before them. They galloped across the land, fantastic, threatening. His Majesty's Carrousel teams flowed down the slope, gathering speed, cutting the switchbacks, gaining fast.

The cart-horses plunged onto the flat, labouring into the mist of the river-plain. Marie-Josèphe fantasied that they could cross the bridge, block or burn it, leave the cavalry behind, and escape.

They'd only ford the river, Marie-Josèphe thought. *And never mind the ruin of their costumes.*

She held Sherzad. The wagon jolted over ruts, bouncing wildly, its wheels lifting from the ground as Lucien urged the exhausted horses to one last effort. They must only reach the bridge, where Sherzad could leap to freedom. Five hundred paces, and His Majesty's troop still a thousand paces behind. Two hundred paces to the bridge. The torches sizzled, trailing sparks; the Carrousel headdresses waved in the air with the menace of demons.

Fifty paces. The wagon hit a rock. It jolted into the air. It crashed down. A wheel splintered. The wagon jerked sideways. Yves grabbed Marie-Josèphe and Sherzad, holding them in the wagon. The axle screamed along the road, digging a furrow through the rocks and ruts. Lucien drove the wagon onto the bridge, but where the road rose the axle caught; the wagon slewed and stuck, leaning lopsided between the stone ramparts.

'Whoa, whoa.' Lucien stopped the horses. One stumbled and fell to its knees. The other trembled, its head between its legs. The horses flinched at Sherzad's cry of dismay, but they were too spent to try to escape her. His Majesty's riders thundered toward them, five hundred paces away.

'If we surrender,' Yves said, 'before we're shot—'

'No! Help me! Sherzad—' Marie-Josèphe slid over the leaning corner of the wagon. Lucien clambered down. Sherzad writhed and fell onto the bridge, snarling.

Lucien ran to the road. His sword slid sharp from his cane. He waited.

The fantastical shadows of the Carrousel teams galloped toward him. The horses' hooves beat the road to dust. Burning pitch and sweat and dirt hung pungent in the air. The King led; alone, magnificent, he stopped so close that Lucien's sword touched his horse's chest and the beast's hot breath ruffled the plumes in Lucien's hat. The teams drew up behind the King. The Nubian hunting chariot brought up the rear. The cheetahs flowed from it like a river, baring their teeth and snarling.

The sun blazed from the King's shield.

'You fought bravely beside me, Lucien,' Louis said. 'Will you now fight against me?'

Lucien could not reply. Marie-Josèphe and Yves laboured to help Sherzad to the crest of the bridge. The sea woman moaned with anticipation and snarled with defiance. Her tails scraped against stone.

Hurry, Lucien thought, *please, hurry, I cannot make this choice.*

With a shriek of triumph, Sherzad leaped from the bridge and plunged into the river.

'Swim for your life!' Marie-Josèphe cried. 'Good-bye, dear Sherzad!'

His Majesty pointed downstream. Monsieur, his kimono sleeves flying like wings, galloped along the bank, his team close behind and the others following. His Majesty faced Lucien with only Lorraine and the young princes to attend him.

Lucien saluted His Majesty with his sword. He surrendered. Bourgogne and Anjou dismounted, took the sword and his cane, and presented them to their grandfather. Louis sheathed the sword.

'Will you give me your parole, M. de Chrétien?'

387

'Yes, Your Majesty.'

Louis returned his sword. Lucien bowed, grateful to the King for treating him as an enemy, rather than as a traitor.

River-water closed around Sherzad. It was thick with the filth of animals and land-humans. She surfaced, spat with disgust, dove again, and set out swimming. She was bruised and sore, tiring quickly after her long imprisonment. The current helped, but she was far from the sea.

The sounds of the river changed. The silt was so thick she was nearly sound-blind. She surfaced for an instant; she kicked hard to raise herself above the mist. At the next bend, men and horses blocked the river. A long net stretched through the current. She dove again, hoping to find a way around it or beneath it. She slid past plunging hooves. When she touched the horses they screamed and thrashed and unseated their riders. The dangerous game gave her away. Riders jabbed with pikes and fired their muskets. Shot rushed past her, boiling the water with its heat; a ball snatched away a lock of her hair.

She dove. Stones weighted the net to the river bottom. Pushed into the net by the current, she fought to slip beneath the mesh. The hunters felt the strain. They pulled the net around her, tangling her, pushing her into shallows.

She erupted through the surface, burst through the mist, and flung herself over the net.

A piercing pain slashed into her foot. A furred and spotted predator growled and dragged her onto the stony bank. Sherzad writhed into the water, pulling the creature with her. Her blood filled the water, mixing with the predator's musky pungent scent.

When the predator was submerged and vulnerable, Sherzad shouted out a sharp hard shock. Her voice, transmitted by the water, slammed into her attacker's heart. The creature convulsed, bit hard, and fell dead.

Its mate leaped and fastened its teeth in Sherzad's throat. She could not shout. She could not move. The predator's canines pressed against arteries. One nip, and she would bleed to death. One hard bite, and the creature would sever her spine.

388

Sherzad went limp. Chaos and clamour swirled around her, the shouts of men and the blows of the pikes. The men of land beat the predator away and dragged her to the shallows. All she knew for sure was the touch of the net.

The Hurons, wearing their diamond suits and greatly amused, galloped toward Marie-Josèphe.

'Be still,' Lucien said quietly.

Marie-Josèphe was too distraught for fear. The Hurons raced past. The older man brushed a feather across her hair. The younger did the same to Yves. The old man galloped by again, leaning down to touch Lucien.

'They have claimed our hair,' Lucien said. 'For my part, this perruke is ruined; they may have it.'

When the King rode away to meet his brother, Lorraine tied Marie-Josèphe's hands to the traces of the cart-horses. Bedraggled, despondent, she made no objection. Yves struggled — a futile exercise — when Lorraine directed the musketeers to tie him at Marie-Josèphe's left hand. Lucien bore the inevitable disgrace with arrogant disdain. Chartres and Maine bound him at Marie-Josèphe's right.

'Someone in a high position could be of use to you now,' Lorraine said to Marie-Josèphe.

She raised her head and glared at him.

'A foolish reply.'

The horses lumbered forward. Lucien struggled to keep up, supporting himself awkwardly with his cane. The cart-horses plodded toward dawn.

'M. de Chrétien,' Lorraine said, 'you are brought low.'

'And yet still you may slither beneath my foot.'

Lorraine slapped the rump of the near cart-horse. It lurched into a trot, pulling its pair with it. Lucien stumbled, recovered, scrambled.

'Whoa, whoa,' he said softly. The horses slowed, more out of exhaustion, he thought, than obedience.

It would please Lorraine, he thought, *to drag me all the way to Versailles.*

'Lucien—' Marie-Josèphe said.

'Shh.' He could not bear pity.

Marie-Josèphe twisted around, squinting into the darkness. 'Did she escape?'

Splashing out of the shallows, His Majesty appeared through the mist. Monsieur and his teammates followed, carrying Sherzad. She was trapped in a net and suspended on poles. Marie-Josèphe sang; when the sea woman struggled, her song broke off in a sob. Sherzad wailed. Her eyes shone like a cat's.

The young Carrousel riders, giddy with exhaustion and conquest, sparred with each other, jostled and joked, and jeered at Lucien. Old friendships dissolved without trace in the acid of the King's disapproval. Lucien had seen it happen to others, this public humiliation. He had crafted his life so it would never happen to him. His painstaking work lay in ruins.

His Majesty stopped when he saw what the Chevalier had done. His gaze passed across Yves, and Marie-Josèphe, and the Chevalier, and fell finally upon Lucien.

'You have all gone insane.'

The sun was rising. The King sounded old, and exhausted.

Chapter 27

Lucien and Yves rode the cart-horses, bareback, their hands unbound by the King's command. Spent from her struggles and restrained by the net, Sherzad droned an eerie hum of grief that spooked riders and horses alike. Marie-Josèphe rode in the hunting chariot. Cheetahs shouldered and snarled, rubbing against her bedraggled petticoat. One sat on its haunches and watched her, its gaze on her bloodstained bodice.

The trip to Versailles took forever; it took no time at all. Marie-Josèphe pushed away exhaustion and despair, seeking escape. She matched her stance to Lucien's: proud, shoulders straight, head up. Schemes occurred to her, each a more fanciful fairy tale than the next. If she could release the cheetahs from their collars – they might confuse the cavalry, they might frighten all the horses . . . but they might equally tear out her throat, or pounce on Sherzad when the riders dropped her carry-poles. If she could overpower the driver – she could gallop away in the chariot . . . but Chartres and Lorraine would make short work of catching her, their powerful war-horses against the stolid zebras. No matter how she escaped, in her fantasies, only Apollo dropping from the sky in his dawn chariot might free Sherzad. No matter how she escaped, the Carrousel riders surrounded Lucien and Yves.

We failed, she thought. *Sherzad's life is forfeit. I drew Lucien into a scheme he never meant to support, with what consequences to him?*

She wiped her face indelicately on her sleeve, hoping her captors would think she had dust in her eyes.

Fire burst along Lucien's spine.

He gasped and clutched the cart-horse's mane. His sword nearly slipped from his fingers. All his senses turned toward the pain, shutting out the world. If he remained very still, he might not fall, he might not drop his sword, he might not lose consciousness.

'M. de Chrétien,' Yves whispered, 'what's wrong?'

'Don't touch me, if you please.'

'You're very pale—'

'It's fashionable,' Lucien said.

Yves fell silent, for which Lucien was also grateful. Fire burned in his back, remorseless, worse than torture. If he were being tortured, he could recant or confess or convert and the torture would stop. When his body betrayed him this way, nothing, neither wine nor spirits nor loving caress, would stop the pain.

The procession plodded toward Versailles, past the Grand Canal, past the Fountain of Apollo; it continued up the Green Carpet, bearing the sea woman to the chateau.

Lucien reclaimed himself from his affliction long enough to understand the significance of their path. He could not see Marie-Josèphe's face, but he had no doubt she understood too.

His Majesty has decided, Lucien thought, *to end the sea woman's life.*

The procession stopped beneath the chateau's north wing. Yves dismounted and walked stiffly around his horse. Lucien clutched the mane of his cart-horse and lowered himself to the ground before Yves could reach him. He leaned heavily on his cane, catching his breath.

He could not even claim an honourable injury. The careening crash of the wagon, the lurching gait of the cart-horse had not affected him. When the ache he suffered constantly rose to agony, the change struck after no particular action and no particular insult.

The only pattern Lucien had ever detected was inconvenience.

And that, he thought, *is because any moment would be inconvenient. I must admit this moment is worse than most.*

The King dismounted and entered the chateau. His companions closed in around him. They left no place for Lucien to stand; they had already obliterated his position. When the guards came, the rest of the courtiers rode away with the horses, never casting a backward glance. Lucien could not blame them. Anyone who defended him risked sharing his fate.

The guards surrounded the captives and marched them to the guard room of the State Apartments. Lucien leaned heavily on his sword-cane and managed to keep up, but only because the musketeers had to carry Sherzad. The sea woman lay limp in the net, keening an uncanny dirge. In the guard room, the musketeers dropped their burden and moved away, unnerved.

'She needs water, sirs,' Marie-Josèphe said, 'or she'll grow ill. Please be so kind as to give her a drink.'

'Be so kind as to give us all a drink,' Yves said. 'And allow us to sit. We've been travelling all night.'

Yves' plea irritated Lucien.

Do you embrace your suffering, priest, Lucien thought, but he resisted the temptation of speaking the irony aloud.

Scrupulously polite, the musketeer captain sent for wine and water. His men brought chairs. Yves sagged into his, leaning forward with his elbows on his knees and his head down. Marie-Josèphe sat so gingerly that Lucien wondered if she had been hurt in the wagon crash. He wanted to go to her. He wanted to comfort her; he wanted her comfort. But the guards would stop him; he had all he could do now to maintain his demeanour.

The captain offered Lucien a chair.

'Do you expect me to sit in the presence of His Majesty?' Lucien asked, his tone severe. He thrust his walking-stick toward a portrait of Louis. Pain stabbed up his back into both shoulders.

'I beg your pardon, M. de Chrétien,' the captain said. 'But will you take wine?'

One of the musketeers poured the wine. Yves drank thirstily.

'I will drink to His Majesty.' Lucien lifted the goblet to Louis' portrait in a pure arrogant salute and tossed the wine down in one gulp. The captain joined the toast.

'No, thank you,' Marie-Josèphe said, when one of the guards offered her the wine. 'I mean no disrespect to the King, but . . . I cannot.'

Lucien realised why she was so uncomfortable, why she would not drink though her lips were dry and her refusal full of regret, and why she was so embarrassed.

'Allow Mlle de la Croix the use of the privy,' Lucien said quietly to the captain.

393

The captain hesitated, but he knew as well as everyone at court, the endurance of His Majesty's bladder as well as His Majesty's habit of travelling without thought for the comfort of ladies. He bowed to Lucien and ordered his men to escort all three captives to relieve themselves.

'Quickly, though, His Majesty will want them soon.'

Alone, Lucien leaned against the wall, letting the stone cool his face. He shivered.

The captain sent in water and towels. Lucien wiped away the worst of the mud, brushed the dirt from his gloves, and straightened his clothes. He wished for a change of linen. He was not fit to face the King, and he was soaked with cold sweat. He never grew used to the cold that accompanied hot pain. The flask of calvados in his pocket tempted him, but the fire of the liquor would do nothing to quench the fire in his back. He pulled a white ribbon from his Carrousel hat, now sadly bedraggled, and tied back his equally dishevelled perruke.

'What about the sea monster, M. de Chrétien?' the captain asked when he returned. 'Will it piddle on the carpet?'

'Mlle de la Croix is the expert.'

'I don't know.' Marie-Josèphe drank deep from her goblet, and did not refuse when the captain refilled it. 'Sherzad's never been in a house, she's never seen a carpet, she wouldn't know what to do in a privy.'

'It won't drink.' One of the musketeers stood over Sherzad with a water bottle; the sea woman had not piddled on the rug, but the bottle had dripped upon it.

'Let me sit with her,' Marie-Josèphe said.

The captain allowed Marie-Josèphe to kneel beside Sherzad. Lucien joined her. Yves hesitated, then followed. Lucien put his hand on Marie-Josèphe's shoulder. She covered it with her fingers, warming and thrilling him. He imagined that the fire of her touch burned away a fragment of his pain.

'My dear friends,' Marie-Josèphe whispered.

Her voice failed her. She stroked Sherzad's shoulder, her bruised hip. The web of Sherzad's hand was torn. Clotted blood covered her

394

ankle; bruises covered her neck. She lay with her eyes closed, her dirge nearly inaudible. Marie-Josèphe held the water bottle to Sherzad's mouth. The sea woman did not respond.

'Sir, may I have the wine?'

The captain handed her the bottle. She poured a few drops on her fingers and wetted Sherzad's parched lips. The sea woman dreamily, delicately, licked away the wine.

'His Majesty requires your presence.'

Marie-Josèphe walked beside Lucien into the Salon of Apollo. Yves walked alone, his head bowed, his hands folded in his sleeves. Guards flanked them, and carried Sherzad with them. The sea-woman's moaning echoed in the chamber.

Lucien faced His Majesty. Seated on the throne, the King gazed down at his former favourites. Monseigneur and Maine, Lorraine and Chartres stood around him, stern and silent. Only Monsieur offered a sympathetic glance. Only he could dare to, but even he could not help.

Sweat covered Lucien's face, and his hand clenched around his walking-stick; he had to push himself upright from his bow.

Marie-Josèphe offered His Majesty a deep curtsy, but her attention remained on Lucien. *Is he injured?* she thought. *Was he hurt in the wagon crash? I've never before seen him succumb to his pain.*

'I respect my opponents in war,' Louis said. 'But I despise friends who betray me.'

'Sire, I'm the one at fault!' Marie-Josèphe exclaimed. 'My brother, and Count Lucien—'

'Be quiet! Do you expect mercy because you're a woman? I'm no fool, mademoiselle, no matter how you've played me.'

'I expect no mercy for myself, Your Majesty.' But she had hoped to beg mercy for Sherzad, for Lucien, for Yves.

'And you, Lucien. Will you explain yourself?'

'No, Your Majesty,' Lucien said.

Lucien's curtness to the King shocked Marie-Josèphe.

'Will you not ask me for the favour I promised?'

So furious, so affronted, that he took a moment to reply, Lucien said, 'I asked it of you already, Sire.'

'Stop that noise!' the King cried to Marie-Josèphe.

'I cannot. Sherzad is singing her death song.'

'M. Boursin!'

M. Boursin hurried forward in his shambling bony way.

'Take the creature. Butcher it. Now.'

'But, Your Majesty, the banquet is almost about to start, Your Majesty, there's no time to prepare it, Your Majesty, if it didn't please you I should kill myself—'

'Do as you like,' Louis said. 'Spare me your protestations. We'll eat the monster raw and bloody.'

'Your Majesty, I, I will think of something, Your Majesty—'

Marie-Josèphe began to cry, silently, with grief.

Lucien took her hand. Marie-Josèphe could not stop crying, but she had never been so grateful for the comfort of another human being.

'You cannot come in! You must not come in!' The usher's voice penetrated from the next Salon. 'Guards!'

A pigeon fluttered wildly into the Salon. It dashed back and forth, it saw the sky through the window, it flung itself headlong toward the glass, it swerved at the last moment. It fluttered to the royal pigeon-keeper, who held it and cradled it against his chest. Other birds rested in his shirt and on his shoulders.

Without anyone's leave, Lucien approached the pigeon-keeper. Leaning heavily on his stick, he held out his hand.

The pigeon-keeper dug in his pocket. He tipped a fistful of silver message capsules into Lucien's palm.

Lucien did not condescend to open one. He returned to his place before the King. The tears in Marie-Josèphe eyes created a halo around the gleaming silver. She dug her fingernails into her palms, trying to stop crying, trying not to shout, Open one, read the message—

His Majesty plucked a single capsule from Lucien's hand. He opened it. He tipped it, but nothing came out. He shook it.

An emerald hit the polished parquet with a bright sharp tap. The ember of green sparks skittered across the floor and came to rest in the fringe of the Persian rug. A guard scooped it up, knelt at the King's feet, and returned it.

His Majesty read the scrap of paper from the message capsule. He dropped it.

Each message capsule contained a jewel more beautiful than the last, or a perfect jade bead, or an exquisite gold bangle. His Majesty littered the floor with the messages. Marie-Josèphe pieced together the words:

'Aztec gemstones. Spanish gold. Glorious prize.'

His Majesty closed his hand around the treasure.

'The sea monster wins its life.' His bleak voice unnerved Marie-Josèphe.

'Your Majesty—' M. Boursin whispered.

'M. de Chrétien, give him—' Louis caught himself. 'M. Boursin, I'll reward you as I promised. You may retire.'

M. Boursin bowed his way from the throne room.

Louis gazed down at Lucien, and for a moment his impassivity failed him.

'Lucien, my valued adviser . . . Who will replace you?'

'No one, Your Majesty.'

Lucien's pride and sorrow moved Marie-Josèphe so deeply that she nearly burst into tears again.

His Majesty called Lorraine to his side. 'Take the sea monster to its cage.'

'Your Majesty!' Marie-Josèphe cried. 'Sherzad gave you a treasure ship.'

'And I give the monster its life.'

'You promised to release her.'

'Do you dare to argue with me?'

'Yes, Your Majesty.'

'I promised not to serve the creature's meat at my banquet. If I cannot grow immortal on its flesh, it must make France immortal with its treasure.'

Sherzad tumbled down the wooden steps and plunged into the Fountain of Apollo. The shock of the fetid water roused her from the daze of her grief song. She thrashed and twisted in the net. As it unwound, as she gained some freedom, she slashed at the cables with her claws.

The mesh fell away into the inadequate current and drifted toward the drain, spreading and creeping like an octopus.

Aching, ravenous, bruised, scraped, she kicked through the surface. She landed, splashing hard. The door of the cage clanged shut and the lock snapped fast. The wings of the tent hung closed. She was alone. Frantic, she scraped at the sides of the pool with her broken claws; she wrenched at the grating over the drain until her hands bled.

She found no escape.

Musketeers took Lucien and Yves away, forbidding Marie-Josèphe to exchange a word with either of them. Two guards marched with Marie-Josèphe to Madame's apartments.

In the dressing room, Madame stood with her arms outstretched. Her ladies in waiting tightened her corset-strings. Mademoiselle had already dressed, in magnificent ecru satin studded with topazes. Haleeda put the finishing touches on her tall ruffled beribboned fontanges.

Haleeda dropped the ribbons and ran to Marie-Josèphe and embraced her wordlessly. Lotte followed. Marie-Josèphe clung to her sister and her friend. Elderflower trotted toward her, snuffling; Youngerflower followed, yapping. They sniffed at the hem of her petticoat. Scenting Sherzad, they barked hysterically.

'Stop it!' Lotte toed the dogs away.

Madame ignored the musketeers while her ladies dressed her in a cloth-of-gold grand habit.

'You may retire,' she said to them.

'But, Madame—'

'Do as I say.'

They glanced at each other; they backed out of the dressing room. No doubt they waited in the vestibule, for even Madame's robust presence could not counter His Majesty's orders.

Madame pressed her cheek against Marie-Josèphe's.

'Oh, my dear,' she said. 'This is worthy of a tragic ballad. The King is furious, and he commands you to attend his banquet.'

'Madame, what am I to do?'

'Obey the King. Sweet child, that's all any of us can do.'

*

Marie-Josèphe helped Haleeda dress Madame's hair, holding hairpins and the few jewels and bits of lace that Madame would allow. She could take no comfort in the ordinary actions. Her hands trembled. The other ladies in waiting whispered about her disobedience and about her bedraggled appearance.

Sherzad is alive, Marie-Josèphe thought. *As long as she is alive . . .*

But she knew her friend would not long survive in the prison of the fountain.

Madame held out her arm. Marie-Josèphe fastened the King's diamond bracelet around her wrist. The tears in her eyes redoubled the brightness of the facets.

'And now,' Madame said, 'what are we to do with you?' She looked Marie-Josèphe up and down, sternly. 'You cannot dine in the King's presence, wearing a muddy dress.'

'Don't tease her, mama,' Lotte said. She led Marie-Josèphe to a wardrobe and flung open the doors.

The gown inside was the most beautiful Marie-Josèphe had ever seen, gleaming silver satin and silver lace, a bodice paved with moonstones.

'Mademoiselle, I cannot—'

'M. de Chrétien sends it, with his compliments.'

I have destroyed him, Marie-Josèphe thought, *and still he treats me with kindness*.

Lotte hugged her and kissed her and gave her hands a hopeful squeeze, then left her alone with Haleeda. Lotte and Madame and their retinue departed, leaving behind the rustle of petticoats, the fragrance of rare perfumes, the echoes of their whispers.

Haleeda pressed a scrap of paper into Marie-Josèphe's hand. Marie-Josèphe unfolded it. She caught her breath when she recognised Lucien's writing.

We will see each other soon. I love you. L.

'Do not cry, Mlle Marie,' Haleeda said. 'Your eyes are red enough already. Sit down, I must comb the rats nests from your hair.'

'Mlle Haleeda, I must send a reply. Do I dare – is it possible?'

'It might be managed,' Haleeda said. 'Count Lucien has many agents.'

I love you, Marie-Josèphe wrote. I love you without boundaries, without limits.

Haleeda whispered to a page boy and sent the note away, then turned her attention to helping Marie-Josèphe into the moonstone gown. The mirror reflected her image, engulfed in silver-grey light.

'It's no more than you deserve,' Haleeda said with satisfaction.

Marie-Josèphe tucked Lucien's note into her bodice.

'Sister,' Haleeda said, 'will you let me dress your hair properly?'

She picked up one of Mademoiselle's several headdresses and held it out to Marie-Josèphe. Marie-Josèphe tried to restrain herself, but at the idea of balancing the tangle of wires and ribbons and lace all evening, she burst out laughing.

'Don't you approve of my creations?' Haleeda asked sternly.

'I'm sorry!' She pressed her hands against her mouth, stifling her laughter. 'Mlle Haleeda, I don't mean—'

And then Haleeda was laughing, too, at the absurd edifices she had designed, at the fashionable ladies who wore them.

Haleeda put down the fontanges. She arranged Marie-Josèphe's hair in a simple style.

'You must wear these.'

Haleeda looped a long string of jewels into Marie-Josèphe's hair.

'Your pearls—!'

'I must have them back,' Haleeda said, 'for they will buy my passage home.'

The source of any gift from Mary of Modena was in truth His Majesty. Marie-Josèphe took some comfort in knowing that if Louis would not free Sherzad, he would contribute to Haleeda's liberty.

The afternoon sun poured through the windows of the Hall of Mirrors, reflecting from the expanse of mirrors with blinding brightness. Rainbow spectra sparkled from crystal chandeliers. The sigil of the King, the golden sunburst, gleamed from every wall. Gods and heroes frolicked and made war on the ceiling.

Long banquet tables crowded the floor; the aristocracy of France and all its allies crowded the tables. The clothes, the food, and particularly the seating at His Majesty's banquet would occupy court gossips for months afterwards, as it no doubt had occupied the Introducer of Ambassadors and his assistants for months beforehand. Music filled the room; orange trees perfumed the air.

'Mlle Marie-Josèphe de la Croix.' The usher announced her. Unescorted, she entered the hall. She walked, alone, dazzled by the light, into a hum of speculation. When her guard appeared, the whispers ceased. She held up her head and glided forward.

They would whisper just as furiously, Marie-Josèphe thought, *because my hair is dressed unfashionably or because I am unescorted, as because I am under guard.*

She almost burst out laughing. Perhaps they were exclaiming over the simple arrangement of her hair. Haleeda's grotesque and fantastical headdresses loomed over all the court's most fashionable women, like a forest of lace towers.

Marie-Josèphe took her isolated place at the farthest end of the banquet table, grateful to be out of the gaze of so many people. She did not want to be here; she wanted to be with Sherzad, with Lucien. Lucien's note rested inside the glowing moonstone bodice, against her breast.

'Father Yves de la Croix.' Yves had put aside the King's medal. A severe sketch in black, he joined Marie-Josèphe. Guards accompanied him.

'Lucien de Barenton, count de Chrétien.'

Lucien entered, the equal of any guest in attire, in demeanour, in pride. He had put aside his blue coat; instead, he wore silver satin and diamonds. He might have been a foreign prince, with a bodyguard of the King's musketeers. His place at the foot of the banquet table, as far from His Majesty as one could be seated, might have been the place of honour.

'You have neglected my footstool,' he said coolly to the lieutenant of his guards.

'I beg your pardon, M. de Chrétien.'

Lucien waited patiently, indifferent to the uneasiness of the musketeers, who must be wondering if they should take orders from their prisoner. His smile to Marie-Josèphe was so luminous, so full of love

401

and humour, that she accepted it as real, not a facade created by his pride.

When the footstool arrived, when Lucien had climbed onto his chair, the guards retreated behind the orange trees. Their tobacco smoke drifted out. Marie-Josèphe envied them.

Yves sat at Lucien's right hand, Marie-Josèphe at his left. Their nearest neighbours edged their chairs away, leaving a no-man's-land. Marie-Josèphe wondered if they would build a wall of candelabra, knives, and salt-cellars.

Marie-Josèphe put her hand over Lucien's.

'Thank you,' she said. 'Thank you for everything. I'm so sorry. I wish—'

He raised her hand and brushed his lips against her fingers; he kissed her palm. Her thoughts tantalised her: *What must it be like to kiss him, if his touch to my hand speeds my heart?*

'It's been too long since my last adventure,' he said.

'Is that the only reason?'

'The reason is, you let me see your spirit, and I love you. Without boundaries. Without limits.'

'I wish we could trade places with them,' Marie-Josèphe said softly, nodding toward the hidden musketeers.

Lucien smiled.

'Control yourself, sister,' Yves said.

Despite Yves' glare, Marie-Josèphe rested her hand against Lucien's cheek. He leaned into her touch, closing his eyes. He shivered.

'Lucien—?'

'Never mind,' he whispered. He straightened up; reluctantly, she dropped her hand.

'You must tell me.'

'You understand my ordinary situation. At times, my situation becomes extraordinary.'

'The cure—?'

'There's no cure for this, but patience.'

The usher announced the visiting monarchs. One after another they entered the Hall of Mirrors and took their places at the high table. The jewels and gold on their costumes weighed them down.

402

Marie-Josèphe caught a glimpse of Queen Mary, moving stiff-necked beneath the weight of an enormous fontanges of gold lace and ribbons, diamonds and silver embroidery. Powder turned her skin dead white, while thin lines of blue paint meandered across her temples and across the curve of her breasts, following her veins, accentuating her paleness.

'His Holiness Pope Innocent, Prince of Rome.'

Innocent turned away from the high table. The usher, horrified, looked around frantically for assistance, found none, ran after Innocent and whispered, received a quiet answer, stopped and bowed and backed away. Slowly, proceeding through the silence of shock, Innocent approached Marie-Josèphe. She rose and curtsied; he allowed her to kiss his ring. Yves knelt before him. Lucien remained where he was.

'Bring another chair.'

'Your Holiness!' Yves exclaimed.

Innocent's command jarred the stunned servants to obedience. Yves seated Pope Innocent in his own place and took the new chair in the no-man's-land at Innocent's right hand. While the guests marvelled in horror at the Pope's breach of etiquette, servants rearranged the high table, whisking away Innocent's place and leaving the King's gold setting in the centre. The usher looked faint.

'His Majesty, Louis the Great, King of France and Navarre, the Most Christian King.'

Everyone rose; everyone bowed. His Majesty, in cloth-of-gold, rubies, and diamonds, took his place without acknowledging that something terrible had happened. He gazed down the Hall of Mirrors, impassive. One moment of his glance raked Marie-Josèphe, and her brother, and Lucien, and pierced His Holiness.

'Your Holiness . . .' Yves said. 'Your place—'

'Our Saviour ministered to lepers. Can I do less?' Innocent regarded Lucien. 'Though Our Saviour was not required to traffic with atheists.'

Marie-Josèphe blushed with anger at the insult.

'If He had,' Lucien said, 'no doubt He would have been gracious about it.'

403

'You are gracious, Your Holiness,' Yves said quickly, 'to share our dishonour.'

'My royal cousin is very angry,' Innocent replied.

'We deprived him of a meal,' Marie-Josèphe exclaimed. 'To keep him from committing murder.'

'We feared for his soul, Your Holiness,' Yves said.

'Perhaps you've protected a demon,' Innocent said, addressing Yves. 'Or perhaps you deprived my cousin of immortality.'

'Sherzad cannot give anyone immortality, Your Holiness,' Marie-Josèphe said. 'Only God can do that.'

Innocent ignored her, ignored her impudence. 'You claimed the sea monster's flesh had the power—'

'I lied,' Yves said miserably. 'God forgive me, I lied. I made no tests, Your Holiness. The truth doesn't matter—'

'Yves, how can you say such a thing?' Marie-Josèphe exclaimed.

'All that matters is what the King believes.'

'And he believes in immortality, because you told him it was true. Now he'll wonder, he'll be tempted – he'll break his word and kill her.'

Lucien met her gaze, but he said nothing.

I hoped he would deny it, Marie-Josèphe thought. *I hoped he would say, His Majesty never breaks his word. Even if he rebuked me, I'd know Sherzad would live.*

'You could save Sherzad, Your Holiness,' Marie-Josèphe said. 'You're revered for correcting the Church's errors, for stopping the corruption—'

'Be quiet!' Yves cried.

'Allow me a moment of praise, Father de la Croix,' Innocent said. 'Allow me to indulge in a moment's sin of pride. I did stop corruption.'

'I beg your pardon, Your Holiness.'

'God gave us beasts to use, the devil to oppose, and pagans to convert. Which is the monster?'

'She's a woman.'

'I am not speaking to you, Mlle de la Croix. Father de la Croix, the monster claims death is everlasting.'

'Your Holiness,' Yves said carefully, 'would a beast understand death?'

'If devils existed,' Lucien said, 'surely they'd affirm life after death, Heaven and Hell. Otherwise, where would they live?'

Fighting her urge to giggle, Marie-Josèphe dared to speak to the Pope again. 'Your Holiness, you could teach Sherzad about everlasting life.'

'Stop meddling, Signorina.' Impatience and anger tinged Innocent's voice. 'Women must be submissive, obedient – and quiet. It is God's will.'

Lucien leaned toward Innocent, making a sharp, angry gesture. He froze; when he recovered himself, even his lips had paled. Marie-Josèphe feared he might faint.

'If you believe in your God,' Lucien said, his voice harsh, 'then you must accept that He made Marie-Josèphe de la Croix both audacious and brave.'

'You—' Innocent said. 'You and the creature both are unnatural!'

The disc of the sun touched the western horizon. The light turned scarlet, filling the Hall, blazing from the wall of mirrors like fire, streaming all over with blood.

Chapter 28

The Spanish treasure arrived, heavily guarded. The wagons passed, creaking with the weight of gold. Marie-Josèphe sat on the steps of Sherzad's prison, imprisoned herself. Guards watched the tent; they watched her rooms; instead of taking their ease when she arrived to visit Sherzad, they intensified their vigilance.

She could have escaped at night though her window and over the roof, as Lucien had shown her, but once she escaped she would have nowhere to go. If she escaped, Sherzad would be alone. If she escaped, Lucien would be left behind.

The sea woman lay with her head in Marie-Josèphe's lap. The spreading ulcer on her shoulder oozed. The bites on her ankle remained raw. She fasted, in silence.

'Please, Sherzad, listen. If you give His Majesty more treasure, perhaps he'll relent . . .' Her voice trailed off. She could not make herself believe the King would free her friend. She certainly could not convince Sherzad.

'Mlle de la Croix.'

At the musketeer's approach, Sherzad slipped away from Marie-Josèphe and submerged. She lay underwater, face up, staring blankly, waiting to die.

'Come with me.' The guard unlocked the cage to let Marie-Josèphe out, and locked it again behind her.

To her surprise, Zachi waited for her. The mare nuzzled her, accepting her caresses.

I expect everything to be taken from me, Marie-Josèphe thought, *even Zachi. Sherzad's life, my brother's affection, my sister's companionship. And Lucien.*

She had not seen Lucien since the end of the banquet, which despite the lack of sea monster flesh had been a wonder, stretching past sunset, when the servants whisked away the flowers from the candle-stands and replaced them with candelabra, and beyond midnight, when the servants replaced the guttering candles and carried in another course. Marie-Josèphe had not been able to eat a bite.

At the end of the banquet, His Majesty gave the Chevalier de Lorraine a purse of a thousand gold louis. In Lucien's place, the Chevalier rewarded M. Boursin.

At the same time, guards bowed courteously to Lucien and ushered him away.

'Don't worry,' he said.

She had done nothing else. She mounted Zachi. The mare pranced, offering to run, offering to outdistance the plodding mounts of the King's guard. Marie-Josèphe stroked her neck and calmed her. Zachi might carry her over the rooftops of Versailles, but she still had nowhere to go.

The musketeers escorted her to the top of the garden and into the chateau.

She gasped when she entered His Majesty's council room. The King sat surrounded by bars of silver and gold bullion, by chests of gold coins, by heaps of jewelled chains.

The King played with a heavy golden chalice. Marie-Josèphe curtsied; she knelt before him.

'What does your monster say?'

'Nothing, Sire. She won't sing, she won't eat. Her death will be on your hands if you don't let her go.'

'Many deaths are on my hands, Mlle de la Croix.'

'Deliberate murder? We saved you from that, Lucien and Yves and I. We saved your soul.'

'Why do you persist in this delusion?' he cried.

'My friend Sherzad is dying of despair.'

'Beasts know nothing of despair. If the sea monster doesn't please me, I might as well give it to my cousin's holy Inquisitors.'

He put down the chalice. He wore dark brown and black, with only a little gold lace.

He offered Marie-Josèphe his hand. She took it and let him raise her to her feet, as if they were back on the floating platform in the Grand Canal, about to dance.

'Or I could eat it, which would be a kinder fate.'

Marie-Josèphe wanted to cry, You promised! You're a great King, how can you break your word, how can you betray me, and Sherzad, and break Lucien's heart?

'Your Majesty,' she said, as calmly as she could, 'you have the power to destroy her. To destroy me, and my brother, and Lucien, who loves you.'

'Do you say you do not love me, Mlle de la Croix?'

'Not as Lucien does.'

'He loves you more.'

'I know it, Your Majesty. It doesn't mean he loves you less. Please, Your Majesty, is he all right?'

'He lives.'

'You haven't—'

'I've done nothing but ferret his men out of my guard. Why should I trouble myself? His body tortures him.'

'May I see him?'

'I will see.'

'Sire, you have the power to show mercy to us all.'

'You're even more stubborn than your mother!'

Marie-Josèphe's outrage exploded. 'She—you—my mother submitted to you entirely!'

'She refused . . .'

Marie-Josèphe watched, in amazement, as his expression grew sad and his eyes filled with tears.

'She refused everything I wished to give her.' He turned away until he recovered his dispassionate expression. 'Come with me. Persuade her to carry out my will.'

For an eerie moment, Marie-Josèphe thought the King meant to refer to her mother.

His Holiness stood beside the cage. He sprinkled holy water through the bars. He chanted, in Latin, a rite of exorcism.

'Cast off your pagan ways,' he said. 'Accept the teachings of the Church, and you will receive everlasting life.'

Sherzad snarled.

'If you defy me, your soul will never rest.'

Marie-Josèphe ran to the cage. 'Let me in!'

Agitated, wild, Sherzad swam back and forth. Louis pushed himself from his wheeled chair. The musketeer unlocked the cage. Marie-Josèphe dashed in ahead of the King, oblivious to etiquette or simple manners.

'Sherzad, be easy, dear Sherzad—'

'Don't interfere, Signorina de la Croix,' Innocent said. 'You ignore my counsel at your peril!'

Marie-Josèphe ran down to the platform, while His Majesty remained at the top of the stairs.

Sherzad saw him. She shrieked.

'Sherzad, no!'

The sea woman propelled herself toward Marie-Josèphe. She swam with desperate speed. She launched herself, snarling, her claws extended, straight toward the King. Marie-Josèphe flung herself at Sherzad. They crashed together and fell in a heap. The edge of the stairs knocked the wind out of Marie-Josèphe. Sherzad lay in her arms. Blood poured from a splintery gouge across her forehead. Marie-Josèphe tried to stop the bleeding. Her hands, her dress, turned scarlet.

'Suicide is a mortal sin,' Innocent said. 'She must vow obedience and repent before she dies, or I'll know her for a demon.'

Marie-Josèphe looked up at the two men, the holy man who thought Sherzad had tried to kill herself, and the King who must believe she had tried to murder him. Perhaps they were both right.

Sherzad raised herself and sang furiously. Blood streaked her face. She looked like a monster.

'What did she say?'

Marie-Josèphe hesitated.

'Tell me!'

'She said – forgive her, Your Majesty – she said, "Toothless sharks amuse me". She said, "Will a fleet of treasure ships buy my life?" '

'Where?'

'She'll tell me – after you free her.'

'With what assurance?'

'Mine, Your Majesty.'

She thought he would dismiss her, call her a thief, accuse her of lying.

'You do not ask me for leniency? For yourself, for your brother, for your lover?'

Marie-Josèphe hesitated, then shook her head. 'No, Your Majesty.'

Sherzad thrashed in the basin, splashing water through the net that restrained her. She cried and struggled, smelling the sea, desperate to reach it.

'Sherzad, dear friend, don't injure yourself.' Marie-Josèphe worked her hand through the rough mesh so she could touch and comfort the sea woman.

Marie-Josèphe sat beside Sherzad's basin, under a canvas canopy on the main deck of His Majesty's flagship. On the upper deck, the King sat in a velvet armchair, shaded by tapestry. He spoke a word to the captain, who shouted to his men. The sailors burst into activity, preparing the ship to sail.

The flagship's skiff cast off from the dock and rowed toward them. Marie-Josèphe whispered encouragement to Sherzad. She tugged her hand free of the net. The skiff came alongside. Lucien, elegant in white satin and gold lace, handed his sword-cane up the side and climbed the ladder to the deck. Marie-Josèphe ran to him; she caught his hands, fine and strong in deerskin gloves. No one would ever guess he had come straight from prison.

'Lucien, my love—'

'Pardon me,' he said. He walked unsteadily to the leeward rail and was sick over the side.

'The ship hasn't even raised anchor!' Marie-Josèphe said. She brought him some water. He did not drink, but splashed it on his face.

The anchor cable groaned around the capstan. The sails fell open; the wind whipped them taut.

'It has now,' Lucien said, and leaned over the side again.

'My poor friend,' she said. 'You'll feel better soon.'

'No, I won't,' Lucien said. The ship rolled a few degrees. He groaned. 'I wish I were on the battlefield . . . in the rain . . .

410

unhorsed . . . without my sword. I wish His Majesty had left me in the Bastille.'

'How can you say that!'

'Do me the kindness,' he said, 'of leaving me alone.'

On the rough crossing from Martinique, many of Marie-Josèphe's fellow passengers had been seasick, but none with the marvellous sensitivity of Lucien. The galleon sailed through calm coastal waters with barely enough breeze to make headway, but Lucien's illness intensified. Marie-Josèphe worried as much about him as she worried about Sherzad. The King showed no sympathy for either of them. Even when the ship sat pitching and yawing at anchor all day while the skiff searched for Sherzad's rocks, Louis showed no impatience. Marie-Josèphe became convinced that he found malicious enjoyment in stripping Lucien of his position and his blue coat and subjecting him to misery.

She tried, unsuccessfully, to coax Sherzad to eat a fish; she tried, unsuccessfully, to persuade Lucien to drink some broth.

The captain came to her under her canopy. He bowed.

'My respects, mamselle, and His Majesty demands your presence.'

In the King's luxurious cabin, Marie-Josèphe curtsied.

'Where is this treasure you promised me?' he said.

She fancied that the King felt sick because of the ship's slow erratic dance, and she felt glad of it.

'Your Majesty, Sherzad can't see the ocean from the deck. Please free her. If she can hear the ocean properly, she'll lead me to the right cove.'

'I will see,' His Majesty said.

Sometimes he meant it, but all too often he meant to refuse but did not care to say it. It was pointless to try to change his mind. Marie-Josèphe curtsied again. The King turned away, dismissing her.

'Your Majesty,' she said, pausing in the hatchway. 'M. de Chrétien's of no use to you here. Put him ashore, send him back to Versailles—'

'Where he has too many friends!' His Majesty exclaimed. 'He'll stay here, in my sight, until you find the treasure.'

Marie-Josèphe fled. She understood: His Majesty held Lucien

411

hostage to illness on the flagship, he held Yves hostage under guard at the chateau, until Marie-Josèphe succeeded and the King returned safe to his court.

On deck, she bathed Lucien's face with a wet cloth.

'I don't like you to see me this way,' he said.

'You saw me after the surgeon bled me,' Marie-Josèphe said. 'If I only stand with you during good times, what kind of a friend would I be?'

He managed to smile. 'You're a friend without boundaries.'

'And without limits,' she said. She took his hand. As yet, they had done no more than touch each other's hands. She wondered what would happen when they could do more.

My heart can hardly beat faster, she thought.

'Are you otherwise recovered?' she asked. 'From your extraordinary situation?'

'There's something to be said for sea-sickness.'

'What's that?'

'It takes one's mind off one's other misfortunes.'

His Majesty's guards approached Sherzad's basin. One carried a musket, another a club. Sailors followed with a net and a coil of rope.

Marie-Josèphe leaped up. 'What are you doing? She enjoys His Majesty's protection!'

'It's His Majesty gave the orders, mamselle,' the lieutenant said. 'Stay back, now.'

'Are you freeing her?' Marie-Josèphe cried, amazed, overwhelmed. 'You needn't threaten her.' She sang to Sherzad, joyously, a simple child's song. 'Lie quiet, Sherzad, as you did when they freed you into the Grand Canal. The King is keeping his word!'

Sherzad obeyed restlessly. The sailors loosened the net and used it as a sling. Sherzad's hair was dull and tangled, her eyes sunken, the swellings on her face deflated and venous. Pallor greyed her mahogany skin; her wounds were red and swollen.

Marie-Josèphe followed Sherzad. The sailors carried her to the bow. Sherzad growled and hummed and trembled.

'Farewell.' Farewell, she sang, her voice breaking.

Instead of opening the net, the sailors tightened it, holding Sherzad fast, pinioning her arms, restraining her clawed feet. Sherzad screamed. Marie-Josèphe cried out in protest and seized the net. The mesh ripped her skin.

A musketeer grabbed her and pulled her away, indifferent to her struggles. Dazed with illness and lack of sustenance, Lucien staggered to his feet and drew his sword. He tripped one of the guards with his cane and stumbled toward Marie-Josèphe.

The lieutenant aimed his pistol at Marie-Josèphe's head.

'Surrender,' he said to Lucien.

Lucien stopped. He put down his useless sword and raised his hands. A sailor shoved him to the deck. Incredulous, Lucien tried to rise. A cutlass grazed his throat. Marie-Josèphe kicked the lieutenant's knee. He cursed and flung her down. She crawled toward Sherzad, dizzy from the fall.

Lucien's sword-cane rolled across the deck and bumped against Marie-Josèphe's hand. She snatched it up and scrabbled to her feet, flailing around her with the sword. The musketeers backed away, laughing. She barely noticed the pistol aimed at her.

'Stop or he dies!' the lieutenant shouted.

A drop of blood flowed down Lucien's neck, staining his white shirt.

Marie-Josèphe and Lucien were overpowered, outnumbered, each held hostage for the other's safety.

Marie-Josèphe lowered the sword, defeated and betrayed. In a fury she jerked away when the musketeer took her arm. She could only watch as the sailors slung Sherzad between the arms of the golden figurehead and left her hanging beneath the bowsprit. The guards lowered musket and sabre, and allowed Lucien to rise.

'Now she can see and hear the ocean.' His Majesty took Lucien's sword from Marie-Josèphe's hand. 'You gave me your parole, M. de Chrétien.' The King grounded the sword's tip and stamped his boot on the Damascan steel. The sword rebounded. The edge gouged the deck. The King stamped again. His expression grim, he attacked a third time. The steel snapped. Lucien never flinched and never looked away.

His Majesty flung the handle to the deck, and kicked the broken blade over the side.

Sherzad hung suspended in the net. The ropes cut cruelly into her breasts and hips; the figurehead's absurd bosom pressed painfully against her back. The salt spray cleansed and revived her. She opened her mouth to take it onto her tongue, the taste and smell of her home.

She was dying. She did not want to die.

She kept her silence all afternoon, refusing to reply to Marie-Josèphe, refusing to direct the ship. As night approached, she sang. Her voice was hoarse and ugly.

'She agrees! She'll take us to the cove!' Marie-Josèphe, foolish trusting Marie-Josèphe, interpreted.

The sun touched the horizon. Sherzad sang, listening to the shape of the sea-bottom as best she could. The wind hesitated, in the moment of calm between day and night, and shifted as dark fell. The ship's captain argued against sailing blind so close to shore. The toothless shark, the King, commanded him to obey.

The ship plunged through the water. Sherzad trilled with excitement and fear.

A jagged stone reached from the sea bottom and seized the ship, grinding along its keel. Timbers crashed and splintered. Sherzad lurched against the net. The rough cables cut her skin.

But they did not break, they did not free her. The ship hung stranded, the captain shouted in fury, Marie-Josèphe cried out in shock. Sherzad laughed, wild and terrible, ready to die, for her plot had failed.

They left her hanging before the figurehead as the waning moon followed the sun into the sea.

Chapter 29

Marie-Josèphe huddled miserably on deck, a blanket around her shoulders. She had tried to persuade Louis that Sherzad had not deliberately run the ship aground. She did not believe it herself, so her protestations only convinced the King she knew what Sherzad had planned.

What does he expect, she wondered, *but betrayal for betrayal?*

One good thing had come of the stranding. As the tide went out and the flagship settled, the groan of insulted timber replaced the erratic pitching. Lucien slept for the first time since the voyage began. His white-gold hair gleamed in the starlight. To Marie-Josèphe's great relief, the sword cut on his throat was neither deep nor long.

Nothing had changed. The ship was not badly damaged. The captain said it would float free at high tide.

And then what? Marie-Josèphe wondered. *They'll never trust Sherzad to guide them, they'll never trust me. Will they torture her, or kill her, or return her to Versailles and give her to Pope Innocent?*

A quiet song floated through the night. Sherzad sang a lullaby that the sea people sing to their babies.

Marie-Josèphe matched her voice to Sherzad's. Dew collected in droplets on the blanket and on her hair and on the ship's gleaming paint and gilt.

Nearly asleep, Marie-Josèphe caught herself. She raised her head, fully awake, singing softly.

The guard near the bow nodded, caught himself, checked his pistol, nodded again. He had orders to shoot Sherzad if she tried to escape. He nodded a third time. He snored.

Marie-Josèphe slipped from beneath the blanket. She stealthily picked up Lucien's sword-cane and twisted its handle. The sound of

415

its release was as loud as the crash of the ship against the rock. Yet no one responded.

She drew the broken blade. A handsbreadth of steel remained, its edge transparently sharp. In her stocking feet, singing the soothing lullaby, Marie-Josèphe crept across the deck. She passed the guard and climbed onto the bowsprit. She crept along it, afraid the rustling of her petticoat, or her awkwardness in her long skirts, would awaken the guard. Sherzad's song charmed him into sleep. The sea woman's song enfolded her.

Sherzad's eyes gleamed red.

'Carry my life in your heart,' Marie-Josèphe whispered.

She slipped the broken blade beneath a cord of the net. The cord parted at the touch of the steel. She cut another cable, and a third. The sword was never meant to slice through cable. The harsh mesh dulled it quickly. She sawed harder. Sherzad grew excited, agitated, writhing, pushing her foot through the hole in the net, tearing at the mesh with her claws. Sherzad's song faltered and dissolved into a moan. Behind them, the musketeer snorted and woke.

'No!' he cried.

Sherzad shrieked in triumph. She burst through the net and tumbled into the sea. A pistol ball screamed past Marie-Josèphe's ear and sizzled into the water. Marie-Josèphe caught her breath and clutched the broken sword in one hand, the bowsprit in the other. She gazed into the darkness, terrified that Sherzad had been hit.

A splash sprayed Marie-Josèphe's face with cool salty droplets. Sherzad laughed, cried a challenge, and vanished.

The ship creaked and shifted. Marie-Josèphe clung to the bowsprit, shaken, intoxicated.

'Come onto the deck, Mlle de la Croix.'

She obeyed the King, crawling backwards, embarrassed that His Majesty and his men could see her legs all the way to her knees. When she reached the deck and turned around, two musketeers held their pistols on her; three sailors stood ready with pikes.

'Give His Majesty my sword, if you please.' Lucien was bareheaded, unperturbed, wide awake. 'Pass it hilt first.'

Her life, perhaps Lucien's, depended on capitulation without

416

threat, even with a broken sword. She did as Lucien said. Louis accepted her surrender.

The sailors led Marie-Josèphe away.

Shut up in the locker with the slimy seaweed-covered anchor chain, Marie-Josèphe lost track of time. She thought it must be day again, then night; but when the ship shifted and moaned beneath her, she knew it was only dawn.

Have they left the ship to break up on the rocks? she wondered. She hoped they had taken Lucien away with them. Anyone who disliked the sea so intensely should not have to drown.

The pumps groaned and rushed. The ship floated free. As the ship settled into the water, Sherzad's voice travelled through the sea and touched the planks, resounding like a drum. Astonished, overjoyed, Marie-Josèphe replied. Sherzad spoke again, begging her to answer. *Hurry, hurry,* she cried, *I cannot bear to wait for you much longer.*

Desperate, Marie-Josèphe pounded on the bulkhead until her scratched hands bruised.

The hatch opened. Light poured in, dazzling her.

'Stop that noise.' The King stood before her. 'You've exhausted my patience three times over.'

'Can't you hear her? I freed her — she'll keep her promise, she'll lead me to your treasure.'

'I hear nothing. She has disappeared.'

'Shh. Listen.'

The King listened in sceptical silence. The ship rocked and complained around them; the pumps rumbled. Beneath the noise, Sherzad sang in a delicate low register.

'She promises. She says, "The sand is covered with gold and jewels." She gives them to you, for my sake, despite your betrayals and your broken promises. Afterwards . . . she declares war on the men of land.'

'I wonder,' Louis said, 'if she's declared war on you.'

The King would never forgive her, treasure or not. Nor could Lucien hope to return to his proper place in the King's esteem. Marie-Josèphe wondered if Lucien would ever forgive her.

On deck, Lucien peered into the dawn brilliance of the sea,

searching for Sherzad. He had locked his dulled and broken sword in its sheath. He leaned on it and grasped the rail as well, preparing for seasickness.

Marie-Josèphe joined him.

Lucien glanced up. 'You are perfectly magnificent.'

She sank down beside him and took his hand.

The captain bowed to His Majesty. 'The ship may return to Le Havre, Your Majesty,' he said, 'but I can't answer for any hard sailing.'

Marie-Josèphe searched the horizon and the silver sparks of sunlight. She called Sherzad, but heard no answer. *She's out there*, Marie-Josèphe thought. *It's so hard to find anything on the whole wide sea—*

'Very well,' His Majesty said. 'Return to Le Havre.'

A distant splash marred the perfect pattern of the surface of the sea. 'There!' Marie-Josèphe cried. 'She's there.'

'It's only a fish,' the captain muttered. If the lure of treasure could not overcome his fears, the will of the King did. The captain sailed his ship in pursuit of Sherzad, though he set a sailor on the bow with a sounding-line. When Sherzad led them to a cove, he refused to take the ship inside.

'It's treacherous, Your Majesty,' he said. 'Look at the chart, the wind. We'd go in. We'd never come out.'

Marie-Josèphe fidgeted unhappily while the sailors lowered the skiff. They objected to her presence, even to Lucien's, but the King climbed into the skiff and commanded Marie-Josèphe to accompany him, and he said nothing when Lucien climbed down the ladder too.

He believes my friend will be even more miserable in a smaller boat, Marie-Josèphe thought uncharitably. To her relief, Lucien's discomfort eased.

The sailors rowed nervously after Sherzad. They whispered to each other, when they thought their passengers could not hear. They were afraid of Sherzad, afraid of more duplicity, afraid of ambush. Marie-Josèphe could not blame them. What's more, she would not have blamed Sherzad if the sea woman fulfilled the sailor's fears.

She caught only an occasional glimpse of the sea woman. Sherzad was frightened, too, of nets and guns, of explosive charges to stun her back into captivity. She hovered by the mouth of the cove, ready to flee at any threat.

In dangerous water among submerged fingers of stone, Marie-Josèphe stopped the skiff. At the mouth of the cove, Sherzad leaped from the water, flicked her tails in the air, dove, and disappeared.

'Here,' Marie-Josèphe said.

Sailors stripped and splashed over the side.

'Send all your men into the water.'

'Your Majesty,' the captain said, 'the rest cannot swim. They must keep their strength – and their lives – to row us back.'

His Majesty acceded with reluctant grace. 'Very well.'

The divers submerged, and ascended, and vanished again. Soon they were shivering. One surfaced coughing and half drowned. Louis allowed him five minutes' rest.

'The sea monster has played you an ugly trick, Mlle de la Croix,' the King said.

'The treasure fleet is here,' Marie-Josèphe said.

'Dive again,' the King said to the exhausted sailor.

Marie-Josèphe sang to Sherzad, asking for more direction. She received no answer.

'She's gone. Perhaps I'll never see her again.' She wept. Only the touch of Lucien's hand kept her heart from breaking.

As far away as she could see, a tiny splash burst from the ocean, and another, and a third, all in a group. Suddenly frightened, Marie-Josèphe trembled.

The exhausted sailor splashed through the surface, thrashing, kicking, shouting incoherently. His mates surfaced with him. The rowers thrust pikes and oars over the side, fearing sharks.

'For His Majesty's glory!'

The divers raised their arms. The weight of handsful of gold and jewels pushed them back underwater. They struggled to the skiff and poured their treasures in a heap before the King.

A closed carriage drove Marie-Josèphe and Lucien to Versailles, at the end of a procession of wagons filled with treasure. His Majesty led in an open caleche. Aztec gold covered him like armour and decked the harness of his horses and spilled out to the wheels. A hundred musketeers guarded the convoy. People lined the road and cheered their King and stared at the treasure in wonder.

Marie-Josèphe peeked past the heavy curtain. Dust and shouts filtered into the carriage.

'He must admit he was wrong,' Marie-Josèphe said. 'And we were right.'

'No,' Lucien said. 'Right, wrong – what's important is that we defied him.'

'But that's nonsense.'

'He can't afford to forgive us.' Lucien sighed theatrically. 'I accept His Majesty's wrath . . . as long as he doesn't sentence us to the galleys – and send us to sea for the rest of our lives.'

Marie-Josèphe managed to return his smile. Lucien twisted the handle of his sword-cane and drew the broken blade.

'It served me well,' he said.

'And Sherzad. And me.'

He sheathed it and locked it. In the dimness of the carriage, his clear grey gaze touched Marie-Josèphe as gently as he had held her hand.

Marie-Josèphe moved from her side of the carriage to his. She took his hand, drew off his glove, and removed his rings. She hesitated when she reached the heavy sapphire, but he did not stop her. She slipped His Majesty's ring from Lucien's finger. She pressed her cheek against his palm.

They leaned toward each other. They kissed.

Marie-Josèphe drew back, touching her lips with her fingertips, amazed that such a simple touch could reach all the way to her centre.

Misinterpreting her surprise, Lucien smiled sadly. 'Even your kiss can't change me to a tall prince, with dainty feet.'

'If it did, I'd say, Where is Lucien? Give me back my Lucien!'

He laughed, with no trace of sadness.

Guards took Lucien away as soon as the carriage reached the chateau. They conducted Marie-Josèphe to her attic room and left her with only Hercules for company. If Yves was in his bedroom she could not speak to him through two locked doors and the dressing-room.

Hercules miaowed for cream, despite the mouse stomachs and mouse tails left over from his hunts.

'You may ask for cream in prison,' Marie-Josèphe said, 'but you may hope prison rats are tasty.'

She comforted herself with her last sight of Sherzad, leaping with joy in the sea, and with her memory of Lucien's kiss.

His Majesty will forgive us, she thought. *He'll forgive me because I was right, and because he loved my mother. He'll forgive Yves because Yves is his son. And he'll forgive Lucien because he never had a better friend, a friend who defied him once, to help him.*

She spared no more thoughts for the soul of Louis the Great.

The key turned in the lock; the door opened. Marie-Josèphe leaped to her feet, her heart pounding.

A scullery maid slipped inside, put down a tray laden with wine and bread and a pitcher of cream, and faced her. Haleeda had put away her finery and tied a cloth over her hair.

Marie-Josèphe flung herself into Haleeda's arms.

No one who took a second look at her could ever mistake her for a scullery maid, Marie-Josèphe thought. *But . . . no one at Versailles ever takes a second look — or a first — at a scullery maid.*

They sat together on the window seat. Hercules butted his head against Haleeda's hand until she gave him his cream.

'What are you doing here?' Marie-Josèphe whispered. 'If His Majesty finds out, he'll be angry—'

'I don't mind, I don't care,' Haleeda said, 'for I'm leaving Versailles, leaving Paris, leaving France in a moment. As soon as I change these awful clothes!' She grew sombre. 'I cannot help you, Mlle Marie, but I had to see you.'

'I've failed you, sister.' Marie-Josèphe took the parchment of Haleeda's manumission from her drawing box and gazed at it sadly. 'I never had a moment to ask Yves to sign it. To make him sign it!'

Haleeda took the parchment. 'He'll sign it.' She kissed Marie-Josèphe. 'I'm sorry I cannot free you.'

421

'Only the King can do that. Sister, I'm so afraid for you. Where will you go? What will you do?'

'Never fear. I am rich, I will be free. I can make my way in the world. I'll go home to Turkey. I'll find my family, and a prince.'

'Turkey! When you marry they'll put you in a hareem, with another wife—'

Haleeda sat back and regarded her quizzically. 'Sister, how is it different from France, except that my sister wives will be acknowledged instead of hidden and lied about and put aside at whim?'

'But it—I—' She fell silent, unable to answer, terrified for her sister.

'How is it different from Martinique?' Haleeda said.

The blood drained from Marie-Josèphe's face, leaving her cold and faint.

'Oh,' she said. 'Sister, do you mean—'

'I mean we are sisters – how could you not know? Our father owned my mother, she was his, he did as he pleased, without a thought to what would please her. Or what would horrify her.'

Marie-Josèphe's shoulders slumped. She stared at her hands, limp in her lap.

'Do you hate him terribly? Did she? Do you hate me?'

'I don't hate him. It is fate. I love you, Mlle Marie, though I'll never see you again.'

'I love you too, Mlle Haleeda, even if I never see you again.'

Haleeda pressed a knotted kerchief into Marie-Josèphe's hand.

'Your pearls!'

'Not all of them! We promised to share our fortunes. I must go.'

They kissed each other. Haleeda slipped out the door. She was gone, to embrace an unknown fate that frightened Marie-Josèphe even more than her own.

Lucien dreaded the approaching interview. The King was too angry with him, too disappointed, to put his fate in the hands of his guards or his jailers. Lucien had every material thing he wanted, clean linen and food and wine. He was treated with scrupulous courtesy. His back hurt only in its ordinary way.

He had everything but liberty, communication, the comfort of intimacy. He hung suspended at a great height, waiting only for Louis to let him fall. He hoped he would not take Marie-Josèphe with him to the depths.

The musketeers took Lucien to the guard room outside His Majesty's private chamber, where Marie-Josèphe and Yves already waited.

How strange, Lucien thought. *The joy of seeing her is equal to the ecstasy of her touch*.

He took her hand. Together, they went to face the King.

Treasure filled the room, stacked and tumbled in heaps like an ancient dragon's hoard. Gold bracelets and pectorals and armour lay in jumbled piles, with headdresses, medallions, and strange flared cylinders. Impassive jade statues clustered on the parquet. One of them eerily resembled Lucien's father.

His Majesty gazed into the eye sockets of a crystal skull. Pope Innocent sat beside him, indifferent to the treasure, counting a rosary of ordinary beads. The beads tapped against a wooden box in his lap: Marie-Josèphe's drawing box. A table piled with books and papers stood beside him.

The King picked up a gold pectoral, lowered it over his head, and arranged the curls of his black wig. The wide flare of gold covered his chest.

The strange eyes of gold statues stared from every direction. Louis regarded his prisoners in silence.

'I loved you all.' To Marie-Josèphe he said, 'You pleased me with your beauty and your charm and your music.' To Yves he said, 'I marvelled at your discoveries. I was proud to be your sire.' After a long pause, he turned to Lucien. 'I valued your wit, your bravery, your loyalty. I valued the truth you told me.'

He flung the skull to the floor. 'You betrayed me.' The crystal smashed. Shards exploded across the parquet.

'Father de la Croix.'

'Yes.' Yves cleared his throat. 'Yes, Your Majesty.'

'I give you to His Holiness, and I command you to obey him without question.'

423

'Yes, Your Majesty,' Yves whispered.

'Mlle de la Croix.'

'Yes, Your Majesty.' Her voice was as strong and as pure as the sea woman's song.

'You've offended me and my holy cousin as well. You must accept punishment from us both.'

'Yes, Your Majesty.'

Innocent made her wait until he had finished the rosary.

'I forbid you this ridiculous desire to compose music,' Innocent said. 'Not to save your modesty, for you are lost, but as a punishment. You must be silent.'

Marie-Josèphe stared at the floor.

'Very well,' Louis said. 'Though it's a shame, for she might have been very good if she were a man. Mlle de la Croix, my punishment is this. You desire a husband, and children. I thought to forbid these to you, to send you to a convent.'

Marie-Josèphe paled.

I'll break it down, Lucien thought. *I'll lay siege to the walls as if it were a prison, an enemy city in war—*

'But that is too simple a solution,' Louis said.

He turned away from Marie-Josèphe and addressed himself to Lucien.

'You will leave court.'

I was right not to hope for a lesser punishment, Lucien thought.

'You will resign the governorship of Brittany to M. du Maine. You will resign your title and your lands to your brother.'

Lucien's plans for the good of his family trembled in his hands.

'And you will marry Mlle de la Croix. You may live on the dowry I promised her. If you do not give her children, you will break her heart. If you do give her children, you will dishonour your sworn word, to the woman you love – as you dishonoured it to me.'

'Yes, Your Majesty.' Lucien's pride finally failed him. He could barely speak.

'I've condescended to spare your lives – but I wish never to see any of you again.' He nodded graciously to Innocent. 'Here is your priest, cousin.'

'Did the sea woman repent?' Innocent asked.

424

'No, Your Holiness.'

'She declared war on the men of land,' Marie-Josèphe said. 'And then she disappeared.'

'I should excommunicate you all.'

Yves fell to his knees.

'I shall not. Father de la Croix, you will have use for your priestly authority. Holy Mother Church faces a terrible threat. The sea monsters—'

'They're people, Your Holiness!' Marie-Josèphe said.

'Yes,' said Innocent.

Lucien was as surprised as Marie-Josèphe and Yves, that the holy man would admit something so damaging to his influence.

'Your Holiness,' Yves said, 'they're nearly extinct because of the Church. Instead of offering them the word of God—'

'That is why—'

'—we tormented them as demons—'

'—history must be—'

'—and we preyed on them as cattle. I—' Yves cut off his words when he realised he had interrupted Innocent.

'—corrected.' Innocent nodded. 'History must be corrected,' he said again.

Innocent opened the drawing box. He drew out a handful of pages: Marie-Josèphe's dissection sketches. He crumpled one. He thrust its edge into the candle flame. It burned to his fingers. He dropped the ashes in a golden Aztec dish.

'Father de la Croix, your penance is this. You will search out every mention of the sea monsters.'

He snatched M. Boursin's book from the table beside him, and flung it to the floor.

'Every book.'

He scattered a sheaf of letters, the current prize of the King's Black Cabinet, waiting to be read, many addressed by Madame's bold handwriting.

'Every letter.'

He ripped a handful of pages from the current volume of M. de Dangeau's journal.

'Every chronicle of this self-indulgent celebration of the monsters. This week of Carrousel must vanish utterly.'

He flung down a handful of broadsheets, the Stories of Sherzad.

'Every painting, every myth, every memory of the creatures. The decree of the Church that raised them from demons to beasts.'

He handed Yves a roll of vellum, inscribed with black ink and illuminated with gold and scarlet.

'You will erase the existence of the sea monsters from our conscience. And from our posterity. You will do as you know you should.'

Yves bowed his head. He unrolled the vellum and held it to the candle flame. It smoked, contorted, burned. The stench of burning leather filled the chamber. With blistered fingers, Yves dropped the ashes into the Aztec dish.

Innocent rose.

'Who gives this woman?'

Yves remained silent.

'I do,' His Majesty said.

I am married, Marie-Josèphe thought. *Married by the Prince of Rome, given in marriage by the King of France and Navarre . . . and I'm perfectly indifferent to the honour. I care only that I love Lucien, and he loves me.*

But he did not look like a man in love. Sitting on the window-seat while she packed her few things, absently stroking the cat, he stared into space. Marie-Josèphe readied a basket for Hercules, who watched suspiciously.

'You may live apart from me,' Lucien said.

Marie-Josèphe stared at him, stunned.

'You'll have your dowry, your liberty, time for your studies. I must leave court – I'll never trouble you—'

'You'll be my husband, in all ways!'

'But, my love,' he said, 'I'm no longer M. le comte de Chrétien. Only ordinary Lucien de Barenton.'

'I don't care.'

'I do. I have nothing. I can give you nothing. No title, no comfort – no children.'

'We'll have more than nothing – I promise you! But I'd choose nothing, with you, over everything, with anyone else. Nothing, with you, is liberty and affection, consideration and love.' She took his hands, stripped of their rings. 'I'd find only joy in a child with your spirit. But I'll never torment you.' She stroked her fingertip along his eyebrow, down his cheek. 'I will hope for you to change your mind.'

Lucien kissed her palm, her lips. He drew back reluctantly, sharing her anticipation.

Yves strode in, carrying his bag and Marie-Josèphe's drawing box. He was smiling. Lucien tried to remember the last time he had seen Yves smile. On the dock, at Le Havre, such a long time and such a short time ago, when he gave the captive sea monster to the King. 'Are you ready?' Yves said.

'Marie-Josèphe,' Lucien said, provoked, 'how can we be happy? My position is gone. My resources. You're forbidden music—'

'Innocent thought to torment me, but all my music belonged to Sherzad,' Marie-Josèphe said to Lucien. 'He never noticed that what I want is to study and learn and discover . . . and the King gave me what I love most.'

Lucien glared at Yves, who shrugged.

'I have what I wished for, as well,' he said. 'To spend all my life searching for knowledge—'

'To destroy it!'

'To . . . do with it as I know I should. To employ intelligent obedience.'

Marie-Josèphe looked from Yves to Lucien.

'Does His Majesty know what he's done?'

'His Majesty always knows,' Lucien said.

'We're cruel in our happiness, sister,' Yves said. 'Lucien has lost everything—'

'The King has lost Lucien!' Marie-Josèphe said. 'And Lucien has gained me.'

Epilogue

In Paris, on Midwinter Night, Yves de la Croix strode through sleet and darkness to his tiny house. He dropped his heavy cloak, lit a candle, opened the secret door, and stepped into the library.

He opened his satchel, drew out his most recent discovery, and unwrapped it from its covering of oiled silk.

In the illuminated manuscript, sea people leaped and played in waves of cerulean blue and sunlight of pure gold. He admired the illustrations, closed the book carefully, and placed it on the shelf next to Marie-Josèphe's exquisite opera score, now bound in calfskin, M. Boursin's dreadful cookbook, and the sheaf of Madame's letters.

Candlelight gleamed on the sea monster medal, and on the frames of two of Marie-Josèphe's drawings: One of Sherzad, the other of the male sea monster, haloed with scraps of gilt and broken glass.

The skeleton of the male sea monster lay in a reliquary of ebony, inlaid all over with mother-of-pearl.

For now, I must protect the sea people with secrecy, Yves thought. *For now. But not forever.*

Lucien's Breton ship sailed through moonlight. Lucien stood at its stern. The wake glowed, a widening arrow of luminescence.

Lucien feared the return of his seasickness. He had endured the Atlantic crossing better than he ever dared hope. The choppy waters of France's north coast brought misery to him, but the soft calm sea of the Tropic of Cancer caused him little distress.

I shall worry about hurricanes, Lucien thought, *when I have a hurricane to face*.

Marie-Josèphe joined him, sat on the deck beside him, and laid her hand along the side of his face. He kissed her palm.

I cannot regret my decisions, he thought. *I'm too proud — too arrogant — to rue leaving court, if His Majesty believes he can find a better adviser, which he cannot. I cannot live in Brittany with my fortunes so reduced.*

He missed his position, and his wealth. He maintained his dignity; he could not have behaved in any other way and kept it.

Returning home to Brittany had been difficult. Lucien could not, by the terms of His Majesty's order, make any claim on the resources of his former title. His own pride prevented him from asking his father for help. All Marie-Josèphe's dowry, and most of Haleeda's gift of pearls, had gone to fitting out the ship and buying a small stud farm, where Jacques now had charge of Zachi and Zelis and the other Arabians, and Hercules the cat had charge of the mice in the stable.

Returning to Brittany had been difficult, leaving it again even harder. He worried about his home, placed under the control of M. du Maine.

Lucien still battled fits of despair, and yet they came less and less frequently.

With all I have lost, he thought, *I wonder at my joy*.

He smiled.

'Tell me,' Marie-Josèphe said.

'I believed I had finished with adventures,' he said. 'I planned my life at court, and a quiet retirement in Barenton after my nephew came of age. Yet here I am, on a mad quest. Why not seek new fortunes, with men from my homeland, still loyal to me? Why not sail away to fight pirates, with the woman I love?'

She smiled, and twined her finger in a lock of his fair hair. He had put aside his perruques. He let his hair grow and tied it back with a white ribbon. His clothing was of plainer stuff than satin or velvet, worn with only a little Spanish lace. He never wore blue.

Marie-Josèphe giggled.

'Tell me,' Lucien said.

'I wish I could see Versailles – just for a moment – to see your sweet brother paying court to His Majesty.'

Lucien laughed. Marie-Josèphe's description was true, and fair. She was as fond of Lucien's preposterous brother as Lucien was himself. But Guy was no courtier.

'If Guy makes himself sufficiently impossible,' Lucien said, 'and sufficiently annoys the King, His Majesty might persuade my nephew to become count de Chrétien, even as I planned.'

'The King might persuade himself he's been a fool—' Marie-Josèphe exclaimed.

'Shh, shh, he is the King.'

'—and beg you to return. Then I'll have to share your attention with him. I'm selfish. I want you to myself as long as I may have you.'

Lucien smiled. He gazed back across the wake, which rippled like milk in the moonlight.

He gripped the rail and peered more closely.

A ship appeared in the moonlit dark.

'You may have to share me with pirates,' Lucien said, his voice grim.

The pursuing ship drew closer.

The Breton ship sailed valiantly, but it would never outdistance the larger, faster hunter. Nor could Lucien's ship hope to vanish in darkness, for the full moon illuminated the sea.

We shall have to fight them, Lucien thought. *If it is British, it will take us as spoils of war. If a privateer, as I suspect, it will simply take us.*

In the first case, all his and Marie-Josèphe's resources would be forfeit. In the second, they would lose their lives or worse.

The master of the ship called for weapons to be handed out. A sailor brought Lucien cutlass and pistol. Lucien kept the cutlass; though he preserved his sword-cane, he would not re-forge the blade unless he returned to Damascus. He offered the pistol to Marie-Josèphe.

'Could you shoot at a man?'

'If need be.' Marie-Josèphe glanced toward the pursuing ship. She caught her breath. 'Lucien, look—'

The ship's sails filled with wind, but the ship had ceased to make way. It shuddered.

'It's run aground,' Lucien said, but he thought, *How is it possible?*

For the ships sailed along the indigo depths between Great Exuma and Andros Island.

'No,' Marie-Josèphe said.

★

430

The moon hovered at the horizon, full and bright. The great current of stars flowed across the surface of the sky.

Sherzad swam free in the wild wide ocean. Her baby clung to her, listening to the songs of its young cousins, learning the music of their passage through the sea. She stroked her long webbed fingers over her baby's back, over the little one's warmth. Her baby had learned so quickly how to swim, how to breathe, how to fall into languor. She welcomed her introduction to the sea.

Sherzad's brothers and sisters had survived the assault on the mating haze in which she was captured, but their mother and their uncle and their aunt, the elders of their family, all had died. Sherzad grieved, singing phrases of her mother's death-song, singing an image of her mother to look upon her granddaughter, Sherzad's child.

Her brothers and sisters swam past her, arced around, dove beneath her, all anxious to make their way to the depthless ocean trench where the sea people gathered for the mating haze.

Sherzad, too, anticipated the approaching Midsummer Day. At the gathering, the other families would rejoice at Sherzad's return; they would admire and welcome her child. All the children would play with the tame giant octopuses, and tease the dolphins. The adults would join the whirlpool of the mating haze. For a time, the haze would ease their grief.

But never again would they mate beneath the sun. They could no longer risk the enormous danger. They were too vulnerable to the men of land. Too few sea people remained, to withstand another assault.

This year they would gather at sunset, as Midsummer Night coincided with the dark of the moon. On the shortest night of the year, in moonless dark, they would dare to rise together to the surface of the sea. Amidst the waves, whispering songs, they would bathe in luminescence. Their bodies glowing in the darkness, they would come together and experience the brief bliss of their mating haze.

They would not gather again for fourteen years, when the dark of the moon next accompanied Midsummer Night.

Before Sherzad could turn her desires and her course toward the meeting place, she must discharge another obligation.

Far ahead, two ships plunged across the waves, digging their keels into the domain of the sea people. The first ship fled, the second pursued, gaining rapidly. Sherzad's younger sister sang of an encounter she had witnessed between two ships. They battered the air and the ocean with their noise for half a day; their iron balls plunged into the water, sending the sea people in a dive to safety.

In the end the two ships sank each other, and all the men of land drowned.

Sherzad's sister laughed, and hoped these two new ships would ride the same wave. She hoped all the ships of land would destroy each other, if the sea people did not destroy them first.

The sea people stalked the ships. Soon they swam beneath the barnacled bottom of the pursuer. Sherzad sang at it, feeling it out with her voice, searching and questioning, finding nothing of interest and nothing worth saving. In the past, she would have swum away.

She gave her baby to her young brother to guard, and swam closer to the pursuer.

Sherzad and her companions plunged their spears of narwhal tusk into the bottom of the galleon. The ivory bit into the wood. Holding the tusks, they rode along with the ship.

Sherzad shouted at the planks. Her focused voice crashed against them. She shouted again. Her spear quivered in the quaking wood.

Sherzad and her brothers and sisters shouted together. The wood cracked and split.

The bottom of the ship disintegrated.

Men shrieked and dove into the water. Sherzad and the others made sure they never surfaced.

Waves washed over the deck. Singing their triumph, the sea people called their allies. A shadow rose, flickering all over with tiny sparks. The octopus stretched its tentacles into the moonlight and entwined them around the mainmast, and inexorably pulled the ship into the depths.

The skiff scraped upon the beach of a tiny cay. Marie-Josèphe and Lucien climbed out onto white sand that shone in the light of the full moon.

'I do not like to leave you here alone, sir, madame.' The master of the Breton ship was still shaken by the sinking of the privateer. 'There are krakens, and sirens. And snakes—'

'Never fear,' Lucien said.

'Except for the snakes,' Marie-Josèphe said, and laughed with joy and anticipation.

'Come back at dawn,' Lucien said. 'I trust we won't have been eaten by snakes.'

The master bowed; the skiff rowed back to the ship at anchor, out of sight on the other side of the cay.

'Come,' Marie-Josèphe said. 'Sit with me.'

They sat on a driftwood log. Marie-Josèphe luxuriated in the warmth of the night. She leaned toward Lucien and kissed him, a long sweet kiss. Her sight blurred for a moment with tears of love and gratitude.

'You have awakened me,' she whispered.

Tonight nothing could frighten her, not snakes, or pirates, and certainly not kraken.

They waited.

Restive, impatient, Lucien gazed out to sea. 'This is madness,' he said softly. 'They have declared war.'

'Not on me,' she said. 'She promised, if she lived, she would meet me here, tonight, at the full moon.'

A breath of song murmured over the waves. Marie-Josèphe leaped up, kicked off her slippers, and ran down the gleaming wet sand to the water.

Ripples washed her toes. The life of the ocean vibrated against the soles of her feet. She sang Sherzad's name-song.

Sherzad replied.

Marie-Josèphe cried out in delight. She pulled her dress over her head and flung it onto the sand. In her shift, she ran into the sea.

The sea-people swam toward her, sleek and untamed. Sherzad led the band to Marie-Josèphe. She swam around her, splashing cool water onto her face, her arms, her breasts. Marie-Josèphe flung off her soaked shift and let it drift away, a plaything for the younger sea-people. Naked, she waded deeper, till the water washed her legs, her sex.

Sherzad was recovered, healthy, strong, and beautiful. Her hair spread dark and glossy around her.

A baby clung to her. Sherzad floated on her back and sank slowly, encouraging the baby to swim. Laughing and splashing, the child paddled to Marie-Josèphe.

Marie-Josèphe picked her up and cuddled her and kissed her silk-smooth swimming webs and her tiny sharp claws.

'She's lovely, dear Sherzad, the most handsome baby I've ever seen.' She turned. Lucien's boots and stockings lay on the sand; he stood in water to his knees.

'You are a wild sea creature yourself,' Lucien said. 'You are Venus, waiting for your cockle-shell to float by.'

He waded a little deeper, then stopped.

'Come closer to shore, love,' he said, 'so I can greet Sherzad and her child. Some other day, I'll learn to swim.'

She joined him where he stood in the shallows. She sat beside him and leaned happily against him and slipped her wet arm around his waist. The sea-child babbled and splashed and played. Lucien stroked Marie-Josèphe's hair.

Sherzad dove and vanished. The other sea people followed her, swimming to a treacherous shoal where many ships had met their ends.

When Sherzad surfaced again, moonlight sparkled on the tips of her fingers. She wore lost treasure on her hands; she took the rings off one by one, ruby, diamond, emerald, pearl, and placed them on Marie-Josèphe's fingers. Her brothers and sisters followed her, all decorated with golden girdles and sapphire pendants, jade beads and diamond bracelets. Their ivory spears gleamed with chains of gold and ropes of amber.

In Sherzad's stories, Marie-Josèphe thought, *the sea people never carried spears. They truly have declared war.*

The sea people tipped their spears before her, pouring gold and amber into her lap. Laughing, Sherzad's baby grasped the shining treasure and waved her tiny fists.

The sea people crowded together around Marie-Josèphe, singing their gratitude for the return of their sister, singing their love.

434

They dropped the treasure at Marie-Josèphe's feet, they placed strings of jewels around her neck and around her waist and ankles and arms. They nestled diamond and ruby earrings in Lucien's hair, and tied them to his hair-ribbon. The younger sea-people brought drifts of shining shells, mixed with golden coins, for though they were willing to share the most beautiful things with Sherzad's friends, they did not want to give away all their seashells.

Sherzad poured handsful of carved jade necklaces into Lucien's pockets. She found his calvados, opened the flask and whistled with pleasure and drank it and shared it with her brothers and sisters. When she returned the flask, her brother had filled it with black pearls.

The sea people sang, and bared their sleek mahogany skin. They adorned their friends with their finery, enriching Lucien and Marie-Josèphe beyond measure, trading jewels for the shimmer of clearest moonlight.